King of Swords

Book One of The Starfolk

Also by Dave Duncan

The Starfolk

King of Swords (Fall 2013)
Queen of Stars (forthcoming)

"The Dodec Books"

Children of Chaos
Mother of Lies

Chronicles of the King's
Blades

Paragon Lost

Impossible Odds
The Jaguar Knights

Tales of the King's Blades

The Gilded Chain
Lord of Fire Lands
Sky of Swords
The Monster War

A Man of His Word

Magic Casement
Faerie Land Forlorn
Perilous Seas
Emperor and Clown

A Handful of Men

The Cutting Edge
Upland Outlaws
The Stricken Field
The Living God

The Great Game

Past Imperative
Present Tense
Future Indefinite

"The Omar Books"   *The Reaver Road*
                           The Hunters' Haunt

The Seventh Sword   *The Reluctant Swordsman*
                           The Coming of Wisdom
                           The Destiny of the Sword

Stand-alone novels   *Against the Light*
                           West of January
                           The Cursed
                           A Rose-Red City
                           Shadow
                           Strings
                           Hero!
                           Wildcatter
                           Pock's World
                           Wildcatter

The Brothers Magnus   *Speak to the Devil*
                           When the Saints

Writing as Sarah B. Franklin *Daughter of Troy*

Writing as Ken Hood   *Demon Sword*
                           Demon Rider
                           Demon Knight

King of Swords

Book One of The Starfolk

by Dave Duncan

PUBLISHED BY

47N★RTH

Text copyright © 2013 by Dave Duncan

Published by 47North
P.O. Box 400818
Las Vegas, NV 89140

ISBN-13: 9781477807392
ISBN-10: 147780739X
Library of Congress Control Number: 2013936766

Cover illustration by Chase Stone

To those fans the faithful few
who have stayed with me all the way,
for a quarter of a century.
You know who you are.

Chapter 1

The sign said CAMPGROUND CLOSED in large letters, but three successive visitors ignored it on that chilly spring evening.

The first was a lanky young male riding a bicycle laden with two packs, a bedroll, and a guitar bag. The barrier was a single beam, pivoted at one end and secured at the other by a chain and padlock. He lifted the bike over the beam, scrambled over it himself, guitar and all, and then cycled off in search of a picnic shelter where he might spend the night without being rained on.

The second intruder was a bear, ravenous after its winter sleep. Gaunt, mangy, and ill-tempered, it had been foraging in the forest for fresh plant shoots and tearing open rotten logs in search of grubs—poor fare that did little to relieve its hunger. As darkness fell, it caught the scent of something delicious and nourishing, possibly a newborn fawn. Summoning its reserves of energy, the bear hurried off to wherever that tantalizing

1

odor might lead it. It reached the campground at much the same time as the boy, but did not enter by the gate.

━━━━━━━━━━━━━━━━

Third was a twentysomething female driving a shabby, well-used Winnebago. She pulled to a stop just short of the gate, jumped down from the cab, and hunched down to inspect the muddy ground. She was tall and solid, but she moved as if her bulk came more from muscle than fat. Her hair and eyes were dark and gleaming. She wore jeans and a plaid flannel shirt.

The cedars and hemlocks were no longer dripping, so the last rain had to have stopped several hours ago. Since then a single truck had gone through and returned later with a much lighter load, judging by the depth of its tracks. Fragments of bark on top of the mud suggested that the rangers had delivered a load of firewood for summer visitors. After the mud had dried enough to become much stiffer, the only other traffic had been a bicycle whose rider had dismounted at the bar. His footprints indicated a tall man, size thirteen cowboy boots with a hole in the right sole.

A troop of Hells Angels might have deterred her, but little else. The padlock was no problem, either. It took her all of four seconds to open the lock and swing the bar up on its counterweight. She drove through, leaving the gate wide open behind her.

Where the trail divided up ahead, she found the washrooms and the woodpile—two joys of the unspoiled wilderness. Having parked at the nearest campsite and built a generous fire, she perched on a folding chair and attempted to eat the gas station sandwich she had unwisely brought along for supper. The Winnebago stopped its clicking and dripping, leaving only the barely audible trickling of a nearby stream and the crackle of the fire as it shot red stars up like decoys to lure in the wild variety. Soon she could see the first of those peering down at her through gaps in the forest canopy, and she knew that millions more would join them shortly. In a badly abused world, the Canadian wilderness still offered wide tracts of solitude and forest, and Vancouver Island's were among the most accessible. The evening was cool and pleasant, heavily scented with conifers, spoiled only by the vile sandwich and the twenty ounces of revolver dragging down the pocket of her coat.

She had little time to enjoy her solitude before a shaky lamp beam flickered through the trees. Soon the cyclist pedaled into view, heading toward the gate and going slowly on the rough track. He stopped beside her campsite, setting one size thirteen bare foot down on the mud. His boots were slung on his back now, alongside the guitar. His hair shone silver in the firelight, but it was a youngster's hair, long and thick, pulled back over his ears and secured in a ponytail at the nape of his neck. He wore jeans, a checked shirt, and a lightweight jacket, which hung open in denial of the cold. In spite of his height, he looked young and vulnerable when he smiled.

"You should go inside, ma'am. Or leave. There's a bear. They can be dangerous at this time of year."

"Grizzly or black bear?" she asked.

"No grizzlies on the Island, but even a black can be nasty."

"And are you sure it wasn't an elk or a moose?"

"They can be dangerous too." He flashed white teeth in another smile. "I saw bear tracks earlier, and I just heard something moving. That's enough for me. I'm gone, lady."

"You think you can outrun a bear on a bicycle?"

"You'd be amazed how fast I can pedal when I'm moti-vated!" Laughing, he pushed down on a pedal and wobbled into motion, disappearing around the bend in seconds.

The woman rose and walked over to the edge of the trail, pulling the S&W Special from her pocket. She stared into the darkness in the direction where the cyclist had disappeared.

Two minutes . . . three . . . She heard the rattle of the bike just before his light flickered back into view. Pedaling furiously, he yelled a warning to her, which she ignored. A bear could outrun a horse over a short distance, so the biker would have had little chance even on a concrete highway. On that rutted, stony mud, it was a wonder that the bear hadn't already caught him. As they came level with the watcher, it did. Boy, bear, bicycle, and guitar crashed a screaming, snarling tangle in front of her.

The bear was on top, with a boot in its mouth and one paw stuck through the bicycle's wheel. A handgun was not a hunt-ing rifle. She had to make the first shot count by putting it into the correct skull. Jostling for position, she put a foot on the guitar, crushing it. As she watched, a paw raked the boy's chest in an explosion of blood that made her cry out. The bi-cycle was being ripped into scraps, and it seemed that its owner would suffer the same fate. But then the bear shook its head, spat out the boot, and rolled over on its back, stone dead. Gripping the revolver firmly in both hands, the woman shoved the stubby barrel between its open jaws and fired. The shot barked obscenely loud, leaving her ears jangling in the deadly silence that followed.

From the bottom of the heap came a whimper of pain. The boy tried to sit up. In a remarkably steady tenor voice he said, "Can you get this damned thing off my legs, please?"

That was no trivial problem, given that the carcass weighed as much as two big men. Had her supplies included a rope or chain, she would have been tempted to tow the brute off with the truck, but they didn't. It took several minutes to free the boy, and he did most of the work. Although his face was coated with mud and probably bruised from hitting the ground, it seemed to have suffered no more than that. His left forearm was bleeding, but his worst injury was the savage clawing that had raked him open from neck to belly, four parallel slashes streaming blood. His clothes were in tatters, and his thick leather belt had been snapped in half. She gripped his good arm to help him upright and tried to wrap it around her shoulders, but he resisted.

"Can walk," he muttered. "I'll be all right." He pulled his arm free to hold up the tattered remains of his jeans.

She held his elbow and guided him back to her chair by the fire. Amazingly, he seemed to be shaking less than she was.

"You shot it?" he mumbled.

"I certainly did! What do you think I did—hit it with your guitar?"

"Just that I thought . . . Never mind." He slumped down onto the chair.

"Stay there!" she said fatuously, and ran to the door of the Winnebago. She disappeared inside, then returned with a bundle of towels. "Here, let me see."

He was crouched in the chair, doubled over, head down, blood dribbling onto the ground. "I'll be all right."

"No, you *won't*! You'll bleed to death if you don't get any help. *Now sit up!*"

Reluctantly he straightened up. She spread a towel over his chest wounds, and blood soaked through it instantly, black patches in the firelight. He used another to wipe the mud off his face.

"You don't have a cell phone, do you?" she asked.

"Wouldn't work out here. Thanks for the rescue. I'm Rigel Estell."

"Mira Silvas. I'll bandage you up as best I can, and then we'll get you to a hospital."

"No hospital." He spread the second towel modestly across his lap. "There's a pump by the washrooms. If you bring me a bucket of water, I'll get cleaned up. I have a spare pair of jeans . . . or at least I did." He peered past her at the remains of his bicycle, crushed under the bear. He was either remarkably calm for a man who had so narrowly escaped a nasty death, or he was already in shock.

She disappeared into the Winnebago and returned with two bottles of mineral water. "This isn't distilled," she said, "but it must be safer than campground water."

To her annoyance he wasted the first by tipping it over his head, drenching his body in a tide of liquid mud. His face was narrow and bony, with high cheekbones, and pale, slightly almond-shaped eyes. Most people would have described him as "a good-looking kid" when he wasn't grimacing with pain and covered in swellings and scrapes. His flaxen hair had fallen loose and hung in tangles around his shoulders.

She pulled away the bloody towel so she could empty the second bottle over his chest, exposing the long scratches. With absurd modesty, he tried to pull the remains of his shirt over them. She pushed his hands away.

"I'm no doctor," she said, "but I think it's mostly superficial. Just flesh wounds." But there had been little flesh there to start with and some of the cuts had gone down to the bone. "You're lucky you had that belt on, or the brute would have disemboweled you."

She reached for the tatters of his jeans. He pushed her away and doubled over.

"For heaven's sake! I'm a married woman. I've seen dicks of every size and damned near every shape. I've played with more balls than a golf pro. You don't have anything I haven't seen before. You still have it, don't you? You didn't lose anything irreplaceable?"

"No. But close enough," he mumbled. He was speaking to his blood-soaked thighs. "I need more water and some bandages, that's all."

"You are going to hospital. Have you any idea where the nearest one is? Tofino? Port Alberni? If we can find a phone, I'll call for a helicopter ambulance."

"No hospital," he repeated. "No hospital and no doctors."

"You'll bleed to death."

"I won't. I heal quickly. Please just get me some more water."

"Is this some religious nonsense? Are you one of those fanatics who doesn't believe in medicine?" When he did not answer, she tried again. "It's not medicine you need; you need stitches to close those gashes."

"No hospital," he muttered to his knees.

"You'll do as you're told! I'm going to bandage those cuts and then get you to medical help."

"No!"

"Yes. Only a hospital can give you what you need. Hell, you need antibiotics, and rabies and tetanus shots too. You'll probably go into shock before we even get there. Stop behaving like a maniac, Nigel."

"Not Nigel. Rigel." He kept his head down. "Mira, I am grateful for your help, but I can't go to a hospital or see a doctor. I'd rather die. That's final."

"No it isn't. What happens to me if I let you die? You'll have to give me a very good reason. Are you on the run?"

He did not speak. She wondered if he was about to faint.

"Rigel! Answer me. I have a gun, remember."

He made a muffled sound that was close to a chuckle. "You'll shoot me to stop me from bleeding to death? All right. I'll let you help me, but you must promise not to take me to a hospital."

"I'll promise anything. Stack of Bibles. Believe it. Now sit up."

He straightened up with a whimper of pain. "Look, then." He gestured down at his chest.

"Look at what?"

"No nipples."

"Oh."

"Or a navel," he said. "Now do you understand?"

She laughed nervily. "You trying to tell me you're some sort of alien?"

He didn't answer.

Chapter 2

The woman reacted better than Rigel had expected she would. She snorted and pushed his wet hair aside to look at his right ear. "Not pointed," she said. "Or hairy. Perfectly good ear."

"It's set too high on my head."

"Nonsense! You're just being hypersensitive. As far as your chest goes . . . well, you must've had some kinky plastic surgery. To hide a bad burn, maybe."

She had found the most obvious solution.

He said, "No scars."

"Doesn't mean a thing, especially if you were very young when it happened. As a working hypothesis that's better than thinking I'm crazy . . . and right now the only thing we need to focus on is saving your life. Let's go inside, where I can see better."

If she wasn't a matter-of-fact, no-nonsense type, she was playing the role well. But why did she carry a gun? He had made it a lifelong rule not to trust anyone, and people who carried guns were dangerous. Something about that fight with the bear had felt wrong.

He let her help him up. He felt shaky now, and tried to focus on fighting the pain load. He could deal with that, but not doctors, not a hospital. His lack of nipples and a navel wasn't all of it. He was different in other ways. His hair and eyes were white. And as soon as they tested his blood group or DNA, they'd lock him up in a zoo.

"Can't tolerate drugs," he said, leaning on her shoulder as they walked. She was a square, solid girl, easily able to bear his weight. "Painkillers, antibiotics . . . I shot a roofer's nail through my foot when I was a kid and they gave me a tetanus shot. I went into anaphylactic shock and damned near died."

"An allergy can do that. Doesn't mean anything." Still steadying him, she opened the door to the Winnebago.

He resisted. "I'm going to get blood everywhere."

"Doesn't matter."

He climbed in shakily, and she followed. One side was lined with miniature cupboards, a sink, and a refrigerator, the other with a narrow bench covered in rumpled bedclothes. Two large suitcases filled the double bed over the truck cab. The place looked clean as a whistle, but had an old, fusty smell.

"Lie down." She turned up the propane light. "Damn, boy, you need about two thousand stitches."

He stretched out on the bench and it felt good to lie down. The pain was growing worse, making it hard for him to think straight. "You got a needle and thread?" She was younger than he'd realized, with big dark eyes and black hair, either curly or curled. She wore jeans and a parka, open to reveal a checked flannel shirt. She was probably not much older than he was. She removed the parka and tossed it up on the bed.

"Happens that I do, but I'm not a doctor and it's not sterilized."

"Doesn't matter. I don't get sick—not unless someone tries to give me medication."

"I can't stitch you! I know some first aid, but I'm no surgeon."

"Then watch me bleed to death."

She chewed her lip. "Rigel, the only disinfectant I have is a mickey of bourbon. And no anesthetic, unless you want to use the bourbon for that."

Oh, crap! His penis was getting excited by the exposure. If he didn't end this conversation soon, he was going to get an erection, which would be worse even than the mauling. "Don't need it. Honestly, infection doesn't frighten me, but if it bothers you, boil the needles and thread and wash your hands in the bourbon. Meanwhile, I'm going to put myself to sleep. I'll wake up in twenty minutes and check on how you're doing."

She started arguing even louder, but he ignored her. He hunted through the forest of pain to find his point of focus, then began tucking the world in around it. He'd learned how to do that when he was tiny and had been surprised when Gert told him other people couldn't do it. Twenty minutes. Reality folded and shrank and swirled down to nothing.

"I'm back."

The woman yelped. "Oh! You startled me." She held a needle and thread in her gory hands; there was blood on her clothes and even her face.

He raised his head enough to inspect the damage to his torso. He hadn't lost anything vital, but two of the scratches reached the edge of his pubic hair. Mira had stitched him up in pink and blue and green silk like he was an embroidery

11

project. The bleeding had almost stopped, and his dick was behaving itself again.

"Thanks," he said. "That should do. I like the pink best." He had the pain under control now. That was another trick humans couldn't master.

"I'm going to get jailed for practicing medicine without a license."

"I won't tell." He tried to sit up, and she pushed him back down.

"Can you do that self-hypnosis trick again? It slowed your bleeding a lot. I felt your pulse, and your heartbeat went down to about thirty."

"As long as you promise not to hijack me to a hospital."

She nodded. "I promise, Sir Alien. What planet did you say you were from?"

"I wish I knew," he said truthfully. She hadn't locked him in and started driving hell-for-leather, so he'd trust her for a little longer. "I'll look back in an hour."

Focus . . .

She had bandaged him up like a mummy and covered him with a blanket. Otherwise he was naked; he rubbed his feet together and felt the dried mud on them. She must have wrestled his dead weight around like a parcel to get him trussed up like this—it was intimate but not romantic, not even erotic. He was wearing nothing but his bracelet, and it would take a blowtorch to get that off him. Turning his head, he saw that she'd spread the ruins of his worldly goods out on the floor and the tiny kitchen counter: some clothes, a knife, a fork, a spoon, a groundsheet, a Swiss Army knife, a couple of cooking utensils, a money clip with twenty-five dollars in it. He wondered if she'd noted the absence of a wallet or ID. No shaving kit, either. She had brought in the folding chair and was sitting on it, thumbing through the *Complete Works of William Shakespeare*, but she must have been watching him.

"How are you feeling?"

"Much better, thank you." He could hold the pain down to a tingle now, and he'd adjusted to the shock. He was alive, whereas he might have been dead and half eaten by now. It was another memory he'd keep with him for life, long might that be! He wondered if the scars would stay, but figured they'd probably disappear like all the rest had. Even the nail through his foot had left no trace. "Thank you *very much*."

She brought him a glass of water. He sat up and drank greedily.

She said, "It's from the pump, but I put some Aquatabs in it."

She was still worrying. He tried a goofy grin that he was rather proud of. "I never get sick, not like you humans."

"The bear ate half your left boot."

"That's what killed it, then." He wasn't sure what *had* killed it.

"The bike's been recycled into paperclips. Your sunglasses were smashed."

"I'll get by. I'm still alive, thanks to you. Nothing else matters."

"And your guitar. That was my clumsiness, I'm afraid. It wasn't the bear."

"Then you're a better music critic."

At last she smiled. "You amaze me. And so does your taste in reading material. The *Complete Works of William Shakespeare, Star Spotting for Beginners,* and Machiavelli's *The Prince*? You have unusual taste, Alien."

"They all came out of library dumpsters. Please don't call me that."

"Sorry. Rigel? That's your home star?"

"It's just my name. I feel badly taking up your bed."

Mira laughed. "It's about time I had a man in my bed again, but I'll sleep up there on the shelf. You do your trance thing, because it seems to help you. We can move on in the morning. I won't leave you here to walk. Which way were you heading?"

"Doesn't matter. I'm a hobo. All roads are the same to me."

"I'm heading back to Nanaimo and the Vancouver ferry. I want to get an early start, so if you wake up and we're moving, that's where we're going. Don't assume that I'm trucking you off to a hospital."

She was watching his face. He tried not to let his fear show, but he had never felt so vulnerable. She joked about a man in her bed but she didn't mean a freak like him. He reacted to human girls the same way human boys did, but the reverse wasn't true. The only other person who'd learned his secret—besides Gert, that is—was a girl named Enid, who'd let him touch her breasts. Afterwards, she'd said, "Tat for tit," and slid her hand inside his shirt. When she'd felt what was there—nothing—she'd told him that nipples didn't matter on a guy but then the fun had stopped, and a few minutes later she'd asked him to take her home. She'd never told anyone, so far as he could tell, but that was probably because she was worried that people would laugh at her. *My boyfriend the alien.* Now he was completely at the mercy of a woman he didn't know.

On the other hand, she couldn't tie him up without waking him and the lock on the door would be designed to keep people out, not in. If she did try to kidnap him, he could escape at the first red light, and he could run as fast on bare feet as he could in shoes.

"Why a hospital?" he said. "Why not a TV station? Or *Ripley's Believe It or Not*? Or the *National Enquirer*? They'd pay big bucks for a story like GIRL KILLS GRIZZLY WITH HAND-GUN, RESCUES ALIEN."

There was no harm in letting her know that he could spill secrets too, if he had to. She caught the threat right away and her eyes chilled.

"It was a black bear, and I have a license to carry that gun."

Oh, did she? A license for a *handgun*? In *Canada*? It was hard to shrug while lying down. "I'm glad you had it handy."

"An autopsy on that bear might be interesting. I'm pretty positive that the brute was dead when I shot it."

So he hadn't just imagined it, then. "You accusing me of strangling it?"

"When I went out to get your stuff, I saw that it had been stabbed. Right through the heart, I suspect."

"Yeah, sure. I ran it through with my trusty Swiss Army knife, which I then wiped clean and slipped back in my pack. Get real, lady."

For a moment she just stared. Sometimes humans were hard to read. So were aliens—he stared back.

"Let's talk it over in the morning, you and I," she said eventually. "I need some sleep."

"What time will you leave?"

"Before dawn."

"I'll be here," he said.

In fact he was down at the stream, naked except for the silver bracelet on his right wrist and a rubber band on his left. Dirt he abhorred—he showered three times a day when he could. His stays at Tofino and Ahousaht this spring had been heavenly because he'd had the beaches all to himself. The Pacific in March was too cold for humans, but not for him. *This* stream would have frozen a human man in minutes. It was a bit nippy even for him, but dried blood was utterly repulsive, and had to go. His wounds had scabbed over nicely—they just itched a little around the stitches—so here he was, sitting waist-deep in icy water, quietly snipping the silk away with the scissors on his Swiss Army knife.

He'd always been good at moving quietly, but sneaking out of the Winnebago in the dark without waking Mira had been an interesting exercise. His every step had set the truck to rocking. He'd left all his possessions behind except for his soap, his towel, and his formerly-second-best-and-now-only jeans, so that she'd know he was planning to return.

Sudden realization that he was being watched made his head whip around. She was standing on the bank in the predawn gloom, staring at him. *"Voyeur!"* he said, trying to hide his anger behind cheerfulness.

"You don't feel cold?"

"Not much. Heat slaughters me."

"And you've healed already?"

"Almost. I'm not quite well enough to try rape yet, but stick around."

Surprisingly, she laughed out loud. "Rigel, you are the most interesting b . . . man I have met in years! I have a couple of doughnuts, and I'll make some coffee."

"Turn around," he said. He rose, squeezing his hair to get the water out of it. He combed it with his fingers so that it covered his ears, and then fastened it at the nape of his neck, wading ashore toward the towel and jeans.

Mira was standing with her back to him, her eyes fixed on the trees. "I believe you, you know. We can't heal like you can, and we can't turn ourselves off the way you do. You're either an alien or a Superman."

"Flattery won't help," he said, close enough behind her to make her jump. "And ET can't call home when he doesn't know where home is. Actually my mommy was a Sasquatch."

She turned her head to smile up at him and did a double take. "Never seen white eyes before?"

She smiled and patted his arm. "I don't care what planet you're from, you're a nice guy, Rigel, and that's what matters. Okay?"

"Okay, for starters," he said. "We are fully compatible with your species, earthling female."

She smiled politely. Human females had an infallible instinct for detecting male virgins, and he'd never had any success with pickup lines.

Chapter 3

As Mira was making the Winnebago shipshape, ready to roll, Rigel inspected the dead bear and even deader bicycle to make sure that he had left nothing that could identify him. His name had never been on the guitar or its bag. His blood must be distinctive, of course, but even if anyone thought to analyze the stains in the mud, there would be no way of tracing it back to him. His DNA might match with some X-File in the Flying Saucer Department, of course, but that would do them little good.

The campground workers were going to get a nasty shock when they found a bear killed out of season with its brains blown out of its head and a bloody stab wound in its chest. Inquiries Would Be Launched. Even the Mounties weren't likely to assume that the bear had been riding the bike and playing the guitar . . . or that it had somehow managed to shoot and stab itself. Small wonder that Mira was eager to make an early start.

He couldn't turn the brute over to see if there was a matching wound on the other side, but what he remembered was a sensation of driving a blade in about fifteen centimeters, not all the way through. He had had no such blade, and he would have written the memory off as an illusion, wishful thinking caused by the stress of the attack, except that *something* had obviously made that wound.

As they drove off along the highway and the sky turned to blue, Mira said, "Tell me about yourself."

"I'm an ecotourist from Aldebaran Seventeen. Why do you carry a gun on vacation?"

She smiled at the road ahead. "Fair enough. And it's only fair to warn you that even being seen with me can be dangerous. I'm a private eye. I worked for a man who ran a detective agency in San Francisco. I fell for Micah's line and married him. It went sour after a couple of years, and he's one of those possessive types who just can't let go and accept that I'm not *his*. I've had court orders and injunctions galore, but he knows all the tricks. Two of the guys I dated after the separation were beaten to jelly in dark alleys. Nothing was ever proved—either Micah hired goons to do his dirty work or he bought alibis, no way of telling which. He knows lawyers who make pretzels look like straightedges. I couldn't stand it any more, so I decided to run. I came up here to Canada."

Her story was fishier than a salmon farm. "Is he so bad at his job that he won't be able to track you down, then?"

"He's extremely good, but I know all the same tricks he does, because he taught me. I avoid using credit cards or cell phones or phone cards. I bussed to Port Angeles in Washington, and took a ferry across to Victoria. I showed forged ID, and they waved me through. I bought the Winnebago second-hand with the plates on. I'm driving without insurance, admittedly, but as long as I stay out of highway trouble I won't leave tracks. I went to ground in Tofino for a few days to let my scent grow cold, and now I'm heading for the big city,

Vancouver. From there I can fly or bus to anywhere, and he'll never know."

"I'll stay out of dark alleys while I'm with you." Her story still stank, but she was the only lifeboat in the present storm.

After a moment she said, "As soon as we see a restaurant, I'll buy you all the breakfast you can eat. That's a promise. You don't have to sing for it, but I'll admit that I'm curious about your background."

"Detectives are all naturally nosy, I suppose," he said, trying to make it sound like a joke. He had never confided in anyone before, but she already knew enough about him to sell him to a circus and if she really was a detective, she might be able to help him track down his past, or at least give him valuable advice. The chance was irresistible—in fact, it seemed tailor-made for him, and luck like that always aroused his suspicions. *I am the cat who walks by himself. Every silver lining has its cloud.*

"I can't tell you much," he said, "unless you want me to make up something about flying saucers or mad scientists. I was raised by a woman named Gert. Her last name was whatever she fancied, usually the same as whatever man she was living with at the time. One was called Estell and I liked that, so I kept it even after he threw us out. She was a prostitute and an alcoholic, a crackhead when she could afford it. She wasn't so much a compulsive liar as one of those people who can't distinguish between dreams from reality. She claimed to have First Nations blood in her, but she'd be Mohawk on Tuesday, Haida on Wednesday, and Métis on weekends. She was human wreckage, but the only family I've ever known and very dear to me in spite of her faults. She died a year ago, and I still miss her terribly."

Mira did not comment, but obviously that was not enough story to buy a decent breakfast. The thought of food was making his mouth water enough to gargle.

"She claimed I was her son, but she was short and fat and I was always skinny as a willow, even when she had us shacked up with a john who could afford to feed us right. Her eyes and hair were black and mine are white. She'd never stay in one place for long, because she was terrified that some welfare busybodies would take me away from her. I've lived all over Canada, from St. John's to the Yukon, but Gert knew enough not to try crossing the US border. I have no close friends, had no proper schooling, and wasn't kidding about fishing books out of library dumpsters. I'm a graduate of Recycle U."

"Why did she name you 'Rigel'?"

"She didn't. As soon I could talk, I insisted it was my name. I'd fly into tantrums if she called me anything else. She never figured out where I first heard the word. She didn't even know it was the name of a star until someone told me, years later, and I ran home to tell her."

"So what name did she use when she registered your birth?"

"I'm certain she didn't register my birth." He couldn't imagine Gert going near a government office or filling in a form. "She could barely write her own name. If she did, she had forgotten about it by the time I was old enough to ask. She couldn't even remember the name she had tried to give me."

"So you have no clue who your real parents were?"

"Or *what* they were."

After a moment, Mira said, "*What* they were . . . You're like that man not born of woman that Shakespeare wrote about."

"Macduff."

"Whatever. Where did Gert get you?"

He sighed. "I have a million answers for that one. On Thursdays I was her love child, sired by the King of the Elves." That was the story he'd liked best when he was a young child. "Honestly, Mira, she had more fairy tales than H. C. Andersen. One that turned up a lot, the one that I'm inclined to believe, was that she gave birth to a stillborn son. When she came home from the hospital, all alone and heartbroken, there I was on her bed, crying to be fed. It's a variation on the changeling myth, of course, so you don't have to put much stock in it. She could have dreamed it. On the other hand, if you had an unwanted nonhuman baby on your hands, that would be the kindest way of disposing of it."

"Would it? Would you give an unwanted human baby to an alien?"

He was angry to hear himself sounding so bitter. "Would you rather hear the angels story? Or the one about the Virgin bringing me down the chimney? How about the flying saucers? *She didn't know!* By the time I was old enough to question her properly, her mind was so screwed up by drink and horse and shit that she didn't remember squat all."

A blue SUV went sailing past them, and the lady detective frowned after it as it disappeared into the distance.

"Yes, it did pass us earlier," Rigel said.

"I thought so too. What else has?"

"Two silver sedans, three pickups, a bus, and two guys on motorbikes."

"You're observant."

"Just careful."

For the next five kilometers or so, neither of them said a word. Rigel was wondering about her predatory husband, if he really existed. Perhaps Mira was doing the same, or maybe her concerns were about something else entirely.

"Do you know where were you born?"

Rigel laughed. "In Canada somewhere. You do know that Canada is bigger than the United States?"

"It certainly doesn't lack for scenery. That view's stupendous."

They were driving along the side of Sproat Lake, all blue and silver beneath them, the sun glowing off it. Rigel could see eagles soaring, but he didn't mention them in case Mira drove off the road. City folk got excited about eagles.

"How old are you?"

"Guess."

"Twenty."

"Reasonable. I may be a year older or younger. Once in a while I run into people I met during one of Gert's brief attempts to school me, and they're about that age now. I haven't the slightest trace of fuzz on my lip. Seems that males of my species don't grow facial hair."

"Well, that's not so unusual, some Indians don't. So you have no birth certificate. That must be a problem?"

His laugh was quite genuine. "Lady, that is the worst problem of the bunch. I can't get a driver's license, a passport, *nothing*. No health care or social security. I'm a nobody. I don't exist. I tell you, it's creepy! If they catch me, they'll extradite me to Mars."

"There are procedures for applying for a birth certificate, but I suppose you don't even have witnesses who've known you for any length of time, and what jurisdiction is going to accept your application when you don't know where you were born? Yikes! No family physician? No documents or photographs?"

"Zilch. In good times we lived out of two suitcases; otherwise out of a shopping cart."

"So how do you make a living?"

"I busk mostly—sing, play the guitar. I do gigs in bars if they let me in." Everything from flamenco to Joan Baez stuff to the Mad Wriggles, whatever the customers wanted. He was good too, although he wasn't about to brag. For the last few years he'd lived with Gert, he'd been the breadwinner. Times were going to be tough for a while now, because last night he'd lost almost everything he owned in the world: bike, guitar, half his clothes.

"You must want to know who you are and where you came from?" Mira said, shaking him from his thoughts.

"More than anything. Where do I start?"

She said, "That's the problem, of course. If I dared to go on the web . . . but I won't, not now. Let me think about it."

Chapter 4

At Port Alberni they stopped at the Best Western hotel for breakfast.

"These places usually say, 'No shirt, no shoes, no service,'" Rigel said, turning his half-eaten boot over in his hands. "One boot doesn't count as no shoes, though, does it? Or will they claim that I'm bear-footed?"

Mira laughed, then slammed the cab door. "More puns like that and I withdraw my offer to buy your breakfast."

He had a thick sock that would serve, although at any time he preferred to stay barefoot. His soles were so tough he could win bets by running over sharp gravel; he might have hustled a living at it, had he dared to draw attention to his oddities. There weren't many people in the restaurant, and none of them looked at his feet—they were too busy studying his hair, probably wondering why he bleached it and how he'd managed to get his brows and eyelashes to match. Mira led the way to a booth. A waitress flashed an automatic smile at them and dropped two menus on the table, which made him salivate harder than ever. This would be the third time in his life he had eaten in a restaurant.

"I ought to be treating you, for saving my life." How wonderful it would be if he could afford to do that.

"No. My treat. All you can eat."

Gods, that was tempting! "Well, thanks, but I have money."

"Not much."

"I don't want your charity."

She flashed him a look more exasperated than pitying. "Rigel, you are the most interesting thing that has ever happened in my life or ever will. You lost a lot of blood last night, and you need protein to make it up. I should have reacted more quickly last night. If I'd fired my gun sooner, I would have scared that bear away before it pulled you down. So your problems are partly my fault. I was the one who wrecked your guitar and I'm going to pay for that too. In the meantime, I'm going to get you breakfast, and that's final!"

"I do not beg. I do not accept charity." Why couldn't she understand that a man had to have some pride?

Her sigh definitely expressed exasperation. "Let's do it this way, then. I'll make a bet with you. I'll pick up the tab, and for every dollar's worth of food you can put away, I'll pay you two dollars. But if you get sick to your stomach, you have to pay for my granola. How's that?"

He wanted to argue, but hunger won out, and he returned her smile. "I'll eat for free. Thanks." He opened the menu.

When the waitress came by, he ordered, but Mira told the waitress to bring him double.

While he was wondering how to start questioning her on how he should be tackling his identity problem, Mira said, "May I see your bracelet?"

"You didn't look at it last night?"

"I did, but I didn't have enough time or enough light to examine it properly."

He stretched his right arm across the table so she could peer at the wide silver band on his wrist. To his embarrassment, she pulled a portable magnifying glass out of her purse but fortunately the restaurant was almost empty and no one was watching. She turned the bracelet slowly, examining the inlaid markings with a furrowed brow.

"How long have you had this?"

"As long as I can remember. Since I was born, according to Gert."

"There's no join in it that I can see."

"No," he said. "I've never had it off. Some of my earliest memories are of being hassled for wearing it. Sometimes other boys would try to take it from me, but it would never pass over my hand."

Mira gave him a hard look. "A one-size-fits-always name band put on by the Central Galactic Maternity Ward?"

He thought of it as more of a personal security service from the Cosmic Life Assurance Corporation, but he wasn't ready to tell her about that yet.

"It's as much of a mystery as I am."

"So we must assume that the two mysteries are related." Mira went back to examining the bracelet. "It isn't silver. Silver would have scratched and tarnished by now. Maybe platinum or tungsten? I don't know what sort of material they used to inlay the writing. Red, blue, green . . . The surface of the symbols is perfectly level with the metal, as if all the materials are exactly the same hardness. How many letters?"

"Forty-one, or nine times that many if color makes a difference—six colors plus black, gray, and white."

"How many words?"

"At least a hundred. They change all the time, like a used-car lot marquee. See these three blues together? Now turn it once around my wrist. They're gone, see? The words change. They come back, but never in the same order. Nobody knows what language or script it is, or if it's writing at all. Is a red fish the same as a green one? It could all be decorative for all I know."

"Or instructions on how ET can call home?"

Rigel retrieved his arm, and Mira slipped her magnifying glass back into her purse. The waitress arrived, bringing them their drinks. Rigel drained his glass of orange juice. Then the food arrived, and he had to talk between gulps.

"What do you think?" he said. "About the bracelet."

"It does look like writing. You should try to get a complete text; see if the order ever does repeat. If it's as long as you think it is, it may yield to cryptography. You can write a whole book using less than a hundred words. Who have you asked about it?"

He shrugged. "Anyone I thought I could trust. I've spent hours in libraries reading up on alphabets. Back in Toronto I saw a plaque in an art store window that looked somewhat similar. They told me it was seventeenth-century First Nations work from the west coast of Vancouver Island, so I went out to Tofino, where they stock stuff like that to sell to tourists. What I found there wasn't historical, but they directed me to an artist in Ahousaht, on Flores Island. Interesting guy. He didn't want to talk at first, but he loved the bracelet and when we got to know each other, he admitted he'd invented his own script, basing it on Rongo-rongo, but I already knew about that."

"Where's Rongo-rongo?"

"Nowhere. Rongo-rongo is a form of writing found only on Easter Island in the middle of the Pacific. It's not the same as this—it's just the most similar I've ever found. Since no one can read Rongo-rongo, it doesn't put me much further ahead, except that whoever made the bracelet may have pirated it, like that guy in Ahousaht."

Mira said, "Mm. And does it do anything else, this bangle, other than advertising best buys in secondhand flying saucers?"

"Everything all right?" asked the waitress.

"My friend isn't slowing down yet," Mira said. "Bring back the menu." When they were alone, she said, "Well, does your little gadget do other tricks?"

That was a creepily perceptive question, and she was a spooky person all around. Even her apparent willingness to believe in him and his bracelet was hard to swallow, but he was fairly sure that she wasn't about to turn him in to the authorities, and if she was working on the shady side of the law, she might be just as vulnerable as he was. He was in over his head already, so he might as well tell her the rest. Besides, he owed her for the best meal of his life.

"Yes, it does. When I was about seven or so, I was hanging out with a gang of kids playing by a river somewhere in northern Ontario. I forget the name of the river, but they were using a fallen tree as a raft. They said I could join them that day, but something kept pulling me back. I got scared, because there was nobody there, just this tug on my wrist. The harder I pulled, the harder *it* pulled. So I wasn't on the tree with the others when it broke loose and drifted away. It rolled, of course, and two of them drowned."

Mira shook her head. "Seven's not very old. I don't mean to be insulting, but I'm not sure that's proof of anything."

He smiled to show her that he didn't take offense. "I have more."

"I want to hear more, but my reaction so far is that a seven-year-old might have dreamt the memory in afterwards. If the gang *didn't* let him play on their raft, he could have invented the story of the magical warning. A psychologist might suspect that he felt guilty because the others drowned and he didn't. But keep going."

"The next two are even weaker," he said, although he didn't believe that his younger self had invented the first warning. "There were a couple of times after that when I felt the bracelet sort of tingle, which made me turn around and walk another way. Once I found out later that there was a pedophile molesting boys in the area that the bracelet had steered me away from. Doesn't prove a thing, I know.

"The fourth case is a lot less fuzzy. About a month ago I was cutting through East Hastings in Vancouver, which is about as rough a locale as anywhere in Canada, and the bracelet began to tingle. I started to turn around, and . . . This is hard to explain. The turn became a pivot, if you know what I mean. I just spun around on the ball of my foot and threw a punch. I never knew I had it in me—I swear it lifted the guy right off his feet, and he must have outweighed me by ten kilos. There was no warning shout, the sun wasn't casting any shadows, and there were no store windows to show me his reflection. It was a completely inexplicable thing for me to do."

"He had a gun, I hope? He wasn't trying to hand you a copy of the *Watchtower*?"

"A piece of lead pipe. A *nasty* looking thing, about this long, and he had it raised to bash my head in."

"Any witnesses?"

"Yes, but I didn't stick around to take names." He hesitated, but then said it. "And if you want to know more, I hit him full on the mouth. I know that's the stupidest place to hit anyone."

She nodded. "A good way to get a fistful of broken teeth."

Rigel held out his hand for her to see. "There were teeth and blood splattered all over the sidewalk, but I didn't have a mark on me, not even a bruise."

"And last night, when the bear tried to make you its dinner?"

"I didn't feel a thing. The bracelet didn't quiver at all. Nothing. But when Bruin pulled me down, I had this weird sensation of stabbing it. I had no knife, but your gun sure didn't make that hole over its heart."

She nodded. "OK. Add it all together and it does make sense. I can't explain you, and I can't explain your bracelet. Micah's team keeps up with all the latest in weapons technology, and I'm damned sure that anything that high-tech is at least twenty years away . . . on this planet."

Two sixteen-ounce steaks, six eggs over easy, two hash browns, four hotcakes with maple syrup, a ham and cheese sandwich, three helpings of pie and ice cream, and about a liter of orange juice later, he said, "No thanks," when the waitress brought back the menu yet again.

Mira held out five fifty-dollar bills and told him to keep the change.

He managed to refuse. It wasn't easy.

"You can pay me back later."

"Not unless you give me your permanent address." And her real name. He knew she'd refuse.

Her smile told him that she knew exactly what he was thinking. "Let's do it this way, then. Honor system. You have no boots, sonny. You need this money now. Don't pay it back, pay it forward: when you don't need it anymore, pass it along to someone who does."

To his shame, he thanked her and stuffed the bills in his pocket.

Chapter 5

By the time they reached Nanaimo's urban sprawl, rain was pelting down.

Rigel said, "Noah's Flood, the remake."

"With an all-new cast."

"We have lots of time for the ferry. There's a Walmart on Aulds Road," he suggested hopefully. "I need new jeans and boots. And sunglasses."

"Won't be much of a run on those today. Does the light bother you?"

"No, the stares do."

"Oh, Rigel! People just think you're an albino."

"Albinos have red eyes."

"But how many people know that? Very pale gray eyes aren't that rare. Keep a shirt on and you're a high-octane stud with the cutest buns this side of the Mississippi. If I were in the mood for cradle robbing I'd have had your diapers off long ago."

"*Ahem!* You did, last night."

"And you went to sleep on me. How do you think that makes a girl feel?" She smiled at him, and then after a couple moments of silence, she said, "Are you sure you're okay with going back to Vancouver?"

"Vancouver is great." Joey Lotbiniere would lend him a guitar, and he earned as much busking in Granville Island Market as he ever did anywhere. He would go back to public lamentation for lost loves he had never known and sins he had never been able to afford.

The Walmart parking lot was surprisingly crowded for this early in the morning. Mira parked as close to the door as she could and sprinted across the tarmac. He followed more slowly out of respect for his still-tender wounds. He needed new boots, jeans, and if the money would stretch, a spare shirt. He preferred to buy at thrift shops when he could, but a guy over 195 centimeters and under seventy kilos had trouble finding new clothes that fit, let alone castoffs. He joined Mira inside the mercury-lit blimp hangar.

"I need another suitcase," she said. "See you back here in fifteen?"

He said fine and strode off in the direction of Men's Footwear, weaving in and out of clusters of strollers, chattering women, bawling toddlers, and elders on walkers. The store wasn't crowded, but it still held more people than he'd seen in one place in the last three weeks. A small lady asked him if he could lift down one of *those* for her, and he happily obliged. That happened at least once every time he entered a big-box store like this one.

Coffeemakers: hundreds of coffeemakers! Scores of different sizes and brands. Who needed all of them? Who bought them? Did they need one in every room? Did coffeemakers go out of style after a month or so? Or just fall apart?

He was cruising along a Kitchenware canyon between columns of plastic containers towering up on his right and cliffs of stratified china and glassware on his left when he felt a sudden tingle from his bracelet. He spun around but saw nothing untoward behind him. Imagination! *With paranoia you are never alone . . .* He decided to go back, though, moving cautiously. The bracelet kept tingling without getting stronger or weaker. Should he head for Gardening, say, and arm himself with a pitchfork or whatever else looked lethal? Or should he just trust the bracelet, which seemed to have an appropriate response for every possible danger? Or should he just shift his butt the hell out of the store and wait for Mira at the Winnebago?

He reached a cross-aisle. Looking both ways like a child crossing the road, he made eye contact with a burly, unshaven, dirty-looking man about five meters away. The man snarled at him, ripped open the package he was holding, and pulled out a carving knife. He bawled out an obscenity and charged.

Nobody can undo store packaging with their bare hands, Rigel thought inanely. He took to his heels and ran straight ahead, ignoring stabs of pain from his scabs. Halfway up that aisle a pregnant woman screamed at him and released the stroller she was pushing so she could grab a toaster off the shelf beside her and throw it at his face.

He batted it aside with his iron glove and kept right on moving. Still screaming, she hurled a stainless steel coffeepot and he treated that the same way. He did register the fact that he had not been wearing a gauntlet a few seconds ago, but he was in too much of a hurry to consider the ramifications; he just had time for the fleeting thought that it was the same glove that had formed around his fist that time in Vancouver. As he jostled past the woman, she tried to claw his eyes out, so he had to elbow her out of the way more roughly than he would have liked. Another man came rushing around the corner ahead of him. This one was younger and better dressed than the first. He was armed with a wood ax.

Another missile struck Rigel in the back, but did him no harm. He continued to run, heading straight for Wood Ax, who raised his weapon two-handed to strike. Rigel extended his sword at arm's length—where had that come from?—and realized too late what was about to happen. His feet and arm had taken on a life of their own, and all of his muscles were out of his control. The sword ran the man through cleanly. The worst part was that it met with almost no resistance any-where; it was like stabbing soft ice cream. Human beings should not die so easily! Their combined momentum slammed the two of them together. Rigel cried out in horror, but Wood Ax just collapsed, convincingly dead.

Rigel yanked his sword free, wasting no time on wondering where the damned thing had come from or the mailed gaunt-let that held it. He turned—it felt more as if the sword turned him—just in time to parry a downward jab from Carving Knife, who had followed him. The man was obviously no fighter, for he was clutching his weapon like a tennis racket, but he was certainly a dangerous maniac, spitting foam and curses. The sword took no chances with him. Before he could strike again, it slashed him across the throat.

Appalled, Rigel backed away from the second corpse. He hadn't meant to kill anyone. *The sword made me do it!* How could he ever explain that? Had these men been sent by Mira's jealous Micah? So soon? And the pregnant woman, who had abandoned the stroller and was even now struggling to pick up the knife? This was madness. Nobody hired pregnant women to beat people up!

Mira! Rigel jumped over Wood Ax's body and raced off in search of Mira. There was definitely something odd about

Mira. Two mysteries—the woman who had appeared so dramatically and inexplicably in his life and this mob insanity. She was the one who had told him to assume that the mystery of his bracelet and the mystery of his parentage must be related. Perhaps she had somehow caused this riot. If so, she was probably the only one who could put a stop to it.

The madness had spread. Women were screaming, men shouting. Rigel himself was splattered with two men's blood and brandishing a gory blade that was more than a meter long and apparently razor sharp.

Luggage . . . luggage . . . where would they keep the luggage? He rounded a corner and almost ran into a middle-aged, blue-rinsed female employee engaged in restocking stationery. She looked up with a smile, which turned into a shriek when she saw the blood-spattered monster looming over her.

"Luggage?" he said. "Where can I find luggage?"

She leaped at him and tried to claw out his eyes. He pushed her aside so roughly that she sat down hard on the floor, while he fled back the way he had come. He found a broader thoroughfare in the middle of the store. His appearance was greeted with screams of triumph as a crowd of fifty or more people surged at him, many of them pushing shopping carts ahead of them like tanks. Some in the back of the mob began lobbing mortar bombs of merchandise over the heads of those in the front.

A fire alarm erupted in intolerable clamor. Someone must have dialed 911 by now, and cops would soon be swarming the store like ants. Guessing that Mira would head for the front door, he went in what he thought was that direction.

But another mob promptly spilled toward him around a corner—shoppers, clerks, cashiers leaving their tills, many of them wielding wire shopping baskets like weapons. For some reason, he had become a leper and the sight of him was enough to arouse a lynch mob. Trapped between the two ravening hordes, he dived into yet another merchandise canyon. Mira was facing in his direction with her feet apart, both hands gripping her damnable gun. She wasn't aiming at him, though, but at a man in between them, who was striding toward her with a golf club raised to strike. Rigel was pleased to know that he wasn't the only pariah, but why had the entire shopping population of Nanaimo gone homicidally berserk? And why were they only attacking him and Mira? *Attention shoppers! The drug-peddling pedophile terrorist in aisle nine . . .* Mira's mouth was moving. No doubt she was shouting at her assailant and possibly he was shouting back at her, but whatever they were saying was inaudible under the cacophony of the fire alarm and the mob.

Rigel wanted to scream at her to put the damned gun away. The Canadian judicial system went ballistic at the slightest hint of handguns. Handguns implied gang warfare; they were illegal, smuggled in from the United States, and they carried extra penalties. More urgent was the fact that he was directly in her line of fire. The sword lurched forward, taking him with it. He turned his face away, but couldn't avoid feeling the impact as the blade sliced into the would-be golfer's back.

He looked again. Mira was still shouting inaudibly, but now she seemed to be shouting at him. The golfer squirmed on the floor, horribly wounded and probably dying. She lowered her gun, freeing one shaky hand to point. The head-splitting tumult suddenly shrank to a distant whisper, as if a glass bubble had closed around them. No, Mira was not looking at Rigel; she was looking past him, at a tidal wave of men and women—mostly women—that had jammed into the aisle in a frenzied effort to reach their intended victims. Those in the front line were being buried by people scrambling over them and by avalanches of merchandise toppling from the high display racks.

"You all right?" he asked, and he heard his own voice perfectly well. Another mob was coming from the other direction. The two of them were about to be stomped into mush.

But no! That mob, also, suddenly stopped advancing. It began piling up higher and higher, beating itself against nothing, as if an invisible sheet of glass had intervened between it and its desired victims. Rigel saw missiles bounce off the intangible barrier, saw people being squelched against it, as the mob kept trying to surge forward. The same thing had happened on both sides, as if he and Mira were enclosed in a science fiction force field.

He felt sick. *Stop! Stop!*

Then they had company.

He was not accustomed to looking up at people, but the newcomer was certainly taller than he was, likely more than two meters, not counting the huge, pointed ears set on top of his head like a cat's. Even so, he might weigh no more than Rigel, because he was slender as a wand. That he had neither nipples nor a navel was immediately evident because his only garment was a shimmering kilt set low on hips that didn't look capable of holding up a rubber band. Nice beachwear, but not really practical for shopping. He sported numerous metallic bracelets on his wrists and ankles, many jeweled studs around the edges of his feline ears, and a thin staff of polished wood taller then himself, bound with bands of many colors. His hair was a velvet cap of spun gold, and his irises shone amber to match. He loomed over Rigel like a string colossus, frowning down at the bloody scene around them. Despite his bare feet and near-nudity, he projected an aura of power and authority that made a man's knees want to buckle into obeisance.

But Rigel wanted to scream with joy. Whatever or whoever this newcomer was, he obviously belonged to the same species as Rigel, or close to it. *Rigel Estell was no longer alone in the Universe!* Unable to offer a hand to shake, because his right hand was still enclosed in a steel glove and clutching a bloody sword, he bowed. "Delighted to meet you, Mr. Fomalhaut."

"You know this monster?" Mira wailed.

"I never set eyes on him before. But that's his name."

"Correct." The stranger's voice was pure song, as sweet as the call of a flute. "You having presently no further requirement for that gruesome weaponry, Rigel Halfling, I do demand that you now diligently decommission it."

Rigel glanced guiltily at the bloody blade. "I don't know how to do that, sir."

"*Lower it,* you incompetent freak!"

Rigel pointed his sword at the ground, and both sword and gauntlet immediately vanished. His arm was spattered with blood down to his bracelet, but his hand and wrist were dry and clean.

"Where did you come from, halfling? Who is your sponsor, and who granted you the authority to extrovert?"

"I regret that I have not the slightest idea what your lordship means." Rigel could hear sirens. They were barely audible over the muted fire alarm, but he strongly suspected that the police were just outside in the parking lot. He hoped there were ambulances there too, because there must be dozens of injured people in those writhing heaps of humanity. At the same time, he felt a certain urgency about taking his leave before people began posing questions and asking for ID.

He glanced at Mira, who was still staring openmouthed at the apparition.

The giant said, "Who gave you that amulet?"

"What amulet?"

"That bracelet!"

"I do not know, sir. I would *love* to know!"

"Then you will come with me."

Oh, yes! Anywhere but here! "I am at your lordship's command," Rigel said giddily. "And my friend must accompany us."

The alien curled his lip at Mira like something that had crawled out of a landfill. "What is she? Your servant? Your concubine?"

More police sirens were shrieking all around them. Every badge on the Island was going to be pouring in there in a few minutes, waving guns and bullhorns.

"Ms. Silvas is a friend, who saved my life just yesterday."

"She's an earthling!"

Earthling or not, Mira must not be left behind for the police to torment—not after all she'd done for him.

"She knows too much. She comes or I stay."

Fomalhaut shrugged his inhumanly narrow shoulders. "You are hardly in a position to dictate terms, Halfling Rigel, but your analysis is plausible. Very well. Grip this!" He held out his curiously banded staff.

Rigel shrugged. Both he and Mira took hold of it. The world around him vanished in a flash of darkness and bitter cold. For a moment there was an agonizing wrenching and twisting sensation, but it was gone before Rigel could even scream.

———

Then the world started up again.

The three of them were standing in a grassy, sunlit meadow, just a few meters from the edge of a small lake. On the far side of the lake, waterfalls sprayed down mossy cliffs, and a couple of stringy, golden-skinned youths had just leaped off in parallel dives. A dozen or so similar looking youngsters of both sexes were romping around in the water itself amid a welter of foam and high-pitched laughter, and the entire scene was framed in trees, flowers, songbirds, and boughs laden with multicolored fruit. The air was perfumed, and exactly the right temperature. It all looked like a travel poster for some tropical paradise, but the kids in the water all had high, pointed ears like bats'.

"Where is this?" Mira cried. "Where are we?"

Rigel sighed with an almost unbearable joy. "I don't know where you are," he said, "but I think I just came home."

Chapter 6

Their arrival had been noticed. One of the bathers shot up out of the water like a dolphin. Instead of falling back, he began running over the surface toward the visitors.

Rigel's mind instinctively rejected the image. He looked away, but the scenery seemed as far-fetched and unrealistic as a child's drawing. The grass was too long for a lawn and too short for pasture; the ground was uneven, but the hollows and hummocks were oddly regular; and the deep blue of the sky didn't fade to a paler shade near the horizon. No obvious path or road led out of the clearing. The only building in sight was a freestanding doorway just a few meters away— two pillars, a threshold, and lintel, all made of marble, framing a grandiose double door of white enamel and gold trim. None of your suburban glue-and-sawdust, hollow-core trash here! He resisted the temptation to go around it to see what was on the other side.

"My gun!" Mira cried. "What did you do with my Smith and Wesson?"

"It remained behind," Fomalhaut said, "like your watch."

She howled in outrage, staring at her wrist. "That was a genuine Rolex Perpetual!"

"Doesn't matter. Machinery cannot be introverted."

"Welcome, welcome!" shouted the boy running over the water. His name, quite obviously, was Muphrid, although Rigel had no idea how he knew that. He was as tall as Fomalhaut, with the same large bat ears and iridescent loincloth. The major difference was that his hair was grass green. His playmates were following in a more orthodox fashion, arms flailing, moving like Olympic champions.

"My God!" Mira said. "They're *elves*!"

"Watch your mouth, earthling!" Fomalhaut barked. "Use that word here and you will regret it dearly."

"If you're not elves, then what in hell are you?"

"We are the starborn, the starfolk, and impudent earthlings get soundly flogged here."

"And just where is 'here,' your lordship?" Rigel asked. *I've a feeling we're not in Canada anymore, Toto.*

"We are in the Starlands, the realm of Queen Electra."

That told him nothing much.

Mira uttered a strangled yell and screamed, "You did this!" She was accusing Rigel, not Fomalhaut, which was ironic because Rigel had suspected her of causing the riot in the Walmart.

"Steady!" he said, putting an arm around her—his left arm, not his magic-bracelet arm. "Wherever we are, let's wait and see what happens before we panic, okay?"

She was trembling violently, wide-eyed and chalky pale, looking ready to faint. He could not doubt her terror, but though he understood it, he did not share it. In a sense he had been waiting and hoping for something like this all his life; it was a childhood dream come true.

Muphrid trotted ashore and bowed low to Fomalhaut, sweeping his arms out to the sides in an expansive gesture as if he were about to leap off a diving board. When he straightened up, his huge smile displayed white teeth with far too many sharp points. He was puffing, every rib visible and working hard. "Welcome to Alrisha, my lord! You do my home great honor."

His eyes shone greener than emeralds, the same lucent color as his hair. That fitted—Fomalhaut had gold hair and gold eyes, Rigel's were both white, and why shouldn't a person's hair and eyes match? It was a tidy idea. Elfin eyes were slightly slanted, their chins were more pointed than normal in human males, and body fat was definitely *out*. So was body hair, and the growth on their scalps looked like flat-lying fur.

"Such is not my intention."

Muphrid gulped and seemed to shrink. He clasped his hands together under his chin, elbows together, and his ears went flat. His friends, who were just starting to wade ashore, stopped dead at the sight.

"I have displeased my lord?"

"Prince Vildiar is enraged by your territorial rapacity in annexing Starborn Dubhe's Moon Garden."

"But she never uses it!" Muphrid wailed. "Not once in the last fifty years. Parts of it were being forgotten!"

"Nevertheless, such larceny is reprehensible, and Dubhe has influential connections. His Highness is considering denouncing you to the regent, and you know how *he* will react to such egregious larceny."

With a loud wail, Muphrid collapsed on his bony knees and tried to kiss Fomalhaut's toes.

His lordship stepped back hastily. "Desist, you groveling maggot. I do not wish to be embroiled in so sordid a contretemps.

Possibly you can make redress by dealing with this halfling." He gestured toward Rigel, who still had his arm wrapped around Mira.

Muphrid sprang upright like a jack-in-the-box and looked Rigel up and down. He scowled. Rigel scowled right back.

The elf's ears went even flatter. "What must I do with it, my lord?"

"Quarter him for a few days. He is probably older than he looks, but he is fresh out of the mud and as ignorant as a newborn."

"That is *blood* on him, isn't it?"

"Only earthling blood, but he is armed and may be dangerous. If he proves obdurate or recalcitrant, apply whatever force is needful to restrain him. Otherwise proceed to instruct him in the rudiments of civilized behavior and deference to his betters, so that he will have some minuscule chance when he appears in court."

Rigel lost his temper. "Just a minute! I was attacked by a crazy killer mob! Are you suggesting that I was wrong to defend myself?"

The two elves looked down at him with open contempt.

"You did not defend yourself, halfling," Fomalhaut said. "Your amulet did. Whoever gave it to you is the party at fault, and the court will endeavor to determine the miscreant's identity so that he or she can be suitably penalized."

Aha! "I shall cooperate fully with the court in that, your lordship. My greatest wish is to learn my father's name."

"Then this is the right place for you." Fomalhaut turned back to Muphrid. "Educate him in our ways as best as you can. Excessive ignorance on his part will waste the court's time."

"My lord wants me to treat a halfling like a *guest*?" Muphrid's face retained its golden shade, yet his expression would have better suited a bilious green color, like his hair.

The audience at the edge of the water was exchanging grins and smirks. Some were holding hands, even cuddling, as they watched, and Rigel decided that these gangling people were not the children he had originally thought them to be. They were all skinny as ropes, their faces were unlined, and they had been romping and screaming, but they were not behaving like children now. They could be any age—twenty or sixty or even a hundred. Maybe it was just Fomalhaut's arrogant bearing that made him seem older than the rest.

"Within reasonable limits. The earthling female may be called as a witness, but in the interim you can billet her in your mudling barns and put her to work."

"My lord is most generous." Muphrid displayed his shark teeth again.

"You understand," Fomalhaut concluded, "that if the halfling is awarded status and you have properly instructed him in the procedures of gentle manners, we can present him to His Highness as a token of your contrition in the Moon Garden affair. If His Highness gains a valuable servant as a result of your efforts, he may be more inclined to overlook your indiscretion."

Muphrid's fearsome smile flashed again, and his ears sprang fully erect. "You may rely on me, Starborn Fomalhaut. You know that serving you is my greatest pleasure and honor. May I present my friends?"

"Some other time. I am busy today." Fomalhaut gestured with his staff and abruptly vanished.

"Someone should teach him some manners," Rigel said.

"Silence, rubbish!" Muphrid said. "You speak of one of the great mages of the realm, a trusted underling of Prince Vildiar himself!"

So now he was rubbish, was he? Rigel glanced again at the elfin audience, all of them displaying those feline ears and shark-tooth grins. On Earth he had been a freak, but it hadn't been obvious so long as he kept his clothes on. And few men had called him rude names since he'd reached his full height. Here, he realized—wherever "here" was—he was still a freak, and more openly so. That "halfling" term was worrisome, and neither his ears nor his teeth were standard. Passing as a local would be harder here, if not impossible, and every male in sight was taller than he was.

But the lifelong mystery of who or what he was might be solvable here in these Starlands in a way that it never had been on Earth. Rigel's best strategy must be to stay polite and learn as much as he could by keeping his eyes and ears open, even if neither were the right shape. He could not play the game until he knew the rules.

The other starborn clustered in closer to inspect the visitors. In every case, Rigel knew their names at first glance, and still did not know how he was doing that. Even many of the women were taller than he, and they all had hair and eyes of the same color, which could be any color at all; their skins were golden, without a single mole, scar, or freckle in sight. He realized with a shock that none of them wore more clothing than a skimpy, glittery loincloth and a vulgar over-abundance of jewelry. *Help, I am being held prisoner in a vacation commercial.* Males and females both were laden with bracelets, anklets, rings, and earrings. No necklaces, though—why not? Like him, none of them had navels, but the girls certainly had breasts. And nipples. And areolas, large and tinted hot rose pink. Suddenly there was nowhere safe to look.

"If Fomalhaut was all that great he wouldn't wear so many amulets," remarked Alniyat, whose hair and eyes were shiny silver. Of the dozen or so gorgeous women there, she was probably the loveliest, although he'd want to stare at each of them for a long time before reaching a definite conclusion on that. She caught Rigel admiring her and smiled; he looked away quickly, feeling himself blush.

The males were not smiling.

"Even for a halfling, he's ugly," said Gacrux, who stood over seven feet tall and had some rather un-elfin beef on his bones.

"Careful," Muphrid said. "Starborn Fomalhaut warned me that he is armed. Show us your amulet, tweenling."

Presumably tweenling was another word for halfling. By amulet, Muphrid was undoubtedly referring to the bracelet that had transformed into the sword that had killed three men in the Walmart fight, the close-quarters dagger that had stabbed the bear, and the armored glove that had punched the would-be mugger. A weapon for all seasons, evidently. Releasing Mira and stepping clear of her, he held out his wrist to let them see.

"Well, show us, boy!" Muphrid said.

"Show you what?"

"It's a weapon isn't it? Old Foamy said you were armed."

"I can't make it appear to order. It only becomes a weapon when I need to defend myself."

The overgrown brats tittered as if he'd asked them to tie his shoelaces.

"You say its name, halfling," Muphrid said with exaggerated patience.

"I don't know its name."

Muphrid grabbed his wrist and raised it to read the inscription. "Denebola, Rukbat, Rastaban . . . *Stars!*" he yelled, jumping back. "It's *Saiph!*"

There were shouts of disbelief, but suddenly a space had cleared around Rigel. He said, "Saiph?" and instantly his hand was enclosed in a shiny metal gauntlet clutching a sword, more than a meter of sun-blazing steel. It sagged because he hadn't been ready for the weight, and the circle of onlookers grew even wider. No, the sword was not steel, he decided—it had been wrought of the same silvery, tempered metal as the bracelet. It bore no fancy inscriptions or jewels—it was a simple, deadly killing machine as he had proved, but a thing of beauty nonetheless. He turned it to reflect the sunlight, squinting along its glowing length, and wiggling it to feel the balance.

He glanced down at Mira, who was staying very close to him, as if he could somehow defend her from this nightmare. He winked reassuringly. "You need a knight protector, my lady?"

She managed to return a tiny smile and a nod, although she was blue-lipped and shivering, her arms wrapped around her body. Part of her trouble must be the temperature, although he felt overdressed and envied the elves their near-nudity.

"How did you get that?" Muphrid shouted. "Saiph is a Lesath!"

"A who?"

"An amulet of massacre potential. It is illegal to make or own a Lesath."

"Not where I come from," Rigel said, wondering how a Lesath would rank under Canadian firearm laws.

"Who gave you that thing, boy?" big Gacrux demanded.

Rigel looked him up and down. Then up again. "An admirer."

Gacrux scowled, raised his right hand, and said, "Taygeta!" Then he too held a sword.

Saiph jerked Rigel's hand up to an on-guard position.

"You idiot, Gacrux!" Alniyat shouted. "There isn't a sword in the realm can beat Saiph. Put it away before you get yourself slaughtered."

Gacrux lowered Taygeta and it vanished.

Rigel disposed of Saiph the same way and could breathe more easily. "What were those other names you read out, Muphrid?"

A couple of the girls tittered and their host scowled. "Manners!" he said. "I have to teach you. Lesson one is that children and halflings address purebloods like us as 'starborn,' or—and I do recommend this, at least until you get status—as 'my lord' or 'my lady.' Never 'your lordship.' Got that?"

"What were those other names you read out, starborn?"

"The names of famous heroes and kings of old who were slain by that sword. Saiph," Muphrid added sourly, "is *ancestral*."

"Ancestral to what, starborn?"

More sniggers.

"I mean it is storied, legendary. It is unthinkable that it should be wielded by a mere halfling boy. The court will certainly regard this as a most serious matter."

"I may be what you call a halfling, but I am not a boy."

"They'll never grant him status with those eyes," Nashira said, blinking her own, which were purple, like her hair. "They're dead as paper."

"You suppose he has ears under that mane?" That was big Gacrux again.

"We'll see," said Muphrid. He selected one of his finger rings and turned it. "Take off those awful rags, halfling."

Rigel raised no objection. He knew he'd be more comfortable without his clothes, and the starfolk were very close to naked. He pulled off his bloody shirt. The half-healed scars on his chest provoked screams of horror.

"A bear," he explained.

"Didn't Saiph protect you?"

"Yes. Oh, I killed it. I mean Saiph did. We just weren't quite quick enough."

His audience exchanged puzzled glances, as if that did not make sense, but he wasn't going to explain about boots and bicycles and guitars getting in the way.

Knuckles tapped politely from the other side of the door, one of the gold handles turned, and the flap opened just enough to admit a man. Seemingly human, he was portly and balding, probably in his sixties. In the company of the youthful giants he seemed old and small. Surprisingly, he wore a toga with a purple border and red shoes like a character in a Hollywood gladiator epic. He bowed to Muphrid.

"How may I serve, starborn?"

"We have an extra guest, Halfling Rigel. Bring a mooncloth wrap for him, and find someone to cut his hair. Take the earthling to staff quarters, and see that she is washed and suitably dressed and put to work. We'll eat in the Versailles room in an hour or so. And, Senator . . .?"

"Starborn?"

"Treat the woman well as long as she behaves. She may have to testify in court. We don't want any unpleasant accusations flying around."

Senator bowed again. "Indeed not, starborn." He gestured for Mira to follow him.

Mira squeaked.

"Wait a minute!" Rigel wrapped his arm around her shoulders again. "We are both strangers here, and we wish to stay together."

"Your wishes are of no interest or importance," Muphrid declared. "And hers even less. You will both do as you are told or you will both be chained up. I extend courtesy to you, halfling, merely because Starborn Fomalhaut asked me to. Now, which will it be?"

Rigel raised his right hand with the shiny bracelet . . .

Mira said, "No, don't! My lord, I trust that I will be allowed to attend my master this evening to perform my usual duties?"

Attend her *whom* to do *what*? After a moment of confusion, Rigel picked up on the cue she was giving him. "I certainly hope so! I have no objection to my concubine helping out in the kitchens by day, starborn, but I naturally expect to enjoy her services at night."

The entire audience exploded in shrill titters.

Muphrid shuddered. "Oh, it is impossible! It will take a hundred years to train this tweenling. Rigel Halfling, you must not *say* such things! But, very well, I promise. Get her out of my sight, Senator."

Mira flashed her "owner" a sickly smile and followed the portly man through the door, which closed behind them before Rigel could see what lay beyond it. Assuming that she was planning to cooperate until she had gathered more information, he could only hope to match her courage.

"What exactly happens if the court does *not* grant me status, starborn?"

"Then you'll have to wear clothes!" Nashira jeered, as if that were a threat.

"Let's see if there is any hope at all," Muphrid said. "I told you to strip, boy."

Rigel balanced on one leg at a time to discard his boot and sock, and then dropped his jeans, leaving himself dressed in nothing but the rubber band in his hair, Saiph, and his jockey shorts, which were white and clean, but too snug for comfort under the present circumstances. He would have preferred to be wearing his loose boxer shorts with the pink cupids, which he'd purchased for a dollar in a thrift shop.

"Yes, he isn't a boy," remarked Dabih, a female with bluish hair.

"Obviously," agreed purple-eyed Nashira. "For a tweenling, he's not bad below the neck. He doesn't have girly nipples or an ugly birth scar on his belly."

"What would you know about those?" Alniyat demanded, provoking an angry blush on Nashira and hoots of laughter from the male starfolk.

"He's a runt, though," Gacrux said.

"And you're a fatso."

"Fatso?" the big elf bellowed over the sniggers.

Playground talk! Rigel trotted over to the water and splashed in. As soon as it was over his knees he plunged in deeper and started to swim. He had been a good swimmer back on Earth, but in moments he was overtaken by what seemed like a pod of dolphins, all streaming through the water far faster than he could manage. Admittedly his cuts stung so he wasn't at his best, but even the women left him feeling like a barnacle. He had been a freak on Earth, and he was a freak here, wherever this was. There was nowhere in the universe where he'd truly feel at home.

Chapter 7

Having shown up Rigel's incompetent swimming, the starborn grew bored of him and returned to their horseplay beneath the waterfalls. Convinced that this fairyland must have more interesting things to offer, he paddled back to the meadow and went to see what lay on the other side of the big door. It wouldn't open for him when he tried the handles, and when he walked around it he discovered a blank stone wall.

Baffled, he turned to the flowers and shrubs. Some were almost familiar—a daffodil tree was certainly a good idea—and others were totally weird. Various shrubs bore flowers like fried eggs, tiny pink horses, or red mouths that smiled when you looked in their direction. A few had gold and silver roses. Some were too bizarre to be anything but deliberate inventions, and yet even those were inhabited by large, multicolored insects and spiders. He had truly been transported to a completely different world, like Alice, or Thomas Covenant, or Wendy Darling.

Then he noticed that Senator was waiting patiently by the door, holding a shimmering length of what looked like shrink-wrap but felt like the finest wool when Rigel wound it around his hips. It stayed there comfortably on its own, glittering in the sunlight, just on the respectable side of translucent.

With a pained expression, the servant gathered up Rigel's discarded clothes. "Someone is ready to cut your hair, if this is a convenient time, halfling."

"Lead the way, Senator. Is that your real name or just Starborn Muphrid's nickname for you? How should I address you?"

"'Mudling' is customary, halfling. 'Butler' if you need to distinguish me from the other servants."

"A mudling being . . . ?"

Senator's well-disciplined face barely managed to hide his shock at Rigel's ignorance. "My remote ancestors were earthlings, halfling, but their descendants have lived in the Starlands for many generations."

"Ah, thank you."

The toga-ed man opened the door and ushered Rigel out onto a balcony. Beyond a dangerously low balustrade, the ground fell away about ten thousand meters to a landscape of hills and forests stretching to infinity. There was no sane way to reconcile this topography with the sprawling parkland on the other side of the door. The temperature was also a good ten degrees lower, and the sun had shifted. Rigel staggered, partly because an icy gust of wind struck him, and partly because something that resembled a Cessna with talons soared past about a hundred meters away, much too close for comfort.

A young male elf named Izar was waiting on the balcony, watching the airborne monster. He was tall enough to be a human adolescent, but might be only a child by starborn standards. His hair and eyes were as white as Rigel's, but his ears were enormous, seemingly full adult size. He turned and recoiled at the sight of the scars on Rigel's chest. The ears flattened back against his head.

The butler said, "I was instructed to explain that the starling will cut your hair, but is forbidden to speak to you." He departed, closing the door behind him.

"You're not hairy!" Izar said suspiciously.

"Are halflings usually hairy?"

"Some are *horribly* hairy. Real starfolk aren't, never. And we don't grow manes like that." He pointed to Rigel's.

"I came here so you could cut it off for me."

The starling hesitated, then grinned to show adult-sized teeth like daggers. "You bet!" He pointed to a spindly chair, which looked as if it had been borrowed from the History Channel and might blow away at any moment. Rigel sat down apprehensively.

"May your progeny outnumber the stars, Rigel Halfling." The starling peered intently at the rubber band securing Rigel's hair.

"And the same to you, Starborn Izar. Is that the correct response?"

Izar broke the band and spread Rigel's locks out with his fingers. "No. I outrank you, so you should have said, 'May the stars shine on you forever, most noble Izar Starling.' Or 'noble Starling Izar' if you prefer; it doesn't matter."

"May the stars shine on you forever, most noble Izar Starling."

"Good. Remember it." Izar lifted a thick tress of hair. *Snip!* There was to be no ceremony with white sheets in this barbershop. *Snip!* again. Although Rigel's hair was still damp from his swim, the gale was so strong that it removed every strand the moment Izar released it. *Snip! Snip! Snip!*—a contrail of white hair swirled off into the void. Rigel sighed for all the years he had spent growing that hair.

"This is fun," Izar remarked. "How often do you need to be pruned?"

"It took me about five years to grow this much."

"*Schmoory!*"

"Yours?"

"It doesn't grow any longer than this. What tried to eat you?"

"A bear."

"You kill it?" *Snip!*

"You bet."

Snip! "Good." *Snip!* "Why did Saiph let you get wounded?"

"I don't know. Why were you forbidden to speak to me, most noble Starling Izar?"

Izar considered the question for a moment. "Prob'ly in case I wouldn't. She didn't want me clamming up. She thinks it's clever to order me not to do 'xactly what she wants me to do; so I will, but sometimes I do what she says, just to keep her guessing. Or maybe she actually meant it this time, though, because she was worried that I'd tell you all sort of things you mustn't know, like what status is." *Snip!*

"What's status, most noble Starling Izar?"

"It's when the court decides whether you're too ugly to be a halfling, so you must really be an earthling or a mudling." *Snip!* "Then it decides who owns you and he has to keep you dressed so you don't show your disgusting deformities. And if it decides you're too dangerous to live in the Starlands, then it'll order you to be put down." *Snip!* Big grin.

"And if I'm not too ugly or too dangerous?"

"Then it'll list you as a halfling, but you'll have to find a starborn to sponsor you. That's status. Are you dangerous?"

Rigel decided that his behavior while shopping in Nanaimo could justify classifyng him as extremely dangerous. "So-so. Usually I'm a cuddly kitten, but I turn into a man-eating tiger at the full moon. What if I don't get status or can't find a sponsor?" Saiph wouldn't allow him to be "put down" easily, if that meant what he thought it did.

"Don't even ask!" Izar said darkly. *Snip! Snip!*

"I do ask, most noble Izar Starling."

The starling pulled a face. "I don't know. That's why I told you not to ask. I 'spec it's pretty horrible, though." Izar stepped back to admire his work, and Rigel realized that he was cutting the hair with two fingers, pretend scissors. They made the right *snip* sound, and they cut through the hair like a razor. More magic.

"What do you do when you're not cutting hair?"

"All sorts of things."

"Like what? What do you enjoy most?"

Izar went back to snipping. "White-water swimming. Rock climbing. Unicorn riding. I have my own unicorn, and his name's Narwhale. My dog's name is Terror, and I teach him tricks. And I like kite riding, way up high, and training my puma and playing my lute and doing magic. I'm good for my age."

"I can see that."

Izar glanced up to smile at whoever had just come through the door behind Rigel. "How's that look, Greatmother? Don't blame me for his ears, they were that small when I started. He still looks savage enough, doesn't he?"

Rigel wished he had a mirror, but the gale was making his eyes water so much that it might not have been of use anyway. He rose and turned to meet the lovely Alniyat's silver gaze.

She smiled. "He's done a wonderful job for a first attempt. But let me . . ." She gestured, and a mist of hair cuttings swirled away into the air. "That's better. Come along and I'll take you to a mirror." She offered a long-fingered hand.

Rigel said, "Thank you for the haircut, most noble Izar Starling."

"Oh, really! Izar, I told you not to speak to the halfling."

"Sorry, Greatmother." The dagger teeth showed in an unrepentant grin. "He looked scared, and I wanted to cheer him up."

"Imp!" She opened the door, and this time it led into darkness and warm, heavily scented air. Sunlight streaming in from the balcony illuminated a path of fieldstones. Alniyat and Rigel's shadows cut across it like bars on a dungeon window. When the door closed behind them, they stood still for a moment, waiting for their eyes to adjust.

"You don't look at all scared," she said. "Or savage." She squeezed his hand.

He squeezed back encouragingly—as the proverb said, when in Rome, do whatever you can get away with. Once he had adjusted to the lighting, he turned to look at her. Their eyes were exactly level, although her ears made her taller. They did not look foolish on her—they were exactly right; she was perfect in every way and breathtakingly beautiful.

"Oh, she doth teach the torches to burn bright!
It seems she hangs upon the cheek of night
As a rich jewel in an Ethiop's ear:
Beauty too rich for use, for Earth too dear."

Her silver eyes opened wider. "Where does that come from?"

"Shakespeare."

"Where's that? Never mind. I'm not Izar's greatmother, you know. I'm his sister, stars help me. You mustn't believe a word that imp says."

Maybe. "I could tell you weren't his greatmother just by looking at you."

"No you couldn't." She pressed close to him and her free hand stroked his back. "Would you like to kiss me?"

No one had ever asked him that before. There had to be a first time for anything, but under the present circumstances he found the question so inappropriate and alarming that his hair would have tried to stand on end if it hadn't already been doing so.

"Very much. But do you want me to?"

She sighed and released him. "I might if I knew you a little better. You smell nice. Nashira bet me that you would try if I encouraged you."

"And what would have happened then?"

"I would be branded a promiscuous hussy and spurned by all my friends. If it came out in court, it would ruin your chances of gaining status. Shall we go?"

"Lead on." It was hard to *think*.

She led him along the paved path flanked by phosphorescent flowers, whose scent hung heavy in the air. The many-colored twinkling lights in the trees were presumably Starlands fireflies. A full moon shone low in the sky, illuminating filmy clouds that perfectly complimented Alniyat's silver hair. Even allowing for the dim light, this place seemed much more real than anywhere he had yet seen in the Starlands. A great white shape swept past overhead, silent as an owl, which it might or might not have been.

"This is the celebrated Moon Garden?"

"One part of it. It's huge, famous. Ancestral. One of Dubhe's greatfathers imagined it centuries ago."

"Greatfather?"

"Father, grandfather, then greatfather. It works the same way with greatmothers. As soon as the moon sets on one side, it rises again on the other."

"And Muphrid stole this place?"

"He flew a portal of his own in a couple of years ago, which is trespassing. Then he closed Dubhe's portals, which made it grand larceny." Alniyat sighed. "But Fomalhaut was bluffing when he threatened him. Dubhe is a Talitha supporter, so the prince will do little to help her. And the regent does whatever the prince tells him to."

The night was very dark, in more ways than one. "Um? Prince?"

"Vildiar. This is where I'm staying."

It seemed more like a cave than a room to Rigel, being a small hollow hill, but it had several entrances, either doors or windows as one pleased, plus its own pool and waterfall. The floor was cushioned by moss and trees grew on the roof. If you had unlimited magic to throw around, as the starfolk seemed to, why not build a nice cool, damp cave?

Alniyat sat on a couch-shaped rock, sinking into the moss. "There's a mirror behind those ferns."

Rigel found the mirror where moonlight conveniently shone on his face. It was an unfamiliar face, with its funny little human ears exposed. With Alniyat's help, the little starling had given him a buzz cut that looked a little like elfin fur, but his eyes didn't sparkle as the starfolk's did. Nashira had called them "dead."

Sprawled back against mossy cushions, Alniyat was staring absently at the roof. "This gathering is a crushing bore. There isn't one interesting male among the lot of them." Her pose was as blatantly provocative as her words.

Beauty too rich for use. Rigel had quoted the words Romeo had used upon his first glimpse of Juliet, which now felt like a serious indiscretion. "I thought I had already passed the seduction test?"

"Yes, you did." She sighed and sat up. "Time to go. We'll be late for dinner. If you are given status, I may let you kiss me, just once, to celebrate. But you must promise faithfully not to tell anyone."

"They wouldn't believe I could ever be so lucky."

"No, they wouldn't." She smiled.

Her teeth were two ivory saws and her ears as big as her hands, but she was unbelievably gorgeous in spite of that.

"Do we have to change our clothes for dinner?"

"No. Just rinse off in a fountain." She fixed her silvery gaze on him and angled her ears at him too. "You do realize that they're all afraid of you, little tweenling?"

"Frightened of *me*? Why?" That was crazy.

"Your scars and the blood that covered you when you arrived. I know Fomalhaut said it was just earthling blood, but we starfolk don't go in for fighting and killing all the time like earthlings do."

He wished she hadn't reminded him that he was a mass murderer. Who was this Fomalhaut, anyway, and why had he turned up to rescue him right after the killings? Rigel hadn't had time to wonder about that strange coincidence yet, not to mention the mystery of what had motivated the strange mass violence in the first place.

"We don't do it all the time either," he said. "I've never killed anyone before, but I was attacked, and Saiph defended me."

"Well, earthling blood doesn't count for much here. We starfolk never die, you know?"

Of course not. Goddesses were immortal.

"Lucky you. How long do halflings live?"

"Not long by our standards, just a few centuries, but much longer than mudlings or earthlings. We can be killed by violence, of course. One of my greatmothers was eaten by a kraken, and my grandfather drowned. But we don't go around killing one another. No wars, no murders." She pulled her feet up, hugged her knees, and stared fixedly at him. "You know why?"

"Because you're more civilized?"

"Oh, no, we're not. Because any starborn who kills another dies of guilt, that's why. It takes all the fun out of blood feuds."

She paused, waiting for his reaction. He was pretty sure now that Alniyat's childish, dreamy manner was a velvet sheath on a steel stiletto. She was dangling something important just out of reach. Now it was time for an IQ test apparently.

He said, "Suppose you hired a killer? No, you couldn't. You couldn't hire a starborn killer, anyway—same problem. How about arranging an accident, a leaky boat, say?"

She shook her head, lighting up the cave with a hint of a smile. "Indirect murder is still murder."

"Hiring an earthling, then?"

"That's absurd. No earthling or mudling would stand a chance against a starborn. Besides, they're only tools, so the curse would fall upon their owners."

Now he saw where she was heading. "Halflings, then? Do we tweenlings die of guilt if we kill starfolk?"

"Not usually." She flashed her teeth again.

"And we're not tools? We have free will?" Rigel looked down at the Saiph amulet. It was like owning Excalibur, Naegling, Durendal, or the sword of Welleran . . . or, rather, it was like being owned by them. "How do I ditch this damned thing?"

"Just by dying. Most amulets can be put on or off like ordinary jewelry, but defensive amulets are different. Saiph wouldn't be much good if you could be threatened or blackmailed into taking it off, now would it?"

"Of course not," he said, although the logic was obscure.

"Poor Rigel! They won't give you status, not ever." She floated to her feet and drifted close to press her breasts against him and touch the tip of her tongue to the end of his nose. "They won't dare. Halflings make good assassins and you're impossible to defeat. They can't let you loose. It's out of the question. You have the white hair of a child before his color comes in, but you're not a boy, are you?"

No he wasn't, and she knew it. This was her third attempt at seduction. "You really want me to prove it? Lie down."

"You already have proved it," she said. "You're a man and you wear Saiph, the king of swords. I have to decide what to do about that. In the meantime, let's go to dinner."

Chapter 8

Muphrid explained that he had created the Versailles room as a copy of the Hall of Mirrors in that what's-its-name French palace, but the huge paintings were blurred and the gold frames were half-melted, giving the room the same phony, half-baked appearance as the swimming glade. Whereas the Moon Garden had felt real, this place was strangely out of focus.

"They were still building it, then," he explained. "King Louis the something or other?" He peered inquiringly along the table at Rigel.

"Fourteenth, probably," Rigel said, that being the only Louis he could recall.

"Sounds too low. It was about three hundred years ago. What number are they up to now?"

"I don't think France has kings any more, starborn."

"Queens are better," Muphrid agreed, nodding.

He and his dozen guests were dining under a row of chandeliers the size of Honda Civics, all of which blazed with candlelight, even though afternoon sunlight was streaming in through the huge arched windows. The meal was being served by about twenty footmen in historical costume—knee britches, silk stockings, powdered wigs, and so forth—under the direction of Senator, who wore a similar outfit with extra gold and scarlet trim on his frock coat. All the servants were human, and they seemed grateful for their heavy wool garments, for the hall was cool even for Rigel. Some of the full-blooded elves in their trifling moon-cloth wraps had drunk enough to become loud, flushed, and sweaty.

King Louis of whatever number would have disapproved of the diners' dress and recoiled at their choice of food. The live starfish, for instance. The trick, as explained to him by Nashira, was to pop the wiggly beasts into your mouth and hold them there while they thrashed around, emitting an unpredictable spectrum of flavors. If you bit them, they would sting, and when they turned bitter you had to swallow them quickly or they would nauseate you. Rigel found that such eating required extreme concentration, and he was seriously distracted by the presence of beautiful bare-breasted girls on either side of him and another directly across the table.

His left-hand neighbor was the purple-eyed Nashira, who amused herself between courses by stroking his thigh under the table. This activity had been noted by Alniyat, who was directly across from him, and she kept sending him warning signals, which might mean that she'd kill him if he responded to Nashira or that Nashira would if he didn't. Or perhaps if he did. Some of the foreplay going on around the table was even more blatant.

Most of the conversation bored him, for it was vapid gossip about the rich and famous of the Starlands. There was trivial chatter about royalty: Princess Talitha, Prince Vildiar, and Regent-heir Kornephoros, who was designated to succeed Queen Electra when she retired "soon," meaning in a century or two. Some starborn with an unpronounceable name had created the *most fascinating* ice park, complete with penguins and polar bears—one *must* see it. My lord This had lost several subdomains, apparently by absentmindedness, and my lady That had reportedly been found in bed with a human boy, which was much worse. This confirmed Rigel's suspicions about Alniyat's attempts to make a pass at him earlier.

The talk that should have interested him made no sense. Starborn Icalurus, who had pink hair, announced that he had found an intriguing temple park in Japan and was planning to imagine something like it in his domain as soon as he completed his new thunderbird aviary. Nashira cattily asked if he had been extroverting after those geisha girls and he angrily told her that two good friends of his had been convicted of extroverting recently, and the regent had confiscated half their domains as a penalty. The others expressed sympathy but generally agreed that the ban on extroverting made good sense, and then began to argue about friends who had been stoned to death. It was all gibberish.

Desperate to make conversation, Rigel asked about maps. The starfolk looked blank. Geography, he explained. Blanker. Eventually he got his meaning across, and they all burst out laughing. Geography was an earthling idea. They had no geography and didn't need it. *Where* depended on *who*, they said, and that was that.

He considered asking how many halflings there were and decided not to risk it. Did he even want to be granted status, assuming that it was some sort of residency or work permit? Would he be happier going back to Earth to face at least three murder charges? Was that even an alternative? The starfolk might be quite happy to banish him back to the real world, but he suspected they would not want to lose their legendary Saiph.

The thought of Earth reminded him of Mira. What was happening to her?

He was being asked a question, something about minotaurs . . .

"No, starborn, never," he said.

"Great sport!" Muphrid proclaimed. "We'll find you a good young one."

"He'll be able to show us Saiph in action!" That was Nashira, of course. When she wasn't too busy caressing his thigh, she never missed a chance to snipe at him.

Playing toreador with a minotaur? Would he have to wave a red cape?

For years Rigel's highest ambition had been to find his parents. It still mattered to him, and now he was making progress. Now he knew that one had been human, the other starborn. Maybe Gert had been his mother after all, and her story of the King of the Elves close to true except that her supernatural visitor had probably not been royalty. She wouldn't have cared who he was or how strangely his ears were shaped so long as he paid well. "You're growing tall like your dad," she had told him when he was young. After the baby was born, his elfin father must have given him Saiph to defend him in his youth.

Or had the amulet served another purpose? Could the use of magic be detected by some sort of elfin direction-and-ranging system? The first time Rigel had needed it . . . no, the third time. And that made sense. Fomalhaut had turned up much too promptly for it to have been a coincidence. Rigel punching out a mugger's teeth in Vancouver might have alerted elfin watchers that the amulet had been activated, killing a bear would narrow down his location, and then slaughtering three men in Walmart would lead them right to him. Which sort of suggested that his father's name was Fomalhaut, a conclusion even less appetizing than the toasted ivy salad.

The first dozen courses were followed by an intermission, during which a flock of eight imps, including Izar, came in to entertain the grown-ups with an act they'd been rehearsing. They varied in height from about one meter to more than two, and only the tallest had any trace of color in their hair and eyes—the rest had the same white pigmentation as Rigel. The imps brought two sorts of harp, three lutes, two woodwinds, and a zither, setting up the large harp at one end of the line and the zither at the other. They then began to play, dance, and sing, all at the same time. As they wove in and out, they tossed instruments back and forth, so that a child might strum a few bars on a lute and then toss it to another in return for a woodwind. The older ones added back flips and other acrobatics. They never missed a beat and they all sang like angels when they weren't blowing into oboes. See it and weep, Cirque du Soleil!

Rigel had always believed that he was musically gifted, but now he realized that he had inherited only a small part of true elfin talent. At the end of the performance, he wanted to leap to his feet and cheer, yet the audience's applause was no more than polite.

After the banquet ended, the adults collected around a grand piano farther along the hall; they all sang and some of them played. Fortunately the halfling was not asked to join in.

Chapter 9

Eventually, as the sky outside darkened, the starfolk began slinking off in couples, but few seemed to go with the partners they had been fondling throughout the dinner. Rigel watched wistfully as Alniyat was hustled away by the giant Gacrux. As soon as Rigel rose from his chair, Senator appeared at his side, accompanied by a young human in the historical livery.

"May I be so bold as to inquire what sort of room the half-ling would prefer?"

Rigel, intoxicated by dinner at Versailles, went for broke. "A beach cabin with good swimming."

"Salt water or fresh?"

"Salt."

"Azmidiske Cove," Senator told the youngster, who in turn bowed and asked if the halfling would be so kind as to follow him.

He led Rigel to another set of imposing double doors. The moment they were opened, Rigel smelled the sea and heard a distant boom of surf. He walked through and then turned to his guide.

"These doors are incredible. Will they take you anywhere?"

The lad seemed surprised at his ignorance. "The portals? To any other portal within the master's domain."

"How do you work them?"

Surprise became worry. The boy developed a stutter. "You j-j-just think of wh-where you want to b-b-be."

"Remember it, you mean?"

He nodded vigorously. "Will these quarters s-satisfy, h-half-ling?"

The room was no bigger than a tennis court, but not much smaller either, and furnished with exquisite taste in a writhing, curlicue style that Rigel had never seen in any book or magazine. A deck outside faced a white sand beach under a quarter moon. Dark palm tree fronds gestured gracefully against a starry sky. Wow! Life on Earth had never been this good.

He said it would suffice.

Reassured, the footman said, "If the halfling has any special preference for breakfast, I can have the kitchen prepare it."

"Thanks," Rigel said. "I'll decide in the morning." The royal treatment was making him so lightheaded that he was tempted to say, "Rigel will decide." He didn't. "What's your name?"

The footman cringed. "My name?"

"You do have a name?"

"It is Sextus, if it p-p-pleases the halfling." His face crumpled. "I have displeased my lord? I mean, the halfling? He wishes to lodge a complaint?"

"Not at all. You have been most helpful. Where were you born?"

"Here, halfling. Not here at Azmidiske Cove, I mean, but within the master's domain."

"And your parents also?"

Sextus seemed thoroughly confused by this personal interest. "My mother was, halfling. The master borrowed my father from another domain."

Rigel felt his scalp crawl. Earthlings were only tools, Alniyat had told him. "Is Starborn Muphrid a good master to
work for?"

Sextus brightened. "Oh, yes. Very fair. We get two whole
days off a month, and this is my nine hundred and seventy-
first day without punishment!"

Puke! "That's good. You must be proud of such a record."

"The halfling is most kind to say so." He beamed. "That is
why I was so worried when I was afraid I had failed to give
satisfaction. When I achieve two thousand days, I shall be permitted to co-habit!"

Rigel wanted to ask if young Sextus would have any say in
choosing his roommate, but the conversation was making his
gorge rise. He dismissed the man.

Then he ran down the sand and hurled himself into the
water. It was wonderfully cool and clean.

Elves were not.

<hr/>

He swam all the way across the lagoon to the reef where the
surf thundered. By the time he had swum back and was trudg-
ing up the beach, the quarter moon was setting, in paradoxical
ignorance of the full moon he had seen earlier in the Moon
Garden. The constellations looked familiar but twisted, as if
either the season or the latitude had changed dramatically. That
was certainly Orion's belt and his name star, Rigel, but he had
never seen the Hunter standing on his head before. The Starlands must be in the Southern Hemisphere, or on another

world entirely, but if this was another world, how could it have the same moon and stars?

There were lights on in his cabin, and when he reached the door, he heard movement inside. He raised his hand.

"Saiph!"

This time he was ready for the weight of the gauntlet and sword. He hurled the door open with his left hand. The woman in the process of removing her bonnet and shawl jumped.

"Oh! You idiot! Put that damned thing away."

He obeyed. "Good evening, Mira."

Even Saiph could not better the dangerous glint in her eye. "You expect the services of your concubine for the night?"

"Certainly." The bed was large, but there was only one of it.

"Dream on." Mira flopped into a chair. She wore a floor-length homespun dress, rather obviously padded out by many layers of petticoat. Her feet were encased in high button boots and she was not in a good mood. "I hope you enjoyed your banquet? I spent all day scraping lichen off rocks to make some sort of salad."

"Oh, is that what that mess was? Nasty! But I may be confusing it with the aphid puree." Rigel sat down. He was desperately tired, but clearly they must exchange notes, and he hoped that Mira's background as a detective had helped her learn more than he had. "Have you the foggiest idea where we are?"

"Not a clue."

"Or why the shoppers went crazy and attacked us in Walmart?"

"No."

"You want to go home, I assume? To Earth."

She nodded. "Can you get these damned boots off me? I forgot to get a buttonhook. Of course I want to go home. Even Micah would be bearable after a day in Muphrid's kitchens."

"I don't know what I want to do." He knelt down to help her. "I need more information, lots more. But what we want may not count for zip."

"There must be police and TV cameras all over that Walmart store," Mira conceded. "And I might be a tad conspicuous if I were dumped back there in this Pilgrim costume. They took my own clothes and burned them!"

No doubt they'd done the same with his. "If I can get them to send you home—to somewhere outside of Walmart, that is—I will. I promise."

"That's a deal, but if either of us sees a chance of escape we grab it, right?"

He chuckled, suddenly realizing how happy he was, in spite of his fatigue. "All for one, but not necessarily one for all? Let's pool what we know. Start with politics."

"You'll have to deal with the politics. You're upstairs, I'm downstairs."

"I'm not much on politics." He summed up what he had learned: "The queen is likely to abdicate and there are three contenders to succeed. I think she chooses the winner, but I'm not sure of that. They might have to fight it out for all I know. We know that Muphrid takes orders from Fomalhaut, and he's a Prince Vildiar supporter, so it sounds sort of feudal. I've read books about the Middle Ages."

"Good for you. It also sounds like gangs—the Mafia and so on."

"That's as far as I got."

"It is?" She seemed unimpressed. "You didn't hear that this world is in danger of falling apart?"

He thought for a moment. "There was some mention of some high muck-a-muck who had lost half his lands somehow."

"And you didn't think that was important?" Mira said acidly. "He isn't the only one. It's happening all over. The servants are quite worried."

"What do they know about it? Why should they care? They're slaves!"

"They know more than you'd expect," Mira said. "The guests bring servants of their own, so there's an exchange of information, a sort of underground telegraph." She glanced uneasily around the room. "I suppose if Muphrid wants to eavesdrop on us, he has ways I can't imagine." She pulled a face in disgust. "They're worse than slaves. They're livestock, Rigel, cattle. They've been bred for docility, like sheep and cows, so don't dream of raising a slaves' revolt, because they wouldn't help you. They wouldn't even *want* to help. And they have no magic. Only the elves have magic."

"Did you find out how magic works?" If Saiph would obey his commands, other amulets should, too.

"No. I was kept busy the whole time. Did you?"

"All I learned was that a starborn female mustn't have love affairs with humans or halflings."

Mira wrinkled her nose in disgust. "But the old double standard applies. Remember how shocked they pretended to be when you called me your concubine? That was pure hypocrisy. Tonight I was brought here 'to serve my master,' and at least one other girl was sent off to entertain a male guest. Just like slavery in the Old South."

"Or like the fur traders who opened up the Canadian west. The voyageurs took native wives, but they would have been appalled if a white woman had married an Indian."

Maybe Gert hadn't been his birth mother after all; from what Mira was saying, he might very well be a changeling conceived in a Starlands slave barn.

Mira said, "I did get the impression that half br . . . that halflings are rare. There are some here, but they don't mix with the kitchen riffraff, so I didn't meet any. The footmen coming back from the banquet hall were commenting that you were quite 'starry-looking' apart from your ears. Your lack of a navel seems to matter a lot. You could be allowed to stay. That's what status means, I gather. You get some sort of second-class citizenship."

"Better than nothing," he said. "Halflings are higher than slaves, because they have free will. I was also told that starborn can't kill one another without dying themselves—it's a guilt thing. They can't get around that effect by using human assassins because humans are just tools, like daggers or swords. But halflings are immune to this. We have free will and our barbarian heritage makes us dangerous. Saiph makes me *extremely* dangerous, like a nuclear submarine."

Mira looked impressed. "Can elves kill halflings?"

"I didn't ask, but my amulet will defend me, so I'm a public threat and I think my only hope of getting status is if Fomalhaut or his Prince Vildiar needs a staff assassin badly enough to bribe the jury, if that's how it works."

"Lucky you! Is assassination a well-paying career?"

"I don't know and I certainly don't intend to find out!"

For a moment neither spoke, then Mira yawned. "Dunno about you, sonny, but I'm tired. Scraping rocks is hard work. We can share the bed, but if you get any fancy ideas about concubinage, I'll stuff that magical sword of yours right down your throat."

Rigel laughed and jumped up. "I'd better not risk it, then. I'd rather sleep on the beach anyway. It's my starborn blood, you know."

He came trotting back to the cabin as the eastern sky began to brighten. His sleep had been haunted by dreams of the massacre at Walmart, and once he had been awakened by a warning from his amulet when something large began circling overhead. He had crawled in under a canopy of thorny branches and gone back to sleep. Nevertheless, he felt marvelously happy. All his life he had been hiding from view, but now his secret was out in the open at last. While this new world offered new problems, it was an immensely exciting and, so far, enjoyable place to be. A halfling who owned the most deadly sword in the Starlands shouldn't have to take crap from anyone. He had begun his day by swimming out to the reef again. If life stayed this good, he was all for it.

The stars here revolved around Sirius instead of Polaris.

When he walked into the cabin, Mira was still snoring away under a heap of covers.

A glance in the mirror revealed that his scars had already faded to faint pink lines. This really was extraordinarily fast healing, even for him.

Hotcakes and bacon? A few eggs on the side? Orange juice! He called up a clear memory of the Versailles Room and opened the portal. He stepped through into . . . *nothing!* . . . not even a floor. Off-balance, he started to fall into outer space, complete with blackness and stars.

He grabbed the jamb with his free hand, but the door swung wider until he was almost horizontal, staring down at stars *below* him. If the sun or moon were there, he was too busy hanging on and saving his skin to bother looking for them. He hauled himself vertical by brute strength and staggered back into the cabin, shaking and streaming sweat. He slammed the door shut behind him. It couldn't really be outer space. There had been air, a cold wind, but not a rush of atmosphere into vacuum. *I'm a stranger here; which way to the edge of the world?*

As soon as he caught his breath, he tried again, this time thinking of the swimming glade and opening the door only a crack. Still there was nothing out there. He went to the nearest chair and sat down to think this over. The portal had worked for the mudling Sextus, so it ought to work for a halfling. Was he in jail? There was nothing landward of the cabin except jungle, nothing seaward except sea.

A light tap, the portal swung wide, and there was Sextus, bowing and ready to take his order for breakfast.

"Whatever Starborn Muphrid usually has," Rigel said. "For two." He watched the slave exit into some sort of pantry. The instant the door closed Rigel lunged over to it and inched it open. He found midnight and stars again, nothing else.

Came a mumble from under a quilt. "Whatimeisit?"

"Just enough time for you to have a swim before breakfast."

Her reply was brief but emphatic.

"My father the elf taught me never to use such words," Rigel said.

Grumbling, Mira sat up, clutching the covers under her chin. "It is *freezing* in here!"

"Just comfortable."

The portal swung open, and she vanished back under the bedclothes. The new arrival was not Sextus, though, but

Gacrux, the beefy elf. He glanced regretfully at the bed as if wondering what he had missed, then at Rigel.

"Ready?"

"Ready for what?"

"To fight the Minotaur. Don't you remember?"

"Only vaguely," Rigel admitted. There had been some talk of showing off Saiph. "You really expect me to kill something in cold blood?"

The big lout sneered. "Scared?"

"No. It just doesn't seem sporting if my amulet never loses. I always thought the Minotaur was imaginary."

"Of course it's imaginary. We're not ready yet, but Muphrid thought you might want to scout out the lay of the land first."

"I suppose that's a good idea. Darling, if I'm not back in time, you'll have to eat breakfast for two."

"Trying to tell me you've got her knocked up?" Gacrux said scornfully.

"I never miss. Lead the way."

The big elf said, "Taygeta!" and his sword appeared in his hand.

Rigel felt no warning tingle at his wrist, so he knew that Gacrux wasn't planning to attack him at the moment. Maybe never, maybe later.

Gacrux opened the portal a crack and peered out cautiously. Only when he had satisfied himself that it was safe did he open it fully and walk through. Rigel followed.

Chapter 10

They were at the top of an ornate marble grandstand whose cushioned seats would hold about fifty people. It stood halfway down the side of a gentle grassy hollow, a natural arena. On the skyline opposite, stark white against the ultramarine sky, stood a pair of stone columns supporting a triangular lintel, what architecture books called a pediment. It had no doors, so it might be just what it seemed, not a magical portal like the one beside the swimming hole.

"That's where it will come from." Gacrux pointed at the arch with Taygeta, then put the sword away, as if suddenly self-conscious. "You should be up there when it does, so that you can lure it down close, where all of us can see the fight."

"Can I go and look over the terrain?" The slopes of this killing ground were tufted with thorny-looking shrubs that might hide all sorts of rough footing. What lay beyond the skyline?

"If it worries you. It's obvious enough, I would have thought. Muphrid sees that it's kept in good shape. There shouldn't be any sharp stones or burrows to trip you."

"Have you ever hunted minotaurs?" Rigel asked suspiciously.

The big elf shrugged. "Smell of blood churns my gut. I've watched it a time or two. There's nothing to it. The more you wave the red cloak, the madder it gets. Just remember what Muphrid told you last night. It isn't a bull. It has hands. It'll try to grab you and pull you onto its horns."

"Right." Rigel trotted down the aisle and vaulted over the rail at the bottom of the grandstand, dropping nimbly to the grass. A staged slaughter was not his idea of hunting and certainly not sport, but refusing to cooperate might endanger his chances of gaining status. He suspected the childlike starfolk just wanted to see him kill something with Saiph. And there was no doubt in his mind that this was also a test—of his abilities certainly, and perhaps of his obedience too. He set off to explore.

He loped across the hollow and started up the slope, checking the footing and the height of the shrubs. There were places where a man or animal could hide from view and he was curious to know why Gacrux had drawn his sword before opening the portal. He glanced back and saw that the elf had gone. The portal doors were closed.

Studying the grandstand from this angle, he decided that it wasn't a secure vantage point. A real bull wouldn't have been able to reach the spectators, but an agile man, whether he had a bull's head or a human one, could easily jump up and catch hold of the railing. Then he could haul himself aboard and turn the tables on those who had come to watch him being slaughtered. Either there were defenses that Rigel couldn't see, or Muphrid had immense confidence in his own magical powers.

He turned to resume his exploration and saw a minotaur sitting cross-legged in a slight hollow no more than ten meters off to his right, watching him. Rigel opened his mouth to summon Saiph, but then realized that the amulet was not tingling and the sword would come on its own if it were needed.

The apparition yawned and stretched its arms. After all the straw-thin elves, its sheer bulk was daunting. From the neck down it would have made an impressive NFL linebacker— probably hairier than most—and its huge horned head must add an extra thirty kilos. It was naked, without so much as a gold ring in its black nose. Rigel gingerly took a backward step.

The Minotaur said, *"Buenos dias."*

"Um, good morning." Rigel went closer to convince himself that he was brave enough. "I didn't expect you to talk."

"Why not? We won't have much time to chat later."

"Probably not. I'm Rigel."

"I'm the Minotaur. All us minotaurs are called *the* Minotaur."

"What did your mother call you?"

The Minotaur snorted explosively. "Darling." His bull's head was Hereford red, but his human body hair was black— Aberdeen Angus, maybe. "Didn't expect a halfling. You're here to prove that you can kill to order, I suppose?"

"I'm sure that's the idea, but it wasn't my idea." At close range Rigel could tell that the monster's name was Elnath. Why had it lied to him?

Saiph was still giving no warning, so Rigel sat down cross-legged and almost knee-to-knee with his soon-to-be adversary. He noticed that the bushes hid them from the grandstand, and wondered if Elnath had been setting up an ambush.

The Minotaur regarded him with a huge and gentle bovine eye. "Well, I'm glad. A halfling should do a nice clean kill. Some of those milksop starfolk can't finish the job properly. They chop and hack and mutilate, and then can't bring themselves to finish us off. My brother was just left there to bleed to death. I call that *escandaloso!"*

"Me too," Rigel said. "But now that I'm getting to know you, I don't want to kill you at all."

"Oh, but you must!" Elnath's face displayed no emotion, but he sounded shocked. "That's what I'm for. For thousands of years we minotaurs have been bred to be killed by heroes. If you don't do it someone else will, and I'd rather be slain by a bloodthirsty savage halfling than a daffodil elf. No offense intended."

"None taken." Rigel pulled his knees up and leaned his chin on them to think. "You insist on this?"

The bull head turned to fix its other eye on him. "Certainly. I don't want to kill you either, but when you wave the cloak at me, the only way I can stop the pain is to try and get it away from you."

"Pain?"

The Minotaur laughed, a monstrous rumble deep in his throat. "They didn't tell you? The cloak is an amulet. When you shake it, it hurts me. Red-hot needles! I go loco. You think any sane minotaur would charge a swordsman without a weapon? No, it's just the only way to stop the agony."

"We could just shake hands and part as friends."

"That merely gives me an hour or so longer in the death paddock while they line up another hero. Muphrid Starborn has to entertain his guests. Besides, that wouldn't help you prove you'll be a good assassin. And I have to think of my sons."

"You lost me," Rigel said.

The Minotaur made a harrumphing noise and studied the enormous dirty, tattered fingernails on his right hand. "The Minotaur must die bravely. He must put on a good show. That's what he's for. You want my sons to grow up with the shame of a father who *made a deal?*"

"I see. How do I help you put on a good show?"

Elnath scratched a furry shin. "Make sure I bleed a lot. You have to disable my arms first, of course—that way I can only try to gore you—and you must be careful not to spoil my legs. Then you spin it out, making it last a good, long time. I keep charging and charging like an idiot. But finally, if you don't mind, put that moment of truth right through my heart?"

Rigel was feeling more like a daffodil elf every minute. "This is all strange to me. I only just arrived in this world. I didn't believe in minotaurs until I saw you sitting here."

The monster snorted. "You wouldn't, of course. On Earth, we're imaginary; here we're real. Like the elves. Reality on Earth is fantasy here and vice versa. And one thing you must understand about the Starlands is that they *aren't* a world. They're a translated state of being. The domains have all been manifested from the starfolk's imagination, and each place is a personal creation. Time is conserved, so life and death stay the same. If you can imagine your own death you can die here—believe it! And even the best mage can't do *nada* about death."

"Magic?" Rigel looked at his bracelet. "Amulets. You said the cloak they give me will be an amulet. The elf, er, starborn, who brought us here carried a long staff."

"That would be his reversion amulet. In order to effect the dimensional transformation, it has to be longer than the user's height, see?"

He didn't. "I'll take your word for it. So all the magic in the Starlands is done with amulets? Rings, bracelets . . ."

The Minotaur sighed hugely. "Not quite. Some elves are better at magic than others, but spells take time to cast, and they can go wrong. You want to remember something, you write it down, right? An elf puts his spell in an amulet, so it's always available."

Aha! "If a friend of mine wants to travel back to Earth, how can she?"

"You don't *travel* to and from Earth. You *extrovert* there. That's unless you just want to seance, of course." Elnath twisted a tuft of long weeds with a big hand, ripped them out of the ground, and tucked them in his cavernous mouth, roots and all.

"Please would you explain the difference?" Rigel Estell really had gone crazy; he was asking a bull for instructions.

"If you want to really *be* there," the Minotaur said, patiently chewing, "and *do* things, then you *extrovert* to Earth. You *introvert* back here again. Think of a dimensional matrix transformation of the space-time continuum with conservation of supersymmetry."

"I'm sure I can't. I'm not educated. All I know is what I read in books people had thrown away."

"Lucky you. Our culture is entirely verbal. We're too hypermetropic to read."

"I've read about imaginary numbers," Rigel said. "They lie along an axis at right angles to real numbers."

"You've got it, then. But even a high-rank mage—red or even Naos grade—won't attempt introversion or extroversion without a staff, and Queen Electra made all reversion illegal a few centuries ago. She's been confiscating every staff she can get her royal hoofs on."

"And seancing is . . . what? Just looking?"

Elnath nodded his monstrous head, then stroked it with a thorny branch he tore off a shrub. "Elves like to think they're ever so frightfully artistic and creative," he said, crunching noisily, "but you'll notice that the stuff they imagine is mostly plagiarism, copied from Earth. Seancing is legal because the starfolk who do it can't be seen, heard, or touched. All they can do is mooch around, spying and stealing ideas."

"You are being amazingly helpful. Now tell me why extroversion is illegal."

The massive bull-man sniggered like a child. "Starfolk like to think they're above all that messy animal sex stuff, but they aren't, and the males like to play around with the livestock, usually the girls. They're not very fertile at the best of times, even with their own kind, but once in a while they make a *mestizo*, er, halfling. They don't admit it, but halflings scare them. Some of you have low-grade magic, even up to blue, and you're not bound by the guilt curse. You make useful servants, because they've bred all the smart out of their mudlings, but you're also scary. So making a halfling is a serious offense. If the father can somehow get hold of a reversion staff, he'll take the baby to Earth and switch it for an earthling one, bringing the human baby back to keep the woman happy. Gets new blood into the servant herds, too."

Changelings! "I'd heard the old myths, just didn't think it was still going on. You're being more helpful than anyone I've spoken to yet, Minotaur. Are we halflings always made in the slave barns, or do the male starborn ever extrovert so that they can seduce human—I mean earthling—women?"

The Minotaur changed eyes again. "It's not common nowadays, since Electra made it illegal, but yes, horny elves used to extrovert to play with the wild stock all the time."

"So they can disguise themselves as human?"

"Dissemble, you mean. The higher grades can dissemble as earthlings, but dissembling's about the only magic that can't be done with an amulet. They have to consciously think about it *all the time*. The moment they let themselves get distracted, every earthling in sight starts screaming. That didn't matter much when the earthlings would decide they were devils and burn them at the stake, but nowadays they'd run forensic analysis and autopsies. Electra didn't want that to happen. It's one of the reasons she banned extroversion."

Rigel rose onto his knees to peer over the bushes at the grandstand, but nobody was there yet. Saiph tingled. He looked around hastily, but Elnath was apparently just reaching for a juicy clump of weeds near Rigel's ankle. He pulled them up and tucked them into his mouth.

"Must be about time for me to get back to the pen," Elnath grunted. "Don't want them to see us talking, right?"

"Right." Why not?

The monster thumped a fist on his enormous hairy chest. "My heart's about here."

Rigel drew a deep breath. "You truly want me to do this?"

"Haven't I been saying so?"

"Does the Minotaur always lose?"

"Of course. The hero must win."

"Then how did you acquire all those scars?" Rigel pointed at thin white lines visible under the black pelt.

The Minotaur shrugged and chewed. "Almost always, then. Don't worry about highly improbable exceptions."

Truth in the Starlands was malleable.

"Saiph never loses."

The Minotaur cocked his great head to look down at Rigel's bracelet. "Truly? The *real* Saiph?"

"Truly. And it's not just your scars. I'm also a little doubtful about your sons story. How many did you say you have?"

The Minotaur sighed. "None. I was simplifying. I've taken out a couple of the weedy elves in my time, so Muphrid promised me that if I won a third time, he'd put me out to stud with the minoheifers. Not that I believe him, really. I just didn't want to worry you. You'll fight better if you have a good positive attitude."

Rigel grinned. Elnath flicked his ears, which might be the bull equivalent.

"Do draws count?" Rigel asked. "Look, I'll leave it up to you. I won't even use the cloak. I swear I won't seriously injure you as long as you just play with me, faking charges and so on. When you want to die, try to kill me for real. Saiph will see you out."

The Minotaur's bovine mouth opened in an enormous yawn, and his massive human arms stretched up into the air. "That's great news, though. Saiph! They must be really scared of me to send in Saiph! Come to think of it, it's been quite a while since they sent up their last hero. I'll get my name on Saiph? *Stars!* Thanks, Rigel Halfling. May the best being win." He held out a hand twice the size of Rigel's.

Rigel clasped it, forewarned by a slight quiver from his bracelet. He watched as the great muscle bulged in that furry forearm. Fortunately Rigel's sword hand was now clad in a steel gauntlet, so his knuckles didn't crumble under the pressure. The monster released him with a grunt, then chuckled. "Even if it isn't the genuine Saiph, it's a good one."

Rigel grinned. "So are you, Elnath Minotaur. Nice try." And no hard feelings, thanks to the amulet.

"Good luck, Halfling Rigel. If you do get that assassin job, kill lots of stinky elves for me." With that, the Minotaur flowed away into the brush, vanishing with amazing agility for such a massive being.

Chapter 11

Rigel rose, wondering if he still had time for breakfast, but before he reached the grandstand, the portal opened to admit a string of starfolk guests, including some new faces. Green-haired Muphrid had a simpering Nashira on his arm, although she was not the partner he'd carried off from the banquet the previous evening, and Alniyat had dropped Gacrux in favor of the one called Icalurus. Behind the adults came the imps, twittering like overexcited birds, and Senator, now dressed in khakis and a bush hat, looking like a clean-shaven Ernest Hemingway on safari. More servants arrived with refreshments.

Rigel stood on the grass below the stand, feeling like a gladiator in a Hollywood toga turkey. Muphrid sat front and center, of course, in the emperor's place. There had been no mention of a thumbs-up signal to spare the Minotaur's life if he fought well.

"There it is!" At the imp's squeal, all eyes turned to the arch at the top of the slope, where the Minotaur now stood in silhouette with a hand on either pillar, like Samson, looking even bigger than he really was, which was plenty big. Was this

contest being staged to test Rigel's nerve, as both he and the Minotaur had assumed? Or was it to test whether Rigel's amulet was the genuine Saiph? The match might not be the sure thing he had been told to expect.

"Oh . . . Halfling . . .," said Muphrid. "You'll need this." He bent to fumble at his feet, and came up holding a roll of scarlet cloth, which he tossed down. "Stars be with you. Give us a good fight, not too quick."

Rigel bowed, spreading his arms in starfolk fashion, then turned and trotted up the slope. The bundle was tied around with a red ribbon in a rather complicated knot, which he suspected might be designed to make sure he didn't unroll the pain-dispensing cloak while he was still close to the spectators. He left it tied, and when he was about three quarters of the way to the Minotaur, he stopped and put his hands on his hips.

"Hey, pot roast!" he yelled. He heard shrill screams of laughter behind him, too loud to be only the imps. "Come on down here, you overgrown cutlet." The Minotaur just stood there, not reacting. "Come and fight me. You're no bull, just an ox." The laughter was thinner this time, as if the adult starfolk were pretending not to understand the reference.

When he ran out of insults, Rigel shrugged his shoulders, turned his back, and walked away.

The crowd started screaming warnings, which he ignored as if he did not hear them. He guessed that the Minotaur could move much faster than he could. He also knew enough to trust dear Elnath much less far than he could throw him, which would be about five nanometers. No doubt the Minotaur would keep to their bargain as long as the temptation to cheat was not too strong, but right now the temptation must look close to irresistible. Rigel had Saiph to warn him, and also shadows, for he was moving away from the morning sun.

Led by Izar, the imps leaped to their feet, screaming at the top of their lungs. Rigel stopped and cupped a hand—his left hand—behind his petite human ear as if he couldn't make out what they were telling him. They shrieked all the louder. "*The Minotaur's coming. The Minotaur's coming!*"

Had it not been for Saiph, Elnath's attack would have succeeded. No second shadow came rushing over Rigel's own to warn him that the Minotaur was charging him from behind. Instead his bracelet yanked his hand aside so hard that he lurched out of the way as a rock the size of a baseball whistled through the space his head had occupied a millisecond before. He spun around to find his opponent almost upon him, wielding a great broken tree branch as a club. Rigel had not expected the enormous Elnath to move so silently, but now he knew what the brute had been doing as he skulked in the bushes prior to the match. No dumb ox, he. How many more missiles and weapons had he hidden away?

Rigel leaped aside and the blow missed.

The watchers in the stand screamed their approval.

The Minotaur slithered to a halt, spun around, and charged again. This time Rigel invoked Saiph so that he could slash at the tree branch, cutting it through while his opponent hurtled by.

More yells of approval from the audience.

Rigel dismissed his sword and started ambling down the slope again. He began to fiddle with the tie on the red cloak bundle, as if he was having trouble with the knot, pretending to ignore the Minotaur. Meanwhile, the Minotaur raced around him to get to the floor of the hollow first and intercept him.

The game had changed. Now Elnath was stalking his prey, great arms outstretched. Rigel dodged around bushes, all the time angling downhill, while pretending to concentrate on untying the red cloak. It was pure playacting, because Saiph stayed out and if the giant had really wanted to win, he could have stormed through the shrubbery like a tank. Rigel expected this mummery to deceive the starlings and amuse the adult starfolk, but even they seemed to be taken in, judging by their alternating cheers and screams of warning.

It would be nice to free the red cloak right in front of the grandstand and throw the audience into paroxysms of agony, but Rigel did not know if the magic would work that way, and had not suggested it to Elnath. Their choreography did not develop in that direction.

Instead, Saiph suddenly quivered and flashed into view. The Minotaur hurtled by, closer than before. "Blood me, you fool!" he said as he went by. Then he pivoted and grabbed at Rigel.

Rigel swung at him, striking his shoulder with the flat of his blade, but giving it enough of a twist to cut the skin. Elnath bellowed in terrible tsunamis of sound, clutching his wound and probably forcing it open to make it bleed more.

First blood! The starfolk screamed and cheered.

Elnath made another pass and Rigel slashed his other shoulder, this time a little deeper than he'd intended. It was still playacting, though, because Saiph was letting him dictate the strokes, so he couldn't be in any real danger. Now the Minotaur was seemingly crippled and unable to use his arms . . . but Rigel knew better than to believe it. Elnath lowered his head and charged, bull-like.

Rigel stepped aside and blooded him some more, much as he hated to do it. He wanted this farce to end as soon as possible, but however it did end, there had to be blood—and lots of it. It suited both his purposes and Elnath's to make this a show that the starfolk would remember for years to come. However much he liked Elnath, Rigel had no illusions about the Minotaur's intentions. If the Minotaur could outwit Saiph, he would kill the halfling and hope to be retired to stud. Again and again he charged, flashing his deadly curved horns, while Rigel leaped aside and whacked him, rarely drawing blood, and then only superficially.

Why didn't the idiot just run away, back to his pen, and call it a draw?

Finally the Minotaur made his move. As was to be expected of a wily and experienced duelist, he launched a complex attack. He first maneuvered Rigel against a thicket of thorns to impede his freedom of movement, and then charged with his head lower than usual to conceal his other ploys, moving much faster than previously. His left arm, miraculously restored to power, hurled a rock; his right, similarly rejuvenated, threw a handful of dirt at Rigel's eyes; and his horned head dipped low enough to disembowel the insolent halfling and toss him across the arena.

Alas, while Rigel Halfling was a merely a promising minstrel—and then only by earthling standards—Saiph was an ancestral defensive amulet. It caused its wearer to leap aside with superhuman agility and plunge his blade like a silver lightning stroke into the base of the Minotaur's neck and down through his aorta and other major organs.

Even so, as Elnath toppled, one of his mighty arms reached out to catch Rigel and drag him to the ground, pinning him. It shouldn't have been possible for any being, whether human, starborn, or minotaur, to speak while spewing torrents of blood both internally and externally. Yet somehow,

in defiance of medical facts, Elnath looked down on Rigel
Halfling with one gentle bovine eye and gurgled: *"Gracias!"*
  And then he died.

Chapter 12

Rigel extricated himself and scrambled to his feet. His sword had vanished, its work done. Judging by the sun, the fight had lasted much longer than he would have guessed. The audience was applauding. The imps at the back were bouncing up and down with excitement, but the adults were more interested in the refreshments being brought out. Only the killer mourned his victim.

Physically exhausted, emotionally nauseated, he trudged back to the grandstand, cloaked in the Minotaur's blood like a flag of shame, with his face full of grit. He wished he hadn't lost the red cloak somewhere in the battle; a dose of that might have done the elves a lot of good.

Muphrid rose and turned to address his guests. "So the murderous Elnath Minotaur meets his just deserts at last! Dear friends, after Rigel Halfling's stirring demonstration of his ancestral amulet, Saiph, we have other exciting acts for you to witness. Our next performer will be Starborn Sadatoni, riding his famous hippogriff, Kabdhilinan, who will round up a fire-breathing chimera to display—*Oh, yuck!*"

Rigel had jumped up and pulled himself onto the stand right beside the host. Muphrid had not expected this dirty, sweaty, and blood-drenched apparition.

"Barbarian! Go get yourself cleaned up immediately!"

"Me?" Rigel offered a gory arm. "I thought you would want to lick the blood."

Starfolk cried out in revulsion and those in aisle seats practically climbed over their neighbors to put distance between themselves and the savage halfling as he stalked up to the portal at the back. The male imps were grinning, of course. Young Izar stuck out his tongue, offering to lick Rigel's arm, but Rigel didn't cooperate. Glancing back briefly, he saw that two slaves had brought out a horse and were tying ropes to the Minotaur's ankles, ready to drag away his corpse.

Senator, in his hunter's bush wear, displayed absolutely no expression as he opened the portal to sea air and the sound of surf.

A few minutes in the ocean washed the blood from Rigel's skin, if not his soul, and the blood did not summon a frenzy of sharks to exact poetic justice, though that possibility did occur to him. Letting the wind dry him, he walked slowly back up the beach to the cabin. He could, he supposed, spend the rest of the day exploring the coast—he certainly had no desire to mingle socially with effete starfolk hypocrites.

On the other hand, he had never seen either a hippogriff or a chimera, and that part of the program had sounded relatively innocent. Leaving sandy footprints across the floor, he went to the magic door and gingerly opened it. This time it didn't lead to empty space or the grandstand . . . it just opened onto the jungle behind the cabin. The door was magic no more. Without it, the cabin was a comfortable prison, but a prison nonetheless. Baffled, he sprawled on a chair on the porch and tried to puzzle out what he would do if no one came to rescue him.

He didn't have long to wait. He heard the door open and turned to meet familiar pearl-white eyes.

"Hey, come and sit down, most noble Starling Izar!" Noting the droop of his young friend's ears, he added, "Something wrong?"

The imp nodded as he fell into a chair. "We're leaving. I came to say goodbye." For a moment deviltry flickered in his eyes, and his ears rose back up. "You missed a mem'rable demonstration of how not to herd a chimera."

"Meaning?"

Toothy grin. "The chimera herded Starborn Sadatoni instead and roasted his famous hippogriff, Kabdhilinan. It was eating Sadatoni when Alniyat dragged me away. Now everyone's going home. Why didn't you let me lick your arm? That would *positively* have sent greatmother into labor!"

"She told me she was your sister."

Izar squealed. *"Alniyat* did? She's my great-great-grandfather's mother! Don't believe a word the old hag tells you."

Rigel decided that there was one starborn he did like—Izar, even if the boy was odds-on favorite to win the Agility in the Abuse of Facts Award. "Why into labor? Is she pregnant?"

"If she isn't, it's not from lack of trying," the imp said darkly. "Why did it take you so long to kill the Minotaur?"

"I didn't kill the Minotaur. I promised him I wouldn't try to kill him, but that he could die on my sword as soon as he made a serious effort to kill me."

"But . . . You *promised* the Minotaur? It could *speak?*"

"Elnath was a lot smarter than I am, and very brave. Even when he knew he was going up against Saiph, he still insisted on fighting me to preserve his honor." That was sort of true. No need to mention that the Minotaur had been bribed.

Izar's ears went flat again. "That's disgusting. That makes it public murder! Nobody ever told me that minotaurs could talk."

"Then make that your lesson for today: You must always ask questions."

"Everyone says I ask far too many. I wish they hadn't canceled the fire fight. I was looking forward to that." He glanced down at the collection of bracelets on his left wrist. "Oh, *schmoor!* The crone's calling me. I have to go or she'll burn my arm off. Rigel, I found out what happens if you don't get status, and it really is pukey horrible!"

It would be pukey horrible if he *did* too. He'd have to earn his living by killing more than minotaurs. "I guessed it would be bad."

"They put you in the Dark Cells!"

"Thanks for the warning, most noble Izar Starling."

Ears drooped. "You don't have to call me that, halfling. I made it up . . . there is no such title."

"You seem noble to me. Give my love to your sister. Tell her I lust after her madly."

The imp's eyes popped wide in mingled horror and disbelief. "You do?"

"No, but she'll enjoy hearing it. Now off with you! No, on second thought, I'll come with you."

He didn't, though. As they reached the door, it opened to admit Mira. She stepped aside and curtseyed to the imp, but servants were only furniture in his world, and he brushed past her without even noticing. He left the door open, but it closed itself behind him. Mira found a chair and set to work removing her boots with a buttonhook.

"They had an accident," she said. "Some elf got killed by some sort of monster. So everyone's going home, and the party's officially over. They told me to go and attend my master." She scowled.

Rigel knelt at her feet to help. "Then I hope your service will be more diligent than any I've seen so far. I heard about the accident. The first event went as expected." He told her all about the Minotaur, and what he'd learned from it.

By the time he finished, they were relaxing on the porch with a bottle of wine that Mira had smuggled out from the kitchens under her petticoats.

"I hate elves," he concluded. "They're nasty, empty, pitiless, worthless, murdering, useless, thieving, promiscuous, baby-abandoning, slave-owning dilettantes. Good-for-nothings."

"Very musical, though," she said. "And remember, Alrisha is only one corner of one domain. The Starlands sound huge. If you had visited one Virginian plantation two hundred years ago, could you have judged the whole United States by it? The whole world?"

"All I want to do," Rigel said, "is find the SOB who sired me and collect the eighteen years of child support he neglected to pay Gert. Then I can go home and hire a plastic surgeon to fake me a couple of nipples and a belly button." He sipped the wine, which was delicious. "And buy a forged birth certificate."

"I don't like your chances of finding Daddy. And you'd better not waste any time. The world is about to end."

"Huh?"

"I told you bits of it are disappearing," Mira said in the tones of someone beginning a lecture. "I gather that starfolk can die by violence, but not of old age. They just fade away, like old soldiers. They aren't seen around as often. They get *rare*. The old queen, Electra, has reached that stage. She hasn't been seen in decades, and everyone is worried. The problem is that the realm was begun by one of her ancestors, thousands of earthly years ago. 'Begun' as an idea, I think—'imagined' they call it, meaning sort of invented, which agrees with what Elnath told you about their reality being our fantasy. Generations of rulers have added to it and expanded upon it, and the lesser starfolk have all added their bits, their 'domains.' Muphrid stole the Moon Garden from Dubhe, but he added that lake park we saw yesterday. He worked on it for years, imagining it rock by rock and bush by bush."

She paused, but Rigel held his tongue.

"Electra's influence is fading away," Mira said. "And the Starlands are fading, too, because Regent Kornephoros can't hold it all together. The servants are seriously worried about this, because part of Alrisha itself disappeared a few months ago. They admit this might be Muphrid's fault, but the West Orchards completely ceased to exist. Portals won't open to it anymore. All of its inhabitants are gone too, not just elves but hundreds of human serfs also. There must be millions or billions of them in the Starlands and they're all going to die if the queen completely loses her grip."

Rigel emptied his glass with a gulp. "So what's the answer?"

"The answer is that she has to bequeath the realm to someone. As you know, there are three contenders: Vildiar, Talitha, and Kornephoros. They're all descended from her, but separated by more generations than humans can imagine. Kornephoros is the most likely candidate, because the queen named him her successor ages ago, making him a sort of vice-monarch. He is doing his best, but that won't be good enough until he's officially king. Everything could just crumble away if Electra loses interest altogether before passing along her duties."

"All the more reason to go home. Or just get drunk," Rigel said, thinking of the Minotaur. He reached for the wine bottle.

A shadow swept over them.

"Now I know I'm hallucinating!" Mira said, staring upward. "That is an aerodynamic impossibility. Are you expecting company?"

Rigel left the bottle where it was. "I wasn't, but I am now."

A white swan the size of a double garage was circling overhead. It carried passengers and one of them was waving.

Chapter 13

The swan dropped its feet as landing gear, and slid to a halt in the lagoon in a long rush of foam. It glided majestically to the beach, then waddled awkwardly ashore on ugly black legs taller than any starborn. When it settled down on the sand it became beautiful again, with its arched neck, snowy plumage, and strong black beak. The open box attached to its back held two adults and a child. The imp leaped over the edge, slid down a wing, and hit the sand running. The man opened a door in the side of the enclosure, and a flight of steps unfolded. Alniyat descended with dignity, and the man followed her down.

Striding down the beach to meet them, Rigel noted the angle of Izar's ears and a mischievous gleam in his eyes just before the imp launched himself like a missile. Rigel caught him, whirled him around, then held him up so their eyes were level.

"*Schmoor!*" Izar had trouble breathing while his chest was being squeezed so effectively. "You're strong, tweenling!"

"No, you're small and puny."

"Am not! I'm big for my age. We've come to *rescue* you!"

Being rescued from the sadistic cathouse of Alrisha would be welcome indeed, but not being rescued out of a frying pan into a fire. Is the devil you know always better than the devil you don't? Rigel bowed to Alniyat, who flaunted a parasol that matched her silver hair, but wore only the usual moon-cloth wrap and a fortune in jewelry. He saw at once that last night's buy-a-boy smile had gone. Today was to be strictly business, and whether she was Izar's sister or great-great-great-grandmother was irrelevant. Not that it would have mattered, with her figure.

Her companion was obviously another halfling. For one thing, he had wrinkles. For another, he wore a sort of Turkish pajama outfit of a loose shirt, baggy pants, and ornate slippers, all of which might be hiding some fearful disfigurement such as body hair. He did have the proper starborn ears, high and pointed, but his eyes were a muddy brown and his hair salt-and-pepper. Whereas every elf Rigel had met so far somehow proclaimed his name, this man's name was hard to make out, as if it was hidden by static.

"Starborn Alniyat!" Rigel bowed. "And Halfling, er, Albireo? You are welcome to my humble cell." He gestured as if to escort them to the cabin.

"Your host would not say so," Alniyat said, not budging. "You must know by now, Rigel Halfling, that you have fallen into the clutches of some very unscrupulous starfolk. You can judge Muphrid for yourself; you heard him confess to grand larceny."

"Muphrid made you kill the Minotaur," Izar said.

"I told you to keep quiet," snapped his sister or possibly greatmother. "It is not you that they are after, Rigel. It is Saiph they want, and Saiph will never leave your wrist while you live. The best that you can possibly hope for from them would be employment as an assassin, and I don't believe that you are that sort of person. Halfling, for your own safety you must appeal directly to Regent-heir Kornephoros, the current ruler of the Starlands. He is honest and upright and a far nobler character than Prince Vildiar. I know them both personally and can swear to it. I am confident that the regent will protect you and see that the law is fairly applied in your case."

Even the Great Ones of the Starlands were willing to fight over him? Life had taught Rigel Estell never to trust anyone, and in this foreign world, he had no way of finding truth among all the lies.

"You told me yesterday that the regent did whatever the prince told him. You meant the same Prince Vildiar?"

"The regent-heir does not stand up to him as much as he should, but he is the best ally you can hope to find." The delectable Starborn Alniyat, like her brother or greatson Izar, tended to see facts more as challenges than barriers.

What was her real motive? She was gorgeous and he would happily exchange all the bracelets in the universe for some serious fondling lessons from her, but she was also a shameless strumpet, vamping every male in sight. She must see Rigel as easy pickings—gain possession of him, and she could sell his right wrist to the highest bidder.

"I am not impressed by Muphrid, I admit," he said, "but he has been a gracious host, and to walk out of here, or fly out of here, without a word of thanks would be rude. No doubt he would dispute your assessment of the two princes. From what I understand, there must be a court hearing before I can be awarded status."

Alniyat dismissed that problem with a twirl of her parasol. "I can explain once we are airborne."

"My lady, I am a stranger here and do not understand your ways."

"Oh, it's simple enough!" she said impatiently. "Any halfling must be sponsored by a starborn. A promise of service and good behavior is exchanged for one of protection and maintenance. That is universal. But if Vildiar sponsors you, the behavior he will demand of you will be far from good. He employs halfling assassins! I know this for a fact." She kept glancing back at the cottage, showing convincing signs of worry. Her anxiety might be genuine and still not stem from honorable motives.

Rigel folded his arms. "And what line of work will Regent Kornephoros find for me and my amulet?" Or Starborn Alniyat, for that matter?

Albireo said, "I was Prince Kornephoros's retainer for almost a hundred years, halfling, and he never once gave me a dishonorable order. He certainly never asked me to kill anyone. Sponsorship is subject to the queen's laws and a sponsor cannot legally order his retainer to commit crimes—quite the contrary! The whole purpose of sponsoring is to ensure that registered halflings behave themselves."

Alniyat took up the story again. "Not only are the regent's ethics beyond reproach, but he is Queen Electra's heir designate. If he agrees to sponsor you, then the court appearance will be a mere formality."

"I doubt if it will impose any restrictions at all other than a hat." Was Albireo bragging about his elfin ears? "When Starborn Alniyat acquired Gienah, there"—he gestured toward the waiting swan—"and needed an experienced swanherd, she offered me employment, I accepted, and the prince transferred my bond to her with no hesitation or rancor."

Piloting a swan was one thing. Wielding an unbeatable sword was quite another. "With respect, starborn, while it does seem that I bear the most deadly weapon in the realm, I have no other skills whatsoever. You have not explained why the honored regent would be so anxious to employ me."

"To keep Vildiar from getting you," Izar said. He was dancing with impatience.

"Exactly!" Alniyat's eyes were still fixed on the cottage. "For once Imp Izar has hit the target. To keep Vildiar from getting you. If you fall into his hands you will either die or become a threat to the innocent."

"And how will I fall into his hands if I remain here? I gathered that Starborn Fomalhaut put me in the custody of Starborn Muphrid until a date was set for my hearing. Is this illegal? Or wrong? Where does Prince Vildiar come into it?"

"Fomalhaut is an underling of Prince Vildiar and an overlord of Starborn Muphrid."

"I am truly sorry, starborn." And Rigel was. To refuse her anything hurt, but her very urgency was just increasing his stubbornness. "I do not understand the ways of the Starlands. Why do you travel by air now instead of by portal? Why should any starborn sponsor a halfling?"

Her silver eyes glanced at him like a flash of steel. "Halfling, I am taking a considerable risk in offering to rescue you. At least let us go to Gienah, and I will explain on the way."

Even that offer might be a trap, but he was frightened now that she might just give up on him and go, and he did not want that. He did not know what he wanted. "Of course," he said. "Coming, Mira?" All of them began heading seaward.

"We must travel by air," Alniyat said, "because portals only work within a domain. Except for root portals, that is, and they are usually kept locked. Alrisha is named after one of Muphrid's ancestors, the one who first imagined it. Perhaps he was an adolescent just coming into his powers and began by imagining a portal leading to some private nook where he could entertain his current girlfriend. Or it may have been his tenth effort. Whichever it was, over the next few thousand years he expanded it, adding subdomains of farm, forest, sea, mountains, cities, and castles, whatever he fancied. His descendants have continued to do so. Muphrid himself imagined the Versailles room, as he was boasting last night, although I would never admit to committing such an atrocity. He isn't even capable of holding together what he's got now—parts of it are disappearing as we speak. Not all starfolk are creative enough or motivated enough to imagine habitable domains, but those who do are eager to populate it with other starfolk and livestock. Do you understand?"

"I think so."

"But the ancestral Alrisha had to *start* somewhere. When he imagined that first portal, he was in a domain belonging to someone else, a parent or friend. The new domain is *rooted* in the older one, like a twig sprouting from a branch, so the system sets up interminable chains of senior and junior domains. Their owners are related as overlords and underlings."

"Like landlords and tenants? Or like kings and barons and serfs?"

Alniyat turned for another landward glance. "Not really. It's mostly a ceremonial relationship. But when Dubhe discovered that Muphrid had stolen the Moon Garden, she complained to her overlord and word went back up the chain, eventually to Prince Vildiar, whose domain of Phegda is enormous, holding hundreds of roots. He threatened Fomalhaut, who threatened Muphrid, as you saw. The regent-heir is the ultimate judge."

The regent-heir was Prince Kornephoros.

They reached the swan, which was even more enormous than Rigel had realized. It was preening its tail feathers, arching its great neck right over the howdah on its back, ignoring the tiny bipeds alongside.

"In theory," Alniyat said, "we could travel by portal all the way to Phegda, which is rooted in Canopus, the capital, and from there by portal to anywhere else in the Starlands, but we never do. Domain owners set up links to their friends' domains. We call them highways, because you must travel by air to use them. Now, *please* can we go, before it is too late?"

Who to trust? Fomalhaut, who had rescued him from the Walmart massacre and then treated him as a potentially dangerous animal? Or the luscious Alniyat, who claimed to lust after him but seemed to lust after every male body around? Saiph was offering no advice. Rigel turned to Mira, who stood on the warm sand beside him, ignored by everyone so far. The detective had seemed odd back on Earth, and she made even less sense here in the Starlands, but he had a feeling she knew a lot more than she admitted.

"Do you have any comments to offer, human female?"

She nodded emphatically. "Oh, yes! I've been thinking about what happened at the Walmart store. I have no reason to suspect her Regent-heir Kornephoros of having played any part in the murders there. That is certainly not true of Starborn Fomalhaut, and therefore, by implication, of his overlord, Prince Vildiar. My ex-husband wouldn't have been able to organize an attack like that, even if he had somehow known where we were. I know of no human device that would have caused those people to run amok and try to kill us. Certain nerve gases have similar effects, but they would have affected everyone, including us. The objective was either to kill you outright or provoke your amulet into defending you and thus make you a murderer in the eyes of human law. Fomalhaut winkled you out under the guise of offering protection, but who created the disaster in the first place? Sometimes the evil you don't know is better than the one you do."

"Succinctly spoken," Rigel said, "and convincing. I will gratefully accept your offer of rescue, Starborn Alniyat. I do have one condition, and you must give me your personal guarantee on it."

Alniyat chilled. "Condition? You do not understand the seriousness of your position. What condition?"

"I don't mind being sponsored, if the words are acceptable and all halflings must be sponsored; but humans in the Starlands are enslaved. My friend Mira has done nothing to deserve such a fate. I want your promise that she will be promptly and safely returned to Earth and set at liberty at a place of her choosing."

"That is easily promised," Alniyat said.

"And easily done," Albireo agreed eagerly. "As regent, His Highness has access to the royal treasury, which is where all the confiscated reversion staffs are stored. The earthling can easily be extroverted."

The swan trumpeted.

A swarm of black objects was rising from the trees inland.

Izar yelled, *"Dragonflies!"* and shot up the ladder like a cat up a tree—obviously a starling with clear personal priorities.

Rigel grabbed Alniyat's arm and urged her to follow. "I'm coming," he promised, but he pushed Mira ahead of him also. Albireo was making strange noises at the swan, half chirping, half warbling, apparently trying to keep it from flying off without them. It squawked back at him agitatedly.

Someone grabbed Rigel's wrist and tugged. He swung around angrily, but there was no one there. Only Saiph. Oh, it was like that was it? He ignored the signal and reached for the ladder. The bracelet pulled harder, but not hard enough to stop him, and he was fairly sure that it could stop him, if the danger were extreme. He continued to climb and the tugging eventually stopped.

The open box on Gienah's back held two benches that faced each other. Izar had flopped onto the rear one. Alniyat joined him there, pulling Rigel down between them, which was a tight fit. Albireo collapsed onto the front seat beside Mira as the steps folded themselves up and the great bird began waddling seaward, flapping its wings in its haste to escape.

"The starling was right," the swanherd said. "Those are indeed dragonflies. I fear we are too late, my lady."

"Keep going!" Alniyat snapped. "Muphrid is playing a dangerous game, but we must call his bluff."

The first dragonfly arrived just as the swan became waterborne. Soon more followed it, circling overhead with the raspy sound of ultralight airplanes. In a world of elves and minotaurs, Rigel had been prepared to find that dragonflies were literally a cross between dragons and flies, but in fact they looked just like earthly dragonflies, except that they were more than a meter long. Their abdomen sections glistened in metallic reds and greens, their wings were a blur, and their heads bore mandibles like shears.

"They're not doing much," he said.

"They won't attack until we're airborne," Izar said. His ears were flat against his head. "Then they'll go for Gienah and bite out her eyes!"

"And we'll crash?"

Alniyat said, "The swan would fall. But Muphrid will never take that risk. We would die and the guilt curse would kill him. Keep going, halfling!"

Looking unhappy, Albireo caroled more noises at the swan. Wings thundering, feet hurling up a trail of spray, Gienah sped across the lagoon. It seemed impossible that she could lift a load of five people and their howdah before she ran into the reef, but at the last possible instant she surged out of the water. White surf flashed by underneath, then the great green-blue swell of the ocean.

An electric blue dragonfly darted at the swan's head. She snapped at it and the broken body fell away. Then another.

"Muphrid's not the one who sent them!" Izar wailed. "It's Hadar!"

"Hadar doesn't know we're here, darling," Alniyat said. She made a throwing gesture and a wad of violet brilliance the size of a golf ball flashed out at one of the dragonflies, which exploded in fire and smoke.

Izar yelled, *"Yeah!* Zap 'em all, Mom!"

She was trying. Fireballs streaked out as fast as she could throw them, about half of them finding and frying targets.

Gienah had gained altitude, perhaps a hundred meters, and turned landward, but the swarm had grown thicker and louder and closer. Soon the bird was having trouble isolating targets, snapping without effect, and every one she did kill seemed to be replaced by three more.

Alniyat was having more success, for she could hardly miss now, but the swan's flight grew erratic, and the howdah rocked and pitched. Izar was alternating between cheering and wailing. Rigel didn't know how to comfort him, because Albireo was obviously terrified. Then one of the flying monsters landed on the side of the howdah. Izar yelped in alarm and almost climbed on top of Rigel. Albireo struck at it with a knife, cutting off its head before it could do any harm. The remains dropped amidst the passengers' feet, writhing. Mira picked it up and threw it overboard.

Another landed just ahead, at the base of the swan's neck. The swan twisted her head around and got that one.

"My lady, we are doomed!" the swanherd wailed. "Starborn Muphrid cannot possibly recall them now."

Never slackening her barrage of fireballs, Alniyat said, "I am afraid you are right. And Izar was right, too. This cannot be Muphrid's doing. Nor any starborn's. A halfling must be behind it, and almost certainly Hadar."

Izar howled in terror. Unable to reach anyone else, he snuggled up against Rigel, who perforce put an arm around him. "Who is Hadar?"

Alniyat was too busy shooting dragonflies, and a chalky-faced Albireo answered for her.

"One of Prince Vildiar's retainers, reputed to be his chief assassin."

"He's a *horror!*" Izar screamed into Rigel's chest. "He murders people."

"But why would he try to kill us?"

"To pick Saiph off your corpse, halfling," said a grim-faced Mira. "Or just to put it out of play so that it cannot be used against him."

Although everyone else in the howdah seemed frantic with terror, to Rigel the action felt more like a staged melodrama, and his next speech was obvious. "Order the swan to land. I will take my chances with this Hadar."

"We cannot land!" Albireo said. The ocean had vanished; there was nothing but jungle in all directions, and no safe landing spots for the swan.

"How long until we reach the highway?" Alniyat asked grimly.

"We cannot find the highway until we gain altitude." Clearly the dragonflies were keeping the swan from doing exactly that.

One of the monsters landed about halfway down the swan's neck. Even the swan wasn't flexible enough to get at that one. Albireo couldn't reach it with his dagger, and Alniyat couldn't zap it without injuring the swan. The horrible thing began crawling forward, heading for Gienah's eyes.

"*Saiph!*" Rigel disentangled from Izar and moved across the howdah to kneel on the bench between Mira and the swanherd. Leaning out as far as he could, he swatted the dragonfly off in two pieces.

Two more promptly replaced it. He got one, but the other was beyond even his reach. He dismissed his sword and scrambled over the edge of the howdah, lowering himself cautiously to kneel on the swan's neck. To his dismay, the plumage proved to be as slippery as ice, an oily, waterproof surface. Keeping a careful grip on to the howdah behind him, he was able to recall his sword and deal with the second dragonfly just before it progressed out of his reach, but clearly this location was not going to be close enough if the giant bugs landed any closer to the swan's head.

He dismissed Saiph again, stretched out on his belly, and began to edge forward, arms and legs spread wide to give him as much balance as possible. Even getting enough of a grip with his fingers was difficult, and he was oppressed by the sight of the long drop on either side of him—there were *clouds* down there. He tried not to think of what would happen if Gienah decided that he was another dragonfly, only bigger. She could easily pick him up and spit him out.

Two more bugs landed ahead of him. He was within easy reach of the first. Bracing himself for the weight, he said, "*Saiph!*" He killed the rearmost dragonfly, and, with a few more one-handed wriggles, managed to get the other one too. Since the swan was not taking offence, he squiggled even farther forward, to the point where her neck was narrow enough for his legs to straddle it like an oversized horse. He still couldn't get a firm enough grip on her plumage with his left hand to risk batting the brutes right out of the air, but he was close enough to her head to defend it from direct attack.

Of course, the area behind him was completely undefended now. No sooner had he realized that than a fly landed directly on his back, claws raking against his bare skin. He didn't dare look at it, for even his instinctive squirm of revulsion nearly sent him on a long one-way trip to the jungle. He buried his face in the swan's musty-smelling plumage and waited as the giant insect crawled over him. Did dragonflies like all eyes or just swans' eyes? It did not bite him, and the second it was clear of him, he killed it. Then something touched his thigh, and he knew he had another passenger to deal with.

Still they kept coming. He soon lost count. A dozen? Twenty? He was dimly aware of Alniyat still igniting the more distant flies, Izar cheering, and Albireo chanting directions or possibly comfort, to the swan.

"Hold tight, halfling," he called. "We have reached the highway."

Rigel spared a glance ahead and saw a strange flat wheel of white cloud, wider than a football field, slowly rotating—the top of a tornado, perhaps? The swan stopped beating her wings and began a long dive toward the center, gathering speed and leaving all the dragonflies behind at last. Soon the fuzzy edges of the mist were rising above them, blocking out the sky. It was cold and damp, even for Rigel, and he felt his ears pop. Abruptly sunlight returned and Gienah was soaring low over grassy hills, sending a huge herd of herbivores stampeding in terror. There were no more dragonflies, and no lingering trace of clouds in the sky far above them. Everyone joined in Izar's cheers. Even Gienah trumpeted.

Rigel banished his sword. He had won the battle, all except the hardest part, which was going to be wriggling backward along the swan's neck wearing only a loincloth. It was unthinkable. Very gingerly he began the dangerous maneuver of turning around, ignoring his companions' cries of alarm. The worst part came when he had turned halfway, head hanging down on one side, feet dangling on the other, and nothing to grip except slippery down. If he started to slide he was done for. If he pulled out feathers and hurt Gienah, would Albireo be able to prevent her from shaking her head and sending her rescuer tumbling a thousand meters into the grassland?

But he did get himself pointed in the right direction, and a few minutes later willing hands hauled him back into the howdah.

Chapter 14

Gienah flew on at an easier pace, climbing gently toward the next highway.

"Go to Dziban," Alniyat told Albireo. "Kornephoros must hear about this attack immediately." She was furious.

Albireo warbled something but the swan just continued beating its great slow wings. The effect was like riding a boat over a long and gentle swell.

"Dziban?" Rigel asked.

"The regent-heir's domain. I was planning to go home to Spica, but I won't abide people trying to murder me and my . . . and Izar."

"Your son," Izar said. "He knows." He took up Rigel's wrist so he could examine the writing on the bracelet. "The guys were saying that Saiph can make a man better than *four* ordinary swordsman! That's if he's strong and nimble. You're ever so strong and nimble, aren't you? Maybe you could beat *five!* If you had your back against a wall, no more than three can get at you at once."

"There are other amulets," his mother said.

"Not as good as Saiph, Mom! How many names?"

Rigel said, "More than a hundred, I think."

"Doggy!" the imp said, apparently a sign of approval. "Is the Minotaur's name on there now?"

"I don't know. I can't read."

Startled, Izar examined Rigel's expression carefully for evidence of leg pulling, and then said, *"Schmoor!* I'll teach you."

"Thanks."

"Can you sing?"

"No."

"I can teach you that too!"

"Not now!" his mother said. "If you're bored, why don't you just put yourself to sleep?"

The imp shrugged, glanced out at the scenery, and surprisingly agreed. "Right. I'll tell myself to wake me when we get to Dziban. But you behave! Remember, he's a halfling." He leaned his head against Rigel's shoulder, closed his eyes, and immediately went limp.

"Is he faking?" Rigel asked Mira, who could see him better.

She was smiling, but saying nothing, playing the perfect servant. "Don't think so. That's the same trick you pulled in the Winnebago."

"I swear I will strangle him," Alniyat said through clenched teeth. "Filthy-minded little pest! Why don't you throw him overboard, as a favor to me?"

"I could roll him up and tuck him under the bench," Rigel said. With more room on the bench, he wouldn't need to squeeze in so closely next to Alniyat, who didn't appear to be enjoying the intimacy as much as he was. Had yesterday's invitations in the Moon Garden been all a fake, or was she just putting it off until they were alone again?

"That seems a little unkind."

Teasing was unkind too. He made more room on the bench by lifting the limp Izar onto his lap, wrapping an arm around him to keep him in place. Then he slid his other arm around Alniyat. She went rigid, and Albireo gaped in horror. Mira was intently studying the sky aft, her eyebrows set high.

Alniyat had her lips pressed tight, but she did not tell the presumptuous half-breed to take his arm away.

"That's much better," he said. It felt very good indeed, except that Izar weighed two tonnes. "How old is he?"

"Nineteen."

End of conversation.

Albireo said, "He was born in the year of black butterflies. Understand, Rigel, that starfolk take about twice as long to mature as earthlings do. They have plenty of time."

"And they never die? How does one recognize an *old* star-born?"

"You never see one. They just fade. You might say they die of boredom, because they've been everywhere and done every-thing."

All the elves Rigel had seen so far had looked young and behaved like children or randy adolescents. "This morning a starborn was killed while trying to herd a chimera at Alrisha. Is that sort of suicidal behavior normal?"

The swanherd winced at such crudity. "I would not go so far as to call it suicidal. Daring . . . ostentatious . . ."

Gienah finished her long climb and dived into another great wheel of cloud. Rigel's ears popped again. The swan emerged in salty wet mist, with breakers and rocks not far below. It seemed as though every link required a drop of about ten thousand feet, and he suspected that going in the reverse di-rection would do the same, because that would make as little sense as everything else in the Starlands.

"I understand that Queen Electra rarely appears in public. How old is she?"

"I am not sure." Albireo's manner implied that he did not wish to comment on that in present company.

"Nineteen centuries," Alniyat said. "Give or take a generation. Prince Kornephoros is a bit over half that; he's starting to plan the celebration of his first millennium. She named him regent-heir about three centuries ago. Prince Vildiar is just past his five-hundredth birthday. He has no real claim to the crown except ambition and the argument that Kornephoros is too old to inherit, which is absurd."

"And the third claimant, Princess Talitha?"

"Count Talitha is out for the best of all possible reasons—she doesn't want the job. She insists that her reign would not last long enough to boil an egg. I don't suppose the old darling has ever boiled an egg in her life."

"Good for her," Rigel said. "But Electra must have been born while the Caesars ruled in Rome. If she's so old, why does she only have three living descendants? A human ruler of that era would have thousands by this time."

"It doesn't work that way." Alniyat seemed more relaxed now. She had either decided to overlook the offending arm over her shoulder or was enjoying it. "Electra has many descendants, although starfolk do not reproduce as fast as humankind and many of us die by misadventure, as you guessed. The qualification to rule is a special talent called *Naos*. Are you aware of the grades of magic, halfling?"

"I'm not aware of anything," Rigel said except the warm pressure of the girl tucked into the crook of his arm, the sweetness of her scent, her silken softness, and the sheer never-let-this-end pleasure of being allowed to hold her. Nothing else mattered. Someone had come within a hair's breadth of murdering him and all he could think about was her.

"Magic comes partly from bloodlines, and partly from hard work. It develops in adolescence, like hair and eye color, and is graded by the six colors of the rainbow. Halflings can usually reach violet, rarely blue. You can perceive the names of the starborn so you already have a trace of talent, and with some training you may be able to strengthen it. Most starborn achieve green or even yellow. One does not ask, of course. Orange is rare and red extremely so, because it requires both innate talent and centuries of study. Your amulet must have been created by a red, and it has grown stronger as it aged."

"So does a starborn's hair and eye color indicate his or her grade of magic?"

"Oh no, except that they develop at about the same age."

Another silence, and this time Albireo broke it. "There is another kind of power, called Naos, which crops up unpredictably, with little regard for bloodlines. It is named after the legendary founder of the Starlands, who must have lived sixty thousand years ago, if she lived at all. The only three starfolk who presently possess Naos are—"

"By the way, those lakes down there are the Ascella Lakes. They have the most superb fly-fishing in the entire realm. I have even heard people say that there is no finer fishing anywhere in the continuum than the Ascella Lakes. Have you ever tried fly-fishing, Halfling Rigel?"

"No," Rigel said. "But I know a lure when I see one. What were you saying about Naos?"

"I don't remember."

This time the pause was chilly and lasted long enough to be uncomfortable. The swan flew on with its gentle rocking motion. Just as Rigel was about to comment on the mountains coming into sight ahead, Alniyat spoke up angrily.

"The halfling was about to tell you that Naos magic, which the monarch requires to hold the realm together, confers a distinctive 'mark of Naos.' At present Vildiar, Talitha, and Kornephoros are the only three Naos starfolk."

Mira had been keeping a respectful silence, as befitted a slave, but now, surprisingly, she was smirking. "And does this mark of Naos have something to do with a starborn's hair?"

"And eyes," Alniyat agreed. "He can't dissemble when he's asleep."

Rigel looked down at Izar's head where it rested against his chest. The boy's eyes were closed, and his huge ears were as limp as a spaniel's. His scalp fur, while still white, had taken on a faint rainbow sheen, like the back of a CD or a milk opal. No adult elf at Alrisha had sported hair like that, nor any of the imps who had performed at the banquet.

"So he was telling the truth after all when he told me to address him as 'most noble' Izar?"

"No, he was not!" Alniyat stormed. "We have no titles below those of royalty. Izar is merely a starling like any other. He will become an adult starborn at forty-one. If he has developed the full mark of Naos by then, Electra will name him a prince. And it does look like it's going to happen. I made him promise to dissemble while we were at Alrisha. It's good for him to be just another imp around other imps sometimes."

"He wasn't dissembling when a gang of them raided the kitchens yesterday," Mira said. "The others knew what he was. He was giving them all orders, and even the biggest of them deferred to him."

"I will skin him!" his mother growled.

"So Izar may be in line for the throne?" Rigel asked.

"In a few centuries, maybe. Stars help the Starlands if that happens!"

"He's a good imp," Rigel protested. "He has spark. Who's his father?"

"His father isn't around much," she said, suddenly sullen.

"I sympathize. I never knew my father." He might soon meet him at last, but he did not expect to like him.

Alniyat sighed and nodded. "That may be part of the reason why Izar has taken to you like a cat to cream. It was your scars at first. Then the fight with the Minotaur. And that insanity just now with the dragonflies. But . . ."

But nothing, apparently.

Rigel smiled down at the child he held. "Have you ever heard the expression 'role model'?"

"Does it mean 'hero'?"

"I suppose it does." He held her worried gaze. "I won't betray his trust, starborn. I don't prey on children! I have other weaknesses, but never that. If I have to find work in these Starlands of yours, I'd rather be a babysitter than an assassin."

"An easy choice, I'd think," she said coldly.

Izar twitched. His left ear was flattened against Rigel's chest, but the right one straightened up. He blinked.

Alniyat said, "That is Dziban straight ahead, home of Regent-heir Kornephoros."

Mira turned around to see and said, *"Holy shit!"*

Rigel could not speak because his jaw was hanging open.

Chapter 15

G ienah was flying over scenery that could have been copied from some traditional Chinese watercolor—little
thatched villages set in misty blue-green wetlands of lakes and
paddy fields, while great sugarloaf peaks with impossibly steep
sides soared in the background, an array of giants fading back
into the distance. But the peak that was obviously their destination defied belief. It was capped like a mushroom with a
vast and intricate web of crystal, shining in spikes of brilliance
and flashes of rainbow. Towers and minarets and domes were
massed all over the top, while the sides beetled out in ribs,
arches, ledges, terraces, and buttresses, seemingly all constructed of crystal. Even beneath that, icicles of glasswork extended down the rock like roots, some almost reaching the
lakes. The sheer size and impossibility of it grew ever more
pronounced as the swan approached. Soon Rigel could make
out battlements and staircases, balconies and windows, fountains and waterfalls.

"That's the Crystal Castle," Izar remarked, stretching his
pipestem arms and launching a huge yawn. Then he realized

that he was sitting on Rigel's lap and turned to grin at him with eyes of mother-of-pearl that shone as bright as that miracle hilltop city ahead. "Aren't I heavy for you?"

Rigel leaned close to one of the great bat ears and whispered, "Any minute now my bladder will explode."

Izar beamed. "Really?" He bounced sadistically a few times to find out.

It didn't.

"You promised me," Alniyat said, "that you would dissemble your hair and eyes the entire time we were at Alrisha. I am told you broke that promise."

Izar's hair turned white as snow. "Well, it's isn't easy for me yet, Mom! When I get caught up in a game or something, I forget. And when some of the guys know, there isn't any point in pretending for the rest, is there?"

His look of innocence was so obviously fake that Rigel choked back a snigger that made Alniyat glare and no doubt raised him another hundred points in Izar's approval.

"We're at Dziban now anyway," the imp said breezily. "Why don't you stop *your* dissembling and let the cute tweenling see who he's cuddling?"

"Oh, you just wait," she muttered, but her anger was no longer convincing.

Rigel was quite sure he already knew, anyway.

The swan soared in under a vast arched roof and braked to descend into a long crystal pool. Waves surged up the sides, and then slopped back. Rising and falling in the swell it had created, the huge bird folded its wings and paddled to a landing stage. The servants who rushed forward to assist with their disembarkation were fully clothed and must therefore be human or halfling.

"I wanna show Rigel the castle!" Izar demanded.

"Can't you even wait until we get ashore? Don't forget your lute."

Izar retrieved his lute from under the bench and led the way up a gangplank to the quay. Alniyat issued orders. "Halfling Albireo, take the earthling and find accommodation for her. You, Starling Terrible, go and put your lute safely in your room and harpy word to your grandfather that we've arrived and would like see him as soon as possible; then come back here. Rigel will wait for you."

Izar glanced at her, and then Rigel, and then back again. His ears pricked up. "Are you going to kiss him?"

"*GO! Or so help me . . .*" Her roar startled even him, and he fled.

So then Rigel was alone with the woman who called herself Alniyat. This had to be the moment of truth—and he saw at once that she was still the businesslike Alniyat of the beach, not yesterday's seductress.

"Halfling, I am sorry."

"Don't apologize for Izar, or you won't have time for anything else."

"I am apologizing for me. That moment in the Moon Garden . . ."

Oh, that moment in the Moon Garden! How had he ever managed to refuse her? "My fault. I started it! I quoted poetry at you. It can happen to anyone. Half the books that libraries throw out are stuffed with poetry raving about love at first sight. No one believes in it until it happens, but it's as real as lightning." He was babbling. Helplessly adrift in a strange new world, he had fallen hopelessly in love because a beautiful woman had shown him a moment's pity. She had not intended anything more than sympathy.

"I know," she said softly. "But you still don't understand how foolish I was. You must know by now that I am dissembling both my name and my appearance. All the other guests were doing the same—Muphrid runs that sort of party, opportunities for anonymous romance. Fomalhaut may have seen through me, because he's a mage, but he wouldn't betray me. I forgot that our ways are not your ways and you would not know all this. You must have thought me a terrible slut. I promise you that I do not normally go around vamping every handsome male I meet."

Handsome maybe, dumb for sure. He shrugged. "Singles bars, we call them." And the word was *fornication*, not *romance*.

She chewed her lip. "I had an unfortunate . . . Never mind. Yesterday a crazy mob tried to kill you, you said. Today, someone else did, and I am certain it was Hadar or one of his gang. If they had known my true identity, they probably would not have targeted Izar and me, although I am not certain of that. I do think it was your amulet he was after."

"He'd kill five people for a bracelet?"

"Five or fifty or five hundred—no matter. That's why I think Hadar was behind it. You said earlier that you would rather be a babysitter than an assassin?"

Aha! That would be an honorable use for a sword. "Certainly! You have need of a bodyguard, my lady?"

"Izar does. The moment I saw a boy wearing Saiph, I wondered if he might be man enough to use it as it should be used. I arranged for Izar to cut your hair because he has reason to fear halflings, and I wanted to see how the two of you got along. You passed that test, so I ran another, and you saw right through me. And as for what you did just now on the swan—I have never seen such courage in my life. I am forever in your debt."

"No courage required. It was my life I was saving. I had no choice."

"It looked like courage to me, halfling." Alniyat's wistful smile would have made the Mona Lisa weep. "I am sorry that I insulted you. Look."

As her dissemblance faded, he was amazed to see the glory of a fully developed mark of Naos. Her hair turned from silver to opal, but a far richer, fierier polychrome than her son's, rippling with reds and blues and greens and gold. Her eyes flashed as if her irises were set with rainbows, too dazzling to look upon. Her true name was revealed . . . and it was what he had guessed it would be.

He dropped to his knees so she could not see the tears prickling out from under his eyelids. Romeo's chances with Juliet were far better than Rigel Halfling's with Princess Talitha. *Stop dreaming!* Even if she were not a princess, she was Izar's mother, and Izar was about the same age as he was. By elfin standards, Rigel was only a child, and she could be centuries old. But she had not looked at him as she would look at a child, and he had not felt like a child when he held her.

"Up!" She glanced around. There were workers on the dock and more people walking in galleries high overhead, but no one was paying attention to the princess and the lovesick half-breed. "Halfling Rigel, I want you to guard my son."

It was a better offer than any he could have imagined. It held out hope of an honorable life in the Starlands, a life with some purpose. "Your Highness, I would be greatly honored to serve both of you, but you know I cannot defend against magic."

"Of course you can," she said, smiling again. "We'll load you up with amulets until you rattle."

It was too good to be true. Life had taught him to beware of good fortune. "You have known me for barely a day. How can you possibly trust me with such responsibility?"

"Because I offered you a bribe few young men would have refused." Her eyes not only shone like diamonds, they could cut as hard. "You did, so I already trust you more than I trust his present guard. I've noticed him wearing amulets I did not assign him. There may be an innocent explanation for that, or a very bad one."

"You may trust me, Your Highness. I will swear whatever oaths you ask of me."

Her smile was a fanfare of roses. "You will be good for Izar, and I should be able to protect you, in turn. You see, the regent-heir is my father. You will certainly have your work cut out for you with that imp of mine. It's only in the last few months that his hair and eyes have started changing, and his magic is growing in strongly. Don't tell him I told you that! My excuse for going to dissembling parties is that I want Izar to be just another brat among strangers sometimes. It's also nice not to have people groveling all the time."

There had been other reasons, but it wouldn't do for her servant to comment on such matters. "Izar is a great lad. Guarding him will be a pleasure, but why does he need guarding?"

"I really fear that his—Look out, here comes the Terror now."

Izar skidded to a halt in front of them, gasping for breath. "Oh good, Mom, you've dropped your disguise. Are you two all done?"

"From now on Halfling Rigel is going to be your bodyguard."

"*DOGGY!*" Izar's grin showed at least two-dozen needle-sharp teeth.

"So you will obey his orders exactly."

"What?" The great ears curled in horror. "Orders from a halfling?"

"You heard. From now on when you disobey, I shall have Rigel put you across his knee and apply the hand of wisdom to the seat of learning as hard and often as I think you deserve. You have been warned." Talitha smiled and floated up into the air. She gathered speed, heading for the roof.

Gaping after her, Rigel realized that there were dozens of people soaring around under the great arches.

"Will you?" Izar asked anxiously.

"Will I what?"

"Beat me if I misbehave?"

"Mercilessly. It's the human savage in me. But you can behave when you want to. I've seen you do it for as long as a minute and a half. Now show me the Crystal Castle."

Izar wrapped stringy fingers around Rigel's wrist. "Hold your ears on! Oops, sorry. Didn't mean that." He pointed his other hand straight up, and up they went.

In Dziban everyone wore a finger-ring amulet that would take its wearer wherever that finger pointed. Izar was quite incapable of supporting Rigel's weight, but his ring could transport both of them as long they stayed in contact. Rigel soon discovered that he felt more secure if he kept his own hand on the imp's shoulder. He could trust *himself* not to let go in a fit of absentmindedness.

Izar's idea of a great tour was to soar all the way up to the uppermost gallery, Stars Gate, then descend to the palace's foundations via a seemingly endless succession of slides: straight slides, curved slides, roller-coaster slides, and scare-the-bowels-out-of-you slides, which were obviously the best. Then do it again and again by different routes.

The imp also had odd ideas on points of interest. The zoological gardens, known as the Bestiary, he dismissed as kids' stuff, not worth a visit. Libraries and art galleries were boring, and he could not yet see the benefits of lingering to admire feminine beauty, of which Dziban had no shortage. He also refused to stop at an amphitheater where an orchestra was pouring out spellbinding music to an audience of several thousand. On the other hand, he felt that a trip on a gondola along a canal and over a couple of waterfalls would be highly educational for Rigel.

Twice Izar ran into friends and went into great detail describing the Minotaur battle so that he could brag about his new bodyguard and let them see the legendary Saiph. His friends were much too respectful toward him for boys of their apparent age, which was, of course, why his mother took him to parties where his identity was disguised.

Once he detoured to a stall and pushed past a line of waiting earthlings to demand a bag of candied lizards. Rigel was ravenous, but he played it safe and chose strawberry ice cream instead.

"Don't you have to pay?" he asked. The humans were paying.

Izar smirked. "Not with my hair."

His bodyguard made a mental note to run that excuse by Talitha.

The slides soon grew monotonous, but the ascents were slower and usually through magnificent buildings, some of which were surely bigger than any hall or cathedral on Earth.

Sunlight beamed down through elaborate stained-glass windows larger than building lots, each displaying a picture of some famous scene, either historical or mythical, if there was any difference between those terms in the Starlands. Crystal statues towered three or four stories high, supporting higher cities on their shoulders.

Not all of the walls were transparent; some were prismatic, mirrored, or colored. Rigel saw into several living rooms, but never a bedroom. He noticed many earthlings relaxing on balconies or rollicking in swimming pools. If they were slaves, they had little to complain about, particularly in comparison to the pour souls in Muphrid's domain.

So far as he could tell, most of the inhabitants were human, dressed in a wild variety of costumes. Perhaps a fifth were starfolk, always fresh-faced and youthfully lithe, wearing nothing but skimpy moon-cloth wraps and often dashing about in groups, shouting and laughing like earthly teenagers. All elves, it seemed, were overgrown children, so those he had met at Alrisha had not been the exceptional rich butterflies he had supposed them to be. They had human cattle to provide muscle, they had magic galore, and they never grew up. Life was play, and eventually they died of boredom.

Halflings were rare, but he caught sight of a few beings that seemed even rarer—stereotypical dwarves with gray beards, once a hulking young cyclops, and flocks of birds with human heads, which Izar confirmed were harpies.

Izar was dismissive of all these minorities. When Rigel suddenly said, "Isn't that a centaur down there beside that fountain?" he just said, "Yes. If we were any closer you'd be able to smell it."

"I thought centaurs were supposed to be smart."

Snigger. "Their front ends are, but they can't house-train their own rears."

―――――――――――――

Then Izar announced that they must go and see the jail. Rigel assumed that he had just wanted to try the slide, which was an absolute terror, a transparent tube dropping out of the bottom of the city and swooping down around the supporting mountain in heart-stopping vertiginosity until it at last deposited its passengers on a narrow platform halfway to the marshes below. On one side rose a sheer cliff, the first ten meters or so as smooth as glass. On the other was nothing—no wall, no railing, only loose air.

"Doggy!" Izar headed for the edge.

His bodyguard whipped him back and pinned him against the rock face. "You can see perfectly well from here."

"I want to know what's underneath!" His ears drooped.

"You stay there and I'll tell you." Rigel had no abnormal fear of heights, but there *was* a gusty wind blowing. He took two careful steps to the edge and looked down. He went, he saw, he returned smartly. "About four hundred meters of nothing and then a scree slope."

"What's a meter? What's a scree slope?"

"Two hundred times my height, then. And scree is jagged gravel. If you fell over there, you'd probably die when you hit it, and you would certainly die rolling the rest of the way down on that stuff."

"That's why they call it 'the escape' then," Izar said gloomily.

The platform itself seemed pointless. At the far end it became a flight of stairs enclosed in a transparent tube that angled slowly upward until it disappeared around a rib of rock.

"Do we have to climb all the way back up?" Rigel demanded
in disgust.

"Some of it. We're out of range for my ring to work. There's
supposed to be a door . . ."

They found the door, solid and forbidding, set in the rock.
Izar used an anklet amulet to open it, though he had trouble
doing so. The door's hinges uttered a loud, cliché groan, and
then it creaked open to reveal a dark interior with a musty,
sour smell.

"Are you really allowed in here?" Rigel asked suspiciously.

"You have to see this," Izar said, slickly evading the question. "This is 'portant!" One of the jewels in his left ear began
to emit a powerful beam of yellow light.

He led the way into the mountain, Rigel following directly
behind him. After a few steps the passage turned at a right
angle and continued parallel to the rock face. Water ran silently along a shallow gutter at the base of the right-hand wall,
soon disappearing down a drain hole, which apparently passed
under the floor, for water emerged on the left and followed an
identical gutter on that side. Then stream and trough changed
back again to the right. After passing three or four such
switches, the Izar-Rigel expedition heard a trickling noise
somewhere up ahead, and soon came to a wide rectangular
hole in the floor, extending almost the full width of the passage. The water vanished for good into the opening, splashing
down on something far below. Beyond the opening lay a massive slab, sized to fill it exactly.

"Schmoor!" Izar said in horror. "This is one of the Dark Cells! No one could levitate a block like that once it's in place! Not even Mom!"

"I expect that that's the idea."

Imp and guard hit the floor simultaneously, and leaned over the edge, scanning the pit with Izar's light. The cavern was about four meters deep, tapering up to the exit, but even at the bottom it was so narrow that Rigel wouldn't be able to stretch out full length, and he was shorter than male elves were. The tiny waterfall drained away through a hole in the floor, but not before soaking every inch of the miserable cell.

"Let's see if I understand this, great and noble Izar. A star-born who commits a serious crime cannot be sentenced to death, because then the judge would die, and the executioner too, unless he was a mudling, in which case whoever owned him and ordered him to do it would. So the prisoner is sentenced to a long term of imprisonment instead . . . How long?"

"Two thousand years."

"Two thousand years in a pit. Water sprays over him all the time. Air? I suppose air circulates through the notches in the cover, and that hole in the floor serves as a toilet." Rigel shivered. "He faces two thousand years alone in this stone tomb, with the hatch closed. He cannot stretch out. He has air and water, and I expect his food is dropped to him in small chunks through the air hole, so that he must grovel for it in the dark like a beast. I assume that the jailers who bring the food are forbidden to speak to him?"

"And they're blind, so they don't use lights," Izar said glumly.

"Shine your light over that way. Yes, in the corner. That sphere?" It looked like a cannonball. "Could a starborn levitate it?"

"What's it made of?" the occult expert inquired cautiously.

"Stone, I think."

"A red or a Naos might."

But who would manage to confine a starborn with that much power? "So when the prisoner has had enough, he can roll that ball over to the drain. And once it has fallen in, there's no way to get it back up, and of course it fits snugly. So in a day or so the cell fills up with water. The prisoner drowns, but that's suicide and not the judge's fault."

Imp and halfling wriggled back from the pit and stood up. Izar's light was just bright enough to reveal the corridor stretching out before them, with dozens of other pits and lids waiting for inmates.

"Let's get outta here!" the boy said squeakily.

"Good idea!" Rigel set off toward the distant gleam of daylight from the entrance. "How many convicts prefer to jump off the platform outside on their way here?"

"Baham says that almost all of them do. *Schmoor!*" Apparently this place exceeded even Izar's taste for the gruesome.

"Who's Baham?"

"My old bodyguard. I *hate* him."

"Does he beat you?"

"The last time he tried, I set his fur on fire."

Rigel turned the corner and blinked at the welcome sight of the empty sky. "So this is where they put unsponsored halflings?"

"Maybe," Izar said, never willing to admit to ignorance. "But Mom will get you status, won't she, Rigel? Won't she? They won't put you in a Dark Cell, will they?"

"I doubt it very much," Rigel said with much more confidence than he felt. "I am the Saiph-bearer. I carry the king of swords. Nobody is going to mess with me." Besides, he had another card to play. It might be an ace, but he wouldn't play it until he knew more about the rules of the game. He didn't know yet whether aces were counted as high cards or low ones.

Chapter 16

The Gazebo had obviously been inspired by the Parthenon in Athens or some other ancient Greek temple, but whichever olden-time lord of Dziban had imagined it had dispensed with the intricacies of internal structure, creating instead a soap bubble miracle that would drive an earthling engineer into therapy. The exterior walls were rows of huge pillars of crystal, supporting an architrave beam on which rested a gable roof of stained glass, spanning at least fifty meters without even rafters to hold it together. Impossible or not, this glass big top was a fine place to hold a party, and that was what Regent-heir Kornephoros was doing that evening. The moonlight reception in honor of some minor relative's coming of age had been going on for hours and had barely gotten started.

Just under the impossible roof, along the inside of the architrave, ran a line of spacious theater boxes for spectators. Rigel Halfling, Talitha Starborn, Izar Imp, and Mira Silvas sat in one of them, a lounge that would have comfortably held twenty people. They were waiting for an audience with the regent-heir and might be kept waiting for a lot longer yet. Rigel had no complaints so far. The chairs and couches were comfortable, although higher than terrestrial furniture, and the tables were laden with exquisite food and wine, served on request by two pages dressed in classical Greek costume, muslin draperies that were nearly as revealing as their normal wraps. They looked little older than Izar and were the first starfolk whom Rigel had seen doing anything resembling work, but royal service probably counted as an honor. No matter. They had just provided Rigel with an excellent breakfast, three-course lunch, and four-course dinner. He felt almost caught up.

On the floor far below them the elite of the realm glittered and shone. A full orchestra played music that made his feet tap and his heart ache to join in, while overhead the pages' female counterparts were performing a stunning aerial ballet, trailing colored fire.

It seemed that starfolk didn't dress up for formal dances, they just wore their normal wraps—*Senior Prom, Annual Swimsuit Edition.* Indeed, most of the guests seemed to have dressed *down* rather than up, dispensing with most of their usual jewelry and trinkets, which was probably the magical equivalent of leaving their weapons at home. A few of the participants flaunted jeweled collars, wide disks of beads with a central hole to encircle their slender elfin necks. The collars extended out to their wearers' shoulders and hung down in front and back like bibs. He had seen some of these earlier, during his tour of the city, and Izar had told him that they were badges of office.

This was still only the earthling hobo's second day in the realm and he was about to meet the head of state. Now *that* was social climbing on steroids! So why had Saiph suddenly begun to tingle? It was only a faint shiver, but it must be a warning of something brewing. Saiph hadn't let him down yet.

Mira was wide-eyed. Relieved of her Alrisha servant duties, she had been issued a change of clothing, a Mother Hubbard–like brown tent and a poke bonnet so absurd that Rigel had to exercise all his strength of will not to smirk when he first saw it. Junoesque by human standards, she looked squat and beefy in elfin company. Whatever she had been doing since arriving in Dziban, she was now enjoying her visit to the surreal realm, even dropping hints that she would enjoy a longer vacation in the Starlands. He didn't know why she had been included tonight; if it was because she'd witnessed the Nanaimo massacre, his fate might be decided right here and now. The court appearance might be a mere formality.

Talitha seemed tense, but perhaps she was mad because her father was keeping her waiting, or because she hadn't been invited to join the party, or because she hadn't yet had a chance to explain to her son's new bodyguard exactly what he was supposed to be guarding against. Izar was always right there, big ears akimbo.

The imp had spent the second hour there trying to teach his bodyguard to perform magic, but Rigel had proved unable to levitate even a feather above the palm of his hand.

"Three-year-olds can do that!" Izar yelled when he ran out of patience. "*Babies* can do it!"

"Not this baby. How much can you lift?"

Izar looked askance to see if his mother was listening, which she was. He muttered, "Lots. But even halflings can reach blue! Can't they, Mom?"

"Some can, if they have been taught, dear."

"If magic develops late," Rigel said, "then perhaps I'm not old enough yet. I'm only a year or so older than you are, you know."

Izar refused to believe that, and had to be told how earth-lings aged faster than starborn. He found it even funnier that Rigel didn't know his own birthday, but it was clear that he was rapidly becoming bored to insanity, levitating cushions and people's drinks, rolling balls of cold fire across the floor.

"Why did Grandsire tell us to wait here?"

"I told you," Talitha said patiently. "He was busy earlier. It is good of him to take the time to see us at all tonight."

"Can't I go to sleep now? Just for a little while?" Sleep was his escape from the unwelcome.

"No," his mother said for the third time. "It would be disre-spectful to your grandfather. He will see us as soon as he can, but he must attend to his guests first. He has told you often enough that royalty has an obligation to set an example of good manners."

"Tell me, Oh exalted starling," Rigel said. "How is sponsor-ing arranged? What will happen at my hearing?"

"Dunno," Izar said grumpily. He knew that Rigel was try-ing to distract him and wasn't about to cooperate.

Talitha said, "After the court determines that you are a half-ling, not an earthling or a starborn deformed by a curse, Fom-alhaut will be asked if he's willing to sponsor you. If he refuses, you'll have seven days to find a sponsor. During that time, you will be housed in a reasonably comfortable jail."

How was he supposed to find a sponsor if he was locked up? "And after the seven days? Unsponsored halflings go to the Dark Cells?"

"Sometimes, but usually they're just humanely put down—you're not protected by the guilt curse." Talitha smiled. "But that won't happen to you, because I shall be there."

"And if Fomalhaut says yes?"

Her smile inverted into a frown. "Normally you would agree and that would be that. But Vildiar is his overlord, and he'll want to get his claws on Saiph. He will pressure Fomalhaut to transfer the bond to him. Again, your consent is required, but if you don't give it, you won't have a sponsor."

"Meaning I'll be between the devil and the deep blue sea? An earthling expression," he explained in response to her furrowed brow. "Between a rock and a hard place?"

"You will be between a slow death and a quick one. *That* is why we have to talk to the regent-heir. He is everybody's overlord. He must take your bond and then transfer it to me. If that is agreeable to you?"

"You mean I'd have to put up with Izar all the time?"

Izar punched him in the arm.

"If that's the hardest you can hit," Rigel said, "I'll have to give you lessons."

Izar growled, bounced up and down on the couch a few times, and then shouted, "Jabbah! Bring me a chocolate mouse."

"Wait!" Talitha said as the page moved to obey. "Izar, that was not good manners. You do not give orders to people older than yourself. And you are never to give orders to servants; you must always ask them. And Jabbah is not a servant anyway. He is an officer of the castle. So now you must apologize to him."

A black silence descended.

Rigel rose, went over to the serving table, and politely asked Jabbah Starling if he might have a chocolate mouse—they were mouse-*shaped* chocolates filled with cream rather than rodents—and returned to the couch he was sharing with Izar. Then he ate the sickly thing himself, risking instant diabetes and chronic heart disease. Jabbah came over to remove his plate and offer a refill, which Rigel declined.

Izar said nothing, but looked ready to levitate his bodyguard over the balustrade and let go.

"Why," Rigel asked, looking around the great hall, "is this the only box that is occupied?"

In her cautious, Izar-is-listening voice, Talitha said, "In Electra's time they were usually full of the guests' unofficial relatives. Known but not recognized, if you follow me."

"She means bastards, gigolos, and concubines," Izar explained.

His mother pretended not to hear. "Regent-heir Kornephoros does not approve of relationships outside of formal pairings. If he ever wore lace he would keep it very straight."

"Grandsire wears *lace?*"

"No he doesn't, Big Ears."

"Formal pairings?" Rigel murmured. Izar had a father, still unnamed. Did Talitha have a husband? "There are also informal pairings?"

"Dozens," Izar said. "Two a night."

"Watch your mouth, imp!" his mother said menacingly.

"Where I come from, formal pairings involve oaths of lifelong fidelity. You can't have those, surely?"

Talitha said, "Hardly! A formal pairing is a contract to produce and rear a child. Traditionally it is for thirteen years, but it can be renewed as often as the parties wish."

"She's free," Izar said helpfully. "But she can't pair with a halfling, so don't get your hopes up . . . or anything else up for that matter."

"*Izar!*"

"I am quite certain your mother will never pair with anyone again," Rigel said. "After what happened the first time." He caught Izar's fist before it connected. "The next time you try to punch me, imp, I will punch you instead."

"You insulted me!"

"You insulted your mother. That deserves several punches."

Izar put on his hard-done-by expression. "Sorry, Mom. I shouldn't have said that. It was a vulgar remark. It's just that I am 'stremely bored! Why can't I go to sleep? I'll tell my self to wake me quick when Grandsire comes."

Talitha sighed to admit defeat. "A light doze, though. Just enough to stop your whining."

Izar promptly swung his feet onto the arm of the couch, rested his head on Rigel's lap, and melted like hot butter. His ears went as limp as wet tissues.

"Little devil!" his mother said. "He's put himself out cold. You'd better waken him. Father will . . . Father has rigid views on manners."

Any thousand-year-old regent-heir could be expected to have an old-fashioned outlook. "Izar! *Izar!* Wake up!" Rigel shook him, shook him harder, then appealed for instructions. "Do I slap him, tickle him, or send for a doctor?"

"Starling Jabbah, please bring Rigel Halfling a glass of ice water."

But at that moment the door opened and three mile-high boys walked in. No, not boys; perennially juvenile starfolk lords—Mekbuda, Kornephoros, and Rasalhague. All three wore disk collars as well as the usual collection of amulets, and the one in the center had opalescent hair. Rigel hastily extricated himself from the pliable Izar and knelt before the regent-heir, as his companions were already doing. Saiph was tingling more strongly.

"Up, Daughter." Kornephoros scanned the company with distaste and gestured for the pages to leave. He did not look like a man who'd been born back in the Middle Ages. He looked like a high school basketball player with an attitude problem. His collar was a golden disk of glittering chain mail that had to weigh a tonne. "Why is this creature not wearing a hat?"

"He has not yet had his status confirmed, Father. No restrictions have been placed on him."

"That is no reason to let him run loose displaying those obscenely deformed ears. And what exactly was he doing with my grandson?"

"Being a pillow. The boy was tired and I allowed him to go to sleep."

"Did you choose his bedding?"

"No, Father. He did."

"Indeed? How well do you know this unsponsored half-breed?"

Izar chose that moment to yawn and stretch. "What'ch you doing down there?" he asked sleepily, when he noticed that Rigel was on his knees. "*Schmoor*! Grandsire!" In a whirl of stringy limbs he flopped off the couch and into a kneeling position.

"You may rise, starling," said the basketball player. "Daughter, my lords, pray be seated. Earthling, you may stand. Now I want to hear the whole story."

Rigel, the only one left kneeling, had no need of Saiph to warn him of danger now. He was certain that Prince Kornephoros had already heard the whole story, or a version of it—in all likelihood, it had not been a version that was very kind to him.

"Your Highness—"

"Silence. I shall hear it from my grandson. Come here, Izar, and tell me about that tweenling and how you met him." The regent sat down and made Izar stand in front of him with his back to the onlookers.

Talitha protested, "Father, Izar is only a—"

A royal glare stopped her.

Izar was beaming. "He wears *Saiph*, Grandsire, the sword that killed Rukbat and King Denebola! He killed a great big bear that attacked him! See the pink lines on his tummy? He doesn't have any magic, but he's ever so strong. He fought the Minotaur at Alrisha . . ."

The more the imp enthused about his new hero, the more the regent frowned and the lower Rigel's heart sank. The orchestra below happened to be winding up a fast and loud fandango. The two peaked together—the orchestra thundering out chords and Izar yelling over it as he described Rigel riding on the swan's neck and fighting off dragonflies.

Both fell silent at the same moment. The downstairs audience managed a lukewarm patter of applause. The upstairs audience did not.

"I see," Kornephoros said drily. "You had an exciting time. You may sit down. No, not near the halfling. Here, by me." He turned his prismatic eyes on Talitha. "Were you not aware that Fomalhaut had put the hybrid in the custody of Starborn Muphrid?"

She nodded. "I was there."

"Then why did you help him escape? Have you no idea of the seriousness of the laws you were breaking? What is he to you that you would take such a risk for him?" He kept his voice low, which made his anger seem all the more menacing. Somewhere inside that virile stripling hid a desiccated husk of a thousand winters. He might not look his incredible age, but his authority sparked like a thunderstorm.

"Father, may we discuss this in private?"

"You are ashamed of your behavior? Or are you merely worried that you will incriminate yourself?"

The hard floor was making Rigel's knees ache. Mira was shooting him warning glances, which were useless without an instruction manual explaining what they meant. Izar had suddenly realized that all was not well. Talitha was pale, but she answered her father calmly, as if she had faced such rage before.

"Neither. The halfling was nothing to me, Father. Not then. What he is now, I shall explain in a minute. I was rescuing his amulet, not him. Fomalhaut is a Vildiar underling, as you know, and Vildiar has been assembling a personal army of thugs and assassins for years. I can tell you where he gets them too. Hadar Halfling and Tarf—"

"Stop! You will not insult a prince of the realm by repeating such baseless gossip and scandal."

"It is not baseless. Oh, Father, even I can remember when we had thirty Naos princes and princesses in the Starlands. Now we are down to three. Poor Aldhibah lost his head while hunting, apparently decapitated by a gazelle armed with a sharp ax. Dear Acubens drowned in her own bathtub although she was an excellent swimmer. Alshat bled to death while picking roses, and Vildiar actually boasted to me—"

"Stop changing the subject. We are discussing your illegal actions at Alrisha today."

Rigel was suddenly aware that he might have bitten off considerably more than he could chew. Twenty-seven Naos murdered? Was that what she was implying?

Talitha clenched her fists in frustration. "My actions were perfectly legal. As a Naos princess, I certainly outrank Fomalhaut. It was always my intention to deliver the halfling to Canopus for a hearing, but I was not certain that Fomalhaut would do the same. I would not, and will not, let Vildiar get his hands on Saiph! However honorable the present wearer of that amulet may be, he is certainly mortal and can be sacrificed on the blood-washed altar of the prince's ambition."

Kornephoros sneered. "How would anyone go about stealing Saiph?"

"Easily, if you don't care about the death toll. By sending a regiment of archers against it. Odds can become impossible even for Saiph. Vildiar's death squad is armed with amulets too. Saiph may be the greatest, but there's one known as Sulaphat that's rated almost as high. Its previous wearer was cut to pieces by persons unknown about five years ago, and Sulaphat mysteriously turned up adorning the disgustingly hairy wrist of Prince Vildiar's senior assassin, Halfling Hadar. The amulet—"

"This is wicked slander."

"Father, Father!" she shouted. "Do you think I don't know him? You forced me into a pairing with that turd and insisted that I endure every horrible minute of it. I know Vildiar a great deal better than you do. But let us talk about my complaint, the attempt on my life and the life of my son today. I was the only one of Muphrid Starborn's guests traveling by swan, and those dragonflies were specifically imagined to blind it and make us crash."

Her father was unimpressed. "What I heard was that the dragonflies were released while your swan was on the beach, with the express purpose of keeping you from abducting the unsponsored halfling. That you took off anyway was reckless to the point of attempted suicide. The person who imperiled your son's life was you. And for what purpose? We need to know how well you know this halfling. I hear that you took him to your room."

Talitha sprang to her feet. "Now you have spies following me around?"

"I do not, no, but you were observed fondling the half-breed."

"I never did! You accuse me of badmouthing Vildiar, and then you spread such filthy lies about your own daughter?" Her face was flaming.

Her father smirked. "You told me a few minutes ago that you had an interest in him."

"Izar has taken a liking to him. He impressed both of us as honorable and certainly courageous. He saved our lives today. I have appointed him as my son's bodyguard, and I will personally sponsor him."

"A woman? A *princess* sponsoring a male halfling? Can you imagine the gossip, Daughter? Whose body will he be guarding, they will ask."

So now Rigel knew what was alarming his amulet. Talitha's plan had collapsed.

She stamped a foot in frustration. "Father, you disgrace yourself by even thinking such thoughts, let alone vomiting them out in public. You assigned me Albireo Halfling's bond without a thought."

"Albireo," the regent-heir said icily, "had been a trusted retainer for a hundred years. This cub is fresh out of the jungle. If you do not enjoy scandal, you should not provoke it with scandalous behavior." He turned his frown on Rigel. "You are a stranger here. Do you know the punishment for tweenlings who desecrate starborn women?"

Saiph was throbbing so violently now that Rigel suspected he would find bruises on his wrist. "No, Your Highness, but if your courts are fair I have nothing to fear. My intentions and actions toward your noble daughter and grandson were, and always will be, completely honorable." *Your grandson, anyway. Your daughter's virtue is still negotiable.*

Talitha tried again. "Father, the problem is not Rigel Halfling, it is the amulet Saiph. That is a royal amulet, and you must not let it fall into the hands of Prince Vildiar! I beg you to sponsor the halfling so that the amulet remains under royal control. I believe he would make an excellent bodyguard for Izar, but that decision can wait. The important thing is to determine who controls that amulet!"

Now the truth was out. *It's not me you love, it's my bracelet.*

Kornephoros ignored her. "Who was your father?"

The change of subject threw Rigel off balance. "I have no idea, my lord. I should much like to meet him, so I could teach him some family values."

"By which you mean seducing women and abducting young boys?"

"I mean loving one's children, Your Highness." It was a good retort, but it was also stupid backtalk to a ruler.

Kornephoros frowned, slit-eyed. "I think we can identify him and bring him to justice." He turned to one of his attendants. "Recorder Mekbuda, what did you discover about the recent history of the amulet Saiph?"

Mekbuda's disk collar was almost as large as the regent's, but made of rubies and emeralds. "I summoned your curator, Highness. The last Saiph-bearer he knew of was Wazor Starborn, who volunteered to destroy a dragon that was ravaging the northern range of the Thuban Mountains some two hundred years ago. Queen Electra assigned him Saiph to aid him in his quest. Wazor slew the dragon but died of burns. We can assume that the amulet was returned to the royal treasury at Canopus, but that must be verified by consulting the records there." He beamed proudly, as if he had just won a Nobel Prize for research.

The regent nodded sagaciously. "We shall do so when we take the prisoner to Canopus for his hearing. His father probably stole it. The charge sheet is filling up against that unknown starborn. Clearly he committed an act of criminal miscegenation. And he either stole a reversion staff or performed an illegal act of red-grade magic, because he hid the mule on Earth, which is another serious . . ." The regent turned to look back at Rigel. "You do realize that you are a mule, don't you? Halflings are invariably infertile, which makes them attractive to starborn women of low moral character."

Rigel had never thought of that possibility. *Mule?* So he was truly nothing: not a man, not an elf, and not even a fully functioning male. It might never matter, since Kornephoros obviously planned to send him to the Dark Cells or hand him over to Vildiar, but it still hurt, and the nasty old man had told him out of spite.

Talitha said, "Come, Izar. We must leave. Your grandfather is drunk."

"Far from it," Kornephoros said. "I am seeing more clearly now than I have in years. Your shameful behavior has opened my eyes at last. So now, Companion Rasalhague, you may open the door."

Baby-faced Starborn Rasalhague's collar was made of silver and pearls; he looked sweet in it.

Like so many doors in Dziban, the door at the back of the balcony didn't lead to anything at all, just the exterior of the building. In this case, opening it was a signal. A blast of cold air swirled in, followed by four men floating up from below: two starborn in the lead, and two halflings in attendance. One of the elves was golden-haired Fomalhaut, who had rescued Rigel and Mira in the Walmart in Nanaimo. The second bore the opalescent mark of Naos and the name of Vildiar. The balcony was filling up.

Izar screamed in terror, hurtled across the room, and threw himself into Rigel's arms. *"Don't let him take me!"*

Shocked, Rigel hugged him tightly and glanced around the faces while he assessed this new disaster. Talitha looked sick, her father outraged, and Prince Vildiar contemptuously amused. Legally, no one else mattered.

But in practice the two halfling retainers might matter very much if the tone of the meeting deteriorated any further. They were dressed, obscenely, in the black uniforms of Nazi storm troopers—jackboots and riding britches, belted tunics with red swastika armbands, and high-peaked military caps. Their names were Hadar and Mintaka.

Hadar, whom Talitha had described as the leader of Vildiar's assassins and wearer of the amulet Sulaphat, was too beefy for an elf and too tall for a human—he had to weigh a hundred and fifty kilos. His ears were wings, big even by elfin standards, their edges studded with jewels, but his jowly cheeks bore a heavy beard shadow that no starborn would ever display. His uniform was slathered with medals, insignia, and miscellaneous gold braid. He was the leading suspect in today's attempted murder.

Unlike the swarthy Hadar, Mintaka had fair coloring and blue eyes. He was as slender as an elf, but small-eared and short even by human standards. Mutt and Jeff. Hired killers, both.

Meanwhile Rigel was clasping a hysterical child. One glance at Talitha confirmed that he had just met the enemy. *This* was why her child needed a bodyguard.

"Izar!" he said. "That is no way to behave. You remember when I was crawling along the swan's neck and the dragonflies were attacking me? Well? Do you?"

Mumble: "Yes."

"When you told your grandfather about it, you said I wasn't scared at all, but you were wrong, Izar. I was, terribly, horribly scared." He waited for a moment, but everyone else was waiting too. "But I did what I had to do. And that's what being brave means. It means doing what's right even when you're frightened, and you don't want to do it. Do you understand what I'm saying?"

Sniff. "Mm."

"Now what should you have done when Prince Vildiar came into the room? Even if you were scared, what would a brave boy have done?"

Silence. The imp was as jumpy as a cricket in a blender.

"You should have greeted him politely, to show everyone how well your mother has taught you. Shouldn't you have, Izar?"

A chin nodded against his shoulder.

"Then do it now. I'll come with you." At least he'd be able to get off his knees. He rose, keeping hold of Izar's hand, and led him over to Vildiar, who was frowning at this unexpected partnership. The prince was bizarrely tall, even for a starborn—close to two and a half meters, Rigel guessed—and absurdly slender, as if he had been stretched like hot taffy. His hair and eyes shone in rainbow brilliance, emphasizing the fish-belly pallor of his skin. He was the least human of the starfolk Rigel had met so far, and yet there was something oddly familiar about his scowling, emaciated face.

Izar released Rigel's hand so that he could spread his arms for a starfolk bow. In a small and shaky voice he whispered, "May the stars shine on you forever, noble Father." But when he straightened up, he kept his eyes lowered.

"And may *our* progeny outnumber the stars, Imp Izar," Vildiar retorted. That was not the correct formula. His two henchmen chuckled at their lord's wit, but nobody else did.

Rigel gave Izar a gentle push. "Why don't you go and stand out of the way beside your mother?"

Izar ran.

Rigel bowed to the prince and strolled back to where he had started. He didn't kneel again. Saiph had almost stopped quivering—now *that* was interesting! He glanced at the regent-heir and decided that the Ancient One had caught every speck of that little dustup. Even a narrow-minded, prehistoric bluestocking like him had to wonder why a boy would be so terrified of his father.

"Prince," Kornephoros said, "we must return to our guests. Outline briefly the petition you presented to me earlier."

Vildiar made a half bow to him, but his words were aimed at Talitha. "I informed Your Highness of your daughter's whorish behavior at Alrisha. I requested that she be forced to surrender the unsponsored halfling she abducted so that he could be dealt with as the law requires. I also stressed to Your Highness the poor moral environment that she is providing for my son, and the reckless disregard for his safety she displayed during her flight from Alrisha."

Talitha looked ready to fry him the way she had fried the dragonflies. "Perhaps you suggested that Izar would be happier at Phegda, where he could play with all of his brothers and sisters?"

The implications of that speech hit Rigel like a falling piano. Talitha was implying that Vildiar was *breeding* his team of halfling assassins. And why not? Starfolk had all the time in the world and the prince undoubtedly owned large herds of human livestock he could choose from. Mintaka and Hadar were physically dissimilar, but they could be just half brothers. It was obvious by now that halflings displayed their mixed heritage in many different ways. The problem with hired guns was that they could always choose to point their weapons in the wrong direction, whereas even illegitimate and sterile sons would probably feel some family loyalty. What Vildiar was doing was undoubtedly illegal, but the prince was probably immune to prosecution as long as he kept on the regent's good side, where he obviously was at the moment.

Suddenly the rest of the orchestra came crashing down too. How could Rigel have missed it? *The regent does whatever the prince tells him!* Obviously, if Vildiar had pruned the Naos royalty from thirty down to three, the regent-heir must know that he was the storm troopers' most probable next victim. For Kornephoros to refuse Vildiar anything now would be tantamount to suicide; the boys would come calling immediately. Vildiar wanted Saiph for his death squad and the regent-heir would see that he got it. If he was willing to sacrifice his daughter's reputation and his grandson's happiness, he certainly wouldn't hesitate to throw an unknown halfling under the bus.

Izar screamed, "No! No! Don't send me back to Phegda!" and tried to climb into his mother's lap. He was much too large to be held like that.

"Izar," Rigel said. "Would it help if I came to Phegda with you?"

He felt Saiph practically spin around his wrist, but a dumb amulet might not understand that sometimes it was better to *pull* than to *push*. Besides, it was well worth the risk to watch how everyone reacted—Vildiar and his SS brutes' smirks turned to frowns as they tried to puzzle out what the halfling was up to, Talitha looked completely baffled, Izar's face was bright with relief and gratitude, and an unmistakable flush of anger rose on ancient Kornephoros's boyish face.

"Are you giving me orders, halfling, or just instructing me in how to rule?"

"I humbly beg Your Highness's pardon. I was distracted by the boy's distress."

Kornephoros growled, but Rigel's ploy had made sending Izar to Phegda a much harder option for him: His grandson wanted a bodyguard when sent to visit his dad? And if Rigel did not turn up in court, then Talitha's claims would be proven correct. That might not help the late Rigel Halfling, but it would expose Kornephoros as Vildiar's lackey. Did the man have any pride left at all?

"Fomalhaut Starborn?"

The mage stepped forward. "Highness?" Was that a hint of a smile playing on his thin lips?

"If I return your prisoner to you, can you hold him?"

"That is largely up to him, I posit, my lord, because, while I have means of controlling most fugitives, I would be loath to wield them against an amulet as ancestral as Saiph, but if the halfling comprehends now that, while he is powerful, he is by no means invincible and submission to properly appointed proceedings remains his best, and indeed his only, chance for a comfortable future life, whereas resistance or flight will inevitably bring him afoul of the state and have serious, conceivably fatal, consequences, then no untoward or regrettable events should occur."

After working his way through the word forest, Rigel decided that it required a response from him. "I do understand those things, my lord. My intention was never to avoid the hearing and Her Highness never suggested that possibility to me. I gladly give you my parole, for whatever a halfling's solemn word may be worth to you—on the understanding, of course, that your lordship will see me safely delivered to the court."

The storm troopers snarled, and Vildiar said, "Watch your tongue, mongrel."

The regent rose as if his time had run out. "Halfling, we return you to the custody of Fomalhaut Starborn, an old and trusted friend and one of the most potent mages in the realm. He will accompany you and the earthling woman to Canopus tomorrow." But he still had not solved the custody problem, and he chose to procrastinate. "Fomalhaut, why don't you take the imp also and bring him to the barge in the morning? We can discuss this over breakfast."

Rigel offered a hand and Izar rushed to him, still teary, but happy again. Rigel glanced to Talitha, who nodded. He raised an eyebrow to Vildiar and suddenly remembered where he'd seen that face before. It could have been the model for all those arrogant, scowling giant stone heads on Easter Island. Instead of staring eternally out to sea, though, this one was looking down at Rigel with the dispassionate, calculating look of a homeowner inspecting mouse droppings while planning what to do about the mouse.

Chapter 17

Before dawn, Rigel went for a swim.

After the meeting in the Gazebo, Fomalhaut had escorted his prisoners through a portal to a guesthouse in the Dziban domain, a "modest" twelve-or-so-room cottage on the edge of a lake with a beech forest behind it. This morning an invigorating rime of frost silvered the grass, luminous fish swam in the dark waters, and great sandstone boulders cried out to be dived off of. The previous evening Rigel had swum all the way across the lake, but this morning he stayed close to shore in case he was summoned.

Mira emerged from the house, took one breath of fresh morning air, and immediately vanished back inside. Then Izar came streaking across the shingle and plunged into the water like an otter. He wanted to see Rigel do "the most difficult, scariest" dive he could. Rigel told him he would need a diving board for that and disappeared underwater. About two minutes later, he grabbed the imp's feet from below and pulled him under in mid-scream.

After that anything went.

Fomalhaut was a problem. The regent-heir trusted and praised him, but he was a Vildiar underling and had almost certainly engineered the massacre in Nanaimo. He was normally long-winded, sometimes curt to the point of rudeness, always arrogant, and could well be Rigel's unscrupulous father.

Suddenly, the starborn himself appeared, and came to stand by the edge of the lake, watching his guests frolic as the sun rose over the forest, backlighting his hair in gold and his ears in pink.

Rigel said, "Race you there!" and let Izar win.

Gasping for breath, the imp made the correct bow and greeting to his host. Rigel waded out behind him and contented himself with a deep human bow, which seemed more reasonable for a nonperson, and provoked no snarl of correction.

Fomalhaut looked down at Izar. "Show me how strong you are now."

The boy frowned. "My noble mother has warned me not to—"

"Your grandsire said I was trustworthy. I am asking for your own good."

"Yes, my lord." Izar screwed up his face in concentration. A pebble rose from the beach and floated in midair. A second joined it. A third, much larger, rose a few centimeters and then all three fell back with a clatter.

"Very impressive! You are well into the blue, very close to green."

Izar flushed bright red with delight.

"Do you have a dog?"

"No, my lord." Izar shot a worried glance in Rigel's direction and mumbled, "Well, just a small one. He does tricks."

"Then I shall give you one now. He's no play dog, though; he's a guardian who will perform only one trick. He will defend you the way that Saiph defends Halfling Rigel. He will respond instantly if you are attacked, although he differs from a sword amulet in that he cannot be made to attack anyone. Also, you will need to use power to put him away again. Can you put an orange in a bottle?"

"Oh, yes, my lord! A small orange."

"Then you should be strong enough to control . . . um, this one . . . or maybe even this . . ." Fomalhaut began pulling rings off his thumb, which held six or seven. He replaced all but the last one. "This is made from human bone, by the way, and you must never take it off, Starling Izar, or your dog could escape your control the next time you call him. Which finger will it go on?"

With his eyes shining almost as bright as his mother's, Izar offered his left pinkie. The simple white circlet closed around it as snugly as it had on Fomalhaut's thumb.

"His name," Fomalhaut said, "is Turais, but you must not speak that word until I tell you to. Like I said, Turais will never attack unless you're attacked, at which time he will appear automatically, but he will appear when you pronounce his name, and will threaten anyone who seems to be bothering you. I warn you not to expect a lapdog, because the sight of Turais can scare yesterday's breakfast out of the toughest thug.

"The cogitation required to put Turais away is very similar to what's needed to impel an orange into a bottle. You can tell him 'Go home!' or 'Heel!' or anything you like, but what matters is that the power of your will compels him back into the ring, so if you are ready, we can introduce the two of you now. Halfling, you stand over there—no, farther back. We don't want the guardian to sense your amulet."

Rigel hesitated, then obeyed. If a "great" mage were up to no good, there was not much a guitarist with a sword could do about it.

"If you find yourself in trouble, I will help you, Izar," Fomalhaut said. "But if you can't control him, you will have to be satisfied with a much smaller dog. Now say his name, point at me with the ring finger, and he will appear to warn me off."

Izar took a deep breath, extended his left hand, and said, *"Turais!"*

If the thing that materialized beside him was a dog, that was mainly because he was the wrong shape to be a lion. His shaggy coat was the color of frost on winter trees, his eyes glowed gold flame, and he could undoubtedly snack on timber wolves. Without moving from his place at Izar's side, he bared teeth the size of chisels at the mage and growled in a rock-grinding rumble that Rigel could feel through the soles of his feet.

Fomalhaut retreated a few feet and the noise stopped. The mage took a step forward and it resumed, even louder. Turais edged forward. Again the mage retreated and peace was restored.

"You see? You may pat him."

Beaming, Izar rubbed the beast's shaggy ears. Barely even raising his head, Turais projected a black tongue the size of a shoe and spread slobber all over the imp's face. Izar squealed with delight and wiped it off with his arm.

But then Turais noticed Rigel and raised a ruff like a hayfield. He growled again and bared his great fangs in Rigel's direction.

"Put Turais away, imp!" Fomalhaut shouted. "He has sensed Saiph."

"Heel, Turais!" Izar frowned and showed his teeth as he concentrated. *"Heel, I say!"*

Drooling, Turais slunk around him and began to stalk Rigel, who now had to decide just how far to trust the mage. Saiph made the decision for him, flashing into view as a long, narrow rapier.

"Put him *away,* imp! He will try to take the halfling's arm off, and then Saiph will kill him."

Izar's face twisted in agony. "Turais, go home!"

The giant dog continued its deadly advance, gathering itself to spring.

"Last chance, Izar!"

"Turais, heel!" Izar screamed. The monster became transparent, flickered in and out a few times, and then vanished for good. Izar burst into tears.

Fomalhaut stepped over and clapped him on the shoulder. "Well done! Very well done! You were well up in green there, mage."

The imp choked, coughed, and said, *"I was?"*

"Easily. Not being his overlord, I would have needed to use red magic to stop Turais and that would have killed him, but from now on you won't have any trouble controlling him as long as you don't treat him as a toy or call him up just to impress your friends."

"No, my lord. I would never! But is he going to attack Rigel every time I call him?"

"Oh! No, I think Turais will remember the lesson you just gave him and will accept the halfling as a friend in the future."

Rigel put his sword away. Given the benefit of the doubt, Fomalhaut had deliberately frightened the boy in order to teach him an important lesson. The alternative was that he enjoyed terrifying imps.

"Oh, and one last thing. If Turais ever kills, you must let him feed before you put him away."

"Feed?" Izar said faintly. Almond eyes stretched wider than papayas.

"Turais is serious magic, imp. He's not a toy." The starborn glanced at the height of the sun above the trees. "Take him over there, well away from the halfling, and let him get to know you. Wrestle with him. He will never hurt his overlord, no matter what you do."

Izar shot off, his feet barely touching the ground. Rigel waited to hear what was about to be revealed for his private benefit. He did not have to wait long.

"Halfling, you are in mortal danger. You are mixed up in matters far beyond your comprehension or control, and have antagonized the two most exalted starborn in the realm. Both Vildiar and Kornephoros want to squash you like a beetle, and one or the other almost certainly will before this day is out. Talitha can no more protect you than Izar could. Historically, mortals who blunder into the affairs of the starborn have very short life spans—a day or two at most. It was my misjudgment to bring you here, and I am willing to make reparation by extroverting you now, while you are still free to go."

"Wearing what I am wearing now, I assume? To Times Square, Trafalgar Square, or Tiananmen Square?"

Amber eyes blazed. "Insolent puppy! I will put you into the menswear department of a large store, after hours, in an English-speaking country, funded with a bag of cut gemstones. You and Saiph can vanish into the teeming anthill of Earth and peace will be restored to the Starlands. The alternative is a very early death. I speak with authority you cannot possibly comprehend."

All his life Rigel Estell had done his best to avoid confrontation. His reaction to attention had always been to disappear into the undergrowth. But now he could not hide and *would* not hide. He offered a small bow. "Yes, I was impertinent and I apologize. Your offer is most generous, but I cannot accept. I have sworn to serve the princess as well as I am able and I must stand by my oath. I do have Saiph."

"Not for long, I think" Fomalhaut sneered. "Your lust for the princess will cost you your life. Believe me, for I have ways of knowing. But if that is your decision, we must dress you for your court appearance, then find the earthling woman and be on our way."

"Starborn," Rigel said, "may I ask you a question?"

The mage's amber eyes blazed like lasers. "No, you may not, Rigel Halfling."

Court dress for an unsponsored halfling comprised a full-length gown and a separate cowl. Fortunately both were cut from moon-cloth, which was cool and almost weightless, but Rigel felt as if he were playing Saint Francis in a Halloween masquerade. He was certain, though, that the holy man wouldn't have approved of the way his flesh glowed through the translucent material.

The mage opened a portal to the harbor basin, and Izar, Rigel, and Mira followed him through it. The dock itself was almost deserted, except for a gang of fishermen unloading a smelly catch. Gienah the swan was scratching herself under one raised wing. On the quay beside her stood Princess Talitha, whose beauty left Rigel breathless and made the giant

bird look positively ugly. She was accompanied by the swanherd Albireo Halfling and a green-haired elf whose name
shortly became apparent as Baham, Izar's previous bodyguard.

Izar's feet began to drag until Fomalhaut put a hand on his
shoulder and urged him forward. Bows and greetings were exchanged while Rigel and Mira waited, ignored, in the background. Izar had said that he "hated" Baham. Allowance for
juvenile exaggeration might translate "hate" into "dislike," but
Rigel was prepared to agree that the former bodyguard did not
impress at first sight. Still, the starborn could not be blamed
for having hair and eyes of a peculiarly bilious shade, and his
fixed sneer owed something to a very short upper lip. Besides,
Talitha must have found some virtue in him or she would not
have entrusted her son to his care.

"Izar," she announced, "Baham and Albireo will take you
home to Spica while Rigel and I attend the court."

Izar clenched his fists and bent his ears to an uncooperative
angle, but Fomalhaut spoke first.

"Last night His Highness instructed me to bring the imp to
the royal barge so that—"

Talitha raised her chin and gave him a megawatt royal glare.
"And this morning he instructed me to send Izar straight
home. Do you question my word, Fomalhaut Starborn?"

Rigel did. Izar had inherited his poetic approach to truth
from his mother. It seemed very unlikely that Regent-heir Kornephoros would have reversed his own orders so drastically
without at least informing Fomalhaut of the change.

Pinned between two royals, the mage chose the safer course
of recognizing a mother's authority over her own child. "Never
for a moment, Your Highness."

"Mom!" Izar squealed. "My warning bracelet just started
itching like crazy, Mom!"

"Yes, darling. Rigel and I will be home by lunchtime, I expect. You go home and have a nice ride on Narwhale. He will be missing you."

Izar looked up at Baham's sneer of welcome and shouted, *"No!* It really is itching, Mom, it's itching like it never has! It's warning me not to go!"

Alas, the shepherd boy must have exceeded his wolf guidelines too often in the past. Talitha very firmly said, "Do as you are told! You go with Baham right now, or no Narwhale for a week."

Fomalhaut drew breath as if to intervene and then released it in silence. Rigel too felt twinges of unease. Granted, the imp was eager to come to the court hearing, but would he lie about a warning bracelet? Izar slouched angrily down the plank to the swan with Albireo and his bodyguard at his heels. Had Baham been informed that he was about to lose his job to Rigel? Would Izar be stupid enough to tell him?

Talitha turned to Fomalhaut. "Starborn, I have a favor to ask."

"Your Highness's lightest whims are inviolable directives to me."

"That's good. I want Halfling Rigel and his amulet to be guardians of my son."

"He would be a good choice."

"Then you will promise to transfer his bond to me right away, as soon as the court grants it to you this morning?"

The mage shook his golden head sadly. "Alas, I have already promised not to sponsor the halfling."

"Promised whom?"

Fomalhaut glanced uncertainly at Rigel and Mira, and then said quietly, "You can guess."

Talitha's eyes flashed polychrome fire. "You are afraid of Prince Vildiar!"

"No, Highness. His Naos magic is far superior to mine, but he will never use his talent against me."

"If you're so sure of that, then what do you fear?"

The mage shrugged. "You want me to list them? Hadar, Muscida, Botein, Mintaka, Adhil . . . and so on. I have lost count, now that so many of the younger ones are growing claws too. They have sent many friends of mine into the dark between the stars, and I have no wish to follow them yet."

Talitha was obviously shaken to hear her own fears so explicitly laid out for her. "They want Saiph!"

"Of course they do. Saiph is a threat to them as long as Rigel Halfling has it, and would be an incredible advantage to them if he didn't. Based on historical records, any attempt to take it by force will cost four or five lives, and may not succeed even then. But that is not my concern, and I have given my word. Shall we join the others, Your Highness?"

Talitha and Fomalhaut set off along the dock to where Prince Vildiar and a couple of his storm trooper thugs were waiting. Rigel and Mira followed.

"This way to the fancy dress ball, Brother Rigel," she said.

"You look like the missionaries got to you."

Just beyond the Vildiar group, the regent-heir was floating down from the roof with two companions.

"I don't like the look of this," Mira murmured. "I'm starting to wish that I'd let the damned bear eat you."

"So am I," Rigel said.

Out in the basin, Gienah the swan was gathering speed, wings and feet racing as she rose from the water, carrying Izar home to Spica.

The prince's halflings, Tarf and Tegmine, were new to Rigel. Both were slightly shorter than he and might be able to pass for human if they remembered to keep their mouths closed to hide the shark-like teeth they were currently leering at him. Tegmine was swarthy and had true elfin ears, which looked ludicrous sticking up beside his SS cap. Tarf had eyes and hair of middling brown. His ears were human, and his fleshy mouth resembled Hadar's.

Talitha pouted up at the inscrutable stare of Prince Vildiar. "Your progeny already do outnumber the stars, starborn. I won't wish you more."

The prince ignored her and addressed Fomalhaut. "The regent instructed you to bring my son to Canopus."

"I have been advised that he has countermanded those orders, Highness."

Kornephoros had arrived, scarlet with fury and hotly pursued by his two minions who had attended him the previous night, Rasalhague and Mekbuda. "That is news to me. By what right do you ignore my orders?"

Talitha's prismatic eyes flashed red and blue. "By the right of motherhood! I will not let this perverted steeple steal my son and turn him into another monster like himself."

"You will do as I say! I am not just your father, due your respect and obedience, I am also regent with jurisdiction over all Naos in the realm."

"Oh?" Talitha said sweetly. "Are you certifying that Izar Starling is a Naos already?"

"No, I am not!"

"Then he is merely my son and none of your business. I sent him home."

"You think you can defy the law?" Kornephoros was turning purple.

"Possibly." Her smile would melt bricks. She laid a hand on Rigel's sleeve. "You won't let them take Izar from me, will you *darling?*"

Rigel distinctly heard the sky fall on him. "Anyone who tries to take Izar away from you, my lady, will certainly find that he has his hands full." He appealed to the mage. "Won't he, my lord?" He wondered if Fomalhaut had foreseen this showdown when he'd chosen to give Izar the Turais amulet.

Regent-heir Kornephoros gave the mage no chance to answer. "Hussy! Stop pawing that halfling and board the barge!"

"Follow!" Releasing Rigel, Talitha marched off along the quay. Rigel hurried after her, ignoring the storm troopers' smirks.

She was seething. "I apologize. I didn't mean that. I just couldn't think of any better way to annoy him."

"I can. Why don't you stop and kiss me?"

She shot him a startled look, and for a moment he hoped she would but then she smiled, never breaking step. "Maybe, I'll give you a kiss to celebrate when you get status. But don't confuse Princess Talitha with Starborn Alniyat."

"I haven't," Rigel said bravely. "But I know which one I prefer."

She sighed. "So do I, but right now you need Talitha."

Chapter 18

The only other vessel in the basin was a flat-decked boat about twenty meters long and five or so wide, lavishly decorated with gold and crimson enamel. It had no masts or superstructure, and the only break in an otherwise featureless deck was a brass railing around a hatchway. The stern bore a flagstaff and flag, probably the regent-heir's personal standard, but the cloth hung limp and unreadable. The bow was adorned with a figurehead of a golden-haired mermaid, about double life size if one assumed that mermaids' human halves would match standard human build. She was obviously another elfin imagining inspired by terrestrial mythology, for even in proportion to her size, her eyes were huge and blue, her lips red and voluptuous, and her breasts loomed enormous compared to any Rigel had yet seen in the Starlands. Her scaly half shone with the silvery iridescence that the elves favored so much.

As he drew closer, he amused himself by speculating how such breasts, if real, would maintain their shape out of the water in miraculous defiance of gravity. He received a considerable shock when one baby-blue eye winked at him.

Talitha stopped. "Saidak, it has been too long!"

"Indeed it has, my lady," the mermaid agreed with a coquettish smile. "How's that stupid bird treating you? I hear you had a nasty run-in with some dragonflies yesterday."

"Gienah works well for my modest needs, but I certainly wished you were with us yesterday. Your regilding looks absolutely gorgeous. I am so happy for you."

The mermaid preened. She sat on a sort of throne, Rigel saw, and was not actually attached to the barge. "Your Highness is most kind. If that is Izar you have with you, he is surely growing fast."

Talitha laughed and flipped Rigel's hood back. "No, just a halfling I am attempting to acquire."

"Oh, very nice," Saidak purred. "A girl needs to keep all her options open, I always say."

Mira, who had followed them on board, chuckled. Rigel hastily pulled his cowl back in place to hide his blushes.

"He is to be Izar's guardian."

"Oh?" Saidak said, even more coyly. "I've been hearing your name linked with Starborn Elgomaisa."

Talitha made warning noises in her throat. "Just a passing fancy, and not even that since he made a pass I didn't fancy. It will be a pleasure to journey with you again today, Saidak. Give my regards to Sertan and the children."

"He will be honored to hear that you remember him, my lady. Have fun with your halfling."

As they moved on toward the gangplank, Rigel heard the regent-heir address the mermaid in what was for him an unusually pleasant tone. It wasn't pleasant enough.

"Canopus?" she shouted. "Always Canopus! Canopus, Dziban. Dziban, Canopus. Why can't we ever go somewhere *interesting*?"

"We can," Kornephoros said quickly, "we can! We had food sent aboard, remember? We have things to discuss, and I want some beautiful scenery to go with our meal."

The mermaid clapped her hands with impacts like gunshots. "Oo, that will be nice! I'll choose ever such beautiful domains to show you."

Talitha strode up the plank and across the deck to lean on the rail and scowl out at the tiny harbor. Rigel went close. Mira tactfully left them some space. The rail—indeed the whole barge—was superbly crafted, every spare surface adorned with elaborate carvings of flowers and birds. The wood itself seemed to glow with life.

The other passengers boarded went below. Silence fell. Rigel waited for Talitha to speak.

Elgomaisa Starborn? Starborn Elgomaisa? Of course she must have starborn friends, male ones. She was at least twice as old as Rigel and was a mother, no virgin. From what he had heard and seen at Alrisha, the only real taboo for starfolk was sex with humans or halflings, and even that seemed to be little more than a forbidden subject for conversation. Amongst themselves, the starfolk were brazenly promiscuous . . . and yet who was he to judge them? They seemed to have no diseases or poverty. Other than a few vague appeals to "the stars," Rigel had heard no mention of any divine overseer threatening sinners with hellfire. None of those hazards had ever done much to keep earthlings chaste, anyway.

Jealousy would be absolutely ridiculous.

But damn Elgomaisa, whoever he was!

After the silence between them had stretched on for several long moments, Talitha said, "I have been looking for a man," seeming to address the harbor at large. "As soon as I was free to leave Phegda, I set up my own domain at Spica so that I could be alone with Izar. He's growing up now, and he needs a surrogate father. But I cannot find a man we both like. Not that I can complain about that . . . For his age, he's an amazingly good judge of people."

That last remark failed to explain why she had just sent the kid off with a guardian he detested. Was she regretting that decision already?

"Going to Alrisha was madness. Neither of us liked a single one of the starfolk we met there, male or female."

But the Halfling . . . !

"Starborn Muphrid and his friends did not impress me either, my lady. But today? Mage Fomalhaut will refuse to sponsor me. When Vildiar offers, what do I do?"

"If you accept him, halfling," she said through her teeth, "he will take you straight home to Phegda and you will never see daylight again. No doubt Hadar will regretfully report that you choked on a fish bone. I must have a serious talk with Father."

"If you and Vildiar both offer to sponsor me?"

"Vildiar wins without question, because he is my senior by centuries. I simply *must* persuade Father to sponsor you himself. It's the only way out."

But the regent was terrified of Vildiar.

The gangplank folded itself up and became part of the side of the ship, and then the royal barge turned away from the quay.

"*Canopus!*" Saidak boomed, spreading her arms wide. She was louder than a military band. "*Canopus!*" The barge accelerated, and the flag stirred limply in the breeze.

"She does know which end is the front, doesn't she?" Rigel murmured.

"She should by now. She's been the royal barge for a thousand years."

"Barge or bargee?"

"Both, I suppose. I don't know if it was named after her, or she was named after it. She finds life a little dull at times, and enjoys adding a touch of drama."

The bow was lifting, the barge moving like a speedboat toward the end of the basin. The great voice boomed again. *"Canopus! His Highness, Regent-heir Kornephoros, departs for Canopus!"* There were splendid lungs inside that memorable chest.

The quay and the buildings at the end of the pool grew misty and disappeared. Then the barge was outside, in sunshine, floating between the peaks of Dziban, about a thousand meters above the marshes, with the Crystal Castle dwindling rapidly astern. Both the royal standard and the mermaid's hair streamed in the rising wind.

"Should be safe to go below by now," Talitha said, leading the way.

"Safe? Meaning?"

"I mean they'll have started eating, so they won't come and sit near us."

From the quay, Rigel had observed no portholes, but the lower deck proved to be a single great saloon walled by slanted windows like a gondola below a dirigible. Everything was red and gold: golden chandeliers hung above tables draped in red cloths and set with gold cutlery. The dining chairs were gilded, the cushions scarlet. Even the benches under the windows were upholstered with red velour. Two imp pages were serving food from gold trolleys, and it smelled delicious, nothing like the strange fare in Muphrid's domain. This was a lifestyle an earthling hobo had never dared dream of.

The rest of the passengers had chosen their seats at the tables, in their original groupings, except that Fomalhaut had joined the regent-heir and his two aides in the bow. Prince Vildiar sat amidships with his SS escort. Talitha led Rigel to the stern and gestured for Mira to join them.

When the young stewards arrived with their trolleys, Talitha took charge of Rigel's food selection. "He'll like this, I think. Give him plenty of that. He should try the squirrel paws too. And some of those."

The pages finished serving and went up on deck to allow the passengers privacy, but for a while everyone ate in silence.

Saidak provided a much smoother ride than the swan. She had coasted over the sugarloaf peaks of Dziban with surprising rapidity, climbing as no terrestrial boat could. A gentle dive through a link cloud brought her down to a rolling, wooded landscape. The next put her above a roiling, stormy sea, heading toward an active volcano spurting fire.

"I still do not understand this!" Rigel said. "How does Saidak know where she's going?"

"I told you," Talitha said impatiently. "You don't ask *where,* you ask *who*—whose domain? Saidak knows her way around so well that she can go almost anywhere in no more than six jumps. Oh stars, there went my appetite."

Tarf had left the Vildiar group and gone over to the regent-heir, apparently in response to a summons, and Kornephoros was pointing at his daughter. The halfling nodded and came marching along the saloon in his jackboots. He shattered the illusion of his humanity by baring his starfolk teeth in a T-rex smile. "Your daddy wants to speak to you, sweetie pie."

Talitha sighed and rose to go. "I wish he'd found a better messenger."

"Impossible." Tarf played carnivore again.

Rigel turned to speak to Mira, ignoring the henchman. "You must ask the prince's chef for his squirrel paw recipe."

"I like the taste, but the smell attracts all sorts of vermin."

Good for her! "Ah, I wondered what was doing it."

Tarf said, "May I have a peek at the celebrated Saiph?"

"No." The bracelet was presently hidden by the sleeve of Rigel's robe and he was strongly opposed to doing anything to oblige a man who would wear that repulsive uniform.

The halfling sneered. "You ever heard of the Dark Cells, sonny?"

By human standards, Rigel would guess that the obnoxious goon was about his own age, but starfolk blood could be deceptive. "They don't scare me, *Untersturmführer.*"

"That's good, because that's where you're going if you don't smarten up real soon."

Rigel forced a smile that he hoped looked serene and superior. "Those who wear Saiph never go to the Dark Cells, and they never die alone. Run along, boy. The sight of you is spoiling my breakfast."

Tarf Halfling, if Talitha was correct, had been bred and reared to do his master's bidding regardless of circumstances. Mere snubs would not discourage him. "Shut up and listen to me, Whitey. Hadar would really like us to have that trinket of yours. It would help us perform our duties better, see? He says he might take you with it, if you're really polite and can persuade him that you're the sort of lad who would make himself useful."

Rigel sighed. He was starting to think that he didn't exist in any world except as the half-breed with the bangle. They were all after his amulet. Even Talitha only wanted an armed babysitter.

"Have you noticed," Mira said, nibbling a very earthlike pear, "how this over-age Hitler Youth reject never mentions Vildiar? It's an old gangster trick. The mafiosi never incriminate their dons."

Yes, Rigel had noticed. "I don't suppose Vildiar even has to drop hints. The boys see to his every need." Now Saiph was a need.

Tarf refused to be drawn. His shark smile stretched his face again.

"What do you suppose," Rigel asked Mira, "I would have to do to convince *Reichsführer* Hadar that I would make a trustworthy employee? Would one murder be enough? Even then, I'd never really be one of the boys, would I? Nothing I could do would make me belong to that gallant band of brothers. What could Prince Vildiar offer me that Prince Kornephoros can't?"

"A long life, lad," Tarf said. "Much longer than you're going to get otherwise. And anything else your heart desires, anything at all. You want it, it's yours."

Rigel shuddered. "Boiled babies?"

"As many as you can eat." The Halfling smirked convincingly. "Try asking for something difficult."

"Go," Rigel said. "Away. Stay," he added. "Away. Or," he promised, "I will personally nail you to a chair from the throat down. Understand?"

The hoodlum laughed. "Big words. We'll see how loud you talk an hour from now, kid. If we can't have the trinket, we'll make sure it's never used against us."

Glumly chewing a suddenly tasteless breakfast, Rigel watched as Tarf strutted back to his prince and fellow thug.

Why wasn't Hadar present? Not his turn for a ride in the royal barge, or was he up to something nasty somewhere else? At the far end of the gondola, Talitha sat with her back to a window, grimly arguing with her father, who had turned his chair around to face her. Elfin ears were real giveaways, and Talitha's showed that she was losing the argument.

Mira had noticed that too. "If you'll pardon my saying so, Mr. Estell, I think you're in a serious pickle. Your friend doesn't seem to be making any headway with her daddy."

For once sympathy was welcome, as was the mere sight of a human face.

"How can she? He obviously has to do whatever Vildiar tells him. If I may say so, Ms. Silvas, you're holding up pretty well yourself. Your situation is even worse than mine."

She smiled, showing human teeth that were a delight to see. "I still kind of think I'll wake up if I pinch myself hard enough. This has been a wild ride of an adventure, but I'll probably sink or swim with you . . . and right now it looks like we're on the *Titanic*. What happens if your fashion model can't persuade her pappy to enter the bidding for Saiph?"

"Nothing nice."

"Well, I hope she's pointing out that he needs a bodyguard even more than Izar does. He ought to set aside his rigid principles just for once and have Vildiar removed before Vildiar removes him. Even if the regent keeps doing his bidding, he'll get sick of him eventually."

The same thought had occurred to Rigel. "I wonder how honest the courts are here?" The judges might be just as terrified of Vildiar as the regent was. "Look, I am quite happy to be a bodyguard, and I would fight to defend myself or my ward, but I will *not* be an assassin for anyone. Never, never, never!"

They ate in silence for a while. Then Mira said, "You're drooling."

"Am not!" he protested with his mouth full.

"I mean that every time you look at Talitha you melt and smoke comes out of your ears. You are in love, sonny! You have a bad case of the yearns if I've ever seen one."

"How can I not be? She is absolutely the most gorgeous woman I have ever set eyes on."

"You wouldn't be afraid of rolling on one of her ears in bed?"

"There is absolutely nothing wrong with Talitha's ears!"

Mira rolled her eyes. "Of course not! Great for fanning bugs away. But I agree. If your taste runs to beanpoles, then she is Elfland poster girl of the year."

A huge gust of wind swept through the cabin as a forward window swung wide. The opening was filled with streaming banners of golden hair and Saidak's enormous head, upside down. *"Canopus ahead!"* she announced in a stentorian bellow, then disappeared again, closing the window with a bang.

Saidak was flying low above an impossibly blue sea speckled by small boats with triangular sails. Rigel could make out a flat green shore ahead and many white buildings. He was so focused on the view that he didn't even notice Fomalhaut's approach. Suddenly the mage was looming over him. "Come up on deck, halfling. You too, earthling. I have to hand you over to the palace guard." He led the way to the stairs.

Rigel followed, wondering which side Vildiar's underling favored. Was he a secret Talitha supporter? He had given Izar a guard dog that could eat Hummers, but even that could be a betrayal if there was some magical password to deactivate the dog just when it was needed.

On deck, the two pages hung over the rail, eagerly pointing and chattering. The barge was moving more slowly as it approached the city. The air was warmer than it had been elsewhere in the Starlands, although not uncomfortably so.

"Canopus is another star name, isn't it?" he asked.

To his surprise, Mira answered. "Yes, but it was also the name of the most westerly mouth of the Nile River and of a city on it, back in the days of the pharaohs." She laughed at his expression. "My parents took me on a trip to Egypt many years ago. I remember our guide telling us that when Alexander the Great founded Alexandria nearby, Canopus shriveled up like a drunk's cock."

"But earthquakes and tsunamis helped," Fomalhaut said. "Those ancient earthly cities have all vanished now—washed away, torn down and rebuilt, or sunk into the mud of the delta, but our Canopus preserves some of their ancient glories. My father visited Alexandria in Roman times, when Canopus was still a suburb with a reputation for debauchery, catering to rich Roman tourists. Some of the buildings you will see are Greek, for Alexandria was a Greek city. Others date back thousands of years before Alexander, and are copies of Egyptian originals from Thebes or Memphis, complete with obelisks and statues of gods and pharaohs and sphinxes."

"If we are going to do the Egyptian number now, I suppose we'll see live sphinxes in this domain?" Rigel asked.

"The sphinxes are the palace guards," the mage said. "Obey their instructions and answer all their questions."

Chapter 19

M*ake way!*" roared Saidak, floating in over the harbor just above mast height. *"His Highness, the most excellent Prince Kornephoros, regent-heir of the realm, enters his capital."* She went on to proclaim Vildiar and Talitha also, and then started over at the beginning.

Rigel peered down at dozens of boats and ships, and at scores of faces staring up at the barge. As far as he could tell, they were all human faces, none of them bearded. Very young boys wore only loincloths, but all the rest were swathed in loose cotton robes and head cloths that hid their non-elfin deformities. By the standards of Vancouver or Montreal, the docks were tiny, but so were the ships. And there were no trucks or cranes or containers here, just carts and wagons and beasts of burden— oxen, donkeys, and humans. Alexander the Great and Julius Caesar must have seen something very similar.

"Kneel for His Highness, the most excellent Prince . . ."

And kneel the people did as the barge floated on into the city, following a wide avenue shaded by date palms and decorated with statuary and fine buildings. The queen's subjects kissed the pavement to honor her regent and the other Naos accompanying him. Saidak kept up her bullhorn roar.

Away from the docks, the crowds contained many starfolk in their usual moon-cloth wraps, which seemed entirely appropriate here, for ancient Egyptians were rarely depicted wearing anything else. Starfolk did not kneel as the mudlings did, but they bowed low as the royal craft swept overhead.

"*. . . regent-heir of the realm comes to hold court . . .*" The mermaid's voice was holding up remarkably well. If anything, it seemed to be growing louder, and it was certainly echoing off the stonework below.

"Hold court?" Rigel said. "Does the regent himself judge my case?"

Fomalhaut looked down at him with puzzled contempt. "Who else?"

So the hayseed halfling had been wrong all along. *Not that sort of court, idiot! The other sort of court!* "I am honored."

"So you should be."

Honored, but probably doomed, for could there be any doubt as to the court's judgment? Rigel paid little heed while Fomalhaut pointed out fine buildings in Egyptian, Hellenistic, and Roman styles. He did notice widespread slummy hovels in the background and was reluctantly impressed by an enormous Egyptian-style edifice that towered over everything and must be the royal palace, their destination.

Gradually dropping lower, *Saidak* floated between two high obelisks flanking the main gate, above massive seated statues of pharaonic style, and along an avenue as wide as any street in the city outside. Now decorative statues of gods and elves were everywhere, and in many cases it was hard to tell which were which. Everything was slabbed or angular, without any arches or curves, and many of the surfaces were inlaid with colored script.

The regent and the others emerged on deck, all except for the Vildiar SS, who stayed out of sight as if they were considered unfit for decent company. The two pages went below.

Gentle as gossamer, Saidak set down in a long reflecting pool flanked by high stone arcades. A large crowd of starfolk had already assembled to greet the regent, and more were hurrying in, many of them wearing jeweled bib-type collars to advertise their importance. Rigel saw his first sphinxes strutting past. A line of musicians armed with silver trumpets exploded into a fanfare as the gangplank was unfolded.

"Stay here until you are summoned," Fomalhaut ordered, and strode off to join the royal party.

"Nice to slip into town unnoticed," Mira remarked.

The spectators knelt as Kornephoros paraded down to the courtyard. He bade them rise. There were speeches and much bowing. Rigel found the rigmarole absurd and quickly lost interest.

"You're the Egyptian expert," he said, nodding at the monumental statues that lined the courtyard. "Are those genuine Egyptian gods?" Many represented human bodies with animal heads.

Mira shrugged. "Most of them have elf ears."

"So they do. The doggy is popular."

"That's Anubis, the jackal god. They probably favored him because he had the right sort of ears to start with."

"And how about the writing on the pillars? Genuine hieroglyphics?"

"Too far off to tell. I'd suspect it's Starlands script, what you called Rongo-rongo. It would be hard to re-create hieroglyphics accurately if you didn't have a camera to document them.

"I wonder what Tarf and Tegmine are up to?"

"Scoffing the rest of the food, maybe."

"I think our tour guides have arrived," Rigel said.

Two sphinxes had just come padding up the gangplank and were stalking across the deck toward them. The front one was male, and looked very much like the great carving at Giza that was featured in every book on Egypt. His human head was larger than a human's—probably about as big as the mermaid's—and although his body was on the small side for a lion, he had to outweigh any cop Rigel had ever met on Earth. While his pelt was tawny, his human hair was black and hung to his shoulders, and a tubular pharaonic beard dangled from the point of his chin, ending in a forward curl. His ears were elfin, their edges studded with jewels. His name was Rasalas, and he looked seriously dangerous.

Chertan, the female following him, was almost as large and entirely similar except for the beard and genitalia. Both sphinxes fixed Rigel with huge yellow eyes and studied him in silence—a cop trick on any world, apparently. Rigel resisted the urge to say that he didn't have his ID with him.

"Rigel Halfling." The male sphinx's voice rumbled about an octave below human bass. *Pause.* "You are summoned to court." *Pause.* "Proceed down the plank, holding your hands behind you so that I can see all your fingers. I will direct you as we go."

Saiph-bearer or not, Rigel was not inclined to argue with those paws. "Certainly, officer."

As he started to move, he heard Chertan ask his companion to confirm that she was Mira Earthling. Purebred humans did not project their names.

Although many of the walls and pillars around them stood taller than a four-story building on Earth, most of the palace was only one story high and much of it was unroofed, as if rulers of the Starlands kept their weather under tight control. The complex was also enormous. Rigel thought he must have walked close to two kilometers with his hands at his back and the sphinx padding behind him, silent except when growling out directions: "Left . . . Right . . . Up the steps . . . Down . . ."

"Stop here."

They had finally reached the throne room, and now it seemed appropriate that all the starfolk called it a *court*. It was about the size of a football field, and open to the blue sky and blinding sun. The walls were slabs of stone at least ten meters high, divided by gaps like enormous doorways, through which could be seen nothing except more stonework. The giant statues lining the sides of the court were no doubt intended to make people feel small, and they did their job well. The only furniture was a grandiose throne at the far end, which stood atop a flight of giant stairs extending the full width of the courtyard. The throne itself was neither Egyptian nor Greek, nor anything Rigel had ever seen in any book or TV show. It was encrusted with jewels and gold stars and bizarre sculptures. Sphinxes and collared starfolk wandered in and out, seemingly at random.

He turned his head just enough to register that both Rasalas and Chertan were present behind him, lying in classic sphinx posture, head erect, front paws outstretched.

"Where's Mira, my earthling?"

Pause. "She is elsewhere," Rasalas rumbled.

Obviously. "May I sit down?"

"No." *Pause.* "The court will convene shortly."

"May I scratch my neck? It itches."

"No."

"I need to pee," Rigel said. That ought to get some action.

"I don't advise it," the female sphinx said. "The penalty for contempt of court is seventeen lashes."

"Minimum," Rasalas explained helpfully.

Chapter 20

First came a strutting line of starfolk in sparkling collars playing a long and stunningly beautiful fanfare on silver trumpets, glorious arabesques of sound rolling across the great court. Behind them the three Naos rode in on magically suspended thrones of jade and silver, followed by a glittering parade of courtiers and officials. Kornephoros floated up the long stairs almost to the great throne itself, turned, and set his lesser throne down one step below it. Vildiar peeled off to sit on the sidelines at the regent's right and one step below him, and Talitha went to his left, one step lower yet. This was not a panel of judges, though. In this sort of court, the ruler alone would decide.

Groups of starborn standing around seemed to be mere spectators or courtiers or perhaps even tourists. There had to be several hundred of them in all, and a few dozen sphinxes too, but the court was so vast that it seemed almost empty. The officials at the front were too far away for Rigel to distinguish their names or the details of their collars of office. Clearly the court was now ready to consider its agenda, and he should feel flattered that his case merited the attention of the ruler himself. He didn't.

"Starborn Fomalhaut may approach the throne!" proclaimed an elf at the front, and magical acoustics carried her words clearly to everyone present. Or maybe the space was not as big as it appeared to be? Perhaps magic was what made it seem so huge and overpowering. Probably not, though, because Fomalhaut took quite a long time to reach the front. The proceedings would be much smoother if they adjourned to a smaller court, but grandeur must be more highly valued than efficiency. The mage eventually arrived at some designated spot, where he knelt, touched his face to the floor, and was given royal permission to rise to his feet again. It was all a big pageant, but then again courts anywhere relied on pomp to command respect.

The official ordered him to state his business.

"Your Highness, while seancing two days ago, I witnessed a disturbance among the terrestrial denizens, the cause of which appeared to be a halfling male. He and an earthling female were being mobbed, and he was defending both of them with the aid of what was obviously a Starlands amulet. It was doing the fighting for him, and he had already slain three male mudfolk. As he was violating so many of our ancient laws, I extroverted and arrested him, together with his companion, whom I brought along as a material witness. I now bring him into your royal presence for assessment and judgment." He bowed.

A nice and succinct briefing, Rigel thought. This court was smelling more and more of kangaroo. Why had Fomalhaut been snooping in Nanaimo at all? It was hardly the center of the universe. Was he implying that Rigel had provoked the attacks on himself? Wasn't a guy allowed to defend himself against berserkers? He turned to his guards, who had gotten to their feet.

"Do I get to question the witness?"

Rasalas gave him a pitying look. "Of course not."

The regent congratulated Fomalhaut on his sense of duty and gave him leave to withdraw. He walked off to the side without another word, and the bailiff, or whatever she was, called for the accused halfling.

The two sphinxes escorted Rigel along the length of the great space, pacing majestically on either side of him. The red granite paving was cool underfoot, spectators exchanged whispers all around him, and he felt strangely conscious of the bracelet hanging around his wrist just as it always had, the protector that might soon lead him to his death. As he neared the steps he noted the inscrutable stares of the three Naos on their thrones, watching him, and a black star inset in the floor, which he guessed was his destination. When he reached it, Chertan told him to stop.

"The prisoner Rigel," announced the official, whom Rigel now knew to be Starborn Pleione. Her bib of office was a mesh of hundreds of pearls and rubies.

"Kneel," Rasalas rumbled. "Kiss the floor and remain on your knees." As Rigel obeyed, his two guards lay down behind him, front paws outstretched, ready to leap if required.

"Stranger," Pleione said, "know that you kneel on the Star of Truth, and if you attempt to lie to the court, your tongue will become a red-hot cinder in your mouth. State your true name and parentage."

"I am Rigel. I do not know my parentage."

And so on. Rigel had to shed his robe and cowl and stand in his loincloth so that the regent could determine his species. He even had to display his teeth, like a horse. It would have been more embarrassing if anyone else who mattered had been wearing anything more than he was, and he kept himself entertained by admiring how the curve of Pleione's pearl-and-ruby collar emphasized the shapely breasts just below it.

"We decree that the prisoner is indeed a halfling," Kornephoros announced. "Record that he can be tolerated in public places so long as his ears are kept covered, and he keeps his mouth closed."

"Prisoner," said Counselor Pleione, "cover your head immediately. Kneel again. His Highness will now determine whether or not the halfling can safely be released into society."

Rigel pulled his cowl up over his head, but in kneeling he managed to wad his robe under him to ease the pressure on his knees. Vildiar continued to stare at him with no more expression than the granite pharaohs lining the walls, but Talitha was studiously avoiding his gaze.

"Not yet." Kornephoros stifled a yawn, understandably bored by the formality of staging a trial when he had already reached his decision. "Before we proceed with that, we shall seek to discover the identity of the original perpetrator of this tragedy, the prisoner's father. Proceed, Counselor."

She bowed. "Rigel Halfling, where and when were you born?"

Wary of red-hot cinders, Rigel said, "I do not know either of those things. I have aged at human pace, and believe myself to be twenty or twenty-one years old."

"Identify that amulet you wear."

"Of my own knowledge I do not know its name."

"How long have you worn it?"

"As long as I can remember. I cannot take it off." His mouth had not burst into flames yet.

"Step aside, Rigel Halfling. Wasat Halfling, approach the throne."

Rigel vacated the Star of Truth. The new witness who shuffled in from the side was short, and wore a collar of office constructed of many strings of amber and onyx beads over an earthling robe. His striped pharaonic headdress covered his ears, but his clothing did little to conceal a human potbelly. He was elderly, with human wrinkles and a stiffness to his movements that already seemed strange to Rigel. He greeted Rigel with a smile, displaying watery blue eyes and crooked human teeth. It was a friendly smile, so Rigel returned it. Then he guessed what was needed, and took the newcomer's hand to help him kneel. Wasat Halfling bowed his head near to the floor with difficulty but did not kiss it.

"Your office, halfling?"

"Starborn, I have the honor to be chief curator of the royal treasury."

"And how long have you held that post?"

"Oh, dear . . . Let me see. Her Majesty appointed me in the year of iron potters. That must be, um—"

"Thirty-eight years," Pleione said impatiently. "You are in fact sole custodian of the royal amulet collection?"

The old man's jowls wobbled as he nodded. "I am."

"Can you identify the amulet worn by the halfling beside you?"

Rigel bent to offer his wrist. Wasat pulled it close to his eyes and turned the bracelet a few times, studying the grisly death toll.

"This is a defensive and offensive amulet of great ancestry and distinction, Saiph by name. It has belonged to the royal collection as far back as we have records. According to legend—"

"Describe the normal procedure for removing an amulet from the treasury."

"Ah," Wasat said thoughtfully. "Normal? I release nothing without royal instructions, of course. Usually His Highness the regent-heir does me the honor of asking my advice on what is needed and available. His aides prepare a warrant for his seal, and the assignee presents it at the treasury in a day or two. By then—"

"So every amulet that is officially assigned is recorded in your archives?"

The old man nodded brightly, as if surprised by her acuity. "Yes, Counselor."

"When you were subpoenaed to appear in court today, were you instructed to search your records for mention of this Saiph amulet?"

"I was."

"And do they show to whom it was most recently assigned and when?"

The archivist smiled again. "No."

"You just testified that all assignations were listed." It was Pleione's turn to look surprised, as if the witness ought to be screaming and blowing steam.

"Saiph was not assigned, Counselor."

"Then it was stolen?"

"No."

"Then where did it go?"

"It was signed out twenty-one years ago, in the year of silver bells."

The counselor looked even more puzzled. "Signed out by whom?"

"By Her Majesty."

Then everyone looked surprised, and the court was filled with whispers.

"Electra?" Kornephoros bellowed, setting echoes booming. "The queen herself?"

"I remember the occasion distinctly," Wasat said, clearly enjoying the attention. "She came in person to the treasury and asked for it by name. Her Majesty does *own* the royal collection, Your Highness! She is quite within her—"

The counselor said, "And you do not know, even by hearsay, what she did with it, or intended to do with it?"

The curator uttered a tiny snort of amusement that probably only Rigel and the two sphinxes could hear, no matter how magical the acoustics. "Starborn, I am kneeling on the Star of Truth. I am not required to guess, speculate, or spread rumors."

Pleione looked to the regent-heir for guidance. Rigel saw his chance to ask a question, whether or not he would be allowed an answer.

"Halfling, could this amulet be used to track the location of the person wearing it? I mean, when I was walking around on Earth with it on, could the person who gave it to me use it to find me?"

Wasat chuckled. "Certainly not! There are such amulets, of course, but a defensive amulet that betrayed its wearer's location would be working against itself, and Saiph is ancestral, the greatest of all protectors, perhaps the most famous amulet of all."

"And it will fit any person's wrist?"

"It will."

"Silence in court," Pleione said grumpily. "You may go, Curator."

Wasat reached for Rigel's hand again. Rigel heaved.

"Thanks," Wasat whispered, giving him another smile. "I have a helmet that would cover your ears, lad. It would look good on you. Come and see me after this." He shuffled off.

"Rigel Halfling, kneel on the Star again," Pleione said. "Prisoner, you were witnessed murdering three earthling males. Do you have any excuse to offer?"

"They were trying to kill me. My amulet defended me from their attack, which was entirely unprovoked on my part." Where was Mira? She was supposed to be a chief witness.

In a grumpy tone, Kornephoros said, "Why would even Earth folk do such a thing? The court must assume you incited the assault unless you can prove otherwise."

Oh, *great*! How could he possibly prove that? "I said nothing and did nothing to annoy them. And I have no magic, unless my ability to perceive names is magic."

The regent-heir snorted. "Talent for magic is easily disguised. Princess?"

"Your Highness?" Talitha asked cautiously. Her obvious surprise at being involved did not bode well for the prisoner.

"You witnessed this halfling slaying the Minotaur Elnath yesterday, I believe?"

"Yes."

"Did he use the red cape to arouse it?"

Talitha stared very hard at her father, shot a poisonous glance at Vildiar, and finally answered, "As far as I recall, he did not."

Kornephoros nodded smugly. "Minotaurs are never stupid enough to attack armed starfolk or halflings unless driven to killer madness. The halfling must have enraged it without the amulet, which means that he has at least that much innate talent. He is accordingly found guilty of interference in terrestrial affairs for slaughtering the earthlings. He is likewise found guilty of displaying magic on earth—a serious crime." Kornephoros then added for Rigel's benefit, "For which the law specifies a term of imprisonment exceeding your possible life span."

The whispering in the court suggested that this verdict was a surprise. It smelled very much like a compromise worked out beforehand between the two princes—Saiph would be taken out of play in the assassination stakes. If Vildiar could not have it, then no one would. That might suit Kornephoros also, because the amulet would become available as soon as Rigel's cell filled up with water. A team of husky slaves or a coven of mages could lift the slab and hack the amulet off the corpse's wrist.

White with rage or fear, Talitha opened her mouth, and then shut it again.

Kornephoros yawned, "Have you anything to say before the court pronounces sentence?"

Rigel sighed. Now he had no option. The time had come to try and unravel the web of lies, to pull on the only thread he could reach. This might solve all of his problems or none, but it could hardly make them worse.

"Yes, Your Highness. I repeat that I did *not* enrage those earthlings to attack me. I say this on your Star of Truth, so if I'm lying, it needs some major repairs. I am not certain who was responsible, although I suspect Fomalhaut Starborn, a mage who would have been easily able to cast a spell of madness. I suggest that Your Highness recall him to the Star, and also summon the apparent earthling who goes by the name of Mira, whom I believe to be a starborn dissembling. She was there, and the previous day—to the best of my belief," he added cautiously, "—she provoked a bear to attack me. I accuse her now of setting the earthlings on me as well. Call her forward and make her testify."

He had played his ace in the hole and would now learn whether aces counted high or low.

Chapter 21

B *ring forth this witness!"* roared the regent.

Supernatural acoustics magnified his voice, but also the spectators' whispering. It would take thousands of people to make that court seem crowded, but there was no doubt that it now held many more people than it had done at the start of the trial.

Counselor Pleione said, "I assume that this is she being brought in now."

Kornephoros was red-faced with fury. Talitha was staring very hard at Rigel—for the first time since she came in. Vildiar was watching him also, but his grotesquely elongated features bore no expression. He certainly extended the boundaries of the expression "poker-faced."

Mira, in her cotton earthling robe, strolled in leisurely fashion along the length of the court, ignoring the efforts of Sphinx Alterf behind her to chivvy her into moving faster. From the way she walked it was obvious that she had discarded her boots and was barefoot, and her bonnet had disappeared also. Her dark hair was longer than the starfolk's, but it did not conceal her human ears. She was cunning and her motives were obscure. Not wanting to get too close to her, Rigel snatched up his discarded robe and vacated the Star of Truth. She halted with her toes just outside of it and nodded to him with mild amusement.

"Nicely done, sonny," she said. "How did you work that out?"

"Lots of little things that weren't right. I wasn't certain until you gave yourself away on the barge."

"You will kneel on the Star!" Kornephoros barked.

Mira looked up at him with a mocking smirk. "No, I won't. But I will tell you this much." She stepped forward, onto the black granite. "Rigel Tweenling did not provoke the mob to attack us. That was the work of a Cujam, one of those fiendishly evil berserker amulets that affect earthlings but not starborn or tweenlings. It was activated by Tarf Halfling, who was begotten in illegal miscegenation by Vildiar Naos." She pointed an accusing finger at the prince. "Tarf was reared by some of his many halfling brothers and trained by them in the art and practice of murder. He can pass as an earthling as long as he keeps his mouth shut, and he had extroverted to the crime scene with the express purpose of killing me. Get him onto the Star and see what you can learn."

The Star was empty. Mira had disappeared.

Aces scored high, and Halfling Rigel had just played the ace of trumps.

The court erupted. Even the sphinxes uttered growls of amazement. Chertan snarled, *"Who was that?"*

Obviously no one knew, but Rigel heard Electra's name being repeated. He kept an eye on Vildiar, worried that he might resort to violence. But if starfolk could use violence, they would have no reason to keep halflings around. He grinned at Talitha, who looked stunned.

The regent-heir waved a hand. A gigantic but invisible gong boomed, jangling every bone in Rigel's body and leaving his ears ringing. It instantly silenced the chatter.

"Where is Halfling Tarf?" Kornephoros demanded. If the long-lost Queen Electra had returned, he would have to be very careful how he proceeded. Voices called in vain for Tarf Halfling.

Seemingly aware that the ceremony was slipping out of his control, Kornephoros tried again. "Then I ask you, *Prince*, where is your retainer Tarf? He was on the barge with us this morning."

Vildiar shrugged. He was leaning back on his throne with his legs crossed, insolently dangling about a meter of bony shin, as if this circus did not concern him in the least. "He was. He attended me until I came ashore with Your Highness, and I have no idea where he went after that. I totally deny that he is any get of mine, or that he is a criminal of any sort. In all the years he has served me, I have never had cause to complain of his work."

Now *there* was a nicely ambiguous statement!

Rigel waited for the regent-heir to order Vildiar down to the Star of Truth to repeat his testimony. But he didn't. He did look very unhappy.

"Fomalhaut Starborn! Bring him back here."

The name was called and repeated. Echoes died away.

"Starborn Fomalhaut appears to have left the court, Your Highness." Judging by her expression, Counselor Pleione suspected that her handling of this case had done her career no good.

Kornephoros glowered at his two fellow Naos in turn. Talitha smirked, looking ready to stick her tongue out at him. Vildiar remained as cryptic as his Easter Island doppel-gangers.

The regent chewed his lip, tapped his fingers, and generally fidgeted. Then he chose the safer course. "Rigel Halfling, have you committed any crimes within the Starlands?"

Was lusting after the regent's daughter a crime? If it was, then surely half the male starborn in the realm must be guilty of it.

"No, Your Highness."

"Then we extend the royal mercy in the name of Her Majesty and grant you status as a permitted dweller within her realm, subject to some reputable starborn sponsoring you. Starborn Fomalhaut, who would normally be asked to serve as your sponsor, is not available, so we call on anyone among the starfolk now present who is willing to perform this task to stand forward."

Vildiar put both size-twenty feet on the floor, grasped the arms of his throne, and unfolded to his full, incredible height. "I will, Your Highness."

Talitha kept silent, face lowered, staring at her clasped hands. Apparently Rigel's ace in the hole was not going to win the game after all.

"Rigel Halfling, Prince Vildiar offers to sponsor you. Do you accept his generous offer?"

Rigel shivered as he looked up at that marble-faced elfin pylon. After what Talitha had told him, he did not need the warnings Saiph was now sending him to know that he'd be stepping into a hyenas' den if he accepted.

"May I ask the court to outline the alternative?"

Kornephoros made a sound indicating exasperation. "If you refuse the starborn's offer, the court will sentence you to the Dark Cells for a term of not less than one thousand years."

Talitha had said he would have seven days to find a sponsor, but this trial was trampling custom and precedent all over the place. Violence was becoming ever more likely. There were three sphinxes within striking distance of Rigel's back. Realizing that he was still clutching his robe, he transferred it to his left hand.

"You know?" Rasalas said softly. "One thing I really hate is licking blood out of my fur."

"Me too," Chertan agreed. They might be offering Rigel a warning or exchanging coded messages about tactics. They would not be indulging in idle humor, because they knew about Saiph and what the likely result would be if the court ordered them to restrain the prisoner.

"I decline the offer," Rigel said and jumped clear of the Star. Saiph spun him around and hissed through the air to intercept a leap by Rasalas. Rigel had a momentary vision of two enormous paws with their claws still retracted, just before the sword cut them both off at the metacarpus joint. He leaned sideways to avoid the hurtling mass of disabled sphinx. The plan must have been for the male to knock Rigel down while his female partner secured his sword arm, because Chertan came in from what was now his left but had been his right. He threw the robe over her face and her claws screeched on the marble as she fought for purchase. Then Saiph crashed into the side of her head with sickening results, visible even through the moon-cloth drapery.

The amulet never wasted a stroke. With total control of Rigel's muscles, it sent him sprawling, then rolling over onto his back as the Sphinx Alterf arrived in a great bound over the writhing, howling Rasalas. She had her claws out, but Rigel's dive threw off her aim and Saiph was extended and waiting for her. The blade slashed into her belly, but it must have hit bone on its way through, because the impact slammed Rigel's shoulder blade against the granite floor so hard he thought it must be broken.

Apparently not, because he was on his feet again in seconds, still clutching the sword, with three screaming, wounded sphinxes around him and a whole pride of the beasts racing along the hall toward him, like an armored division, scattering the fleeing spectators like fenceposts. Three sphinxes had posed no problem, but could even Saiph possibly hold off a dozen?

"*Stop!*"

Everything stopped.

Rigel, facing toward the rear, saw the running starfolk sprawl headlong and the sphinxes roll, tumble, and slide. He tottered but stayed upright, probably held there by Saiph. Then the freeze vanished as quickly as it had come.

"Put up your sword, halfling!" commanded the same voice.

Blade and gauntlet disappeared. Rasalas was howling for someone to help him, blood pouring from his truncated paws. Chertan lay silent, eyes closed, and only the spreading blood around her showed that her heart must still be beating. Alterf writhed and screamed in agony, with shiny loops of bowel spilling from the slash in her belly. It was the Walmart fight and the Minotaur all over again. Was Rigel fated to kill people on a daily basis from here on out? Freed from the amulet's control, he fell to his knees, dry-retched twice, and then vomited convulsively.

Neither Siegfried nor Lancelot would have done that.

"Healers! Healers to the front!" It was not the regent's voice; someone else had taken charge of the hall. "Rigel Halfling, come here."

Rigel went to wipe his mouth with his arm, discovered that his arm was covered with blood, and promptly upchucked again. When he finally managed to stop heaving, he wiped his mouth with his left arm, clambered to his feet, and turned toward the thrones.

The royals had gathered on the steps with Counselor Pleione. It was obvious just from the way they were standing that the towering Vildiar was now in command. Rigel tottered up the steps to join the group. The length of the sentence wouldn't matter, just as long as they'd let him have a quick death by jumping off the ledge on the way to the Dark Cells. But the Dark Cells in Canopus had to be at or below ground level, so there would be no jump. He would just have to drown, then. Even that would be better than going through life as a one-man mass-murdering catastrophe.

He halted a step below the two women and Kornephoros, feeling very small. The towering Vildiar was one step higher yet, a pallid version of the great jackal-god statues that lined the walls.

"The killer!" the regent said, enraged.

"No!" Vildiar was quiet, almost whispering, but his tone cut like a razor. "You were the killer, you idiot. You sentenced the halfling to death, knowing he could not control his amulet." He could be loud when he wanted, though, and he sent commands thundering through the court: "More healers! Scribes return to your places." He returned his attention to the wretched Kornephoros, lowering his voice again. "Now what? You have just sacrificed three sphinxes and blackened the queen's reputation forever by implying that she bore a tweenling baby twenty-one years ago. What happens—"

"I did nothing of the kind!"

"You informed everyone that she was the last person to possess the bracelet before it turned up on the halfling's wrist. You asked questions in public before you had learned the answers in private. Haven't you even learned that simple lesson in all these years? You aren't fit to maintain a flowerbed, let alone a kingdom. The half-breed has refused my sponsorship. What are you going to do with him now?"

Vildiar was calm, austere, a pillar of iced venom; Kornephoros was brick red, trembling with impotent fury. Talitha looked from one to the other with equal contempt.

"I will sponsor him," she said.

Vildiar said, "Do you accept, halfling?"

"I do, Your Highness."

"See that it is so recorded, Counselor. Announce it, *Regent-heir,* and issue a pardon to the halfling so that the sphinxes don't try any more stupidity. And then adjourn your audience, *Regent-heir.* Have you gotten all that? Take his tiny hand and lead him through it, Counselor. Let us see how the wounded fare."

He strode off down the steps. Rigel had to run to keep pace with him. Was the crisis over? Apparently he had status now and was sponsored by Talitha. What's more, he had been pardoned for the fight. Vildiar had arranged all that? Now the villain was on the side of the angels? Who or what, and certainly where, was Mira? The web of lies and deceit seemed more tangled than ever.

Seven or eight starborn of both sexes were tending the sphinxes. Healers wore blue collars. A few more were inspecting starfolk casualties in the rest of the hall, those who had fallen hard or been trampled in the panic.

"Well? What's the toll?" Vildiar demanded.

A bloody-handed healer rose and bowed to him. "Not as bad we feared at first, Highness. Sphinxes Rasalas and Alterf will recover. We were too late to save Sphinx Chertan."

Both of Rasalas's front paws were heavily bandaged. If the Canopus healers could reattach those, they must be using very powerful magic. Seeing that the sphinx's eyes were open, Rigel knelt down.

"I am sorry."

The sphinx smiled faintly. "Don't worry about it. Line of duty." His finely shaped and oiled beard had become an untidy tangle.

"I do worry about it."

"Can you control that amulet?"

"No."

"Thought not. So I shouldn't have tried to be a hero." Rasalas shut his eyes for a moment, then opened them and smiled with pale lips. "But now I can brag that I fought Saiph and lived."

"Halfling Rigel, stand on the Star."

Rigel turned and found himself looking at a furious Counselor Pleione. "What?"

"The oath of sponsorship. Stand there!"

Talitha was standing on the Star already. Rigel joined her, stepping intimately close on the pretext of avoiding a pool of blood. Smiling, she held up her hands and he clasped them.

"Repeat after me: 'I, Halfling Rigel, will be your retainer, obeying the laws of the Starlands and your orders, until I die or you release me from this promise.'"

He did.

Talitha spoke her lines without prompting. "I, Starborn Talitha, will be your sponsor, maintaining and protecting you until you die or ask to be released from your promise."

It was a very simple ceremony, but it was invested with the power of the Star itself.

"Halfling!" said a new sphinx voice, even more sepulchral than Rasalas's. The newcomer's name was Zozma. He was a sphinx and a half, with silver in his mane and murder in his eye. "The regent-heir has just issued you a pardon for resisting arrest." Obviously he did not approve.

Rigel said, "I did not choose to bear this amulet, and I would take it off and throw it away if I could."

Behind him, Talitha said, "I think he means that, commander."

Zozma nodded his great head. "Repentance doesn't undo damage, but it is the first step toward forgiveness. I am glad the prince stopped the slaughter before I lost any more of my officers." He turned his tail on her and paced away. A Vildiar supporter? A *hard-line* Vildiar supporter!

Talitha looked appraisingly at Rigel, as if judging what sort of monster retainer she had just taken on. She did not look as happy over his success as he would have hoped. "Who is that Mira person?" she asked him in an undertone.

"I was hoping you might know. I heard whispers about Queen Electra."

"No." Talitha frowned, shaking her head. "Electra has too much respect for the crown to ever stage a spectacle like that. Your friend might be Acubens, one of the Naos we thought Hadar and company had killed. There were unanswered questions about her death, and she may well have gone into hiding. Acubens played the fool sometimes. Well, you have status. Congratulations."

"Thank you." He was puzzled by her coolness. "So you have a bodyguard for your son."

She said, "Mm. We must find something better for you to wear than that stupid hood."

"The archivist said he had a helmet that would suit me."

"Good. Perhaps the old rascal has some other help to offer us."

Chapter 22

A s they crossed the courtyard, Talitha said, "Father tried very hard to talk me out of sponsoring you, halfling." Her tone was brittle.

"How, my lady?"

"He explained on the barge what Vildiar had told him last night. Vildiar said that 'whoever' had tried to kill us yesterday must have been after you, not me or Izar, so to make you Izar's bodyguard would be putting Izar in harm's way."

They left the courtyard and headed along a shadowed corridor.

"That's an open threat to kill me!" Rigel said.

"Of course it is!" The flush on her cheeks suggested rage, and the backward slope of her ears confirmed it. "Vildiar is a compulsive liar. He doesn't see any distinction between truth and lies. You heard him deny fathering Tarf, but he used to brag to me about his army of halfling sons, and often listed Tarf among his favorites. He had them address me as 'stepmother' because he knew I would hate it."

"But his threats?"

"Oh, you better believe his threats! Father said Vildiar dropped a broad hint that whichever halfling had sent the dragonflies yesterday had been severely punished for nearly killing Izar. But that won't stop them from trying again. Izar is starting to show the Naos mark, and Vildiar wants him back. He doesn't want you and Saiph getting in the way. If you are not going to work for him, he wants you out of the picture."

"So you want me to stay away from Izar?" Rigel's sense of triumph faded. She would send him off to run a farm somewhere, be a slave boss.

"No I do not!" Talitha snapped. "That would be giving up. Hadar and the gang would just grab Izar. And now I've seen what you did to the sphinxes. That was so incredible! More than ever I want you to guard Izar!"

That was better. "With my life, I promise."

"If Hadar and his gang appear, *dice* them!"

They descended a wide staircase. There were few other people around, but those few all cleared a path, kneeling to let Talitha pass and staring in horror at Rigel's bloodstains.

"Vildiar impressed me," Rigel said. "He knows how to take charge in an emergency." The giant had displayed remarkable leadership. Kornephoros had fallen apart, but not Vildiar. By abandoning his efforts to obtain the amulet, he had turned on a dime, conceded a battle but not the war, and shown up the regent-heir as a feckless ruler, if not an outright fool. Where would he strike next?

"Oh, I do not question his competence," Talitha said bitterly. "He's clever, ambitious, utterly unscrupulous. He's not even a sadist, like Hadar and Tarf and some of the others. I'm sure Vildiar regards sadism as a weakness because sadists may let their cravings distract them from important matters. It serves his purpose to encourage perversions in his goons. They can use terror and brutality to bring in the results he needs, yet these very qualities make them hated and feared and vulnerable to the law. So they become more dependent on him since he protects them from retribution or punishment. On the other hand, if sadism were needed—if he had a reason to torture someone, say—then he would be worse than any of them."

"Let's talk about nicer things," Rigel said. "You promised me a kiss when I got status."

"Did I?" she asked, but her doubt was not convincing. "Well, it will have to wait for a more private place. And it will be a very short, maidenly kiss."

"But I shall have to return it, and mine will be a longer, manly kiss."

"Leading where?"

"Let's not plan anything specific," he said. "We can just see where it goes."

Talitha drew a deep breath. "Halfling, the thought of a romance with you is far from displeasing, but it is just not possible. I am very happy to have you as my retainer, and I hope you will remain with me for however many centuries you will live. I have every confidence in your ability to be Izar's guardian, and I promise that you will always have worthy employment and respect in my household when he grows up. I have already apologized for your encounter with Alniyat. That will not happen again."

He wondered how long it had taken her to prepare that speech. And how long he would have to wait for the kiss. He would get it eventually. It would be his life's ambition.

They had come to a long courtyard with a reflecting pool. "You can wash there," she said.

Cleaning off bloodstains was becoming a habit. Rigel stepped down and then knelt. The water was unpleasantly warm. Several starborn in the distance stared at his antics with obvious disapproval. Well, the people of the Starlands would have to get used to him.

"Izar is terrified of his half brothers," Talitha said. "You saw."

"I did. And I don't blame him; so am I. To defend him I must know more about magic. You saw Mira use it. How did she manage that vanishing trick? Can you teleport like that?"

"No one can teleport. What she did was this, and I can't do it as well as she did." Talitha faded and became transparent. She did not quite disappear and her shadow lingered as a prismatic shimmer on the flagstones. "Maybe with another century's worth of practice," she said—and even her voice seemed faint—"I'll be able to go the whole way." She popped back to solidity with a *whoof!* of relief.

"I suppose Vildiar can do that?" Rigel said glumly.

"Certainly. And Kornephoros. It's a terrific strain, though. No one could do it for long."

"Electra?"

"Of, course—if she would still bother."

"Hadar?"

"No. Invisibility is a form of dissembling."

"He can't dissemble, make himself look like you, say?"

"No. No halfling can. Dissembling is an ongoing process, and it can't be stored in an amulet. Only starfolk of at least green talent can dissemble."

That was good news, and it supported what the Minotaur had told him. Rigel climbed out of the pool and adjusted his cowl. They set off along the courtyard. He had much to learn before he could be of real use, but meanwhile he had a future, an important job to do, an enemy to hate—even a girl to love, although he might have to endure agonies of jealousy and frustration for years without getting what he wanted. Nevertheless, every day was going to be bright and new and exciting from now on. He was also drawing closer to the end of his quest.

"I must find Mira again. Is there a magical way to find out who she really is or why she was stalking me back on Earth? Or what both Tarf and Fomalhaut were doing there, if she spoke the truth?"

"She spoke the truth. She spoke on the Star, and I doubt if even Electra herself . . ." Talitha stopped dead. "Halfling! You don't think . . . You can't possibly think . . ."

"Why not?" Why not a human father and a starborn mother?

Talitha laughed, which was an improvement upon her previous worried mood. "Because I know Electra! Not well, but when I was young she took me boating, and we sang madrigals together. I just cannot imagine her doing what you suggest! It's impossible! She's not as straightlaced as my father, but she . . . she just *wouldn't!*"

They resumed their journey. He said nothing, just left wet footprints on the paving. Talitha read his thoughts from his face.

"Halfling Rigel," she said as if she were breaking bad news to a small child, "mudlings are farm workers and porters and latrine cleaners . . . I cannot imagine Electra losing her head over some husky young gardener. They would have absolutely nothing in common."

But she was the last person known to have handled Saiph before it turned up on the wrist of baby Rigel somewhere in Canada. "Would it be possible for an eighteen-hundred-year-old starborn to bear a child?"

Talitha sighed. "Why not? All right, let's just suppose the inconceivable happened, and she conceived a child by a human male. That I could maybe, possibly, perhaps, hypothetically, just for the sake of argument, suppose. But I am absolutely certain that my Greatmother Electra would *never* callously abandon a baby in the way you were abandoned, in another world, in poverty, with no support, no identity. *That* I absolutely *cannot* believe of her."

"I see." He nodded. That argument was more convincing. Whoever his parents were, at least one of them was a first-class swine.

"Forget your royal blood, halfling. This is not a fairy tale. Starborn women do not bear halflings to humans. Look for a male starborn who spends too much time in the livestock barns."

For instance Prince Vildiar? Rigel made a vulgar noise.

Halfway along one of the wide palace streets, Talitha turned through an open doorway into a small, bright room overlooking the sea. The walls of massive stone were inscribed from roof to floor with the strange Rongo-rongo script, all inlaid in bright colors, but the only furnishings were a brilliantly colored rug and a low table under the window. On the rug sat Wasat Halfling, cross-legged, poring over a scroll. He looked up with his crooked-tooth smile.

"Your Highness! What a welcome honor!" He rolled up the parchment and prepared to rise. Again Rigel offered a strong young hand to lift him. He bowed to Talitha. "It has been a long time since you came to beg amulets off of me, Highness." He hesitated, then beamed and said, "Fifteen years, maybe?"

She smiled. "A lot more than that, I think. Halfling Rigel says you have something to cover his ears?"

"Oh, yes. Let us go and see . . ." He stepped over to the wall alongside the door and placed his palm flat against a mural depicting another door. The fake door faded away instantly, leaving a gap. The two adjacent openings led into completely different places. He stepped back and bowed again to let Talitha lead the way through the portal.

"One!" said a voice.

Rigel followed.

"Two!" The speaker was a black statue of Anubis the jackal god standing just inside the door. "Three!" it announced as Wasat entered after them.

Talitha said, "This is Miaplacidus, the royal treasury and archive. It's a great place to swim too."

Miaplacidus was an oasis, a small lake of very blue water surrounded by sand that stretched away in all directions until it met a cloudless blue sky. The air was pleasurably cold on the skin after the sultry warmth of Canopus, although the sun hung almost directly overhead, spilling tarry patches of shadow under the motionless fronds of the palm trees. In among these trees, on the nearer side of a small lake, stood a cluster of small white buildings. The freestanding doorframe that Anubis was guarding led back to the room in the palace.

"Personally, I find Miaplacidus a bit chilly," Wasat confessed, shuffling along in his sandals. "I keep a warm coat here for days when I must spend a lot of time here. But the starfolk like it."

So did Rigel. He stared uneasily at the blank horizon. "What would happen if you just walked away?"

"You would walk until you dropped," Talitha said. "Size is easy enough to imagine. It's convincing detail that's difficult. Whoever first created this place just imagined desert going on forever and that's what you'd find."

The buildings, Rigel now saw, were unroofed enclosures. "It never rains in Miaplacidus?"

"Why should it?" Wasat led the way, pointing as he went. "Those over there are full of books—over-full, I'm afraid. I keep meaning to ask His Highness to imagine another enclosure for me. Those two store all the reversion staffs Her Majesty managed to confiscate . . . of course, His Highness has continued her policies. These are full of jewelry amulets. Weapons . . ." He had arrived at his destination, a structure comprising a sand floor surrounded by four walls of shelves. "This is the garment store." The shelves were laden with steel and bronze armor, hats, shoes, and folded clothing of every color and texture imaginable. Everything was sparkling clean, as if the inventor had never imagined dust.

"All of these are magic?"

"Each one is an amulet," the curator said proudly. "It was your suggestion that Saiph could be used to track you, halfling, that—"

"Please call me Rigel."

"Rigel. You were wrong to think that Saiph could be tracked, but your question reminded me of that helmet, Meissa." He smiled shyly, pointing up to the topmost shelf. "If you would be so kind? Meissa is not as famous as Saiph, but it does have a history, and several celebrated warriors have worn both. When you arrived I was comparing their histories to—"

Rigel lifted it down, as requested. "You expect me to go around wearing *this*?" Meissa was a bowl of hammered bronze, which was a reasonable enough thing for a helmet to be, but a peak on the crown supported a metal arc, which in turn held a cockscomb of stiff white horsehair. It would extend from above the wearer's eyes to the nape of his neck.

Wasat stroked the fringe. "This is called a brush. It was used to distinguish officers."

"Greek?" Talitha said.

"Very ancient Greek," the curator agreed happily. "And the Romans used them too. The originals would have covered the face more, with a nosepiece and cheek pieces, but they probably had some like this for ceremonial wear. I have seen many replicas of Greek art showing heroes wearing helmets like this."

"And what else?" Talitha inquired with an innocence worthy of Izar.

Wasat smirked. "Nothing else. Meissa is technically interesting, because it was obviously not made for a starborn. The archives are vague on—"

Rigel drew in all the air his lungs would hold. "There is absolutely no way—"

"Rubbish," Talitha said. "You'll look good in it. Put it on."

Rigel had sworn to obey her orders. "It's too small," he grumbled. It wasn't, of course. It would fit anyone. It was not even heavy, and when the curator directed him to a silver mirror, he had to admit that it was striking. Mardi Gras stuff, but striking nonetheless. It made him twenty centimeters taller and no one would be able to see his deformed human ears; they would be too busy laughing themselves to death at the great white crest bristling over his head.

Talitha clapped her hands. "Wonderful! He will be a credit to my household. What does it do?"

Oh, what a man would do for love . . .

Wasat showed his crooked teeth again. "It makes the wearer invisible to other magic. People's eyes will still see him, but he cannot be tracked or detected by magic after he activates this. Booby traps or magical guardians will not be alerted."

"I never heard of such a device! In fact I would have sworn that it was impossible."

"It is very rare," the curator agreed. "We have records of only two others like it, and both seem to have been lost or destroyed."

"He activates it by saying its name, I assume?"

"Of course. But do not forget, young Rigel, that your friends will not be able to find you either. If Starling Izar needed you in an emergency, for instance, he would not be able to summon you. You deactivate it by taking it off your head for a moment. Meissa is probably the finest defensive amulet in existence, which is why it has so often been combined with Saiph in the past."

"I can see fifty hats and helmets on your shelves, Wasat Halfling," Rigel said suspiciously. "Why do I need one as rare and precious as this?"

The old man looked at him as if he was a simpleton. "Because Saiph is the most precious amulet of all. It is like the queen on a chessboard, powerful and therefore vulnerable to attack. It will defend you, but you must defend it! Meissa is an added protection."

That did make sense, unfortunately. An aircraft carrier needed an escort of lesser ships to protect it. "It is an invitation to ridicule," Rigel said, removing the stupid thing. "Izar would laugh himself to death. I will not—"

"Yes you will," his sponsor said. "You will wear that helmet in public from now on. That is an order. Thank you, Wasat. What other amulets does he need?"

Rigel replaced the helmet, turned back to the mirror, and invoked Saiph. He lunged at his reflection. Not bad, he had to admit. Sword and helmet did go well together, and he would much rather frighten people out of his way than kill them. On the other hand, what better equipment for an assassin than stealth armor? Had Talitha planned this somehow? No matter. He was her retainer and must obey.

He trotted after the others and caught up as they arrived at an enclosure whose shelves bore hundreds of wooden boxes, each one carved or inlaid or otherwise decorated. Wasat began opening and closing lids.

"A levitation ring, for Dziban. Doesn't work anywhere else and it has to go on a finger. I think everything else we can handle with ear studs. They'll clip into the side of the helmet's brush holder. Very convenient—" he chuckled "—for us poor halflings who don't have proper ears! As you can see, I wear my collection on the neckband of my robe."

Rigel's suspicions were clamoring like fire alarms. "I heard you testify in court, Wasat, that you released amulets from the treasury only on the regent-heir's instructions. Has he given you permission to load me up like this?"

"Mm?" The archivist was poking through a box of gems. "I said 'royal instructions,' I believe. Her Highness's word is good enough for now. I'll have her father countersign the list the next time I go to Dziban. Message stud, one to promote healing, antivenom . . ."

Baffled, Rigel clipped each one to the crest of the helmet.

"Fire protection?" Talitha said.

"Of course! Here. This shields you from fireballs, maybe even up to red grade, but don't challenge Prince Vildiar himself!" The old man cackled, clearly enjoying himself as he handed over amulet after amulet. "Coagulant spells to staunch bleeding—that's another very rare one, we only have two in the treasury at the moment—stamina booster, a light for night work—put that near the front . . . and a fire-thrower. That's another that must go on a finger."

Talitha said, "Remember that fire is useful against things like dragonflies or vampires, but most starfolk carry defenses against that type of magic."

"These amulets are from the royal collection, my lady," Wasat protested. "They are the very best available."

"I shan't remember a quarter of this!" Rigel complained.

Talitha smiled. "We have lots of time to teach you. I'm sure Izar will be happy to assist."

"I'm sure he'll see to it that I burn down a palace or two."

"Very likely. I'll have more amulets to give you when we get home. Keys to various places." Her smile was for him alone. It might not mean as much as Rigel hoped it did, but she did seem to be enjoying herself.

"Four!" said Anubis. Wasat hurried to the doorway to see who had entered the oasis.

"There you are!" cried a raucous voice. "Trying to hide from me? How stupid." A bird the size of a turkey landed on top of the wall. It would have resembled a very bedraggled crow had it not had a miniature human head and chest. In pictures Rigel had seen, harpies had always been female, with human breasts. This one was male, with a straggly mustache and protruding front teeth. It looked as ugly as it sounded.

"Speak your message and then go," the curator said. "And don't try to steal anything this time."

The harpy screeched and spat, ruffling up its feathers. "Steal? Me? That is a foul lie and I wouldn't carry a message to a filthy old half-breed like you if the queen herself—"

"Speak!" Talitha commanded.

The harpy shrank itself back to size. "If I must," it said sulkily. "From Kornephoros the Useless, regent-heir of the Starlands, to his hot-titty daughter, Talitha the Slut: Tell her to stop pawing that latest stud mongrel lover of hers and get her fat ass to the Dolphin Room right now or I'll whip her butt."

"Harpy, tell my father I'm coming. Go!"

"Screw yourself," the harpy muttered and launched with a mad flapping of wings.

Wasat watched from the doorway to make sure it made no detours before it passed by Anubis, which called out, "Three!"

"Charming," Rigel said. "Reminds me of an Internet flaming."

"A what?" Talitha asked, heading for the gate.

"Never mind. Thank you, Wasat Halfling, for all the invaluable amulets. Are you certain that the regent will approve all these?"

"Oh, I'm sure he will, lad. Don't worry about it. Come and see me again sometime."

Talitha went out and Anubis said, "Two!"

Rigel rounded on the curator. "So who did put Saiph on the baby's wrist?"

The old man halted. "You heard my testimony on the Star of—"

"And you evaded the question. In fact you managed that interrogation so cleverly that I suspect you were using some sort of counter-magic. *Who put Saiph on the baby's wrist?*"

Wasat shook his head, looking shrunken and flabby and so pathetic that Rigel's suspicions about defensive magic were reinforced. How could anyone so decrepit and pathetic be entrusted with such treasures?

"You testified," Rigel persisted, "that Saiph would fit any size of wrist, but we were talking about a *newborn baby!* My wrists would have been no bigger than my thumbs are now. Why would any mage make an amulet that's capable of equipping a newborn with a sword? Yet you dared to say it was possible on the Star without ever having seen it tested on a baby?"

"Do not ask me to betray confidences, lad!"

"I am asking you. I have a right to know how I was wronged!"

The old man just shook his head in mute misery.

"Three!" said Anubis.

Talitha had returned through the portal. "Halfling Rigel!"

"Coming, my lady!" Rigel ran to her, remembering to duck his helmet under the lintel.

"Two!" Anubis said. "One."

Chapter 23

The Dolphin Room was probably classified as a small and intimate meeting chamber, but it was as wide as a furniture store and as high as a church. Vast unglazed windows looked down on sails in the postcard harbor, and the walls were ablaze with bright, colorful inscriptions and frescoes, none of which seemed to have anything to do with dolphins. Near the center the regent-heir was slumped into an exquisitely delicate gilded-wood chair, looking as if he had just been thrashed within an inch of his life. Queen Electra strode back and forth across the room bellowing insults at him.

Electra was a large woman, tall even for a starborn, unusually heavyset and full-breasted. Her wide collar of office seemed to be made of diamonds the size of sugar cubes, and it flashed and sparkled with all the colors of the rainbow. Even she, greatest of the starfolk, went barefoot and wore no garment other than a moon-cloth wrap. She could get away with it, because she showed little more than one percent of her eighteen centuries. She could also swear like a goosed marine.

She did not look in the least like Mira Silvas.

She stopped her pacing when she saw Talitha folding into a deep bow, which Rigel thought it wise to copy. By the time he straightened up, Talitha was racing across the room with outstretched arms, shouting, "Electra! Electra!"

Electra smiled and embraced her. Together they indulged in just as many hugs, kisses, and *Darlings!* as earthling women were prone to do after a long separation. Rigel stepped back against a wall and tried to blend into the frescoes, feeling certain that he would be evicted very shortly.

The queen knew he was there, though, and after a few minutes she looked his way, smiled at his helmet, and said, "That is the youth who bears Saiph?"

"Halfling Rigel, ma'am," Talitha said. "May I present him? He would be greatly honored."

"Later, dear. Wherever did you get that hat for him?"

"From Wasat."

"Wasat! How is the old boy?"

"Aging, I am afraid. Halflings . . ." Talitha stopped, and then shrugged.

Electra nodded understandingly. "To business, then, and we can talk frankly until Zozma gets here. I have been away for far too long, I admit. Now I return to discover that my realm is literally falling apart, and a serial killer is trying to seize my throne. *And nothing has been done about it!* All thanks to this starborn sponge." She glared down at Kornephoros, who glowered back resentfully.

Rigel had just realized that what he had thought to be a royal collar of diamonds on her was nothing of the sort. It was part of her, a collar of fire. It pulsed and twinkled like a rainbow aurora, shrinking at times up around her neck, at others spreading down to her breasts and lapping her upper arms, never still, constantly changing color. There, obviously, was the genuine mark of Naos and the model on which all the collars of office were based.

"There were thirty-two Naos when I left," Her Starry Majesty continued, her voice like a trumpet of doom. "And now there are three. Three! The rest, I understand, have been *murdered*. Sit down, my dear." She gestured to a pair of elegant chairs and callously took the one that left her back turned to the regent-heir.

"Perhaps not all, ma'am," Talitha said. "Four or five seemed to be genuine accidents. Another six or seven probably just . . . faded."

"Hastened on their way by the bloodbath, I have no doubt. So you have had only seventeen murders, give or take a few. How relieved I am to hear it. And I understand that you were paired with the monster?"

"Yes, ma'am."

The queen snorted like a dyspeptic camel. "You agreed?"

"Reluctantly."

"Stars, you must have been still only a child!"

"Um . . . thirty-five, ma'am," Talitha said quietly, not looking at Rigel.

But Electra did, and raised an eyebrow. Rigel was busily calculating that Talitha could not be very much over fifty even now, a mere babe by starfolk standards. Why did that seem better than, say, three hundred? He wondered why he had not been ordered out of the room yet. How long before the first hints that he should go and assassinate Vildiar?

"That is absolutely disgusting! Greatson Kornephoros, tell me why you let that ghastly killer steal your daughter from her cradle?" Electra asked without even turning to look at him.

"Because," the regent-heap mumbled, "he argued that the realm was getting dangerously short of Naos, and since both he and Talitha bore the mark, there was a good chance that their offspring would too. Izar is starting to turn already."

"Excellent! Now we just need another five centuries for him to grow up. Was that all? No reason beyond that bit of nonsense?"

Kornephoros scowled as if he were about to flare back, but then subsided into sulks again. "Vildiar also let me know, without actually saying so himself, *why* we were dangerously short of Naos. He indicated that I would be the next to go if I gave him any trouble."

"So you let your daughter be legally raped to save your own skin. Great stars! Did *nobody* in the realm suggest you gang up on him?"

"Of course they did," Kornephoros snapped, straightening up. "Several tried. We gave each of them a state funeral and waited to see who would be next."

The bead curtain clattered and flashed; Zozma marched in, seeming to crowd the room with his presence. He bowed to the queen like a cat stretching, touching his beard to the floor and extending his claws.

"Zoz!" she cried, extending a hand. "You great pussycat! How are you?"

The sphinx stalked over to her and kissed her hand. Or possibly licked it—Rigel did not see which.

"Much better since I heard Your Majesty was back."

"How are your mates and cubs?"

"All very well, thank you, ma'am. More of both since you left."

"I would have been shocked to hear otherwise. It has come to my attention that we have had some troubles, Zoz."

Zozma glanced briefly at the regent-heir and his tail twitched. "Indeed we have, ma'am."

"I understand," the queen said, "that an unidentified star-born masquerading as an earthling testified today on the Star of Truth that a certain Halfling Tarf not only extroverted without royal permission but unleashed a Cujam amulet. Those horrible things have caused some of the worst massacres in earthling history."

The sphinx looked much happier than he had in the court-room earlier. Even the curl at the end of his beard seemed to jut forward more aggressively. "Yes, she certainly accused him of using a Cujam. There were many noble starfolk present, and no one has yet explained to me why her real name and appearance did not become evident the instant she stepped onto the Star."

"Mm?" Electra frowned. "Good question! As I recall, my Greatfather Rastaban told me once that the Star only works on spoken words. The intruder could still dissemble her ap-pearance, but if she had been asked her true name she could not have lied. The question is this, Zoz: Where is this despi-cable Tarf Halfling now? Forget the Star of Truth; I want to hang him up by his ears and ask penetrating questions, with the aid of penetrating instruments!"

The captain's smile was now much more scrutable than a sphinx's was reputed to be. "He arrived in the city with his sponsor and Halfling Tegmine on *Saidak* this morning and the barge has not left yet. I know the prince went to his resi-dence on Front Street after he left the court."

"Find out if he's still there," the queen commanded. "If Tarf or any other halflings are present, arrest them immediately. If Vildiar is there, tell him that he is summoned to court, and that he must bring Tarf. I'd very much like to question that long moonbeam on what he knows about the deaths of all of these Naos. Can you do that for me, Zoz?"

Talitha looked aghast, but only Rigel was watching her.

The sphinx nodded his great head. "I will gladly attempt it for Your Majesty, but that residence is the root portal of the prince's domain, Phegda. If the birds have not flown already, they will certainly have done so by the time we gain access to the building."

The queen used more of her roustabout language and drummed fingers on the arm of her chair in frustration. "The portal is active? Most root portals are kept well sealed."

"When he entertains at Phegda," Kornephoros said, "guests from Canopus walk straight through."

"Mm. It has been ages since I was there. Talitha, child, you were paired with that oversized horror for years. Can you show us what you recall of the house on Front Street?"

Talitha licked her lips. "It is a small residence, Your Majesty," she said. "Long and narrow." She gestured with her hands and a foggy outline began to take shape on the floor beside her. "The gate from the street opens into the central court at this end, and there are buildings around the other three sides, like this."

The dollhouse model became clearer, revealing a rectangular, two-story structure enclosing a long courtyard. An internal balcony gave access to the upper-floor rooms, and all the windows seemed to overlook the court. Uninvited, Rigel walked closer to watch the details develop: trees and shrubs and water, but nothing intruded on the central line, so he had guessed where the portal must be before Talitha told them.

"The portal is here, ma'am, at the far end from the gate. Guests coming in from Front Street can see straight through into Phegda, into whichever subdomain the party is being held. When the portal is not active, it is the door to a small storage area for tables and chairs."

"Very well done! And how many people live in this residence? What is it used for?"

"There is no permanent staff there. It is just treated as part of the domain, ma'am. I used to escape there with Izar sometimes, when he was very small. We often had it to ourselves."

"So the prince may still be there with his henchmen or there may be nobody there?"

Talitha nodded.

"So!" Queen Electra bared her saw teeth. "Can the guard come in over the roofs? Do any of the adjacent buildings overlook the courtyard?"

Surprisingly, Talitha blushed scarlet. "Only the upper rooms do."

"Likes that sort of party does he? Well, Commander Zozma? Why don't you storm the place? Take control of the portal so they can't escape and arrest anyone you find there. If the mice have fled, seal the portal. That ought to get their attention!"

"Gladly," Zozma growled. "But I expect it will be empty by the time I break in."

The queen grimaced. "I suppose so. Well, from now on, Commander, arrest any Vildiar halfling you can get your claws on. We'll put them all on the Star. What will you need?"

"Your royal warrant, ma'am."

"You shall have it as fast as a scribe can . . . Tweenling, go and haul on that bell rope."

"And . . ." Zozma sat back on his haunches and raised a front paw to inspect his black dagger-claws. "And some nimble hands, Majesty. We are permanently short of *hands* in the palace guard. My kind can't open doors; we can only knock 'em down. We have harpies for communication, but we'll need first-class magical defense in case we meet with booby traps or active resistance."

Pause.

Here was the problem. Presumably only a Naos could defend against another Naos, so the queen was waiting for offers—Talitha, who knew the house, or her father, who had let the prince practice his evil ways for so long. Or was Electra prepared to take on the rebel *mano a mano* herself?"

"Greatson?" she inquired sweetly, but without turning. "You are being uncommonly silent."

Kornephoros looked at her back with a scowl. "You really want my opinion?"

"Let's hear it anyway."

"You are about to kill a few fine servants, members of your guard. The front door will certainly be booby-trapped. Yes, it can be defanged, but that will take time. By then the rats will have fled. And the portal itself will be loaded to the lintel with venomous magic. At the end of the day you will have made a fool of yourself and gained nothing except casualties."

Her Majesty was not amused. "I can see why Vildiar has gotten away with so much for so long."

Talitha still looked frightened. Any minute now she was going to be press-ganged onto the assault team, and Rigel could not allow that, not even if this was a setup, which he strongly suspected it was. He had been the kid with the brace-let and now he was the kid with the helmet too, and that fortunate coincidence was much too cute to swallow. He had been manipulated into this, but he would have to see it through or he would despise himself evermore. Returning from the bell rope, he inserted himself into the meeting.

"Let me go in first, ma'am."

Four pairs of eyes turned to him and all of them managed to look surprised, which must have been no small feat. He said, "Halfling Wasat assured me that this salad bowl on my head makes me invisible to magical booby traps. That should allow me to walk through the front gate unchallenged. Once I'm in, I'll run to the far end, and use Saiph to stop anyone from leaving. That should give your mage enough time to clear the traps on the gate, and let in Commander Zozma and his team. If Saiph holds the portal, nobody leaves. Simple."

Without talking her eyes off him, Electra said, "Testicles at last! How much for his bond, Greatdaughter?"

"I'll give him to you, ma'am! Take him off my hands and good riddance." Talitha, regrettably, was not glowing with pride at Rigel's romantic courage. She looked ready to order him flogged. Could she possibly be dissembling that rage? Could she possibly *not* be party to the conspiracy?

But the queen was smiling. "What you are proposing will be extremely dangerous, halfling. I must hear your motives."

Because I was hoping to get royally lucky this evening? True, but not diplomatic to mention and not at all likely now, given the way Talitha was looking at him. "According to the witness Mira, this Tarf tried to kill me two days ago, and caused me to kill three men, probably more. Maybe they were 'only' earthlings to you, but they were fellow human beings to me, ma'am, and had done me no harm. Yesterday he, or one of his litter, tried again to kill me and four other people. This morning he openly threatened me. It would give me great pleasure to loose the wrath of Saiph on Halfling Tarf."

The eruption of hair-raising noise beside him was Sphinx Zozma laughing. "If the halfling can do what he says, we shall have no trouble. I'll try to get Bellatrix to back him up. She can get him there fast and get him out again fast if he meets a watchdog he can't handle. I'll throw a cordon around the house and deploy a flight of harpies for air cover. But we shall still need magical protection, especially if the prince himself is present. He will not readily give up one of his halflings, ma'am."

"You mean his sons?"

"Yes, ma'am, and daughters."

Electra pulled a face. "Disgusting! We need a mage, at least a red. I wonder if Fomalhaut is still in the city?"

"All right!" Kornephoros bellowed, leaping to his feet. "I still think it's a stupid, dangerous waste of time and prestige, and I am not at all sure that I can undo any spell that Vildiar set, but I'm willing to try. Does that please you? You've degraded and insulted me in front of my daughter, a halfling, and the commander of the guard, but where were you when all the trouble was going on? I never wanted the regency; I told you that, yet you insisted. I had no authority to start a civil war. If I'd tried to squelch Vildiar, he would have killed me and appointed himself regent, and then where would you be? Where were you then? You vanish for twenty years with no explanation, and then come back and start bad-mouthing me. But if you want me to take part in this madness, just say so!"

Electra's smile was as deadly as Saiph. "I do say so. Help, then, but for stars' sake, let Zozma call the shots."

Chapter 24

Zozma bounded out the door as if he were chasing wildebeest. Rigel, attempting to follow, caught a glimpse of a mousy human male leaping aside on the stairs to avoid being run over, spilling a shower of paper, pens, and ink bottles. The sphinx's tail vanished around a corner at the bottom, and Rigel was about to barrel after him when he was stopped in his tracks by a bellow from behind him.

"*Halfling!*"

He turned. "My lady?"

Talitha was red-faced and spitting fire. "A retainer does not go plunging into suicidal adventures without asking for his sponsor's permission or giving her advance warning!"

To which the best answer he could find on the spur of the moment was, "You ordered me to defend your son, my lady."

"*My son is not in the house on Front Street!*"

"But his enemies are. Have you never heard that the best form of defense is attack? You expect me to sit around waiting for those goons to keep trying to—*No, let me finish!* I will not wait to be slaughtered at their pleasure. It is time to teach them some respect for the law. And respect for Saiph, which is what you wanted all along, not me. Saiph is needed and it cannot go without me. Now, by your leave, I am on Her Majesty's business."

He tried to leave and she grabbed his arm, digging in her fingers with surprising strength. "You idiot, you don't know what you're getting into! I doubt if any of the amulets Wasat gave you will do any good at all against Naos Vildiar if he's there, and his thugs will be armed beyond anything the law allows."

"Saiph is a Lesath too. It slices sphinxes, remember? Now," he added recklessly, "if you won't give me a good luck kiss, at least show me a smile so I can die happy."

She gaped at him, speechless, her fingers still digging into his arm. Just then Kornephoros emerged from the Dolphin Room. "Can't you ever keep your hands off that mongrel? Stay with Her Majesty but don't gossip. I'll take the halfling down."

So ended Rigel Estell's first romance . . .

A few minutes later, Rigel was standing under a lemon tree in a shady corner of the sphinxes' courtyard, wishing he had not shouted at Talitha so stupidly and that he had more experience with women so he could understand why she had been so angry with him if he was no more than a servant. Zozma was conferring with three of his officers, while a dozen or so harpies lined up on the opposite wall were screeching complaints and obscenities at everyone.

A centaur trotted in through the arch. She was jet-black all over, except for her lips and two large human nipples and areolas, which were blood red—Rigel was too polite to check if she had a mare's teats as well. As a horse she would have measured at least sixteen hands and her human part could have matched a Russian wrestler in sheer muscle, yet her ears were elfin-shaped and bore jeweled studs. Her hair was thick and straight and bound in a ponytail long enough to brush her back.

Horseshoes clattering loudly on the paving, she headed straight for him and stopped a little too close for comfort, looking down at him with undisguised disgust. She set her hands on the part of her body that served as both human hips and equine shoulders; Rigel noted her many rings and bracelets, as he was no doubt supposed to. Her name was Bellatrix.

"I understand I have to help you be the freakin' cavalry," she said.

"Not my idea. Is there another way?"

"If there was, I'da' found it. You're the Saiph-bearer?"

"This is Saiph. What are all your trinkets for?"

"Enif, my bow. Wezen, my sword. Daggers, fireballs, paralyzer, et futon cetera. You done much police work?"

"None."

"Ridden a horse?"

"Never."

"That's a relief." She looked over at the sphinxes and Kornephoros, who had disappeared earlier and had now returned. The harpies were jeering at him because he had shed his golden collar, probably to prepare for battle, but of course they were accusing him of having been stripped of his office. If that ever happened, Vildiar and Talitha were the only Naos available to replace him.

"Stars, I hate those shitty birds," Bellatrix said. "Looks like Zoz is almost ready. You'd better practice falling off a few times." She turned with a clatter of hooves to put her left side toward Rigel, then twisted her human torso around to offer him her right arm. She raised her left rear knee, or whatever that part of her was called.

Taking the hints, he gripped her wrist, put a foot on the step-up offered, and . . . and very nearly fell flat on his face. The harpies shrieked, momentarily averting their attention from Kornephoros.

"Hold my other arm too, you idiot."

Rigel tried again. Inspired by thoughts of what the harpies would say if he failed a second time, he mounted successfully. Or Bellatrix hauled him aboard, whatever.

"Keep your knees higher," she said. "And hold on to my hair. If I tell you to hold *tight*, you can put your arms around me, but touch my breasts and I'll throw you off and kick your head in. Ready?" She walked slowly around the courtyard.

The harpies continued shrieking insults at him. He ignored them, and then survived a brief trot and even a few gentle swerves and bounces.

"Not bad," the centaur admitted over her shoulder. "Great reflexes. Thighs need work, but you're doing well for a first-timer."

"Thanks."

"Now tell me exactly what the helmet does."

He repeated what Wasat had told him.

"That's impressive! Never heard of one like that. So you're really going to walk up to the front door and just open it? Are they paying you or blackmailing you?"

He couldn't see the centaur's face and had only her tone of voice to go on. Was she mocking him or not? "I volunteered."

"Is there much insanity in your family? How will you deal with the lock?"

"Hadn't thought of that. How would you deal with it?"

Bellatrix chuckled for the first time. "With my back feet, if I had to. But I also have this. Take it." She passed him a gold ring with a white stone. "Turn the handle with whichever hand you wear that on, and you'll get through most doors. Vildiar may have double-hexed his, o' course. Here comes Menkent at last."

Another centaur came cantering in through the gate, a young male. "Hey, pussycats!" he yelled, cavorting around the sphinxes and kicking up his heels. "Wake up! Where's the mouse hole? Cough up your hair balls and let's go."

"I do hope we're ready," Bellatrix said. "Any more of his crap and the sphinxes will surely eat him." She carried Rigel over to join the group.

So now he'd joined the Mounties. His life just kept getting stranger and stranger.

Chapter 25

About twenty minutes later, Bellatrix said, "Call a harpy and tell Zozma we're ready."

"Why don't you?" Rigel retorted grumpily.

They were in an alley facing the harbor. She could peer out and see along Front Street in both directions. He could smell the sea, with wafts of cinnamon and coffee and tar; he could hear axles and pulleys squealing, sailors and porters and hucksters shouting; but all he could *see* was the back of her head. He had been sitting astride her too long for his physical comfort.

"Because the next time one of those stinking chickens insults me, I'm going to put five arrows through its crop."

"Sounds reasonable. Harpy!" That command invoked the message stud in his helmet, and a few moments later a female harpy flapped down to perch on a wall beside him.

"Hey, horsey! You got some shit on your back."

"Go and tell Commander Zozma that we're ready!" Rigel said.

"You think he'll care?" the harpy screeched, but it could not refuse the order and took off with a mad tumult of wings.

It was barely airborne before another landed in the space it had just vacated. "What's black and has six legs?" it demanded. "I'm talking to you, beetle."

"*Enif!*" the centaur snarled. A strung bow appeared in her left hand, an arrow in her right.

"Easy, easy!" Rigel said. "Ask it for its message first."

"Talk before I kebab you, vulture!" Bellatrix nocked the arrow.

Either the harpy recognized genuine peril, or it had a high cowardice coefficient. Maybe both. It took off even while screaming its message:

"Zozmasaystogoandmesseverythingupthewayyoualwaysdo."

"*Hold on tight!*" Bow and arrow vanished. Rigel barely had time to wrap his arms around the centaur's waist before they were out of the alley and leaning into a sharp left turn in a frenzied clatter of hooves, amidst cries of alarm from passing humans. He buried his head into Bellatrix's hard-muscled back, while keeping his grip safely below the danger zone she had mentioned earlier. They hurtled by wagons, carts, stalls, laden donkeys, screaming children, and a few outraged starfolk. Then Bellatrix clattered to a halt before an imposing iron-studded timber gate set in a high white-plastered wall.

"Stars be with you, halfling."

"Thanks for the ride."

Rigel dropped to the ground, staggered as he adjusted to being a biped again, and mentally crossed his fingers. Would the gate kill him outright or just char his arm? The multicolored Rongo-rongo script on the brass plate probably said something like, *Residence of Prince Vildiar, Trespassers will be Liquefied.* Rigel reached out his left hand, the one with the ring on it, and turned the handle. The gate opened. As he stepped through into a covered breezeway, he heard the centaur canter away, satisfied that she had played her part.

His heartbeat stabilized at about eight hundred, his blood pressure around a million. He had done it, and now it was too late to stop or go back, although Saiph was vibrating furiously. He must not hesitate or linger. Five quick steps took him through the archway to the courtyard Talitha had described and holographed in the Dolphin Room. It was bigger than he'd expected and she had left out the staircases on either side of the entrance. The trees were higher, and the courtyard was cluttered with assorted furniture and flowers galore. Black swans floated on one of the pools, while headless pink flamingoes stood asleep in another. But there were no people in sight. Maybe everyone had already left the property after all. His sense of relief was enormous; Rigel Estell was not cut out to be a burglar.

Saiph was still throbbing, though.

He continued walking, going fast but not running, keeping his head high as if he had every right to be there. He could see his destination in the center of the wall far ahead, two large double doors painted dark blue. He didn't look up to see if harpies were circling or perched on the tops of the walls, but Zozma had seemed confident that they would keep him informed of Rigel's progress. Or death, although he had not said that.

Talitha had been derogatory about the residence, but it would have made a first-class motel, and to a vagrant earthling minstrel, it seemed like a cozy little palace. Its white stucco walls and red-tile roof gave it a Mexican or Californian air. The portal was set back in an alcove, which might be helpful if Saiph had to hold it against a ravening horde.

That did seem unlikely now, in spite of the bracelet's continued warnings. He was halfway there, and no one had challenged him yet. Menkent would be setting out right about now, bringing Prince Kornephoros to de-magic the gate. By the time he arrived and started his work, Rigel should be at the portal, ready to play Horatio holding the bridge.

There were two men just ahead, on the balcony to his left.

He hadn't seen them when he'd first entered because they'd been hidden by hanging flower baskets. They were leaning on the balustrade, watching something below them, something behind the next bush Rigel had to pass. They wore SS riding britches, but were bare to the waist. The huge one was Hadar himself.

Whatever was holding their attention, they would certainly notice Rigel going past. The helmet hiding his white hair should keep them from recognizing him for a few moments. Even then, their reaction might be guarded until they realized that no starborn could wear a hat that shape. He forced his feet to keep walking, held his gaze straight forward.

A pair of bare feet came into sight on the grass beyond the bush, then ankles, then calves. Hairy calves, so not elfin. Heels up, toes down. Very little of the person underneath was visible other than her legs and arms, wrapped around her friend. *That sort of party!* That explained why Talitha had blushed when the queen had asked her if the court was overlooked, and why the two men on the balcony were being so quiet, not disturbing the performance.

"Who the stars are you?" They had seen him.

Their cries of outrage alerted the couple on the grass, who disentangled instantly. A real assassin would have killed both of them before they could get up, but Rigel just sprinted for the portal.

He reached the double doors and spun around. The alcove was too wide and shallow to force the defenders to come at him one at a time, but it would make it harder for them to get behind him. Here he had to make his stand until the sphinxes arrived. Here he had to block the escape route of killers fleeing justice, desperate men with nothing to lose. Here Saiph had to earn its reputation anew, against odds of three to one, and for the first time Rigel Halfling would be facing other swords, not unarmed suckers. They would undoubtedly try to use magic against him too, and he would need to rely on the defenses Wasat had given him.

No, he had miscounted; it would be four on one. The enraged lovers both came after him, armed from ankles to ears with amulets, wearing nothing except furious expressions. Happily the man was Tarf himself, and killing him would present no problem for Rigel's still-tender scruples. Naked, he looked more human than he had when clothed, aboard *Saidak* that morning; only the absence of a navel and nipples marked him as part elf, and that was masked by an abundance of human body hair. His tumescence was fading rapidly.

The woman was a halfling too—she had an elfin shape, almost-elfin ears, and blue hair, but human teeth and a navel. She was taller than Tarf and looked even more furious. A sword fight with a woman would be a nasty experience. The two of them stopped just out of reach.

Tarf said, "You!" and showed his sawtooth dentition. "Pretty boy Rigel has decided to change sponsors already? Momma didn't waste any time."

Every second Rigel could delay the battle was more time for the queen's forces to arrive. "What makes you think so?"

"Take off your amulets and we'll talk," Tarf responded. Every second he could delay the battle would be more time for Hadar to arrive with reinforcements.

Nevertheless, talking was safer than fighting. Should this moment of confrontation occur, Zozma had suggested, Rigel ought to read out the queen's warrant. Rigel had explained the problem with that plan. But he produced the scroll he had tucked into the waistband of his wrap and tossed it at Tarf's feet, where it was ignored.

"Queen Electra is back, halfling. That is a warrant for your arrest on a whole pile of charges, with an offer of clemency if you surrender peacefully. You," he told the woman, Adhil, "keep out of this."

"I'll have your balls for earrings!" A sword appeared in her hand, flashing sunlight.

Good! The other side had drawn first.

"Wait!" Tarf laughed. He held up both hands. "Oh, please, Halfling Rigel, don't hurt us. We were only having a little innocent fun. The lady will be very happy to have you join our party, won't you my precious? You can go next, and I'm sure we can figure the other matter out before she performs the surgery she has suggested."

He was stalling for time, too. That much was obvious because Saiph was quivering harder than ever. The two goons up on the balcony were probably too high up to jump down without injury, and the stairs were at the far end of the courtyard. Reluctant as he was to attack first, Rigel knew he needed to put Tarf out of the fight before the others could join in.

A harpy swooped overhead. "Hey, pothead! You're outnumbered, boy! You're dead meat." It banked and returned. "Zozma says he's on his way, but I wouldn't count on him arriving in time if I were you."

Halfway through that speech, and very much to his own astonishment, Rigel leaped at Tarf. Saiph appeared in his hand, of course, and about ten centimeters of steel slid into Tarf's belly before the halfling could invoke his own magic sword to parry. Saiph slit him open, then flashed around to parry a clumsy stroke from the woman.

One down. Tarf screamed as he collapsed, clutching his wound and spraying blood through his fingers. That helped pay for the massacre in the Walmart store at least. Rigel went after Adhil, but either his heart wasn't in it, or she didn't represent a real threat to him, because Saiph failed to even nick her.

The two men in the balcony jumped. Rather than risk broken ankles or worse, they leaped into the nearest of the ornamental pools, landing in a huge explosion of water and startled flamingoes.

Adhil's retreat had drawn Rigel away from the portal, so he had to back up quickly as Hadar and Muscida came charging into the fight, both soaking wet and bare to the waist, each armed with both a sword and a parrying dagger. Hadar was an oversized gorilla; blond Muscida would have seemed quite starborn had he not been humanly hairy. Metal rang and rang. For a few moments the battle seemed quite equal. Moving in a blur, Saiph held off the two men despite their additional weapons, and Adhil's efforts to help them just got in their way.

Suddenly an enormous clanging sound flooded the courtyard, like the sound of a giant shaking an iron foundry. Rigel guessed that it was an alarm to warn those inside that someone was using magic on the gate's defenses. So Kornephoros had started work at last. It startled him, but it startled his opponents more, because it came from behind them. That was all the advantage Saiph needed to lunge deep into Muscida's neck and then swing free to parry a haymaker scythe-slash by

Hadar. Rigel did not escape unscathed, though, for the giant's dagger sliced his left shoulder. He registered blood spurting, but he was too fired up by the fight to feel pain.

Adhil screamed, Muscida toppled to the ground, and the action paused for an instant while both sides assessed the situation. Muscida writhed in his death throes—gurgling, vomiting blood, and pumping out arterial rivers of it. Rigel was wounded, but the magical defenses Wasat had given him had already stemmed the bleeding.

Tarf, too, must have possessed healing amulets. He should have been dead or dying, but he was on his feet again, bloody and bloody mad. Baring his teeth, he threw a fireball at Rigel. The ball exploded before it hit, giving him a mild, tingling shock and a momentary glimpse of a multicolored glass barrier. He could not retaliate in kind, because Wasat hadn't had the time to explain how all of his new amulets should be used.

Tarf caught hold of Muscida's right ankle and callously hauled him out of the way of the fight. The dying halfling managed a scream that died in a gurgle and a fountain of blood.

"Adhil, beloved," Hadar said, "you burn his balls off and we'll stick him."

The woman stood aside and began hurling a stream of fireballs. Rigel's amulets protected him from them, although he found them distracting. Saiph, fortunately, did not, and their only real effect was to scorch the door behind him, which smoked and gave off a foul smell of burning paint.

Tarf snarled and stepped back into the fray. For a moment the three combatants stood poised at guard, and then Saiph tried a feint at Hadar. Hadar blocked and lunged high while Tarf came in low. Saiph beat them both off, but they kept coming, and the battle grew fierce. The brothers' resemblance was more apparent when they fought side by side. They moved smoothly together, as if they'd practiced this way for years. No doubt they had.

Hadar was very good. Talitha had classed his amulet, Sulfur-something, as being almost as ancestral as Saiph. It was making the big man move even faster than his small brother, and Tarf was no slouch as a swordsman. Rigel was soon gasping for breath and streaming sweat, as his body tried to keep up with Saiph's inhuman demands.

Thrust—parry—riposte—counter—engage . . . on and on, feet and arms in constant motion. Had any of the amulet's previous owners died of a heart attack? How long could his muscles possibly hold up under this strain? And through it all, he had to stay far enough from the door to leave himself room to retreat, but not so far that the brothers could get behind him.

Why was the idiot Kornephoros taking so long? Were the sphinxes never going to get here? Would that terrible din never stop? How long could Adhil keep throwing the damnable fireballs?

Stamina amulet or not, Rigel was close to collapse, but so were the others. Saiph and Sulaphat were the best. Whatever sword Tarf was wielding was no match for either of those, and he had been wounded earlier. Inevitably, he was the one who failed first. He slowed just enough for Saiph to slash him across the face.

Seconds later, the din came to a sudden stop. With a very different sort of thunder, the gates flew off their hinges, propelled by centaur hooves, and sphinxes poured into the court.

Rigel tried to lunge at Hadar, but was blocked by Tarf's collapsing body. Hadar grabbed Adhil and threw her bodily at Rigel. Her sword flashed into her hand, but Saiph impaled her before she could do any damage. Using Rigel's momentary distraction to full advantage, Hadar dived through the portal. Rigel slumped to the ground exhausted, and the world darkened.

Chapter 26

"M agnificent!" Menkent yelled, scooping Rigel up in his arms as he would a child. "Incredible! The harpies were telling us all about it." He clattered over to a pool and waded across to hold Rigel's face under a stream of water emerging from a marble putto. Rigel gulped it down thirstily. "You got three of them!"

Rigel spluttered, trying to say that Hadar had escaped.

"Had enough?" the centaur asked. "Ready to bathe now?" He released the halfling with a big splash.

Rigel struggled to his feet, cursing. But the cold water felt very good—refreshing, cleansing. His legs were shaking so hard he could barely stand. He drank some more from the cherub's stream.

Zozma stood on the edge of the water, his smile not at all inscrutable. "Well done, Rigel Halfling! A great feat of arms."

No it wasn't. It was a great feat of magic, and Rigel had only been a puppet. He staggered to the edge of the pool, heading back to the scene of the fight, but when he tried to climb out, his arms would not obey him. Menkent, following close behind him, obligingly lifted him out. Though the young centaur lacked Bellatrix's weightlifter build, he had impressive strength. His horse portion was bay, his scalp bore a curly mop of reddish-brown curls, and he had the beginnings of a red-gold beard around what seemed to be a permanent grin.

Rigel forced himself to inspect the bodies—Muscida already corpse-white, Adhil flat on her back with a seemingly trivial wound over her heart, Tarf with his face cut in half. Yet the great gash was still oozing blood, and Prince Kornephoros was kneeling over him, clutching the halfling's head and muttering under his breath. Bellatrix knelt beside him, cutting away Tarf's bracelets with a dagger. A heap of rings and ear studs glittered on the pavement.

"He's alive?" Rigel asked incredulously.

"His Highness is hoping to revive him."

The scorched and blistered portal was closed once more. Only Rigel was invisible to any booby traps it might have. He tottered over to it, and three sphinxes moved in with him to see what he might find. Saiph offered no warning, so he went ahead and turned the handle. He found a closet with a stack of wooden chairs.

Kornephoros rose to his feet, scowling at the bloodstains on his hands and knees. "Hopeless!"

"This portal may still be booby-trapped," Rigel told him. "It should be inspected before you seal it."

"If I need advice on magic, boy, you will not be the first person I turn to. The idea was to arrest them. You staged a massacre."

"I regret that I did not kill all of them."

"That is not how we do things in the Starlands."

It was the way Hadar and his brothers did things. Rigel needed rest—he was going to be as stiff as a tombstone after his exertions—but he had more important things to do first. He turned his back on the prince and headed over to Menkent, the only friendly one in the whole bunch.

"May I ask a favor?"

The centaur widened his ever-present grin a few notches. "Ask away, hero. I'm not great at climbing trees, but I'm willing to try anything else."

"I need to tell the princess something. It's very urgent."

"Always happy to oblige a hero." Menkent turned his tail on Rigel and sat down, reaching both arms back. Rigel offered his wrists to the centaur and was hauled aboard. "Hold tight!" The centaur folded Rigel's arms around his waist, but he kept a firm grip on them so that he would not lose his still-shaky passenger. "Next stop, the palace!" He took off at a canter, cornered sharply onto Front Street, and geared up to a gallop. By then Rigel had put himself to sleep.

"You did say urgent?"

Rigel started awake. "What? Yes, very." His nap must have been brief, but it seemed to have helped. His muscles were not shivering quite as much.

"Good." Menkent cantered past the sphinx at the gate and straight up the staircase, ignoring the angry shouts that followed him. "Always wanted to see what's up here."

He was probably kidding, because he knew exactly where he was going through the maze of corridors. Talitha and a circle of a dozen or so starborn ladies were dining in a hall even larger than the Dolphin Room, each one seated at her own small table. Starling maidens were serving them, while human servants bore platters of food in from the kitchens and tended the heaped sideboard. The queen was not present. Courtly ladies cried out in alarm and disgust at the sight of a centaur invading their banquet.

Talitha shouted, "Rigel!" and came running to his side as he made an unsteady dismount. "Oh, Rigel, Rigel, I was so worried!"

For a giddy moment he thought she was going to throw herself at him, but then she recoiled. "You've been wounded!"

"It's nothing." He had forgotten the cut on his shoulder, which was already closed and healing. He was back on the angel team, apparently, anger forgotten. She was calling him 'Rigel' and not 'halfling.'"

"Zozma sent word! You're a hero! I'm so proud of . . . What's wrong?"

Rigel glanced up uneasily at the centaur's idiot grin.

"Yes," Menkent said, "tell us what was so urgent."

"Would you like something to eat, Menkent Centaur?" Talitha asked.

He glanced longingly at the sideboard. "Well, if you don't mind, Your Highness . . ."

"Please help yourself."

"What do centaurs eat?" Rigel asked as the big fellow headed for the feast. The sight of so much food was a reminder that he had not eaten since dawn and now the sun was setting.

"Anything they can get their hands on. I do hope he stays off the rugs. Now, tell me what's wrong."

"Tarf was there, and Hadar, and one called Muscida."

"Yes, yes. I heard. Hadar escaped, and you killed the other two. What is *wrong*?"

"The first thing Tarf said to me was, 'Pretty boy Rigel has come to change his sponsor already? Momma didn't waste any time.'"

Talitha frowned blankly.

Rigel said, "Tarf and Tegmine heard you say that Izar was going home with Baham." The Baham whom she did not completely trust. "I think you should check on him."

"What?" She lost color. "Why? But . . . Oh, Rigel! No! No! Starfolk do not do things like that!"

"But halflings do. That's what we're for, isn't it? You starfolk only tolerate us to do your dirty work. Hadar and his gang would see it as a fair offer: You send them Saiph, meaning me, and they send you back your son. Except they wouldn't, of course."

"I must tell the queen!"

"Who will do what?" Rigel said. "Send for Vildiar? If you can even find him, he will swear on the Star of Truth that he has no idea where his son is and you're not competent to look after him anyway."

She nodded. "You're right. We must go to Izar immediately!" A dark cloud of worry had gathered around her.

"How?"

"My root portal is here in Canopus. I'm just trying to think of the fastest way to get there."

"By centaur! Come along." Rigel grabbed her wrist and pulled her over to the sideboard, where Menkent was eating his way through an entire roast goose under—actually *over*—the horrified eyes of the palace staff. He looked down at Rigel with a gleam in his eye and a mouth too full to speak.

"Still urgent," Rigel said. "The princess and I desperately need to visit Spica."

Talitha said, "Rigel, it's a terrible insult to ask a centaur to be a horse!"

Menkent gulped his cud disgustingly. "I don't mind. 'Long as it's urgent, so I have an excuse, and you tell me why. Where to?"

"Ascella Square."

"Hop on, then." Still holding half his goose, the centaur reached for an entire ham to go.

Once they were both mounted, with Talitha holding on to him and Rigel holding on to her—which made this the best part of the day so far—Menkent picked his way carefully down the long staircase. "You have no idea how hard it is to balance like this," he said cheerfully, but he continued to alternate bites of ham and goose.

"We're very grateful for your help," Talitha assured him.

"My pleasure. Any chance of a fight in this? My dam promised me one today, and I didn't get it."

Could he mean that Bellatrix was his mother?

Talitha said, "Probably not. You know my imp, Izar?"

"Course! Great colt. Fearless."

"We're worried that he's been kidnapped."

The centaur's roar of outrage startled the sphinx at the bottom of the stairs, who sprang around with her claws out.

"Futon stars! Are you *sure* there won't be a fight? That's one I would *really* enjoy."

The sun had just set. The streets were almost deserted, but Menkent was feeling his load, and kept his pace down to a fast walk, while still crunching goose bones.

"Describe Spica to me," Rigel said. He was close enough to nibble Talitha's ears if he wanted to. He did want but didn't do it. Her scent was intoxicating, all the more so because it didn't come out of a bottle.

"It's still tiny. I started it after my pairing with Vildiar ended—there is a river that provides good swimming and fishing, some trees, half a dozen buildings, and a unicorn stud. That's all, really."

"How many people, apart from you and Izar?"

She thought for a moment. "Six. Over twenty if you include earthlings. A couple of the females . . . Two of the women are expecting."

Rigel was left with the unpleasant certainty that Talitha, like the rest of the starfolk, made small distinction between two-legged and four-legged livestock. She ran both unicorn and human studs.

"What a day this has been!" she said. "Tell me about the fight."

"Not sure I can. I was too busy to notice, and my amulet did all the work for me. There were four of them: Hadar, Tarf, and Muscida, plus a halfling girl called Adhil."

"Another of the brood, one of the worst."

"There must be someone else by that name, because when I arrived she and Tarf were . . . um, hard at it."

"Rigel, Rigel! Any evil or crime or perversion you can imagine, they practice. They make dares to find out who's the worst. Incest is nothing to them; they know they're sterile, anyway. Don't you understand yet why I don't want my son back in their clutches?" She leaned back against him. "I'm sorry I shouted at you earlier."

"Then you owe me a second kiss," he whispered. He slid his hands up her body until they touched the undersides of her breasts. She stiffened, then relaxed when he did nothing more. He said, "And I shouted at you, so I owe you one too."

"We'll see," she murmured. Had she noticed that Menkent's ears were tilted backwards? "That door under the cherry tree, centaur."

They dismounted and climbed the six steps to the door.

Menkent followed right on their heels. As Talitha reached for the handle, he said, "No! Let me go into the house first. There may be a trap, and your halfling's fought enough today."

Curiosity killed the centaur, but Rigel was certainly in no shape for another battle, tonight or hopefully ever. "Good thinking . . . my lady." *He had almost called her "darling"!* "Hadar may be waiting inside. Any servants?"

"No. You think I wouldn't know if the lock had been forced?" But she did stand aside to let the centaur squeeze his bulk past them and open the door. A stud on one of his ears lit up as he went inside.

Rigel winced at the sound of iron shoes on hardwood floors. "I need a lesson in magic. If Hadar and the others did want to raid your domain and carry off Izar, how would they manage it?"

She hugged herself, which was a waste of good hugging. "Easy. By air. I have a link to Dziban, so two hops would do it—Phegda to Dziban to Spica."

Thumps from inside suggested that the centaur was now climbing stairs. Talitha shuddered. Then came a resounding crash and some baritone curses. A few moments later, Menkent backed out of the door. "It's a little tight in there, Your Highness, but there's no sign of intruders except that somebody's knocked over your china cabinet. I'm sure he meant well."

"That doesn't matter. Thank you. Now let me in to open the portal."

"And this time I'll go first," Rigel said.

Chapter 27

Saiph in hand, he stepped through the portal and into a spacious room that was obviously modeled on some North American ranch. Roof, walls, floor, and furniture were all of wood, decorated with bright rugs, cushions, and colorful Mexican hats. A nostalgic odor of wood smoke lingered, although the hearth in the great fieldstone fireplace was cold, and the evening twilight cast a romantic glow over everything—everything, that is, except for the dead body lying almost at his feet.

He backed out hurriedly, pulling the door closed so that Talitha would not see. "Bad news," he said, and told her.

"Get out of my way!"

He let her go, and followed. She twisted a finger ring to make light. The dead man was Albireo the swanherd, and he had obviously been cut down while trying to reach the portal.

"Izar! Izar!" Talitha started racing through the ranch house yelling her son's name, with Rigel right behind her. Then they went outside and explored all the other buildings. It was a fruitless search, as she admitted later, because she wore an amulet that could track her son, alive or dead, and it was not registering him in Spica. Though they did not find Izar, there were bodies everywhere—men, women, starfolk, halflings, children of all species. Rigel counted twenty-two corpses, and there could have been more out in the pasture. Most had blade wounds, a few had been shot through with arrows, and one or two had been burned almost beyond recognition. Every biped who had been in Spica was dead, with two exceptions.

Izar was gone, and Starborn Baham was conspicuously not among the bodies they found.

They finished back at the house, standing outside the front door with Rigel's arms tight around Talitha, who was weeping uncontrollably. He was very conscious of the body contact. Why must what he had wanted so much happen under such horrible circumstances?

"I am being a weak, useless, childish fool!" she mumbled.

"No. You starfolk are not accustomed to atrocities. On Earth we live with them all the time—TV, magazines, newspapers, movies, books, all full of violence, real or invented. You'll be okay in a few minutes, when you can think straight again. The important thing is that they *took* Izar. They didn't hurt him."

They might have frightened the poor imp half to death, though, and they probably had not been gentle.

Menkent, who had galloped off to check on the livestock, returned in a thunder of hooves, breathing hard and shining damp in the starlight. "Fourteen unicorns are alive," he panted, "and one is dead in the field. A puma cub is dead in its cage. There are four live cows, two live swans with some cygnets they wouldn't let me near enough to count—thought they were going to eat me—one dead starborn, and four dead dogs."

"Four?" Talitha said, rubbing away tears with the back of her hand. "We only had three dogs."

"One very *big* dog?" Rigel asked. "Where is it?"

It was Turais, of course, lying in the pasture near the dead unicorn, which Talitha identified as Izar's Narwhale. Having explained about Fomalhaut's gift, Rigel knelt to examine the scene by the light on his helmet. Turais had put up quite a fight, judging by the way the ground was torn up.

"This is more than just dog blood. Turais has blood on his muzzle, see?" He also had bloody flesh between his teeth. "I hope he took a few of them with him." If he had, the attackers had carried off their dead. How many of them had there been? Wishing that he could read the signs like trackers in stories did, he stood up and offered Talitha another embrace, but she had recovered her poise and pretended not to notice the invitation.

"Dead starborn over here," Menkent said

Baham lay with two arrows in him and a sword by his hand, on grass painted silver by moonlight, looking like some romantic lithograph of a fallen hero.

Talitha choked and turned her back. "I misjudged him. He wasn't a traitor. He died doing his duty."

That was certainly the obvious interpretation. Rigel Halfling, that overly suspicious soul, could speculate that the guard had betrayed his charge and then been double-crossed by the killers. With no way to prove or disprove the possibility, he saw no reason to mention it.

"Now what?" he said. "Back to Canopus so that we can complain to Queen Electra?"

"Back to Canopus and burn the royal ear!"

They headed for the house. Neither of them spoke until Talitha stopped to look down at a corpse sprawled a few steps from the front door.

"Caph! She was my nurse when I was a child, Rigel. She is in all my earliest memories. Stars know how old she was, but she had no ambition, only a love of imps. Caph lacked enough magic to imagine her own domain, and I doubt if she ever even paired. She just lived for other people's children. She helped me with Izar and stayed on after he had outgrown her care."

"Then we must see that her death and all these other deaths shall not be in vain. Have Vildiar's thugs ever committed a massacre like this before?"

"Never! I doubt if there has been such an atrocity in the Starlands in the last thousand years."

"So now they have overreached themselves. Thanks, indirectly, to Starborn Fomalhaut, I think. As soon as *Saidak* arrived in Canopus, Tarf or Tegmine must have run to Front Street, portaled home to Phegda, and told Hadar about Izar. Daddy wanted Izar, and Izar had gone to Spica, so the brutes decided to come and get him. Would any of the other halfings besides Hadar have made that decision?"

Talitha nodded. "Botein might have. This bloodbath seems too clumsy for Hadar, but carry on."

"They came here. Izar was waylaid out in the fields riding Narwhale, yes? If Baham was escorting him, he would certainly have been mounted too, which explains why he was shot down with a bow. Perfect. But the kidnappers had not reckoned on the guard dog. They found they had far more of a fight on their hands than they'd expected. By the time they'd dealt with Turais, either Izar himself or Baham's runaway mount had raised the alarm. They were seen. Not wanting to leave witnesses, they killed everyone. But—don't you see?— this was decided before anyone knew that the queen was back."

Talitha laughed thinly. "And she won't stand for it! Oh, do they ever have a surprise—"

"Something's coming," Menkent said, staring up at the skies with his ears askew. "A pegasus, I think." A bow flashed into his left hand.

"The only pegasus I know is Markab," Talitha said. "That means Vildiar."

The centaur notched an arrow. "It'll be a tricky shot in this light, but I'm good. I'll get him for you."

"No!" she snapped. "I want my son back."

The centaur sighed and lowered his bow, but did not put it away.

Rigel had known from his first glimpse of Gienah the swan that she was aerodynamically impossible. A flying horse must be even more so, unless it had a chest a kilometer wide to hold all the muscle it would need. Yet the great beast circling lower in the starlight undoubtedly had the traditional pegasus shape—a handsome white steed with plumed wings. Its rider had seen their lights and was coming in to land nearby.

Land the pegasus did, as lightly as a bee, although it was the largest horse Rigel had ever seen. It folded its great wings and the rider dismounted. Making no effort to tether or hobble it, he came striding over to the group. Inhumanly tall, bizarrely emaciated, pale as a specter—Prince Vildiar was unmistakable. He stopped a few feet in front of them and frowned down at the corpse at their feet.

"What happened here?"

"Twenty-three people were murdered by some of your sons," Talitha said.

Vildiar looked thoughtfully at Rigel—as if analyzing the helmet or wondering whether it was the right time to bring up the subject of the two sons and a daughter who had been slain at his Front Street house—and then at the centaur, who held a feather close to his right eye and a steel arrowhead at his left thumb, the shaft between them pointing directly at the prince's heart.

"Order that idiot monstrosity to lower his bow, or I'll kill him."

"Put it away, Menkent," Talitha said.

"Yes, Your Highness." The centaur's bow cracked like a gunshot, making Rigel jump. The sound was followed by a resounding thump as Markab the pegasus collapsed to the ground. "See that?" Menkent exulted. "Right through it! The arrow went right through its heart and out the other side."

Vildiar raised a hand . . .

"*No!*" Talitha stepped between them. "There has been enough killing tonight. And you deserve it after what happened here. Where is my son?"

"*Our* son," said the giant in a withering tone. "The last I know of him was that you disobeyed the regent this morning and sent him back here to Spica. And before you start screaming, I assure you that I do *not* know where he is. I do *not* know who took him or killed the people here, and I did *not* order it."

Talitha said, "Ha! But if you find him in a dungeon at Phegda, you will return him to me at once, won't you?"

"No. I do not expect to find him at Phegda, and even if I do, I shall wait for a ruling from the throne. The regent was prepared to consider the question of custody in court this morning until your halfling started slaughtering sphinxes left and right. You are not well positioned to argue about massacres, my darling ex-consort."

"But now Queen Electra has returned! The game has changed, Prince."

"It has, although everything Electra has achieved so far demonstrates that her powers continue to wane. She sent her palace guard and this murderous tweenling of yours to storm my residence and kill three valued halflings. You were not the only one wronged today. And now your semi-intelligent horse has slain my priceless pegasus."

"So if you did not come to demand ransom for Izar, why are you here?"

"Ah, yes," Vildiar said sadly. "In the midst of all this useless recrimination I forgot my original purpose. I am the bearer of very bad news, Talitha dear. Your father is grievously stricken. I promised the queen I would find you and bring you to Canopus as soon as possible."

"Stricken? What sort of stricken?"

The giant shrugged. "They are not sure. Some sort of curse or poison. He is in terrible pain and not expected to live."

Chapter 28

Talitha and Vildiar hurried off through the portal. Rigel hung back, staying between the prince and the centaur to discourage any attempts at revenge for the killing of the pegasus. He could easily imagine the starborn hurling a sneaky fireball as a parting shot. He worried about the bodies in Spica needing burial or cremation or whatever the starfolk did at funerals. Who was going to look after them?

When he emerged into Ascella Square, he found it brightly lit by a near-full moon and the ear lights of a melee of sphinxes, starborn, and halflings. Among them stood several human servants—most of them wearing livery that might have graced Hollywood Regency romances—and unicorns harnessed to small two-wheeled gigs little larger than the sulkies used in harness racing. As he watched, Talitha was being driven away in one. He let Menkent precede him down the steps into the crowd, then made sure that the house door was locked before following him. The centaur hurried off into the crowd, probably looking for something else to eat.

The smells of Canopus were already familiar, a blend of spices, desert dust, horses, sweaty people, and a faint tang of the sea. Palm trees showed dark against the moonlit sky.

"Halfling Rigel."

Rigel turned to face the speaker. "Sphinx Praecipua."

"Come with me. You are included on the list."

"What list?"

The guard's beard twitched in annoyance. "The list of persons who are summoned to the palace."

That was good news, for Rigel would certainly have gotten lost on his own. He was in serious need of both food and rest, and he suspected that this night was far from over. "Thank you. There has been a massacre at the princess's domain—more than twenty people murdered. Who will attend to those bodies and investigate the crime?"

"Her Highness has already reported the matter to us. We have it in hand." Praecipua halted at one of the gigs. The unicorn flicked its ears uneasily, as if detecting the scent of a large carnivore nearby.

"What news of the heir?" Rigel asked.

"There has been no announcement about His Highness's condition," the guard said guardedly.

"Halfling!" Prince Vildiar had folded his great length into another one of the gigs and was beckoning to him.

Rigel walked over and offered an insolently small bow. "Your Highness?"

"You testified this morning that you are ignorant of your parentage."

"Yes, my lord."

"Then it is time you heard the true story. Get in." Vildiar took the reins from his driver, who obediently dismounted.

Saiph did not react, so whatever lay behind this surprising invitation was not immediate revenge for Tarf, Adhil, and Muscida. Rigel took the driver's place, and off they went. The prince set a dignified pace into the dark-shrouded streets, steering with his hands between his knees, which stuck up as high as Rigel's helmet.

"Back in the year of orange stars, the regent-heir proposed that his daughter and I enter into a pairing, which is a legal agreement to produce and rear a child. Talitha was—"

"When was that, my lord? I am not familiar with your calendar."

"Or good manners. Do not interrupt your betters. Twenty-three years ago. Talitha was not yet of legal age and very immature. Normally I do not pair with children, but His Highness was concerned about the shortage of Naos in the realm. You are aware of Naos, I hope?"

"Yes, sir."

"We seem to have become rarer over the last couple of millennia and we had recently lost many fine Naos in an unfortunate series of accidents. Such clusters of bad events do happen in nature, like falling stars or droughts, and only the ignorant seek evil, unnatural explanations for them. I agreed to the pairing. Talitha proved less willing, but she has always been headstrong. As a minor, she should have obeyed her father; as a Naos, she was forbidden from entering into a pairing without the consent of the monarch. The same rule applies to me, although neither Electra nor Procyon before her ever refused my requests."

That was hardly surprising, given his murderous reputation. The unicorn was trotting along in its own shadow, cast far ahead by light from an amulet in the prince's right ear. The street was a dark canyon, too deep for moonlight to penetrate, but bats wheeled and whistled overhead, and somewhere a hopeful swain was singing a love song. Someone ought to throw a chamber pot at him.

Vildiar continued his sad sermon. "Talitha was young, as I said, and headstrong. She sought to block the pairing by doing the unthinkable—she deliberately conceived a child by an earthling. In your world's terms, that is worse than a high status lady giving herself to a beggar in an alley. It is almost as vile as bestiality."

Rigel did not ask whether the same taboo applied to starborn males and human females, because he already knew the answer and did not want to be evicted from the sulky and left to walk.

"The pairing ceremony had to be cancelled, of course. The scandal would have been tremendous—even worse than we initially thought, because she had refused to name the father. We eventually discovered that he could have been any one of several minor mudling servants in Dziban. I am afraid that you will never uncover that half of your parentage."

"Half is better than nothing. It is exciting to learn that I have royal blood in my veins."

Vildiar shot him a suspicious glance, and then went back to watching the road.

"The child was born in the year of red pelicans. It . . . *you . . .* obviously had human ears and your other physical features that would allow you to pass for human. We consequently arranged for a skilled mage to take you to Earth and give you to a woman who had just lost a baby. I would have been within my rights to refuse to have anything to do with Talitha, but the scandal had been successfully suppressed, so I accepted the regent-heir's wishes and paired with her as soon as she recovered from your birth. She bore Izar in black butterflies, two years after you. By mutual consent we let the pairing lapse at the end of its primary term. The rest you know."

"Not all, Your Highness. Who put Saiph around my cute little wrist?"

"Talitha, of course." Vildiar lowered opalescent eyebrows in a frown. "This morning that decrepit halfling said that Queen Electra was the last to check it out of the archives store. She did come and go more in those days, but I have no recollection of her being anywhere in the Starlands as late as that. Her last sighting before this morning, that I recall, was at a pairing celebration back in the year of violet fists. She continued to attend pairing parties long after most other topics had palled for her, so I am sure she would have become involved in the matter I just disclosed to you if she'd been around to hear of it."

"But—"

"The Star punishes deliberate lies. Honest mistakes it ignores. The curator reported what he saw in his records. He thought he remembered the queen's visit, but it was a long time ago, and he is aging, as your sort do. Wasat must have been thinking of some other trip she made in search of some other amulet. His wrongful testimony this morning was a considerable surprise to both the regent-heir and myself, and undoubtedly to Talitha as well—a huge relief, in fact, because we were braced for the scandal of the century."

Izar had not inherited all his creative talent from his mother.

Rigel tried not to display his skepticism too openly. "I have seen the archives store, my lord, and I am astonished that even my sponsor could manage to steal anything from there. She is a starborn of great talents, but how did she manage such a feat?"

"Easily. A princess has the right to borrow low-grade amulets from the royal collection. I expect Talitha made some excuse to visit the archives, stole Saiph while the old man's back was turned, and forged the queen's name in the ledger when signing for some minor amulet or other. When she was allowed to hold you for a few moments after your birth, she palmed the amulet and slipped it onto your wrist. After that, it could not be removed."

A touching tale, but a violin accompaniment would have added pathos.

The sulky jiggled along an avenue of gigantic seated statues, so huge that only their moonlit toes and shins were visible from the road below them. Then it turned into the palace by an entrance that Rigel had not seen before. The unicorn's hooves clinked across a great courtyard, and it pulled to a stop in front of a doorway. Vildiar reined in at the steps. A sphinx bowed to him, touching his beard to the ground.

"Three days ago," Rigel said, thinking that it felt like years, "Fomalhaut Starborn introverted me from Earth. How did he find me, and why was he looking for me?"

"For that you will have to ask the mage himself, halfling."

"He refuses to talk to me."

"Not surprising. I never speak to halflings myself, but I have made a reluctant exception in your case. If you recall that the mage delivered you straight to your natural mother at Alrisha, then I think you can deduce the most likely explanation. I suggest you ask the sphinxes to find you a place to sleep tonight. Your mother will be busy tending to her sick father. If she wants you, the harpies will find you. Now you understand, of course, why she has been taking such an interest in you, and why she could not possibly tell you the true reason."

"And why I felt so attracted to her." Rigel dismounted. "It is strange how instincts work, isn't it? Thank you for your kindness and the illuminating story, Your Highness. You have explained a lot that I wanted to know."

He bowed and watched the prince drive away.

"Male ungulate excrement!"

The sphinx said, "What?"

"Just a passing opinion. Do harpies fly by night?"

"Certainly. There is a perching wall over there." He pointed with his tail.

"Thank you." Rigel walked to the place indicated, which had a fusty smell, like a henhouse. He said, "Harpy!"

Several minutes passed before a familiar flapping announced a bird's arrival.

"What crap is this?" it squawked. "Dragged off my roost in the middle of the night to wait on a freaking ignorant half-breed with its head in a bucket?"

Rigel produced Saiph. "Go tell the queen it's time that she and I had a little chat, and if you say one more word I'll fillet you. Go!"

He found a marble bench that looked appealingly comfortable to him in his present condition. He stretched out, primed what Izar would call his "self" to awaken when spoken to, and made the world disappear.

Chapter 29

Halfling Rigel?"

Rigel opened his eyes and sat up with a wince—he was as stiff as a hockey stick. The moon had covered about an hour's worth of sky. The man standing over him was human, wearing a jeweled collar of office with the cotton gown and head covering of a mudling.

"I am."

"What business do you have with Her Majesty that needs disturb her at this time of night?"

He was a youngish man, with a solid build, as far as could be seen under his robe, and quite tall for a mudling. Rigel rose to his full 196½ centimeters and looked down on him.

"What business is that of yours?"

"I am Alfred, Her Majesty's private secretary."

"And did the harpy I sent speak to her or to you?"

"To her, of course."

"Then so will I."

"Follow me." The man turned and stalked away, following a light from a finger amulet.

Rigel caught up in two strides to walk alongside him. "How long have you been her private secretary?"

"I do not see how that concerns you, halfling." But the man's expression showed more amusement than annoyance.

"It doesn't. I was just thinking that if she appointed you before she disappeared twenty-odd years ago, your workload must have increased rather drastically in the last few hours."

"And the stars are many." A Starlands agreement, no doubt.

"How is Regent-heir Kornephoros?"

"Dying."

Alfred opened a door. A rush of cooler air and unfamiliar scents proved that it was a portal, and Rigel stepped through into somewhere very different from the palace at Canopus. Instead of monumental stone, it had hardwood floors, plaster cornices, and thick rugs. The windows were hung with heavy drapes, the walls lined with gilt-framed pictures and animal head trophies. It smelled of dust and old polish. He was led to a long flight of stairs.

"Where in the world is this?"

"We're still in the Starlands, and still in the royal domain. This is Balmoral, a royal retreat, pseudo-Victoriana kitsch. Her Majesty commanded that you wait in here." Alfred opened another door and went ahead to turn on several lamps that were passable imitations of gaslights. They illuminated a vast four-poster bed, two stuffed armchairs, a marble-topped washstand, and two ugly, oversized wood chests. The air was stale, smelling of dust and mildew, and the only charitable thing to say about the gloomy paintings of cloud-racked moors that covered the walls was that they hid some of the wallpaper.

"What happened to whoever imagined this place?" Rigel asked.

"He was extroverted to the Spanish Inquisition."

"Glad to hear it. I have not eaten since early this morning, and murder makes me hungry."

Alfred smiled. "Me too. I shall see what I can do."

He departed, closing the door behind him.

Curious! Why would a royal private secretary be so tolerant of a lowly halfling's sassing? It would be interesting to know exactly what instructions the queen had given him. Rigel flopped into one of the velour chairs, which smelled distinctly musty, and prepared to salivate for an hour while someone made him a cockroach sandwich.

He hadn't reckoned on the power of magic. In a few minutes Alfred returned, wheeling a trolley laden with steaks, hotcakes, fried eggs over easy, hash browns, pie and ice cream, and a large decanter of orange juice.

Imagine that! Rigel ate it all, and was barely finished before the door opened and Electra entered.

He hauled himself off the chair and bowed.

At first she didn't even look at him. "Jesus, what a mess!" she said, as if speaking to herself. "And I used to find running the Starlands boring." She walked over to the washstand and poured water from the urn into the basin. "In all my 1,776 years, I have never witnessed such a fuckup." She rinsed her face with her hands, then turned to face him.

"Hello, Rigel."

"Hello, Mom."

She half-smiled, half-nodded. "Sit. You look beat. I sure as hell feel it."

"How's the prince?"

"Still dying, but he won't be much longer."

Why was he dying? He didn't ask. "I'm sorry."

"No, you're not. Kornephoros was one pissy, stuck-up elf, and you wanted to kick his butt real hard."

And often. "I am sorry for Talitha's sake. This is a bad time for you too. Our talk can wait." He had been given the confirmation he came for.

"No." She waved him back into his chair. "It can't. This is important; you're important. You love Talitha?"

Not the question he had expected. "If it were possible for a halfling to aspire to love a starborn, I would throw my heart at her feet."

"And who would clean up the mess? I asked her about you." She hauled open the draperies on the four-poster. "Close your eyes."

He closed. "And?"

"The hots. No shit. She's head over her pretty little heels for you. She's yours any time you make your move, I'd say. You can look now." Her Majesty was in bed, with the covers pulled up to her waist and her discarded wrap lying on the floor. She arranged the pillows and leaned back on them, looking at least 1,750 years younger than she really was. A billion stars sparkled on her shoulders and neck.

He concentrated on the wallpaper. "It sounds as if the princess's life doesn't need any more complications right now."

Electra made a little sideways, *how-about-that?* motion of her head. "That's not a stereotypical male response. You're a good man, Rigel Estell."

"And you're a good woman, Mira Silvas."

She smiled politely—amused, but not very. "Just a hunch or did I give myself away?"

"Queen Electra was the last one known to have handled Saiph, and she turned up in Canopus right when I did. It was completely obvious after you explained what a Cujam was, because the mob in the store attacked both of us. Mira also happens to be the name of a star."

"I meant how did I give myself away when I was Mira?"

"You were *wrong*. No one specific thing; there were just too many little things that didn't make sense. You claimed you were hiding out, but you'd come to an unpopulated area when everyone knows cities offer safer cover. You claimed to have a license to carry your handgun, and it's just about impossible to get one in Canada. No US license would be valid there, and a detective would know that. You had it with you when you were just sitting by a campfire, as if you were expecting trouble, but you had left the campground gate open, which would advertise to anyone looking for you that there was someone there. Saiph gave me no warning of the bear attack, so I wasn't in danger. You said you had bought the Winnebago, but it had rental company plates and no rental company name sticker, so it was obviously stolen, which explains why you didn't care about getting blood in it. The floor was clean as a whistle, but there had been a lot of rain, all over the island, so there should have been more mud. You were leaving fingerprints everywhere and a detective's prints would be on file with the FBI and Interpol. You had silk and needles handy, but you didn't look like a petit point sort of gal."

He thought for a moment. "And even I never healed *that* fast before."

"Perry J. C. Mason! I wasn't as smart as I thought I was."

"And this morning, on the barge, I mentioned Tarf and Tegmine to you, and you didn't ask who I meant. Humans can't read names."

"G'damn it! I really must be getting old."

"So who sicced the bear on me?"

She sighed. "I did."

"Thanks, Mom."

This time she gave him a real smile. "I deserve that. But I'd tried to make friends with you three times, dissembling a different person each time, and you kept shutting me out. Your defenses were too high. Not that I blame you for that; you had a helluva raw deal, son."

He thought back. "A blond girl on the Swartz Bay ferry?"

"That was one of me."

She had come across as seriously weird, he recalled.

"Yeah, but a *bear*?" Her admission about the bear hurt more than anything else she'd done to him, and she had plenty to answer for.

"Stuff it," she said. "There was no risk—you wore Saiph, and it was a struggle for me to even delay its response. You had about two seconds of terror, and then you knew you'd stabbed Bruin to death. Don't tell me that it didn't feel good. You were able to bring your pain under control in minutes, and if you hadn't been able to, I was ready to give you a fake morphine shot and do it for you. Don't start being a crybaby now, Rigel, my son."

Being 1,755 years his senior made his mother very hard to argue with.

"Let's talk about the rest of the raw deal, then."

She nodded, covering a yawn. "'Scuse me. It's been a very long day and I'm not used to them any more. Okay, here it is. I was never one of those alley-cat types you met at Alrisha, but I've always enjoyed a good tumble. You have two brothers and a sister somewhere—full-blooded starfolk, of course. After I became queen I found that ruling and pairing don't mix. Pretty soon all my partners would start asking for favors for brothers, sisters, cousins, and aunts. I still needed company, though, so I got into the habit of keeping a lusty young bed-warmer on hand. I'd boot them out as soon as they tried playing politics. That worked better, although few of them lasted longer than a couple of months. And then . . ."

What she had not spelled out was that in switching from consorts to gigolos, she'd also switched from starfolk to mudlings. Obviously.

"Then me?"

"You. Stars! Imp impending! I knew I was fading. That's starborn talk for aging. I was dumping more and more of the job on Kornephoros. I hadn't conceived in six hundred years and never dreamed that I still could. I decided I couldn't face all the tattling and scandal. So I slipped away with your father and went to ground. Went to Earth, literally. I picked Canada because it was sanitary and had a nice cool climate— Winnipeg in January is wonderfully bracing."

"And you took Saiph with you?"

Electra nodded. "We took all sorts of amulets, but the birth went terribly wrong, and none of them would stop my bleeding. I didn't dare go to a hospital. Think of the ruckus it would cause if I'd changed into someone else on the table, someone from a different species. Imagine them trying to match my blood group! Type E, Rhesus squared? I should have had more help. Your father did the best he could, but he decided he needed to introvert and bring back a trustworthy mage. By that time I was in no state to look after a newborn. Your Gert had just had a stillbirth, so he . . ."

She saw his doubts and her eyes narrowed. "Something bothering you, *Son?*"

"That was very convenient, wasn't it?"

"Not as it turned out," she snapped. "There's no such thing as baby formula in the Starlands. We had always planned on finding a wet nurse for you, some human welfare case who was due to give birth at about the same time as me, and would welcome a cushy job as royal nursemaid. We had a wonderful domain picked out . . ." She glared. "We would have taken her child there with her, understand? None of that changeling crap! When I went into labor, your father checked on all the candidates and learned that Gert had just lost her child. He more or less told her, 'Look after this for me, I'll be right back.' And that was that."

Silence. This was going to be as close to the truth as Rigel ever got, and he might as well accept it. He smiled.

"She skipped, of course?"

Electra shrugged. "He wasn't gone an hour . . ."

"But she'd already left town." Gert would have been terrified that it had all been a mistake and *They* would come and take her baby away, whoever *They* might be.

"She was gone. And then, to make things much worse, we discovered that your father had put the wrong amulet on your wrist. The one he'd intended to give you would have let us track you. He certainly didn't mean to give a newborn a *Lesath*! Rigel—Rigel, my son—I swear by the stars that I have been looking for you ever since. Twenty-one years I have scoured North America from coast to coast. I knew your name before you were born, and 'Rigel' is not a common name on Earth. I got very close to you several times. *Oh, you mean Rigel Whosit, the skinny boy with the white hair?* But Gert, or whatever she was calling herself at the time, had always moved on already, whereabouts unknown. I knew I could pick your face out of a hundred million male earthlings, if I ever set eyes on you." She chuckled. "I found three halfings, as it happens. The other two were the wrong age, but I delivered them to their proper place, which is here. And they were both musicians. That switched on a light for me. Now it was, *Rigel the minstrel? Sure I know him. Heard he'd gone west again.* By then, I had realized that you had never left Canada."

"You were seancing all this?"

"No, no! I was down in the field, hiring detective agencies, placing ads in newspapers, interviewing people, and scanning every medical journal I could lay my hands on for reports of strange new syndromes. I thought the Starlands could look after themselves, because I never dreamed it would take me so long—and it wasn't long by our standards. Then one day I heard you singing in Granville Island Market in Vancouver, and I knew my quest was over."

It was a cute story if it were true. "I'm not much of a minstrel by starfolk standards."

"You're hell on skates by human standards. I wept to hear singing like that again. The next step was to try to become your friend, and you took to me like Teflon to water."

He thought of Talitha's insistence that Electra would never have abandoned a baby, any baby. He thought of the poor mudling sod, whoever he was, who'd lucked himself into a job as the queen's gigolo. How would the kid have felt when he suddenly found himself watching his lover die in labor in a strange city in a strange land—heck, probably a strange world. Small wonder that the kid had lost it so badly that he'd chosen to trust a screwball like Gert.

He believed her now. Rigel rose and walked over to the bed. He bent to kiss Electra's cheek. "You are forgiven, Mom," he said.

She took his hand and squeezed it. Her eyes glistened, but they *always* glistened. She did not look the way a mother should look, and she wasn't wearing any clothes under the sheet. He went back to his chair.

"So tell me about the riot in the Walmart store. You said it was Tarf's doing."

"Yes."

"Why? What was he up to?"

She sighed wearily. "He was hunting for me. Vildiar's angels must have guessed or found out that I was on Earth somewhere. There are other continua I could have been visiting, but Earth was the most likely. Hadar set his hounds on me. So while I was hunting you, they were hunting me, with much less pleasant intent."

"Vildiar knew about me?"

"Maybe, maybe not. You would have been of no interest to him."

"But they found you?"

"I'm pretty certain they found *you*, a lost halfling of about the right age. They put two and two together. And after that they kept track of you."

Shit! "I led them to you? I didn't know I was being followed."

"As long as they just seanced, there wouldn't have been any way for you to know."

Even so, he hated the thought of trash like Tarf watching his every move. "How long did that go on?"

"I have no idea," she said. "But when I appeared, obviously tracking you, it was time for action. The Starlands would never have learned how I died, but the realm would have started falling apart, and Vildiar would have stepped forward to act the savior, claim the throne, and try to save it. I'm pretty sure that he would not have succeeded. There's a mystical bond between the Starlands and their ruler that must be transferred by a laying-on of hands, but Vildiar has never been overly troubled by scruples or rules."

Rigel was going to have to spend the rest of his life learning the ins and outs of magic, stuff the starfolk picked up in infancy. "So how did Tarf recognize you?"

Electra shrugged. "I told you we can't dissemble all the time, and no dissemblance is ever perfect. I've been a tourist in Byzantium and Chichén Itzá and Kublai Khan's pleasure dome. I've watched gladiators, *autos-da-fé*, and Aztec flower wars. And yet, even after I'd spent twenty-one years in Canada, you saw through me right away. You knew somehow that I wasn't *right*.

"Hadar and his gang decided to dispose of me with a Cujam. Ages ago, some mage imagined an amulet that would drive earthlings crazy without affecting starfolk or even halflings. If they were ever detected, it would allow them to keep their heads and make a clean getaway. But then, by accident or evil design, some other mage twisted that magic to produce an amulet called Cujam, which has been copied so often that 'Cujam' is now the name of a class of amulets. The starborn are still immune, but the earthlings' berserker frenzy is specifically directed against them. A Cujam went from being a getaway to being a deathtrap. All Tarf had to do was leave the amulet on a shelf and introvert to safety. Later, when the store was deserted, he could just extrovert back to retrieve it."

Rigel had never expected to feel happy to have killed someone, but he had certainly upgraded the galaxy by offing Tarf Halfling.

"Why couldn't you just introvert back home?"

"All my amulets were out in the Winnebago."

"But by amazing good fortune Starborn Fomalhaut arrived to save the day. Who was he hunting?"

"No one." Electra was quiet for a moment, studying her hands on the sheet. "Rigel, lad, how serious are you about

Talitha? Are you just looking for another scalp on your belt, or are you ready to make a serious commitment?"

His heart hit the stars. "You mean we *can* make a serious commitment? It is possible for a starborn and a halfling to . . . to pair, as you call it?"

"Not formally." Diamond eyes drilled into him for a painfully long moment before she said, "You would always be a servant by day and a lover slipping in through a secret panel at night, but if you are big enough to accept that humble status and ignore the sneers, then your love can be very long term. I won't say 'lifelong,' because your lifespan is limited, and hers is not."

"I don't know," he muttered. It would be a strange and shameful existence, slinking in the shadows, sharing only a tiny part of her life.

"I think you're up to it," she said. "I've watched you for several weeks on Earth, and several days here, after your whole world went insane, and you impress me."

That felt good, even though he didn't fully trust her motives. "You, maybe, but I've never impressed girls." She was his mother, so she wouldn't laugh at him. "I have no scalps on my belt yet."

Electra smiled. "I'm not surprised. It would have to be hard to explain once they got your shirt off. You haven't told me if you truly love Talitha."

"If she will accept me, I will love and serve her all the rest of my days."

She seemed to reach a decision. "Very well. I will believe you and trust you with a secret. Fomalhaut wasn't hunting anyone. He was seancing Halfling Tarf. Fomalhaut is a member of a small band of high-rank mages who call themselves 'Red Justice.' They have been in the dangerous business of trying to curb the Vildiar assassins. Fortunately, Fomalhaut is an extremely fast thinker. While he was watching the chaos at Walmart, he recognized you for a halfling, extroverted to save you, and then realized that the mob was after me as well. So he introverted all three of us to Alrisha."

"Why Alrisha?" Rigel demanded.

She shrugged in an effulgence of blues and greens. "I don't know for certain. He had to dump us somewhere, and Muphrid is his underling, easy to bully. He must have thought we would be safe there for a day or two, and he was in a hurry to get back to Nanaimo to try and nail Tarf. He didn't succeed, obviously."

"And the dragonflies were not sent by Muphrid?"

"Stars, no! Muphrid is a third-rate panderer and voyeur. I doubt if his magic is even into yellow. But Tarf and the gang tracked us down somehow. Whether they were after Saiph or me or both, the swan was an easy target for them. And I was still vulnerable, having no amulets. You saved your dear old mom from a very vulgar ending. Thank you."

"You're welcome." All very slick! It made sense, and the Red Justice story explained why the mage had refused to discuss his motives with the ignorant boy halfling. But it still wasn't the full truth.

"And who was my father?"

Silence. Then Electra said, "It's late. Let's save that part of the story for another day. We have a few centuries ahead of us to get to know each other, Son, assuming that—"

Knuckles rapped on the door.

She grimaced. "Enter!"

Alfred peered in. "Majesty, you asked to be informed . . ."

"Thank you. I will tell the princess."

The secretary left. Electra stared blankly at the foot of the bed.

"Mother?"

She shivered, as if the room was suddenly too cold for her, and her starry aura faded to pastels. "No, it is you who must go and tell the princess! Rigel, she is losing her father and the weight of the Dziban domain is descending on her shoulders. Millions of lives now depend upon her Naos power. Her child has been stolen from her, and she stands alone in the most dangerous place in the universe—between Vildiar and the throne. She desperately needs people she can rely on. She is resting in the room directly across from this one. Go and tell her that Kornephoros is about to die and she must go to him. And then, for stars' sake, *help* her!"

"What use can I be?" he asked bitterly. "I know nothing about magic, nothing about the Starlands, nothing—"

The queen's eyes blazed polychrome fire at him. "She needs someone she can trust utterly, someone who will not be turned or bought or intimidated by Vildiar and his pseudo-Nazi savages. Are you up to that, my son? Or is your love so frail that it fades already?"

"I am not a hero!" he shouted. "I wasn't brought up to fight battles and duel dragons."

She shook her head. "These are the Starlands, Rigel Halfling. Fantasy is reality. You must be Sir Lancelot or be nothing. Are you truly the son I am so proud to have borne or just a fake on the make?"

More manipulation! Rigel rose and put on his helmet. He bowed to the queen and strode out of the room without another word. *Damn her!*

Chapter 30

The opposing room was very similar to the queen's, being almost as large and furnished with the same elephantine furniture and plaid wool. The bed curtains were closed, but Talitha sat huddled on a straight-backed chair with her hands clasped in her lap. The room's single lamp cast an uncertain glow on pale cheeks and eyes reddened by weeping, and the way she looked up at him reminded him of deer and car head-lights. He knelt at her feet.

"The queen sent me to tell you that you must go now to your father."

She nodded.

Rigel took a very deep breath. "She also told me that you are in need of a helper you can trust completely, someone who will not be turned or bought or intimidated by Vildiar and his thugs. If that is the case, and the position is still open, I wish to apply for it. And I ask to be considered for lifetime tenure."

Her gaze flickered past him just as a voice said, "Brave talk!"

Before the second word was out, Rigel was upright, sword in hand.

Starborn Cheleb was sitting in another of the overstuffed chairs and had been hidden from him by the bed. As always, he could make no guess at her age or character, but even by elfin standards she had a bony face, and her eyes reflected the candle with an unearthly copper tinge.

He dismissed his sword and bowed to her. "It came from the heart, starborn."

"Obviously not from the head. Are you congenitally insane or just driven crazy by rut?"

Not knowing the correct answer, he snapped, "Neither! Are you always so insulting?"

"Insult a halfling?" she mocked. "Oh, my! Well, then, hero, are you willing to join an expedition to rescue Imp Izar from his father's stronghold?"

"I'll do anything my lady wants."

"You're a cocky young braggart, boy."

"You're an evil old cynic."

Talitha rose and quietly kissed his cheek, the part not covered by Meissa. "I accept your offer of help, Rigel Halfling, and will give serious consideration to your application for lifetime tenure." She managed a brave smile. "Now escort me to my father's deathbed."

He offered an arm, she took it, and even that gentle touch of her hand felt like progress. They walked out the door and down the corridor together. Cheleb did not follow. Rigel considered telling Talitha what he had learned of his parentage and decided that the time was not right.

"Who was your acid-tongued friend?"

"One of the oldest of the starfolk, if not the oldest. She jokes that she watched the Egyptians build the pyramids, and watched from a window when Troy welcomed the wooden horse. She is also one of our greatest mages."

"Red Justice?"

Talitha's grip on his arm tightened. "Who told you about that?"

"Electra." He felt rather smug about being able to say so, and ashamed of himself because of it.

"Yes. We are plotting a rescue, and I do desperately want you with me."

"I'm your man."

She squeezed his arm harder. "That too. But later."

As they started down a long staircase, he said, "What happened to your father? All I heard was that he was very sick, and then that he was dying."

"Tarf killed him."

"Tarf? I know your father was trying to revive him, but I was sure he was dead. In fact your father gave up and said he was."

"Poison. His hands turned black, and his knees too, and they began to rot away in front of our eyes. He kept screaming. We called in mages, but none of them could help. They couldn't even stop the pain. It was like acid, horrible, horrible!"

"Hands?" Rigel said, remembering his last sight of the regent. "And knees?"

"Tarf's blood was poison. It was the vilest magic I've ever heard of. The mages tested Muscida's blood, and it was the same. Not the woman's, just the men's. Two sphinxes got blood on their paws and licked it off. They died very quickly."

"I got some splattered on me too! And I must have stepped in it." Menkent had dropped him in the pool very soon afterwards—had that saved his life?

Talitha said, "The amulets Wasat gave you may have shielded you. Father always refused to wear anything like that, but if you ever fight any of that gang again, darling, you must be very careful not to get any of their blood on you."

That was much like telling him not to sweat. *What was it that she'd said? Darling! Talitha had called him darling!*

The moment they went through the portal to Canopus, Rigel caught a whiff of something rotten. The smell grew worse as they proceeded along the corridor, and by the time they descended a short flight of steps into a courtyard, it had become an overpowering, nauseous stench. The courtyard was small by palace standards, brightly lit by what seemed to be half a dozen moons, and had been turned into an emergency hospital. Regent-heir Kornephoros lay on his deathbed in the center, while a few dozen starfolk stood watch in a circle around him, giving the bed a wide berth. Rigel recognized Fomalhaut and, at the far side, Prince Vildiar looming over all of them. The great disk-shaped gold collar of the regency lay like a puddle of light on a table behind the dying man's head.

He was the source of the smell, of course. His legs had rotted away to black goo and his arms had melted to stumps. The question now was how much more of him could decompose before he died. He was mercifully unconscious—had been for hours, Talitha whispered—and the end was obviously very near. His face and chest were a bruised purple, his lips swollen sausages, and every breath was a climactic struggle. After each one the tension in the court would steadily rise. Then he would gasp once more, and the waiting would start again.

Seemingly oblivious of the putrid odor, Talitha entered the circle and approached the bed. She bent as if to kiss her father. Fomalhaut hurtled forward, caught her arm, and drew her back.

"Inadvisable, Your Highness."

"Release me!" she shouted, revealing the strain she was under. "You will not forbid me my last farewell."

"He is right, Talitha," Vildiar said loudly. "The distemper may prove to be contagious, and we Naos are too precious to risk now."

For a moment Rigel feared she would ask whose fault that was, but she ignored the murderer and let the mage lead her back to the circle. When Rigel's gaze returned to the sick man at the center, he realized that Kornephoros had not breathed once during that brief interchange. There was a sigh like a gentle wind through reeds as the watchers came to the inevitable conclusion: the prince's torment was over. One of the mages crept timidly forward to hold a silver dish over the corpse's mouth and nostrils and establish that there was no misting.

Prince Vildiar stepped forward, honing in on the gold collar.

Talitha raced in front of him. "Don't you touch that!"

He raised his hands as if to ward her off. "My sympathy for your sad loss, my dear. He will be sorely missed."

The mockery in his voice was sickening, and Talitha reacted with more anger.

"You will leave his collar alone. It isn't yours yet."

"You are distraught. You should rest. The collar belongs to the realm. I was merely going to take it to Her Majesty with the sad news, which is my duty as the most senior Naos present."

"The most junior Naos delivers the collar. You want precedents? When Albaldah died it was done that way. When Algorab was killed by—"

"You have a wonderful memory, my dear," the giant said, "considering that those worthies died long before you were born. But I can quote precedents too."

"You are both wrong!" Queen Electra stood in the doorway, four steps above them, which made her taller even than Vildiar. She glowed with stars from her ears to practically her waist. Secretary Alfred hovered at her back, no doubt unnoticed by anyone except for Rigel.

Talitha knelt and everyone else followed her lead. "The collar stays with the deceased," Electra continued, "until his pyre is lit." She scanned the crowd, which was growing as newcomers crept in at the back through other doorways. "And when the funeral has ended, I shall bestow it upon Prince Vildiar."

"Your Majesty does me great honor," the giant said. He was within reach of his lifelong ambition, but he displayed no emotion—he was good at that. Talitha could not hide her distress, yet what could she have expected? By Starlands standards she was centuries too young to rule.

For a long moment the court was silent. Electra seemed to be searching for words. "Kornephoros did his best," she said at last, "and we must honor him for that. If his best was not good enough, then the fault was mine for imposing on him an office he knew he could not fill, and which he fervently did not want."

Was that a dig at a prince who wanted it far too much? She sent a meaningful glance then, not at her new heir designate, but at Rigel. What was she trying to tell him? She started to speak again, then shook her head. Alfred stepped forward, a diminutive human alongside a towering starborn. The queen laid a hand on his shoulder and went back inside, leaning on him.

Another piece of the puzzle slipped into place. It fit well.

Talitha had insisted that the queen would never lose her head over a hulking gardener. No, Electra had probably never lost her head over any male, starborn or otherwise, but she was one tough-minded lady, capable of setting bears on people to attract their attention. Rigel had no trouble imagining her cold-bloodedly ordering some young hunk to strip and climb into her bed.

Alfred was still a well-built, handsome man. Using expressions like "pseudo-Victoriana kitsch," he was certainly no gardener. He was most definitely a full-blooded human; he showed no elfin characteristics, and did not even project his name. Starfolk wouldn't notice, for they took no account of age, but Rigel could tell that he could not possibly be older than a well-preserved forty. What qualifications could he possibly have possessed twenty-two years ago to be appointed Her Majesty's private secretary? It was much easier to imagine him playing the role of bed warmer.

He had been curiously tolerant that evening when a certain young halfling had chosen to get cheeky. One gets you ten that Secretary Alfred had last seen that halfling twenty-one years ago, in Winnipeg, when he was a terrified teenager, panicking as his newborn son screamed for care and his lover bled to death. If that were true, the last person Electra would ever admit it to was Rigel himself, who was older now than Alfred could have been then.

Yes, a very tough lady.

And that meaningful look she had given him when she appointed Vildiar her heir? Rigel bore the king of swords. She had arranged for him to be given the helmet Meissa. He had everything that a well-outfitted assassin needed. No starborn could rid the Starlands of the usurper Vildiar and prevent him from murdering again—but Rigel Halfling could, an invisible killer with an invisible sword. It was his duty to both his mother and the woman he loved.

Lies, lies, and more lies. Rigel Halfling, Lord High Executioner.

Chapter 31

Follow me!" Talitha took off at a run.

The portal was just closing behind the queen and her companion. Talitha elbowed past a group of starfolk to reach it before they did. She pulled it open, and Rigel followed her through it into musty-smelling darkness. She closed the door behind them, and opened it onto a place he had never seen before. Then again, and again.

"Um?"

"Just making sure we aren't followed," she said.

Again they went through, but this time he could smell the sea, and moonlight threw a bluish gleam on stone walls covered in inscriptions. They were back in the palace at Canopus. They might never have left the city, but location was irrelevant in the Starlands.

Talitha found an open window with a view of black trees and white roofs in moonlight. "Harpy!"

Rigel could hear the distant murmur of surf, but the only noise from the city itself was the faint screeching of a cat fight. "We're going to rescue Izar?"

"I can't leave him in the hands of those monsters! We have about a quarter of the night left. He'll have to wake up soon."

"You mean . . ." Of course Izar would have put himself into a deep trance; that was his standard way of dealing with any difficulty. "Let's get to it, then."

A harpy flopped down on the window ledge. "The shame of it, the shame of it!" It croaked. "Why are you dragging this poor wretch around the palace at this time of night, when he so desperately wants to get you back into bed? Just look at the bulge in his—"

"Silence! Tell Wasat Halfling to meet me at Miaplacidus immediately. Go now, and don't argue."

Grumbling obscenities, the smelly bird departed.

Talitha started to walk along the shadowy corridor, and Rigel followed. Their bare feet made no sound on the polished granite floor. White moonlight lay in slabs under each of the great windows.

"I feel so guilty," she said.

He took her hand. "About what? Izar?"

"Of course Izar, but I was thinking of Father. I find it very hard to mourn him. He was indifferent when I was a child and tyrannical when I grew up. All my life he was regent, far more concerned about politics than he was about me. Now he's gone, and all I'm worried about is the realm and the politics. It sounds terrible, but I don't think I will miss him."

"Children are eager to share their love. A parent who isn't loved must have worked very hard to reject their child. My foster mother was a terrible person, really, but I still loved her. I needed her; she needed me. We shared hunger and cold often enough, but the sharing was what mattered. Don't feel guilty. It was his fault, not yours."

"Thanks."

"It's true. Tell me about your mother."

"I never really knew her. I was born late in their pairing, after they'd already agreed not to renew it, and she died in a skyboarding accident when I was only two. But I never lacked for love and care. Starfolk are dotty about starlings. I didn't have to rely on Father."

"What are you going to do once we have Izar back?"

"Run away," she said firmly, tightening her grip on his hand. "Extrovert with you and Izar and a sack of gold, and live happily ever after. How does that sound? It will have to wait until Izar can dissemble well enough to hide his ears, but that won't take very long at the rate he's going."

"Sounds like a sad loss for the Starlands, but I'd be happy. Total debauchery. Are you serious?"

"It may be the best way out, except I think I'd always be waiting for Hadar to kick my door in. Have you a better suggestion?"

Better but not good. "I could kill Vildiar for you. Or die in the attempt."

She stopped and swung around to face him. "No! How can you even suggest it? You would be as bad as Hadar!"

The moon was at his back, and the way its light refracted in her eyes was glorious. "But it's your only chance of ever leading a normal life." Or any life.

"Doesn't matter! You mustn't even think it."

"I understand that you can't directly order me to do it, or you'd be killing yourself with the guilt curse, but if you just—"

"No! No! I am ordering you *not* to do it! You're not a mudling, anyway. You have free will and discretion. You could refuse the order, so the curse wouldn't apply."

"Right," he said, pushing the argument to its insane conclusion, "I understand. Don't worry. I'll exercise my free will. And discretion. It will be a very discreet assassination."

"*No!*" she screamed. "I forbid you to kill anyone, anyone at all! Except in self-defense, I mean."

He had the free will to refuse that order too. "Or to save you?"

"I suppose so."

"Or Izar."

"Yes . . ."

"So Vildiar has to go."

"*No!* Oh, Rigel, *stop it*! You're tying me in knots."

He wrapped his arms around her and pulled her to him, pressing his cheek to hers. He was ready to accept a kiss if it was offered, but he wouldn't push his luck. No kiss came, but she did cooperate in the hugging. They were wearing only moon-cloth wraps, so it was very nearly whole-body contact; she had to be just as conscious as he was of the instant reaction in his groin. He kissed the side of her neck cautiously, unsure of whether starfolk could get hickeys.

"Stars!" She broke free. "No, we mustn't! I want to, want to, want to, but we mustn't."

He drew a few deep breaths in an effort to regain control. "Sorry."

She took his hand and smiled wanly. "I'm not, it was wonderful—but not yet, please. Maybe someday. Soon, I hope."

"That's a promise?"

"Almost. We must go."

They set off into the moonlight. He was tremendously relieved to know that she truly did not want him to kill Vildiar, whether it was because she really didn't want him to or because it would be too dangerous to have him do it. He loved her so much for it that he would have to kill Vildiar anyway, of his own free will, just to keep her safe.

<hr />

Soon after that they saw a glow ahead and when they rounded the next corner, sunlight was streaming out from the doorway of the royal archives. The treasury portal had been opened, and it was always noon in Miaplacidus. Shielding their eyes against the glare, they stepped through.

"Two!" said Anubis. "Three."

Wasat trudged over the sand to meet them, looking rumpled, stubbled, and understandably curious to learn why he'd been dragged out of bed in the middle of the night. He bowed stiffly to Talitha; gave Rigel a smile and a nod. "How may I serve Your Highness?"

"Basilisk masks," Talitha said. "Five of them."

"No!" The old man recoiled, shocked. "You are not serious?"

"I am extremely serious and very much in a hurry. Now give me what I need, or I shall order Rigel to chop you into small pieces."

"She means that she will have me shake you vigorously," Rigel said. "It will be very horrible."

Still Wasat hesitated, chewing his lip. "I heard about Izar . . ."

"I shall count to three," said Rigel the henchman. "Starting at two."

Wasat shrugged and led the way to the most distant of his storerooms. He hefted a box down from a high shelf and counted out five strips of flimsy cloth, like silver gauze. Talitha stretched one over her eyes to look through it.

"That will do," she said, removing it. "And the deadliest fire amulets you have."

"Your retainer already has the best there is," Wasat grumbled, but he produced a finger ring for her to wear as well. "You must never use this against a starborn, Highness. It will kill."

"Good. What else do you have that will kill? Something unexpected?"

Shaking his head in misery, he produced yet another box of rings. "Throwing knives," he said. "Only one throw per ring. They never miss, but they are so rare that nobody ever carries a defense against them."

"Rare why?" Rigel asked suspiciously.

"Because it's much more effective to have a bow ring on one hand and an arrow ring on the other. Far greater range, faster rate of fire."

Talitha accepted four of the rings, Rigel three. If those weren't enough to protect him on top of Saiph and whatever the masks did, he was sure to die anyway.

"Remember," the old halfling mumbled, "that an amulet is only as strong as the starborn who made it, and how much it has been used. Most of mine are ancestral, but there are stronger, older ones out there." He had obviously guessed exactly what was afoot. Rigel was sure now that there was much more to Wasat than met the eye: little escaped *his* eyes.

Talitha said, "Thank you. Any other helpful suggestions?"

Wasat shook his head. "I hope you have a good mage to help you?"

"One of the best."

"Then may the stars be with you both." He stood and stared after them.

"Two," said Anubis. "One."

Their next stop was the pool where the royal barge floated. Saidak herself was perched on her throne in the bow, facing aft. If she were a biped, her position would be called kneeling. She was supporting herself by gripping the rail with two enormous hands as she chatted to someone on deck. Looking down at the arrivals, she spoke in the most civil tone Rigel had yet heard from her.

"My sympathy for all your troubles, Your Highness."

"Thank you. My apologies for disturbing your rest."

"Oh, that's nothing. Fish don't sleep. Come aboard."

The person on deck was the mage Cheleb. "Did you get the masks?" she demanded urgently.

Talitha handed them over. "He had a whole box of them."

"Excellent!" Cheleb tucked the masks away in a shoulder satchel, her bag of magical tricks, no doubt. "To Spica, please, captain," she said as soon as the others were aboard.

Rigel waited until the three of them were down in the saloon before he started asking questions. The red and gold tables and dining chairs were gone, leaving the room bare. The lamps were unlit, but moonlight illuminated the red plush window benches, and he was surprised to see the top of an obelisk rush by outside. The barge was already airborne.

"What are we going to do with basilisks?" he asked.

"Nothing," Cheleb snapped. "Can you ride a horse?"

"Only centaurs. Why do we need the blindfolds?"

"When you need to know, we will tell you. Halflings should be seen and not heard, and preferably seen only at a distance."

Talitha did not comment in words, but she sighed wearily and leaned her head against Rigel's shoulder. She settled a hand on his knee. He wrapped an arm around her. So she had put herself where she belonged, and put old Cheleb in her place at the same time. The mage sniffed in disgust and twisted around to peer out the window.

"Why Spica?" Rigel asked softly.

"Because we need red magic to find Izar," Talitha said.

As she clearly did not want to talk, he was content to just hold her and study the silver path the moon had painted on the sea. Suddenly there came the familiar wheel of cloud, the ear-popping descent, and the moon was gone. It reappeared beyond another one of the windows as the barge drifted down to a dark, tree-lined river and a ranch house. Lights were moving around down there, indicating some signs of life.

Rigel was first on deck and first down the gangplank, so he was also the first to spot the great cat bounding toward them, whom he quickly identified as Sphinx Praccipua. The guard inspected him and the two women who followed him, then bowed to Talitha.

Other sphinxes were directing a gang of humans who were building a mass funeral pyre in the moonlit pasture. Two huge cyclops were gathering the bodies, carrying them as if they were sleeping children.

"The pyre will be ready very shortly," Praecipua rumbled.

"Light it whenever you are ready," Talitha said. "I mourn each one of the dead, but I have more urgent troubles that require me to be elsewhere. Starborn Cheleb and I require a moment in the house." She hurried off after the mage.

Praecipua said, "I have a question, halfling."

Rigel halted, remembering that Fomalhaut had warned him to answer all the sphinxes' questions. "I will help in any way I can."

"When we asked her about the dead dogs, the Pythia informed us that you would supply all the information we needed."

Pythia? "Um...As I recall, the Pythia's prophecies were always obscure," Rigel said, needing time to decide how much he should tattle to the cops about Mage Formalhaut's interference.

"But I have a feeling we can rely on this one," Praecipua purred, with just a hint of menace.

"All I know about their dogs concerns the big one, whose name was Turais."

"That is the only one that could possibly matter."

"Turais was a magical shield given to Starling Izar just this morning—yesterday morning now—by a mage loyal to the cause."

"It did well."

Was there no limit to the powers of magic? "You mean you know what happened here?"

"The Pythia informed us," the sphinx said, "that five men and two women arrived here in two air boats at around half-morning yesterday. Regrettably she did not identify them for us. They attempted to seize Starling Izar while he was riding his unicorn in the charge of his guardian, Starborn Baham. The dog killed three of them and wounded another before being itself slain."

"The dog did well . . . better than I did."

The sphinx's laughter was terrifying and powerful. "You must not be ashamed of your efforts, Rigel Halfling. You survived. The dog did not, and there are still a lot more vermin where those came from." He paused, and after a moment of staring at the house, he said, "The princess is understandably preoccupied. Strictly speaking, the palace guard has no authority outside the royal domain, but several of us here are about to go off duty. If you think she could use any help tonight, we'd be more than happy to accompany her." He paused to examine four dagger talons attached to his right forepaw. "In an advisory capacity, of course."

"Your offer is extremely generous," Rigel said. "I will certainly suggest that she take you up on it." Rigel was accustomed to the law looking upon him with suspicion, a young male vagrant. His exploits against Tarf and Muscida must have greatly impressed the palace guard if it was willing to confide in him.

"As for the incident we have been investigating—may I rely on you to convey my report to your sponsor at her earliest convenience?" The sphinx strode away with his tail twitching.

By the time Rigel reached the house, Talitha and Cheleb were already coming down the steps, so whatever they had come for had not been hard to find. He told them about the sphinx's offer to join the expedition. The mage snorted as if it were a ludicrous suggestion.

Talitha smiled wanly and said, "Hardly practical, but it's sweet of them to offer."

They hurried back to the barge; Saidak greeted them with a cheerful, "Where to now, my lady?"

Cheleb said, "Tarazed, the northern coast."

"*No!*" The mermaid's roar echoed faintly off the house. "Never!"

"Please, Saidak," Talitha said. "This is only way we will have any chance of rescuing my son from Phegda."

"You think I'm crazy? Go to Tarazed? *At night?*"

"You won't need to dock," Cheleb said soothingly. "If you can just find a flat spot and hover, we can make it down ourselves."

"*Hover?* Lay to in those winds? I'd be bounced up and down and smashed to firewood."

"Only for a moment. Just long enough for our muscleman to jump down and catch us."

"You call that weedy tweenling a muscleman?" the mermaid said grumpily. At least she had stopped shouting. "Why not take one of those cyclops?"

"If you like," said the mage, "but we can't leave him there, so he'll have to climb back aboard."

"And haul me down onto the rocks in the process? No thank you!"

Again Talitha said, "Please, Saidak? You're a mother. You know I can't leave Izar with Hadar and his goons."

The mermaid sulked for a moment longer, then said, "We can go and see how bad it is. Gales I can handle. Hurricanes and lava bombs, I can't."

"I am so very grateful! Starborn, give her a basilisk mask."

Chapter 32

Ignoring disapproving sniffs from Cheleb, Rigel settled onto the bench next to Talitha and cuddled her tight against him. "You are exhausted," he said. "So sleep. Even a few minutes will help. I'll wake you when we reach Tarazed."

"But—"

"No buts. Sleep."

She sighed and said, "Yes. You're right." Then she was gone, her head heavy on his shoulder, ears limp.

The barge climbed steeply into the night sky. It was well past time for a business meeting. He looked over at the mage.

"Basilisks? Hurricanes? Lava bombs? A short briefing on this mission, if you please, Starborn Cheleb."

She smirked in the moonlight. "I don't want to frighten you, boy. Just do as your sponsor tells you."

"That is absurd and you know it," Rigel said, trying to sound calm and logical, if not exactly respectful. "Talitha must not order me to break the law, but we are obviously engaged in a mission of armed intrusion that may very well lead to violence. She knows I will help in any way I can, but if I don't know what to expect, I may panic at the first emergency."

"You will anyway."

"I haven't yet."

"Your ability to emerge unscathed from fights is a tribute to the potency of your amulet. Don't let it give you exalted ideas of your own strength and courage."

He wondered if the old biddy hated him personally or all halflings on principle. Had she borne halfling sons of her own and watched them die before their first millennium? Or— recalling what Prince Kornephoros had said about mules being attractive to starborn women of low moral character—was Cheleb in denial over her own secret longing for Rigel?

How was that for an exalted idea of his own strength, potency, and so forth?

"Try this, then. Despite the color of my hair, I am not a boy, although I appreciate that anyone younger than Christ may seem so to you. I am an adult male savage motivated by animal lust for the princess, who is cleverly luring me with wiles and promises into aiding her in her illegal purposes. After which, no doubt, she will thank me kindly and slam the bedroom door in my face. So pander to my rutting frenzy and explain what is going on."

"You are a vulgar, ignorant serf!"

"I am her loyal retainer. Whose side are you on?"

"Insolence!"

"Calling me names won't help Talitha's cause."

Cheleb scowled. "It must be quick, then. What do you know already?"

"That Hadar and his gang kidnapped Izar to please Vildiar, who could safely deny any knowledge of this even on the Star of Truth. That his domain must be very big and we cannot rescue the imp until we locate him, which I assume will be your job. Mine will be to sneak into the hyenas' den and steal

Izar back again. I am also aware that Izar was taken hostage to barter for Saiph, meaning my life. As a seasoned killer being hunted by other killers, I intend to be absolutely ruthless. What do we do at Tarazed?"

His ears popped as the barge plunged through a link.

"You came close," Cheleb admitted. "Phegda is very big, perhaps as big as the royal domain. Fortunately the princess has lived there and knows it well. She even has friends there who may help. Finding her son is the first task, and for that we need transportation—something quick, nimble, dispensable, and inconspicuous. Neither her swan nor *Saidak* fits the bill, and her swanherd is dead anyway."

"So we collect basilisks at Tarazed?" Five basilisk masks: Talitha, Cheleb, Saidak, Rigel, and Izar.

"No. But there *are* basilisks on Tarazed, some as small as hawks, some bigger than hunting dogs. Their gaze can kill or paralyze, many species can spit a deadly venom, and at least one breathes fire. Watch where you're stepping at all times, because if you tread on a basilisk, the next thing you hear will be your funeral drum roll. But don't worry unduly about them, because there are a dozen other things more horrible. Including," the mage added with relish, "dragons, wyverns, wasps the size of laundry baskets, whose venom induces paralysis so that—"

"Fascinating. What lives on the northern shore?"

"Cockatrices."

"Is it safe to step on cockatrices?"

"They're more likely to step on you. The cockatrice is a larger variant of the basilisk and will attack on sight. Its stare will paralyze you unless your eyes are covered with a basilisk mask. Fortunately you can daze a cockatrice with a fireball about ninety percent of the time, because those are the creatures we will be riding."

The barge twisted through another highway. "It's a long way to Tarazed?" he asked.

"Of course. How many starfolk would link their domains directly to such a bestiary?"

He should have seen that. "And the other ten percent? Cockatrices who aren't dazed?"

"You move one link down the food chain."

"I do have a fireball amulet but I don't know how to use it."

"Stars bless me! I cannot understand why Talitha didn't manage to find a better helper than an ignorant boy. Ignorant youth, if you insist."

"Because she trusts me more than anyone else. Instruct me."

"Fireballs are easy. You have a ring with a large violet stone?"

"Yes." He raised his free hand. No colors showed in the moonlight, but there was only one large stone on his left hand. "This one."

"You press on the stone with your thumb and move your hand as if you're throwing something. Do *not* practice in here."

Saidak lurched again. The moon disappeared. Now the barge trembled and rolled like a real boat, and Rigel could hear storm winds raging. Rain beat on the windows.

"So who imagined Tarazed?" he asked the gloom. "Why tolerate such a horrible place?"

"Tarazed is where nightmares grow. It's as old as Naos. No one knows who started it, but once imagined, things cannot be consciously unimagined, and it is best to confine them in one spot as much as possible."

The barge dropped, then slammed upward again. Cheleb bounced on her bench and the unconscious Talitha began to slide out of Rigel's embrace. Plunged into pitch darkness, he slithered to the carpet, taking Talitha with him as gently as he could. Although he made sure that she ended up on top, they landed just as the barge hit another updraft and the double impact knocked him flat, crushing all the air from his lungs. As the lamps began to glow, he wriggled free, sat up, and arranged her as comfortably as possible in his arms. She did not wake up. Thump! Severe turbulence, no seat belts. He wondered how *Saidak* compared to a Boeing in terms of structural strength.

Cheleb had also taken refuge on the deck.

"How does one ride a cockatrice?" he asked, thinking how bizarre that question would have seemed to him only four days ago.

"You sit on its back and hang on by wrapping your legs around its neck. Don't let them dangle, or it will bite them off."

"Reins? Stirrups?"

"No. A cockatrice has a fleshy comb and wattles, like a rooster. You control it with those. If you push its head down it cannot fly. If you tug on a wattle, it will turn to that side, and so on. The tricky part is dismounting."

The next highway threw *Saidak* into wild gyrations. Storm winds thundered rain against the windows, blurring vague shapes of red fire.

"We're here!" Cheleb said.

Rigel kissed Talitha's forehead. "Time to wake up, darling. We're at Tarazed."

"Thanks." She opened her eyes, perked up her ears, and yawned. Then she squealed in alarm as *Saidak* rolled. Rigel happily tightened his grip.

Cheleb opened her satchel to find one of the basilisk masks. "Put this on, halfling. Go and see if Saidak thinks she can let us off. She has her hands full."

The mermaid must have her hands full just staying aboard, for the barge was pitching like a rodeo bronco. Reduced to crawling on his hands and knees, Rigel had trouble reaching the stairs at all, and when he slid open the hatch, a bathtubful of water was dumped on his face.

He had never experienced weather like this, not even the great Pacific storm that had blown in while he was in Ahousaht. He clung desperately to the hatch with one hand while reaching for the railing with the other, feeling at times as if his legs were flying free or the deck was higher than he was—and well aware that in a few seconds he would be thumped hard on the deck again. Rain was rushing by like a river, icy cold even by Starlands standards. Explosions of fire in the background cast a fitful glow over a jumble of rocks, but he was being bounced so much that he could not judge whether they were boulders or mountains. Terrified that his fingers would freeze and lose their grip on the wet wood, he clamped both hands tight around the railing in the bow, close by one of Saidak's much larger ones. Even in that monsoon downpour, her hair streamed out like a golden flag.

"It's raining," he bellowed.

She turned her great head to look up at him, and he was astonished to see that she was grinning. "Good exercise. Enjoying it?" Despite the known power of her lungs, he could barely hear her.

"Interesting experience!"

"What?"

He leaned closer. "Can you let us off?"

"You still want to try?"

"Yes."

"You are one crazy imp. I'll try to find a sheltered spot. Alright?"

"*Yieee!*" He had almost been torn loose. "Right, I mean."

"Tell the starfolk to stand by," Saidak bellowed. "When I drop my gangplank, you go first. Then you catch them. I'll only have a few seconds between gusts."

"Right." What else could Sir Lancelot say?

The first problem was getting back to the hatch, but *Saidak* solved that for him by tilting her bow upward, or perhaps Saidak herself did it; he had trouble distinguishing between barge and bargee. He slid, grabbed, and arrived more or less unbroken at the bottom of the companionway. A minor lake was swilling back and forth across the saloon.

"Passengers stand by to disembark," he yelled. "I'll go first and try to catch you. We'll only have a few seconds, she says." He crawled back up the steps and the two starborn followed him with no greater dignity than his.

He let ripples of rainwater chute him across the deck to the gate where the gangplank would appear. There he clung for dear life, sternly telling himself that Lancelot and Galahad had never succumbed to seasickness.

In moments when he was not blinded by wind and rain, volcanic explosions lit the scene for him like strobe lights. As the barge descended, he saw more and more steaming rocks all around them. He wondered if the rain had cooled the ground to a bearable temperature or if contact with it would boil his feet. Off in the distance, he saw breakers and waves leaping up cliffs. By the time he could work out an idea of scale from the rate at which they fell back, the rocks and white water were perilously close. Saidak was taking a serious risk by edging the barge's great bulk lower in search of shelter from the wind.

She found it in the lee of a towering sea stack, just above a rocky shore. The wind slackened, the gangplank unfolded, and Rigel forced his hands to slacken their deadman's grip on the railing. He half scrambled, half fell down the plank and flew off the end like a spitball flipped from a ruler. He landed on one foot, one hand, and a shin, and was instantly blown onto his back by a screaming gust of wind, which carried away his howl of pain and *Saidak* also. The gangplank, with either Talitha or Cheleb clinging on the end of it, went soaring away into the darkness.

Sir Lancelot was now marooned on the island of cockatrices.

Chapter 33

He tried to sit up and rapidly decided that standing would be a lot more comfortable, provided that the rambunctious wind would let him stay upright. His shinbone was not broken, but it hurt even more than his back, which was bleeding in at least two places. The storm was fiendishly erratic, going from dead calm and salty-tasting mist one minute to hurricane winds driving needle-sharp rain the next. He could make out white surf on one side, which he decided to call north, and red fire on the other, although the source of the flames was hidden by a nearby ridge. The ground was jagged, painful even for elfin feet, and it trembled constantly. He could not tell if it was being shaken by the volcanoes or the impact of the surf or both.

Shelter would definitely be a good idea, and an impenetrable blackness at the base of the nearest rock pile looked like it might be a cave. He hobbled across the jagged lava in that direction, struggling to keep his balance as the wind wrestled and needled him. Happily the cave was real, and deeper than he had expected. Unable to see the ground in front of him, he took three cautious steps into the opening, and then stopped to think.

Nice to be out of the wind and rain, even if the air stank most horribly of sulfur.

But now what?

One of his amulets might help, if he knew which one and how to use it. Cockatrices attacked on sight, Cheleb had said, but nothing would be able to see very well on a night like this, unless of course its dinner volunteered by coming to stand in the front door, silhouetted against what little light there was outside. He looked back uneasily. Nothing was visible inside the cave, but of course that meant little.

He was doomed unless *Saidak* returned, and it could not possibly locate him unless Starborn Cheleb had some magical means of doing so. He could not remember if he had spoken his helmet's name since he'd last put it on, but if he had he'd be invisible to any magic the mage might use. He removed Meissa and replaced it.

"Where did you come from?" asked a quiet voice behind him.

He painfully stubbed a toe in his haste to turn around.

The girl was sitting on a stool five or six meters deeper into the cave. She was on lower ground than he was and visible only because she was faintly luminous.

"Who are you?" he asked. "Were you carved out of moonlight, or do you bathe in phosphorescent seas?"

She laughed. "You must know who I am, or you would not have risked coming here. Why are you blindfolded?"

He laughed, embarrassed. "In case you turn out to be a cockatrice in disguise." He left the basilisk mask on.

"Are you elf or Greek?" Her voice was so soft that it should not have been audible over the storm and the volcanic activity. Her image kept flickering and changing—one minute she had elfin ears, the next she seemed more like a young human. Her clothing kept flickering back and forth between a full-length gown and nothing whatsoever. In earthly terms she might be fourteen.

Greek? Her stool had three legs. "You're a pythia!"

"*The* Pythia!"

"One of a kind? Like the Minotaur? You expect me to believe you are the same ancient priestess who sat on a tripod in Delphi in Greece, to prophesy for kings and rulers of cities? Don't answer that," he added hastily. Prophecies were traditionally limited to either one or three per person, so he must not ask the wrong question by mistake. What was the *right* question? "I suppose the same immortal essence of prophecy could materialize in more than one place, especially if some elf imagined you here after he . . . or possibly she, you understand, no offense intended . . . Where was I? Don't answer that either. I mean you could be an imagined replica, like Canopus isn't the same Canopus."

"You are quite the strangest petitioner to come calling on me in ages," the Pythia said, solidifying slightly to peer up at him. She floated closer. "And I do mean ages. Where is your rich offering to Apollo?"

Thunder rumbled in the storm outside.

"I think I must have left it behind," Rigel said vaguely. There was something he ought to be thinking about, if he could only remember what. "Apollo will have to do without, poor guy. I was going to ask you something, but it escapes me. Hadar escaped me. Probably it was about *Saidak,* the royal barge or royal mermaid. Or both. I need to know if she's going to come back and pick me up. That was a rhetorical question. There's no point in asking you that, is there? If she or they either isn't or aren't going to come and get me then I'll die as soon as the cockatrices or basilisks or creepy crawlies find me. I ought to ask you something useful. Ask something useful, I mean, something that you can answer usefully. Usefully for me."

"I like your helmet! Alcibiades had one just like it. The brush was red, though." The Pythia rippled unsteadily, like a reflection in water.

"Don't do that," he said. "You're making me queasy. Didn't you answer questions for the sphinxes last night?"

"Is that really what you want to ask me? Either way, I do wish you would hurry up and then go away. You look awfully sexy in that helmet, Rigel Estell, and I'd hate to see you die here."

"You really can foretell the future?"

The Pythia laughed again. Her laugh was very loud and bold for someone so insubstantial. "I foresee that I won't answer that. I usually give indecipherable answers that would be very useful if you happened to understand them in time."

"I thought you just spoke gibberish, and the priests interpreted however they fancied. I read a book that said you sat on a tripod in the temple of Apollo and breathed in a seepage of ethylene gas, which made you hallucinate."

The Pythia boomed out her great laugh again. "Are you sure you're not hallucinating now, young Alcibiades? You're kneeling there on all those sharp rocks and babbling about inhaling gas. Hydrogen sulphide paralyzes your sense of smell, you know? It's as poisonous as cyanide gas, but at least it keeps you laughing."

"Not laughing gas. Ethylene. Male version of ethyl gas."

"It echoes like Dionysius's Ear. Now, do you want to ask me for a prophecy, and then go, or will you just lie there and die?"

Wasn't sulfur-hydrogen-whatever heavier than air? Rigel struggled to his feet again. "All right, let's presume or assume that I'm going to be rescued, okay? Because if I'm wrong it won't matter. Isn't that logical, Pythia? Take that for granite. Prophesy for me, pretty Pythia. Peanut butter sandwiches. Tell me how best I can serve my adored Talitha Starborn, because I really do want to get laid as soon as possible?"

"That's a very honest question," the Pythia said, clapping her hands inaudibly. She was fading to black. "So I'll give you an easy answer: *It is mightiest in the mighty.* Now get out of here, Rigel Halfling-Estell, because the barge is returning, and this is your last chance."

Chapter 34

A few minutes out in the storm cleared Rigel's head, leaving behind a thundering headache and an overpowering sense of shame. How idiotic could a man be to crawl into a volcanic crevice and not remember that H_2S was poisonous? Not to mention the millions of other gases that were no doubt down there.

The Pythia had been an interesting hallucination, though. Had she been anything more than a warning generated by his own subconscious and memories of what Sphinx Praecipua had said? "What was mightiest in the mighty" might be nothing but plain old stupidity, and even the unmighty, like him, could be catastrophically stupid. He was still debating whether his headache or his nausea was worse when *Saidak* dived out of the night sky at him like a sounding whale.

For one moment of horror he thought he was going to be swatted flat by the gangplank and the solitary passenger clinging to it, but the wind slackened and the mermaid regained control at the last possible instant. Whoever the starborn on the end of the plank was, she did not lack for courage or strength, because she slid over the edge feet first, and then dangled there. The moment she came within reach, Rigel caught her ankles, and she let go.

They hit the ground in a heap, and what felt like the same rocks that had hit him upon his own landing struck him in what felt like the same spots on his back. His cry of pain did not quite hide the sound of a rib or two breaking.

"Well done," Cheleb said, scrambling off him. "Up! Quickly!"

It was all very well for her to say that, but somehow he obeyed and was able to help catch Talitha. He set her down gently as the barge swooped away and disappeared into the murk.

"What a horrible place!" Talitha said. "Oh, you're hurt! Let me—"

Cheleb pulled her hand away. "No, wait! Let him bleed a little more. Unless you want to walk a hundred stadia over this glass heap? The wind is erratic, but it seems to be blowing more or less landward, and cockatrices are attracted by the smell of blood."

"Your sympathy is touching, starborn," Rigel said.

"Impertinence! You must be wearing a coagulant amulet, or you would be bleeding much more."

"Would it help if I cut an ear off?"

"It would help if you kept your mouth shut," the mage shouted.

"You brought me along as bait?"

"You are well qualified. You did offer to help any way you could, so stand there and keep your eyes open. Stay upwind of him, Talitha dear, and be ready to throw fire."

For the first time in the Starlands, Rigel felt truly cold, though some of his shivering was undoubtedly from terror. His feet, leg, and back hurt abominably, and he was surrounded by jagged boulders, any of which might conceal predatory monsters. Just when he thought things were as bad as they could be, hail began dancing off the rocks in all directions like tousled white fur. It rattled deafeningly on his helmet, needled against his bare skin, and cut visibility to a few meters. He felt a sudden tingle at his wrist. Then the gauntlet and sword suddenly sprang into being, and a cockatrice charged out of the hailstone fog.

It was far bigger than he had expected, a horse-sized ostrich at least three meters tall, with outspread wings and a beak that could bite his head off, helmet and all. Its eyes burned bright with evil, painful to look at even through his protective mask.

Saiph cut its head off. Rigel leaped aside as the huge corpse dived into the ground. It somersaulted over him, but a leathery wing swept him off his feet. He landed on the rocks again, and this time his brains would have been smashed out if he had not been wearing Meissa.

Talitha crouched beside him. "Are you all right?"

"Been better," he admitted. "Try to be faster with that fire next time. But—" He gasped as he tried to sit up. "Now that you've got better bait, can you do something about my ribs? And my leg?"

She made a light and cried out at what she saw. "Cheleb! Come here and heal Rigel."

"You do it," the mage said. "We're going to have cockatrices all over us any minute."

"I'll watch for them. *Come here and heal Rigel!*"

Nice to feel appreciated . . .

The headless cockatrice was still flopping and flapping in its death throes, bleeding exorbitantly. If Rigel's few spoonfuls of blood had brought forth that monster, the torrent spilling from its neck stump ought to fetch the entire cockatrice population of Tarazed.

Grumbling disapproval, the mage came to tend to Rigel's injuries, although from the odd way she walked, he suspected that her feet were not touching the ground. She banished his pain and staunched his bleeding with a few gentle touches and some rapid incantations.

"That will have to do for now," she said.

The hail had stopped. The wind died down, as it did periodically. Two cockatrices attacked almost simultaneously, charging into the light cast by the starfolk's amulets. Cheleb's fireball got one and Talitha's got the other. Hit with purplish flames, the monsters staggered and sagged to the ground.

"Hold its head down!" the mage shouted to Talitha. "Come here, halfling! Get on this one's back."

That was easier said than done. Apart from its rooster head and thick, feathered neck, the monster was scaly and slippery. Its two long legs ended in bird-like feet with dagger claws, and there was a vicious barb at the end of its reptilian tail. It lay sprawled at an angle, one side higher than the other, and only its outspread wings kept it from rolling over.

Still, Rigel followed Cheleb's directions and scrambled aboard, wrapping his legs around the beast's neck and gripping its fleshy comb with his right hand. His face was pressed against the beast's feathers, which stank horribly. As long as he forced its head down, it would be unable to move—so the mage said, anyway, and for the moment the cockatrice seemed to believe her. Rigel had no doubt that it was many times stronger than he was, and could flick him off with a shake of its head, but for the moment it just twitched and made harsh piping noises.

A surge of lavender fire announced the arrival of a fourth monster. Cheleb disabled it and then scrambled aboard, but it needed time to recover, and others were arriving fast on its heels. Talitha stunned two, and two more began feeding on the corpse of the one Rigel had killed.

"Prepare for flight!" the mage shouted. "Heads up!"

"You heard her, Gruesome!" Rigel hauled back his mount's comb. It struggled and staggered to its feet, tilting almost vertical so that for a moment he was virtually hanging free, alarmingly high above the ground. When he tugged on its right wattle—copying what Cheleb was doing—it turned to face the wind and spread its giant wings. Then, with surprising grace, the cockatrice rose into the air.

<hr/>

To Rigel's relief the three cockatrices did not immediately scatter into the night, which suggested that they naturally traveled in flocks, but Gruesome wanted to lead and did not favor the direction that Cheleb did. Nor did it want to fly very high. Fortunately the mage was a skilled rider, and she literally flew rings around the other two, shouting out orders like a drill instructor. After a while Rigel mastered the knack of wrenching his mount's head to the correct angle, and then he could lead the expedition on its way across the fiery wastelands of Tarazed with only an occasional shouted course adjustment from Cheleb.

Hot updrafts from lava fountains made for extreme turbulence, and once something that might have been a wyvern or small dragon tried to contest their passage—or possibly grab a halfling snack on the wing—but the combined stare of three cockatrices sent it tumbling into the fiery lakes below.

The mage had not explained where they were going, but her aim was true. A long climb, a wheel of cloud below them, a dive through cold dampness, and the cockatrices emerged above the surface of a calm and moonlit lake. Tarazed was gone, leaving only a lingering sense of horror, like a too-well-remembered nightmare.

Again the cockatrices had to be coaxed to climb into the sky, although they obviously disliked such heights. Even by elfin standards it was cold up there among the stars. The moon was nearing the horizon and dawn would not be far off. They had to make haste. Invading Phegda to rescue Izar would be dangerous enough in darkness; by daylight it must surely rank close to suicide.

Rigel recognized a cryptic cloud gyre ahead as another link and braced himself for the jump.

And another, this time very high . . .

A vast snow-capped range glowered like a march of specters in the last rays of the setting moon. At first glance Rigel thought the great marble monolith ahead was one of the mountains. Then he realized that most of what he was seeing was a single building. It stretched along a high ridge, true, but he could not even guess at its dimensions or how many thousands of rooms it must contain. The only thing he had ever seen that looked remotely like it was a photo of the Dalai Lama's palace in Tibet, the one at Lhasa.

"Land on it," Cheleb shouted, her voice growing hoarse now, "somewhere high up, near the middle."

"Heads down to land?"

"Of course. Head level now, and glide."

Gruesome was probably as tired as its rider; it seemed happy enough to stop flapping and float down onto the staggering stone pile—balconies, towers, endless staircases, and multitudes of empty-eyed windows. Rigel let the cockatrice choose its destination, and it selected a flat rooftop terrace as a suitable runway, spreading its talons. Being as inexperienced at manned flight as its rider, it misjudged its loaded momentum and skidded awkwardly on the tiles, but Rigel managed to stay aboard. He couldn't get the stupid brute to lie flat, though. It stood almost vertical, so his weight rested entirely on his thighs and he had to cling to the creature with his legs, which were not designed for such exercise. His knees ached, but he didn't dare straighten them.

Talitha was able to land quite close to him, and Cheleb ostentatiously came down exactly halfway between them.

"Well?" she said.

"Yes," Talitha said. "No doubt about it."

"Then where do we try next?"

"No doubt about what?" Rigel demanded angrily.

"Izar's location amulet," Talitha explained. "It's here, in Phegda Palace."

"It is?" It would take years to search a place this size.

"So Izar isn't."

Rigel's expression must have revealed his confusion, because Cheleb said, "Oh, work it out, boy. The first thing big, bad Hadar would do after stealing Izar away from his mother would be to take off the boy's ear stud so that she couldn't find him. And if the bad man thinks a certain bold but dumb knight will show up to steal Izar back again, and he wants to get a hold of that knight's sword, then he'll set a trap for him using the ear stud as bait, now won't he?"

Rigel was too tired to bandy barbs. "You're assuming that Saiph was his sole reason for kidnapping Izar. I know Tarf implied that it was before I sliced him open, but Tarf was in a tight place and hardly a reliable witness. The Hadar crew may have taken Izar only because his daddy wanted him. He's their daddy too."

"And they murdered twenty-three people for that? That seems a bit much even for a child custody dispute."

"Please, starborn!" Talitha said. "We don't have time or energy to waste on squabbling. Rigel, the reason we went to Spica before going on to Tarazed is that Starborn Cheleb has a way of locating people that doesn't rely on their amulets. We went to Spica to find a hair from Izar's head. We took one off his pillow, and Cheleb put it into a ring she gave me. That amulet is not reacting, so I know that Izar's not here."

"Thank you," Rigel said. He wondered if he'd be able to straighten his legs, one at a time, if he kept a tight grip on Gruesome's comb so that it couldn't bite him. "So where do we try next?"

Talitha hesitated, and then said, "Let's try Alsafi first. That's the Phegda playground—soft beaches and surf, waterfalls and unicorn rides, all the things Izar loves. If Vildiar himself ordered this and wants to woo Izar to him, that's where he'll take him."

"And if he isn't there?"

"Hadar has his own private fortress, Giauzar. As you might guess, it has a nightmarish reputation. Escape and rescue are probably equally impossible. No outsiders are ever allowed in and the only access is by portal. I've never been there, so I won't be of much help."

"But it exists somewhere in the Starlands," Rigel protested. "It must be within Phegda, right?"

"Yes," Cheleb said, "and I can probably find it. But Hadar is quite capable of playing a double game and taking Izar somewhere else. A prisoner of his age would not be hard to detain. Let's forget about Alsafi for now. We can learn if Izar is in Giauzar by flying over it."

"If Giauzar is impregnable," Rigel said, "you'd better tell me all about it now, so that I have some time to work out how I can break in."

"Pffooey! No doubt Halfling Rigel's celebrated tactical analysis will become a classic of magical lore for future generations to marvel at. First let us scan the place and establish whether or not the starling is there. If he is, we may need to negotiate."

Rigel said, "Thanks very much!" under his breath. Would he be the quid or the quo? Aloud he added, "Let's fly, then, Gruesome," without specifying whom he was addressing.

Chapter 35

The sky was still dark, but the moon had gone and a first breath of morning was snuffing out the stars. All three cockatrices were exhausted. Rigel needed all his newfound skill to make Gruesome fly up the long slope of the mountain; the other two followed, but they hung farther back than they had earlier. When he reached the summit, he let his mount perch on the rocky crown and rest. He gingerly massaged his thighs, which were knotted with cramp.

The crater was astonishing, several kilometers wide and filled with velvet black shadow. What he could see of the walls suggested that they fell sheer to an invisible floor. On Earth he would have intended that "sheer" to mean "extremely steep" but in the Starlands anything might be literally true. A faint lightness in the eastern sky backlit the far rim, and a thin wind blew. Fatigue had turned his muscles to mush and his bones to lead.

The other two cockatrices landed, Talitha on his left and Cheleb on his right, a little too close for Gruesome, which hissed angrily but was too weary to make any real trouble.

"A remarkable feat of imagination," Cheleb remarked approvingly. "Based on some earthly model, no doubt, but tweaked as needed. The rim looks too regular to appear in nature. Have we any idea of what's inside?"

"Swamp and jungle," Talitha said in a harsh voice. "Impassable and deadly, stocked with snakes and alligators and every other horror imaginable. So Halfling Botein told me one night when she was even drunker than usual."

Cheleb sniffed. "From long acquaintance with Prince Vildiar, I am certain that he will not have overlooked the need for aerial defense, so allow for griffins, vampire bats, flying snakes, and such. Our mounts' stony stares should defend us, but I am concerned about their condition. If we fly them down into that hole, they will lack the strength to fly us back out again."

"The amulet is detecting Izar," Talitha said, her voice rising an octave. "He is here."

Cheleb said, "Mmph! Its range is not great, so he must be close. I wish I knew how deep this was."

"A hundred meters at most," Rigel said. "I can see stars reflected on open water."

"I can't."

He was tempted to tell her she needed glasses but contented himself with a sympathetic sigh.

Talitha said, "So can I. You must be at the wrong angle. A meter is about a pace, right Rigel?"

"A starfolk pace, yes. Can I make this stupid reptile walk forward, starborn?"

"Try putting its head down a little and squeezing its comb."

The cockatrice squeaked in protest at that treatment, but did lurch forward a few steps, to the very brink of the cliff.

If Izar was close, he had to be almost directly below the watchers, probably on an island fortified against black-lagoon monsters. *Yes, there was a light down there!* It shone brighter than any star, flickering as if it was partially blocked

by foliage. This was the time at which servants would begin
to stir and light lamps.

"Izar will know how to open a portal to Alsafi?"

Talitha said, "Yes, but . . . Why? No, Rigel! You mustn't—"

"We'll meet you there, then. Do *not* follow me, or you'll give
the game away." Before his nerve could fail, he dragged Gruesome's comb back and the brainless cockatrice jumped off the
cliff for him. *"Meissa!"*

He bent his steed's neck over at an impossible angle to make
it descend in a tight spiral. He was undoubtedly slobbering
crazy, but was his madness intended to rescue Izar from this
horrible place, impress Talitha, or just to get back at the acid-
tongued Starborn Cheleb? As he spun downward like a falling
leaf, an exhilarating rush of air and adrenaline drove out all
thoughts of motives. The ride was better than any roller
coaster. Had the ancient partnership of Saiph and Meissa ever
charged into a madder adventure than this one?

The crater wall was not as close to vertical as he'd expected,
and the light was farther away, which made keeping it in sight
all the more vital. Twice he lost track of his beacon, and twice
he found it. By the time he realized that it came from a brightly
lit window reflected on water, he knew that his way to it led
through a clump of trees. There was no way that an aircraft
with Gruesome's impressive wingspan could get through
there, but by then it was too late to do anything but hope for
the best.

The cockatrice was either too stupid or too exhausted to put
up much of a fight. It made a weak effort to veer right, an even
weaker feint to the left, and finally just folded its wings and

went in like a missile. The lighted window that had attracted Rigel's attention—there were two more to the left and one to the right—overlooked a tiny, stagnant pond enclosed in a dense tangle of trees, undergrowth, creepers, and swamp. His only hope of survival was a small platform under the window, perhaps a boat dock, and it was not nearly large enough for the cockatrice to land on.

Gruesome hit the water at a forty-five degree angle and bounced. *The tricky part is dismounting*, Chelab had said. Rigel hurtled free, turned a complete somersault, and belly-flopped into the explosion of water that his mount had raised. Had he landed on his feet or made a respectable dive, he would have undoubtedly died on the snarl of trunks and branches under the surface, or been caught up in it. He scraped his knees and shins as he struggled to find footing, but there was no footing, only rot and tangle. The fetid water was too shallow for swimming and God alone knew what might be lurking in it. He was a couple of meters away from the edge of the dock, but a man could drown in much less water than that.

He had certainly not landed unobtrusively. Water and debris from the impact had sprayed the side of the building; his struggles to reach safety required a great deal of thrashing and were in full view of the window. Gruesome was splashing too, and its screams were easily the loudest noises Rigel had heard it make all night. It sounded as if something was attacking it, and he didn't even want to think about the kind of beasts that preyed upon cockatrices. Having lost his basilisk mask in the chaos of his landing, he dared not turn around to see.

Just as he gripped the edge of the dock, a door opened, and a man stepped out, with the light behind him. He wore nothing but a towel around his hips and shaving soap on his face.

He had starfolk ears but was obviously a halfling. His name was not apparent.

He watched as the intruder in the grandiose bronze helmet tried to climb out of the mire, and a sword appeared in his hand. "Halfling Rigel!" he said. "How nice of you to drop by! We were warned you might. Hey, Graffias, come and see what—"

At that point he made the mistake of looking up to see what else was paddling in his pond. He toppled forward as majestically as a tyrant's statue pulled down by a mob, hit the edge of the deck with his knees, and pitched headfirst into the water. Gruesome's shrieks of pain stopped abruptly as whatever was attacking it dragged it under the water.

Without any recollection of having done so, Rigel had left the water and relocated himself on the planking. Looking down to see if he could rescue the petrified halfling, he was just in time to watch toothy jaws close around the man's legs, and a tentacle encircle his neck. Whoever he was, he disappeared into the depths in a swirl of dark water, leaving behind nothing more than a few bubbles. Rigel quickly glanced around for a harpoon or a boat hook, but there was no need for boats on a pond smaller than a suburban bathroom. The stage was a fishing platform, not a jetty. A heap of rods, stools, and baskets indicated that fishing must be part of the entertainment package available at Giauzar.

"What's the matter?" said a voice from the interior. Rigel scrambled to his feet and dove behind the open door as yet another halfling emerged from the building. He wore jeans, surprisingly, and from the rear looked entirely human, except that he was projecting his name, Graffias. He said, "Hassaleh? Hassaleh!"

From behind him, a soft voice said, "Do not look around, Graffias Halfling. I have Saiph and any sudden movements or cries for help will send you to join Hassaleh in the monsters' banquet. Now take one step forward."

Graffias had gone as rigid as a marble column, but one step would put him right on the edge of the deck. One more . . . He said, "No!" hoarsely, and then cried out as a sharp point drew blood close to where his left kidney was busily trying to refill his suddenly voiding bladder.

"That is Saiph," the voice reminded him. "I didn't say you were to step off. I don't intend to kill you, but I will if I must, and you will have no chance against Saiph. Now take another step forward, then turn around."

Graffias obeyed. From the front, with the window light on him, he still looked passably human, having nipples and ears more human than Rigel's own. He would not have been notably tall even on Earth, but he had his father's beetling brow and elongated features. He seemed young—young enough to be bullied perhaps.

"You look quite a lot like your daddy," Rigel said.

The kid licked his lips. "Thank you, Halfling Rigel."

"I didn't mean it as a compliment. I know Imp Izar is here and I am going to rescue him. If you help me, I will not harm you."

"Hadar will feed me to the polliwogs." Graffias's crooked smile was a commendable effort, but not convincing.

"If you let him. You have a golden opportunity here. Electra is back, so if you help us escape, and then testify against Hadar and his wolf pack on the Star, she will reward you beyond your wildest dreams."

"I will!"

"That was a very quick surrender," Rigel said suspiciously.

"I mean it!"

"I suppose if I had Saiph at my throat and polliwogs at my ass, I might be eager too. You swear you will help me rescue the imp?"

"Yes, I swear. I tried once before to get out! I don't want to be one of them, Rigel. I *really, really* don't! Do you know what Hadar does to people he considers losers?"

Rigel *really, really* did not want to know. "Where is Izar?"

"In the larder, er . . . I mean the jail."

"How far away is it, and how far from there to the portal?"

"Not far."

"How many men . . . How many people are here?"

Graffias paused, and then said, "Seven. Six now, after what you did to Hassaleh."

"I didn't do anything to him. It was an accident. I wish I had more faith in your arithmetic. Is Hadar here?"

"I don't think so, Rigel. He often comes through at about this time, though, to give us our orders for the day."

"So you really *don't* know how many people there are here?" It was disgustingly easy to bully people when you had Saiph's authority.

"Not exactly." Graffias swallowed nervously. "At least six, counting me. We're only one step away from anywhere in the domain, sir!"

"All right, take me to Izar now. Don't forget that the deadliest weapon in the Starlands is right behind you, held by the man who used it to kill Tarf, Muscida, and Adhil yesterday. Understand?"

"Yes, my lord."

"Not your lord, your friend. Remember whose side you are on now. Lead the way." Rigel wished he didn't sound so much like a bad action movie, but that was probably because his plan was utter madness. On the other hand, fortune favored the bold and wasting time trying to think up a better idea would just give the rest of the Vildiar gang more time to wake up.

Graffias opened the door. Rigel followed him into a very large communal bathroom. The fixtures were of semiprecious stone and the fittings of gold, but those were probably no more difficult for a mage to imagine than ceramic and chrome.

Beyond that lay a wide corridor of thick, soft carpet, richly decorated walls, and intricately carved doors. Rigel had been expecting some sort of dank dungeon in the depths of the infamous Giauzar crater, but nothing was too good for Hadar and his brethren. A few doors farther along, a passage led off to the left.

"That's the way to the mess," Graffias said. "We may be seen. You'll have to trust me."

"If I hear one squeak, I'll kill you deader than Tarf. I swear I will." Rigel distrusted his own oath even more than he distrusted his guide's, but he stopped at the corner. Graffias walked across, looking to see if there were any watchers. On the far side, he halted and turned.

"It's safe."

Rigel crossed. The three steps it needed took hours.

"Do you trust me now?" Graffias asked, eyeing him earnestly. He had blue eyes and blond hair, blue at the roots. He must have extroverted recently.

"Not yet. Keep going."

They reached an open door. Again Graffias halted.

"This is my room. There's no one else in there."

Rigel told him to keep walking, and followed close behind him. As he went past, he glimpsed a large, luxurious, but not very tidy, bedchamber. The corridor led to a dead end, and there Graffias stopped at a door like all the others.

"The imp's in here. There's no guard with him, as far as I know. I'm just a trainee, and they don't tell me much. All I get is orders." Graffias was either the finest actor in the universe, or he was terrified half out of his wits. His jeans were soaked, and he stank of urine.

But Rigel couldn't be very fragrant himself, fresh from a swim in stagnant swamp water and a long ride on a cockatrice. "Any magic? Locks? Booby traps?"

"Not that I know of. Stars! I'm doing my best for you, halfling!"

"Open it and go in, then."

Rigel followed him through. There was no luxury in this room, just bare stone walls and floor, bars on the windows, a slop bucket, and a metal bedstead with a flock mattress. Rigel left the door ajar, and waited a moment to make sure it would not try to close by itself, locking him inside.

Then he went across to the boy asleep on the bed. A brass chain connected his wrist to the headboard; all his amulets had been removed, but otherwise he seemed to be unharmed.

Graffias said, "He's been like that ever since we . . ."

"Since what?"

"Since he was brought here," Graffias finished, his face aflame with guilt.

"I meant it when I promised you a royal pardon," Rigel said. "But stand farther back, just so I don't get nervous. Izar? Wake up, Izar, it's Rigel."

The imp's ears twitched and straightened, and then his iridescent eyes opened and blinked.

Izar smiled sleepily. "Knew you'd come! I told my self it mustn't wake up until it heard your voice."

Chapter 36

It felt good to be a hero to somebody, even a child. Rigel swallowed the lump that had just appeared in his throat. "That's what friends are for. The first thing we need to do is get that chain off you. Sit up. Hold your hand here." He arranged the imp's wrist so that the chain was draped over the top rail of the bedstead. "Now close your eyes for a moment." Saiph cut the metal like wax.

The clang made Izar jump. He inspected the two links attached to his manacle. *"Doggy!* Oo, Rigel, I really need to go pee!" He swung his reedy legs over the edge of the bed. "It was so horrible what—" his voice trailed off in a wail.

"It's all right!" Rigel said quickly. "Halfling Graffias is on our side now."

He was so far, anyway.

"But he was shooting arrows!" Izar said shrilly. "He shot Baham! And Narwhale and—"

"But now he's helping you escape, so he's all right. I'll explain later, but do your pee quickly, because we must hurry." Rigel dearly wished Izar had not made those allegations just yet.

Graffias's face had turned to bone, hard and yellow. He might believe in Rigel's good intentions, but would he be willing to entrust his life to a babbling imp?

"There were other people shooting arrows at Spica, Izar, weren't there?" Rigel asked, desperately hoping that the answer was *yes*. "And you couldn't see which arrows came from which bows. But Graffias was just pretending. All his shots missed, didn't they, halfling?"

"I tried to miss as much as I dared," Graffias said. That would have to be his defense if he were brought to trial.

"And now you're going to lead us to the portal?"

"Yes, I am."

"And we're all going to go join your mother, Izar."

"I need a *long* drink of water," Izar announced, having finished his business with the bucket. "Don't think I've *ever* been this thirsty."

Before Rigel could reply, an angry shout came from just outside the door. "What do you mean you can't find them? You mean they've gone?"

Izar turned as pale as milk and his mouth stretched into a rictus of horror. Graffias looked little better. Rigel doubted if he did himself. The gap between the door and the jamb was too narrow to reveal the speaker, but he blocked the light all the way to the top of it. Only one starborn was tall enough to do that.

The reply was more distant, but still audible. "No, lord. I sealed the portal myself when I left last night, and now Tegmine is keeping watch to make sure nobody leaves. They have to be on the island somewhere." That was Hadar's voice.

Rigel shivered. His plan had been doomed from the start. He had never considered the possibility that the gang would lock Giauzar off from the outside world, trapping both Izar *and* his guards inside.

Vildiar said, "I do wish you'd *find them*, for stars' sake! Or at least find Graffias. If Graffias has gotten away, I'll toast your balls on a fork."

"He can't have escaped, lord. He's a loser. He was heaving his guts out at Spica. My guess is that the guilt curse got him, and he went to feed the polliwogs."

"Your guess is worthless, Hadar. The guilt curse never affects halflings and never leads to suicide. It just kills. I don't care about Hassaleh, but I will be *much happier* if I know for certain that Botein, Graffias, Sadalbari, and Benetnash are all here in Giauzar when you and I leave."

"I like you to be *happy*, Father."

So that was how it was done? A command had just been issued and acknowledged, yet both would be deniable on the Star of Truth.

With a finger over his lips to indicate silence, Rigel tapped Izar's shoulder and pointed to the bed. The imp spun around and raced back to it. He flopped onto the mattress, adjusted the end of the chain under his wrist, and closed his eyes. His ears did not go fully limp, but what a great kid! Rigel stepped behind the door. Graffias moved in behind him. He wore many amulets, any of which could be a sword in waiting. Rigel's trust in the young halfling was being stretched very thin. Considering how hopeless the situation now seemed, Graffias had to be tempted to try to win back his daddy's love by turning in Halfling Rigel's corpse with a hole in its back.

The door began to open, and then stopped. Vildiar spoke again.

"I can't wait here while you search the entire island. Change of plans: I'll take the imp and leave first. *I'll be happiest* if you keep everyone out of the way until I'm gone and if only you and Tegmine know I was here at all. If you can't find Hassaleh, I shan't mind if you leave without him. But I'd really like you to find Graffias or prove that he's dead. And when you have the whole Spica crew in custody here, I'd like you to take the others and go. Today's key to seal the portal is 'Grumium.' You need to say it three times; understand?"

"Yes, my lord. 'Grumium' three times."

"When you've done that, I'd be *happier* if you moved the rest of the family to Zubenelgenubi. I'll be at the funeral in Canopus. And remember that I want *no one* besides Tegmine to know I've been here. Go!"

The door swung open, and His Highness strode into the room, ducking under the lintel. He did not go over to the bed, perhaps not wanting to frighten the imp.

"Izar? Wake up, Son."

Triumph! Rigel had only to raise his hand to that grotesquely long, bony back and then summon Saiph. One quick jab and the problem would be solved—the monster would be dead, and the portal would be accessible. Tegmine could not single-handedly hold it against Saiph, even if Graffias didn't defect back to his daddy's team. *Victory pulled from the jaws of disaster!* But could Rigel Estell really kill Izar's father right in front of him? Could he murder Vildiar in cold blood, evil though the starborn undoubtedly was? What would Talitha want him to do?

"Izar?" the prince said again. "I was very sorry to hear about what happened at Spica, Son. The people who did those terrible things are going to be punished."

This was all a game! Vildiar *must* know Rigel was there. That discussion out in the corridor had been much too convenient. Rigel had always despised stories in which the villains discussed their plans right outside the hero's hiding place. Such things never happened in real life; even in the Starlands that would be stretching fantasy too far.

The prince sighed. "I can tell that you're not really asleep, Izar. I'm going to take you to your mother now, I promise. Why haven't you tried to kill me yet, halfling?"

Izar shot off the bed on the far side and squeezed into a corner, as far from his father as he could get. His eyes stretched as big as his ears.

Vildiar turned around to stare down at Rigel from his impossible height, like a gardener inspecting a bug.

Before stamping on it.

"I was warned not to, my lord."

"You have become a serious nuisance, mongrel. I warned you off last night. I shall not be as lenient next time." He curled his lip at Graffias. "You didn't take long to defect. Whose side are you on at the moment?"

"Justice's," Graffias mumbled, avoiding his father's gaze. He had been tested too, and had failed. He should have tried to save his father by stabbing Rigel in the back when he had the chance. Backstabbing seemed to be out of fashion today.

"You were planning to betray us, your own family? Hadar was right when . . . But you heard. Answer my question, Halfling Rigel. Why didn't you try to kill me?"

Rigel had no idea. Was he just too wimpishly scrupulous to stab someone from behind, even someone as odious as Vildiar? Was Vildiar's magic powerful enough to neutralize Saiph? That was not what people had been telling him about his "ancestral" amulet.

"Because of what the Pythia told me, Your Highness." Let the monster chew on that! Rigel was pleased to hear he had become a serious nuisance, and he wasn't going to flinch under the giant elf's anger. He turned to look at Graffias. "Was Hassaleh present at the Spica massacre?" he asked.

"No."

"But you were. That's why you matter and he doesn't. So, Your Highness, when Hadar has collected all the Spica witnesses and sealed them in, how long will you shelter them from the queen's justice?"

Vildiar studied him with the disgust due a well-trodden dog turd on a Persian rug. "Are you ignorant or just trying to be funny? A prince administers justice within his domain. What happened at Spica was unforgivable incompetence. The guilty will stay here until they have eaten all the polliwogs, or the polliwogs have eaten all of them, or they have eaten one another. I don't care which comes first. If Her Majesty wants to send them to the Dark Cells, I will gladly turn them over to her."

"Tough love? Fatherly discipline? I came to escort Izar back to his mother."

"So did I."

"I wanna go with Rigel!" Izar shouted.

His father shrugged. "As you will. Will you lead the way, halfling, or shall I?"

Nobody moved. Vildiar was making another of his lighting fast U-turns, like the one he had made in court when Kornephoros tried to sentence Rigel to death. Izar was the key, of course. Had he not been here, the polliwogs would already be munching on Rigel and Graffias. But Vildiar could no longer deny knowledge of his son's kidnapping, so he had to put himself on the side of the angels. He always had two roles to play and for now he was portraying the loving, caring father. Anyone who would believe that would try to buy pork in Jerusalem.

Rigel had an uncomfortable feeling that he was playing sixth in a Russian roulette tournament. "I think perhaps you had better lead, my lord."

"And what happens at the portal?" Vildiar inquired scornfully. "Am I to be stabbed in the back or locked up here in Giauzar to die with the incompetents?"

"Neither," Rigel said, "as long as you let us depart in peace."

Vildiar ducked out the door without comment. Izar rushed to Rigel's side and clasped his hand like a small child. They followed Graffias into the corridor and all three hurried after the tall starborn.

Rigel bent toward one of the imp's big ears. "You remember Alsafi, Izar?" he whispered.

"Yes, Rigel."

"Your mom is waiting there for you."

"But you're coming too!" Izar's eyes sparkled as if he had been weeping, but that was just the Naos in him.

"I'm planning on it, but you will have to open the portal."

They reached a large sitting room, furnished with rich rugs and a cluster of chairs and sofas. Its windows looked out onto a jungle faintly lit by predawn light, and opposite them stood a large double door, much like many of the other portals Rigel had seen. The storm trooper halfling who waited next to it walked forward to greet his father. It was Tegmine, who had accompanied Tarf and their father on the royal barge the previous day. He scowled at the sight of Rigel, and then sneered at Graffias.

"We should have left my darling baby brother in diapers, my lord."

Vildiar ignored his comment. "Go and tell Hadar that I have located Graffias." He watched his son leave before saying, "Does Izar know where his mother is?"

Rigel said, "Yes, my lord."

"Then run along, son. I wish to speak with Rigel."

Izar's face fell like a shooting star.

"Rigel will follow you in a few moments," his father said. "I promise."

The imp opened the door, and disappeared into a swirl of salty wind and ocean scent. He left the portal open, but it closed itself behind him. Now the grown-ups could get down to serious business.

"You look bushed, halfling," Vildiar said graciously. "Please sit down." He scowled at Graffias. "You will be more comfortable standing, I expect. Now, Rigel, where did you meet the Pythia?"

Rigel sank into a delightfully soft, velvet-upholstered chair and promptly yawned. "Pardon me, my lord. I've been up all night. On Tarazed."

"Cockatrices? Ingenious! Does that explain what happened to Hassaleh?" The Naos's mind was sharper than razors.

"Yes. He was petrified, and he was attacked by one of the creatures in the lagoon before I could fish him out. It was an accident."

The prince's lips twisted into a cynical smile, one without humor. "My family has had a serious run of bad luck lately. I've never heard of the Pythia prophesying for a halfling before. What did she tell you?" He was being very sweet for a mass murderer—no bluster, no veiled threats, just princely courtesy. He had all the time in the world to get what he wanted, and he was content to wait. He was as deadly as a third rail.

Fighting more yawns, Rigel wished he had chosen a less comfortable chair. "She quoted a poem she knew I would recognize. It's by William Shakespeare. You know of him, my lord?"

"I saw him act once. Tell me."

Rigel said,

"It droppeth as the gentle rain from heaven
Upon the place beneath: it is twice blest;
It blesseth him that gives and him that takes:
'Tis mightiest in the mightiest: it becomes
The thronéd monarch better than his crown.

"'Becomes' means 'adorns' in this case, of course."

Vildiar studied him with eyes of rainbow. He was taking the upstart halfling more seriously now than he had before, which was both flattering and terrifying. "I give up. What's the answer?"

"Mercy. Or, rather, the attribute of being merciful. She was warning me not to stab you when I had the chance."

"You didn't have the chance. Saiph or not, I'd have burned you to ashes."

"But I didn't know that, did I? The Pythia did."

"That doggerel does sound like the sort of thing that Jacobean scribbler spouted, and the Pythia is typically obscure in her prophecies, but your logic escapes me." He paused, and then suddenly changed tack, "Who gave my son the killer amulet?"

Oops! "I am not at liberty to answer that, my lord."

The giant was pacing aimlessly as he spoke. "Never once have I given Talitha cause to hate me, Rigel, but she does—virulently. She has a spiteful tongue and no scruples about telling the most appalling untruths. Despite what she has told you, I am not a monster. I admit I have faults, as we all do. I despised Kornephoros as an incompetent prude and Electra as a wastrel who has neglected her realm for decades. I am eager to show that I could be a better ruler. Is that so terrible?"

The end, perhaps not. The means, yes. Tactfully: "I am not competent to judge either the political problem or your noble self as the solution, my lord."

Vildiar continued on as if he had not heard. "I enjoy earth-ling women, a shameful perversion that I have tried to shake off many times without success. But I am generous. I make sure that the women are willing beforehand and well provided for after, and any children that may result are given an educa-tion and lifelong employment."

Miscegenation sounded like an expensive hobby, but no doubt all those eager young tweenlings managed to earn their keep somehow. Rigel fought desperately against another yawn.

The prince stopped close to him, and stared down at him again. "There are not so very many of them when you consider my age—about one every ten years or so. And they are not as-sassins and terrorists, as Talitha would have people believe. We all know that halflings can be dangerous, don't we? Yesterday you broke into my domain, claiming to have authority from a queen who hadn't been seen since before you were born. Of course my sons challenged an intruder they knew to be armed—what would you expect? Before they even had time to open the paper you claimed was a royal warrant, you drew your sword and disemboweled my son Tarf. Only magic stopped him from dying instantly, and you finished him off later, him and two others. You started the fight. Who bears the blood guilt, Rigel?"

Rigel was in very serious trouble. And Vildiar was standing with one foot between his, so that he couldn't even rise from his chair.

"Your daughter was the first to draw, my lord. That was folly when she knew I wore the ancestral Saiph. Shall we discuss Spica?"

"Spica?" Opalescent eyebrows rose. "By all means, let us discuss Spica. Talitha disobeyed the regent's express orders by sending our child to her domain instead of taking him to Canopus. When she was informed of this, my daughter Botein—who is Izar's half sister, of course, and known to him—went to Spica to explain the situation to the imp's attendant, Baham Starborn. Baham agreed to escort the boy to Canopus as the regent had commanded, but Izar invoked a *Lesath!* You know the term? An especially baneful amulet. It is a capital offense to own or make a Lesath. To give one to a child is utter madness."

"The amulet did not slaughter the entire population of Spica, my lord."

"But it began the bloodshed. I told you how the perpetrators will be punished, but is it a wonder that they went berserk? Three of their siblings were killed in front of their eyes, and Botein herself was horribly savaged. The wonder is that they did not kill Izar out of hand. If the imp had not been given that Lesath, not one drop of blood would have been shed."

Rigel could not bandy words with the starborn. He was out of his league, and every cell in his body ached with fatigue. "Well, he did not get it from me, my lord." He set his hands on the arms of the chair to show that he wished to rise.

Vildiar did not budge. "Even so, here you are, trespassing in my domain again, and now another one of my sons has died. And you dare to call me murderer?"

"By your leave, Halfling Graffias and I will go now, for I must escort my sponsor to her father's funeral."

The prince shrugged, stepping out of Rigel's way. "You are an extraordinarily resourceful youngster, Halfling Rigel. I do wish that you had accepted me as your sponsor yesterday. If you ever change your mind, I will be happy to take you on. I promise that there will be no revenge. And despite all the lies you have been fed, there will be no murders, either." He looked across at Graffias. "You wish to go with him, Son?"

Graffias nodded several times before he managed to whisper, "Yes, Father."

"And you hope to buy your life by selling your brothers' and sisters'?"

It would not take Vildiar long to talk the turncoat into a complete 360 degree revolution. Rigel hauled himself upright.

"I have promised him a royal pardon, my lord."

"Did you, now?" Vildiar tried, but he could no more depict surprise than could his lookalikes on Easter Island. "On your own authority?"

Dangerous question! Royal blood did not turn a halfling into a prince and never would, even if Electra was ever willing to reveal her outrageous secret in public.

"Having just returned Izar to his mother, I am certain that I have enough influence."

The resulting stare went on dangerously long as the prince tried to guess just how much Rigel knew and how much royal favor he might possess.

"Nice helmet," Vildiar said at last. "Take Graffias by all means, but you will need to find another sponsor for him, and he is a pathetic thing, even for a half-breed. This has gone on long enough. I must go to Canopus."

Graffias dived for the portal and swung it open. Rigel bowed to the prince and followed. He did not try to seal the portal behind him with the *Grumium* password, because he was certain that the mage would simply use an override to open it again.

Chapter 37

He stepped through into another starfolk playground, like the Alrisha swimming hole. It was a sheltered bay ringed by steep cliffs with only a narrow channel connecting it to the sea. There were all the usual conveniences on hand: shady trees, a waterfall, a sandy beach, and mossy banks. A few meters away, Talitha was still embracing her son, and the look of relief that swept across her face when she met Rigel's eyes made every moment of the terrible night seem worthwhile. Graffias turned his back on her, hiding his shame.

Rigel said, "Race you, halfling," and sprinted toward the water. They hit the surface together. It was a very brief dip, followed by a quick sprint to the waterfall to rinse off, but it rid Rigel of the swamp smell and turned Graffias's jeans a uniform wet blue. By the time the two of them returned to the beach, Izar was recovering some traces of his customary toothy smile. He had seen horrors, but his ability to turn himself off at will had hopefully saved him from serious trauma.

Talitha gave Graffias a cold glare. "Izar tells me that you were one of the raiders at Spica, but that you're on our side now?"

"I have much to tell, Your Highness."

"That is good, very good. It is long past time. Consider yourself under arrest at present, but I am sure Her Majesty will grant you a full pardon if you answer every question put to you on the Star, in which case I shall be happy to sponsor you." Then she turned to Rigel with a smile that demanded to be instantly and thoroughly kissed.

So he did.

After a while, Izar said, "I thought grown-ups laid down to do that?"

Rigel released her, which wasn't easy. Graffias looked appalled—a princess allowing a mere halfling to take such liberties?

Talitha turned away and headed for the portal. "You left in such a hurry," she said over her shoulder, "that we didn't set up a proper rendezvous. There are a dozen portals in Alsafi. I came here because I knew it was Izar's favorite. Cheleb is watching another. So that is where we must go first."

She led the way to a cobbled yard enclosed by stables and sheds on three sides, and a rambling, thatched house on the fourth. It had a dovecot and pigeons and a sleeping dog, as if inspired by some syrupy calendar art. The only otherworldly touch was the open carriage that sat at its center. It had the customary large wheels at the back and a smaller pair at the front, two upholstered benches, and a canopy, which was currently folded down, but it lacked shafts to hold a horse, and had no visible means of propulsion—unless, Rigel decided, one counted Starborn Cheleb as such. She was dozing on the coachman's box, her back erect but her head down, hair shining copper in the dawn sun, ears drooping.

Izar said, "Where's Dschubba? I wanna see Dschubba!"

"I expect he's still asleep," said his mother. "His father said we could borrow their carriage."

"Doggy! You going to drive, Mom?"

Cheleb came alert, swept her gaze over the arrivals, and deigned to grant Rigel a nod of approval. "I did not expect to see you again, halfling. Very well done."

Praise indeed! He bowed and said, "Thank you, starborn," with all the grace he could muster.

"Will you drive, please?" Talitha asked her. "And let Izar ride on the box? Halfling Graffias has turned queen's evidence. I must hear some of his testimony so that I can properly advise Her Majesty."

Izar's happiness fizzled in an instant. "Wanna stay with you and Rigel. I'm not comp'etely recovered yet. You have to be specially consid'rate of my needs."

"Starborn Cheleb wants to hear all about your adventure."

His lip trembled. "I have to sit between you two so you don't misbehave."

Talitha kept her patience. "You keep telling me you want to start highway training. Starborn Cheleb will give you a lesson. Won't you, starborn?"

"Of course," the mage said, although her expression would have turned princes into things much lowlier than frogs. Izar hesitated while he evaluated the bribe, then he grinned and scrambled up to the box in a swirl of twiggy limbs.

Talitha had a royal knack for getting her own way. Rigel handed her up to the carriage, then joined her on the rear bench, wrapping his arm around her. Graffias sat facing them. The carriage soared upward, narrowly clearing the rooftops, and swung around to the east.

"We don't have long," Talitha said, being very businesslike despite—or perhaps because of—the nearness of Rigel's hand to her right breast. "I don't recall meeting you when I lived at Phegda."

"No, Your Highness. I just graduated from Unukalhai three months ago."

"Tell me what you know. I promise that nothing you say on this journey will be used against you, although you will be interrogated later on the Star. You've been extroverting?"

Graffias nodded guiltily. "It's part of the training. To qualify as full members of the Family . . ."

"Go on!"

"We have to kill an earthling—a wild one, not a domestic."

"*Stars!*" Talitha looked at Rigel in horror.

He shrugged, not surprised. He guessed that there would be even more lurid revelations to come; Graffias would best help his cause by making his testimony top every rumor. "Tell Her Highness about Spica."

"Oh, that was Botein's doing, my lady. She was at Canopus with a squad of us, standing by in case V . . . that's Prince Vildiar, our father. In case he needed us. Tegmine arrived and said that V wanted Izar, and Izar had been sent to Spica. Botein decided to make a grab . . ."

Graffias's story closely followed what the Pythia had told Sphinx Praecipua. Five men and two women had gone to Spica in two carriages. It had seemed like an easy prospect—ambush the imp in the fields, kill or intimidate his attendant, Baham, and leave with both of them. Alive or dead, Baham could be fed to the polliwogs at Giauzar, and there would be no evidence. The plan had gone terribly awry when Izar unleashed Turais.

"We never thought," Graffias said, "that an imp like him would be trusted with anything like that. A *Lesath*! None of our amulets worked on it! It killed Ain and Homam and Haedi and damned nearly ripped Botein's hand off. I put three arrows through its heart before I dropped it."

Graffias did not repeat what Hadar had said about him—that he had heaved his guts out at the scene of the massacre—but by the time he finished the story, he was weeping. He was either a very good actor or a very poor terrorist.

"Frankly, I wish it had killed all of you," Talitha said. "His Highness could not have been pleased."

"Hadar made Botein tell V herself," Graffias said. "I wasn't there, thank the stars. And right after that came the news that Halfling Rigel had taken out Tarf, Adhil, and Muscida at Canopus."

The world lurched. Izar's driving lessons had begun in earnest, and he was at the helm. Rigel tightened his grip on Talitha, for the carriage had no sides to prevent passengers from falling out, although that might be a more pleasant death than whatever Hadar was undoubtedly planning for him. The carriage tilted nose-down and then nose-up.

Then it dropped like a cliff diver.

"That's enough driving for today!" Talitha shouted. "I don't want any more funerals, thank you!" The descent slowed and stopped just above tree height. She continued talking as if nothing had happened. "And now Rigel has rescued my son and helped you defect."

"And killed Hassaleh," Graffias agreed. "You must be very careful in the future, halfling! The Family has very rarely been bested in anything, and will avenge its own. Just because V let you go today doesn't mean that you've been forgiven."

"I never dreamed that it did," Rigel said. "And I don't believe that he's going to leave Botein, Sadalbari, and Benetnash locked up in Giauzar to starve to death, either."

Graffias looked blank. "You don't? But we heard him tell—"

"We were meant to hear him tell Hadar all that. They knew we were inside that door the whole time."

Talitha pulled a face. "Tell us about the Family."

If she was planning to bring all of Graffias's evidence to light that day—presumably right after the funeral, while the court was still packed with mourners—anything might happen. Rigel decided that he was giddy with fatigue and needed to catch some sleep if he hoped to guard Izar during the coming riot or revolution. He was not at all interested in Graffias's description of the prince's nursery at Unukalhai, with its regular output of halfling babies. He leaned his head back and closed his eyes.

Chapter 38

Cheleb landed the carriage in a relatively small courtyard in the palace, one that Rigel had not seen the previous day. He jumped down to offer a hand to Talitha, and by that time sphinxes and starborn were already closing in around them. Izar had moved very close to Rigel, practically leaning on him. Commander Zozma bounded in from a side alley and pushed his way to the front of the throng.

He bowed. "Welcome back, Your Highness. And your noble son is a very welcome sight as well." He bowed to Izar, who grinned delightedly at this homage. His ears seemed to sprout even longer.

"He is indeed," Talitha said. "And this, as you can see, is Halfling Graffias. He is going to give—"

"Her Majesty wishes to see you urgently, Your Highness."

Talitha frowned. "This is urgent too. Graffias is a very valuable and willing witness. See that he is treated with respect, decently clad, and, if time permits, fed. And above all, make sure that he is well guarded! Cheleb, dear, will you also keep an eye on him, please?"

A lobster's smile could not be thinner-lipped than the mage's. "I would do so even if you did not ask me, my lady. I do hate the smell of fried sphinx."

"Thank you. Commander, see that Izar and Rigel are guarded also. Now escort me to the queen."

Zozma started barking orders.

"I hope you're hungry, Izar Imp," Rigel said. "Because I could eat a cat."

"Don't push your luck, halfling," said a familiar voice from behind him.

Rigel turned. "My luck is unbeatable at the moment, Sphinx Praecipua. It carries all before it. How are Rasalas and Alterf?"

"On the mend. We all feel rather inadequate since you came on the scene. And you, imp—congratulations on your adventure. You have an incredible bodyguard."

"He's not bad," Izar conceded, his grin almost as wide as it usually was.

"If you are really hungry, I can catch a harpy for you, but you'll have to eat it quickly. Come along."

Praecipua set off at a lope, with Rigel and Izar running behind him and Sphinxes Kalb and Adhafera bringing up the rear. In moments Rigel and his ward were seated cross-legged on mats in front of a low table, gobbling food that was definitely not raw harpy. The three sphinxes crouched around them, listening intently while Izar recounted his kidnapping and rescue, speaking and eating at the same time and at the same frantic pace. Just as halflings were a seemingly random collection of elfin and human features, so Izar was a curious hybrid of child and adult. Despite his looks, he had almost as much life experience as Rigel did. He babbled out his story in far more detail than Rigel would have considered necessary or even proper, for he was not addressing a formal investigation, just three nosey palace cops. And yet when Kalb Sphinx asked him where he had gotten the Turais amulet, he avoided her question as slickly as any crooked ward boss stonewalling a grand jury. It took Rigel a minute or two to realize what he had done, and that it had not been an accident.

Somewhere a drum began to beat, and the sphinxes instantly jumped to their paws.

"Fill both hands, imp," Kalb said. "Eat on the way. You are needed at the funeral."

Izar contented himself with carrying off a stuffed papaya in each hand. "I don't like funerals," he told Rigel sulkily as they walked along.

"How many have you been to?"

"Three. All killed by Vildiar."

"I *really* don't think you should say that here. I have never been to a funeral in the Starlands, so tell me what happens."

The ceremony was held in the Great Court where Rigel had almost died the previous day, but what happened was not what Izar remembered and tried to describe, because this time he was family. He was herded about by flustered starfolk wearing a variety of dazzling collars, who repeatedly tried to send Rigel away. Others ordered the imp to "*Get rid of that food,*" but were no more successful—Izar just smiled mushily at them until they turned away in revulsion. Eventually the deceased's grandson was inserted into his proper place within the various family groups arrayed on the wide steps before the throne. In nine hundred years a man could produce a sizable tribe of descendants, all of whom were displayed on the right in order of descent. Having died young, Kornephoros was also survived by many ancestors, and they stood on the left. In all, there must have been two hundred family members on display, and that excluded anyone more than seven generations removed, because there were only seven steps. All others had to stand with the rabble on the floor.

As the only halfling present, Rigel was the target of innumerable furious glares. Talitha was not yet in sight, but when she arrived, she would join Kornephoros's half a dozen other sons and daughters on the top step, one up from Izar. Prince Vildiar was down in the body of the court, towering over everyone, the only Naos royalty present. There would have been numerous others if he had not contrived their absence—did he sense their ghosts?

Despite its size, the great courtyard was packed with starfolk, sphinxes, halflings, humans, centaurs, cyclops, and some miscellaneous species too far away for Rigel to identify. They had come to mourn the starborn who had ruled them for the last generation, and to catch a glimpse of their revenant Queen Electra. There was something odd and muted about the light, as if the sun itself was mourning.

The sphinxes officiously herded mourners out of a center aisle that included the black Star of Truth and the catafalque beyond it, where the deceased lay in a plain wooden casket. Although the queen had said that the heir's golden collar of office would stay with him until his pyre was lit, Rigel could not see it on display. He wondered uneasily if Electra might change her mind and present the heir's insignia to Talitha instead. That would surely be a spider kiss, unless the queen was prepared to denounce Vildiar and somehow lock him up in the Dark Cells. And if Vildiar was not chosen, Talitha was the only possible alternative. Damnation! She certainly did not want that honor, and Rigel did not want it for her.

What was going on with the light? The day seemed to be dimming without consideration for the early hour. Rigel raised a foot and flexed his toes to let the sun shine through them. As he had guessed, the image of the sun was distorted. He bent down to speak in Izar's ear.

"Do *not* look at the sun, but there's going to be an eclipse."

"Of course there is."

End of conversation.

The crowd rumbled constantly, as restless as the ocean. Starfolk were not used to being kept waiting, to being bored, to enduring distasteful realities like funerals. The old should just fade away gracefully. Now the light was definitely fading, and it was past time for the ceremony to begin. What was taking so long?

At last silver trumpets screamed their fanfare, quenching all other noise. Out from behind the great carved throne came— Talitha! She walked over to join her numerous half brothers and half sisters, all of them centuries older than she, and none of them Naos. She was bent and huddled like a waif caught in an Arctic storm, as if she bore a world of trouble on her shoulders. Her eyes sought out Rigel's bronze helmet, and the look she gave him was heavy with horror. Something terrible had happened, he had no doubt, but although she was just one step away from him, he could not go to her.

"What's wrong with Mom?" Izar muttered, provoking angry shushing noises from the geriatric beauties who surrounded him.

Rigel put a hand on his shoulder. "Don't worry!" He would do the worrying for both of them, and it would do them no good at all.

The sun had slimmed down to a crescent when the queen emerged from behind the throne, leaning heavily on the arm of her human secretary, Alfred.

"What's wrong with HER?" Izar demanded. Fortunately his shout was lost in a universal cry of dismay.

Izar had never seen Queen Electra before. Nor had he ever seen an old starborn. Nobody ever saw an old starborn. Electra had aged several centuries overnight. Even in the near darkness her starry aura had faded and shrunk to a faint glow around her neck, and her opalescent hair had lost its sheen. Shuffling unsteadily, peering around as if she were almost blind, she let Alfred guide her to the throne. He stepped aside but did not go very far. He was clearly aghast at what had happened, but somehow that made him look younger, not older.

According to the Izar's program, there would now be "a lot of *schmoory* singing" but that didn't happen. Electra cut straight to the end of the program.

"My people," she said. In fact she managed only a hoarse whisper, but the magical acoustics carried the words throughout the vast courtyard. "My friends." She needed a rest then, to catch a bubbling breath.

After a lifetime of searching, Rigel Estell had found his mother last night. He was about to lose her again, this time forever.

"I killed Kornephoros," the queen said. She waited out the hubbub, and then began again, growing a little stronger, but still halting every few words to catch her breath. "I should never have made him my heir. He did not want it, and that was his greatest virtue in my eyes. Others were too old, too young, too lazy, or too greedy for the title. He had no spark, no soul, but I knew young Korny would do his best . . .

"Let that be his epitaph, that he did his best."

She nodded to a group of court officials—Rigel had already spotted old Wasat among them—and more signals were passed. A reverberating drum roll filled the court, and the crowd near the center hurriedly pushed away from the bier. The thunder grew louder and louder.

The light dimmed until the last speck of sun winked out. In rushed the dark and a startling, skin-puckering coldness. A corona of milky shards blazed up around the jet-black moon and then the stars came: billions of them, more and more crowding in with every second, more than Rigel had ever seen or imagined, blazing galaxies and constellations filling the sky. Surely all of the multitudes of heaven had gathered above the court to honor one of their own, Kornephoros.

Here below, wisps of whitish smoke trickled from the catafalque, followed by tongues of flame—first red, then white, and finally an unbearable violet—until in one great rush of brilliance, one column of glory, Kornephoros was gone. A cloud of multicolored sparks sped away into the starry heavens. Then a hairline of brilliance announced the return of daylight, and the stars departed, taking the soul of Kornephoros with them.

Rigel released a long breath and looked at the tear-stained faces that surrounded him. *That* had been some send-off! Not even a speck of ash remained on the paving where the bier had stood. According to custom, the queen should have left then and the congregation dispersed, or so Izar the prophet had told him, but Electra was far from finished.

"Yesterday . . .

"Yesterday I gave Kornephoros an assignment that he . . . he could not handle.

"Again he did his best.

"It killed him.

"And that is killing me."

Rigel was watching Prince Vildiar. So was everybody else as the rapidly brightening light illuminated his monolithic Easter Island features. How sweet the fruits of success must be! Yet he displayed no emotion whatsoever. Rigel could almost admire him at times—the bastard had class.

"I have two things," the queen mumbled, "to do before I go."

"First, I must right an ancient wrong . . . as much as it can be righted."

Oh, no! Rigel braced himself. He wished she was not going to do this. All his life he had stayed in the shadows. Why couldn't she just leave him there?

"I bore a child," the queen said. "And then I lost him, through no fault of my own. I have sought him for more than twenty years, neglecting my realm to make redress. I found him at last, and he is a son to be proud of. Honor him, not for my sake, but for what he has already achieved in his few days amongst us. Rigel Halfling."

Rigel smiled down at Izar's goggle-eyed amazement. "Stay here." He pushed his way through the crowd of Kornephoros's appalled and outraged relatives—to some incredibly remote degree they were all his relatives now too. When he reached the center of the steps, he bowed, Starlands style, to his mother. On Earth he would have removed his helmet, but here he had to conceal his deformed ears.

She smiled and beckoned him closer. "You told me you needed a birth certificate, Son. This is the best I could do." Just for a moment she showed him a hint of Mira Silvas, but then the pain closed in again, crumpling her face under a crust of antiquity. Alfred handed Rigel a thin tube—a scroll bound with ribbon dangling a wax seal.

Certain that she would not be comforted by lies and hypocrisy, Rigel said only, "Thank you for everything, Mother. You did your best too, and I am proud to be your son. Go in peace." He bent and kissed her parched cheek. Nothing he could say or do would ease her guilt; the wound was mortal. He withdrew and returned to Izar, watched by the furiously buzzing hive of courtiers. He tucked the scroll into the waistband of his wrap.

Electra leaned back, exhausted. Alfred whispered something. She shook her head and roused herself for a final effort.

"Vildiar Starborn . . ."

The gangling prince began to move forward.

". . . is a murdering monster."

He stopped.

"Unfit," she said, "to . . . live, let alone . . . rule, so I must lay my . . . burden on one too . . . young. Help her, help her, all . . . of you."

Talitha was weeping as she went forward to kneel at her greatmother's feet. The dying queen closed her hands around her own throat, and then held them out to clasp's Talitha's neck, passing the Light of Naos to her successor. A rainbow galaxy of stars flamed along Talitha's shoulders and halfway down her back. When she rose and turned to face the court, she was a figure of fire, clad in starry majesty from her breasts to the tips of her ears.

Rigel forced himself to keep his eyes on Vildiar, looming on the sidelines. The giant had flushed scarlet with rage, and the starfolk around him were easing away from him. But he did not hurl fireballs or thunderbolts. Nor did he summon his private army to seize the throne for him—that was not the starfolk's way. Instead, he dissembled to invisibility, and then slipped away as an unremarkable, ordinary elf, lost in the crowd.

Clad in her glory, the Light of Naos, Talitha stepped aside. Electra tried to rise from the throne, but then slumped down, as if all her remaining strength had suddenly deserted her. Alfred and Talitha moved forward to help, but she waved them away, her face twisting in pain. To Rigel's horrified gaze she seemed to be visibly aging, as if the loss of her aura had breached a dam, and her eighteen centuries were drowning her. Her flesh was melting away, her features were shriveling, her breasts were sagging, and she was clearly in agony.

Izar turned away from the horrible sight. "What's happening?"

Rigel clasped him to provide what comfort he could, which was nothing. "It is the guilt curse. She blames herself for the regent-heir's death."

"But that wasn't her fault! That was—"

"Sh! Don't say it." Certainly Naos Vildiar was the chief villain and ought to be the one paying the price.

And what a price! The old queen should have been granted privacy for her death throes, but she suffered and shriveled and died in full view of the court. The starfolk moaned like wind in a forest, but they watched, helpless and sorrowing, until there was nothing left of Electra except a hint of skin and crumbling bones, and then even those shriveled away into nothing. Her empty wrap slid to the floor, and Alfred hastily removed it.

Talitha stepped forward and dismissed the court.

Chapter 39

I could use a swim," Rigel said. What he really needed was time—time to think, time to dig himself out from under an avalanche of confusing emotions. He could not pretend to mourn his mother as a son should, for he had barely known her, but he could mourn his friend Mira and honor the queen who had abandoned a kingdom to spend a generation seeking her lost child.

Courtiers were surging forward to engulf Talitha in waves of comfort or congratulations. Nobody was going near the royal halfling monstrosity, which was a blessing, although now a squad of sphinxes was heading in his direction, which was another. Vildiar and his goons were still at large, and probably even more dangerous than before, now that their perfidy was being dragged out into the open.

"I want my Mom!" Izar said in a very small voice, which showed that the cummulative stress of the last two days was finally shaking even his incredible nerve. It was time for the starling's babysitter to attend to his duties.

"She's going to be very busy for a while, great and noble Izar. The kindest thing you and I can do now is to stay out of her way and let her get on with her business."

And if Queen Talitha could have little time to spare for her son over the next few weeks, she would have none at all to break in a lover. A young princess might accept a halfling paramour, but a new queen—particularly a queen who was bizarrely young by the standards of the Starlands—could not dare to flout the ways of her people so drastically. Vildiar was not the only one who had suddenly been exposed to the glare of unwelcome publicity. Talitha would have to send Rigel away. Not only was their romance dead in the bud, but even to retain him as Izar's bodyguard would probably keep the tongues wagging.

"I know a great secret place where we can get a swim without being disturbed."

"Swim?" Izar squeaked. "Stars! My mom's queen!"

"Does that stop you from swimming? Will you sink? Here's Praecipua now."

And with him came his assistants, Kalb and Adhafera, and yet another, Sphinx Algenubi, whom Rigel hadn't met before. None of them seemed happy about the recent turn of events.

"Commander Zozma," Praecipua announced, "has sent us to escort you to a safe place. Queen Talitha will join you there as soon as she can."

"That *soon* won't be *very* soon," Rigel said. "We'll have ample time to visit the royal archives, so that Izar Starling can replace the amulets that were stolen from him."

"Halfling, you are in more danger than he is," the sphinx declared in the heavy, plodding tones of Authority Being Patient. "Several of the Vildiar assassins have been seen around the palace. Thank the stars that halflings cannot dissemble!

We are keeping everyone other than starfolk away from Her Majesty, but we must get you and the imp to safety immediately." His tail swished.

"There is nowhere safer than Miaplacidus, especially if you and your gallant band are guarding the entrance."

"Only the royal archivist can let you in."

"I have no doubt that he will be there," Rigel said. "Let's go and see."

Izar had brightened at the prospect of acquiring interesting new amulets, and was even more excited to be escorted by the Starlands equivalent of a SWAT team, which could plow through even the densest mob in the still-crowded palace. *Four* sphinxes, he confided to Rigel, were the next best thing to a royal guard, which was eight. Rigel told him that he was an important person now. In truth he was merely a vulnerable one, worth a kingdom's ransom.

When they reached the archive room, the portal to Miaplacidus was already open. Kalb went through and Anubis called the tally, "Two!" and then, "One!" as she returned.

"Halfling Wasat is there," she said suspiciously, wondering what Rigel knew that she did not.

"He's entitled to be. Izar and I shan't be long."

Frowning, the sphinxes crouched down to wait for their charges to return.

Izar had never visited Miaplacidus before, and the Anubis statue had to repeat, "Three . . . Two . . . Three . . ." several times before he tired of the game. Wasat was sitting outside the first enclosure, at a table that had been strategically placed so that the bench on his side was warmed by sunlight and the other was in the shadow of a palm tree. He had no books or other visible reason to be there, so he must have anticipated this meeting, just as Rigel had guessed.

"I must speak to that old man," he told Izar. "Your mom says this is a great place to swim, so you start and I'll join you. Then we can choose your amulets."

"Don't be long, then." Izar raced off over the sand. Rigel walked over to the table and sat across from the archivist, dropping his scroll on the table between them.

"I would like to leave this here for safekeeping."

Wasat's robe was dusty and rumpled, and wisps of white hair had escaped from under his head cloth. His watery eyes were red-rimmed. "You haven't opened it," he mumbled.

"I think I know what it says, Dad."

The archivist cringed. "She told me that she hadn't told you."

"She didn't. It would endanger you if the starfolk knew you had seduced their queen, wouldn't it?"

"Seduced? Me?"

Wasat timidly reached for the scroll, but Rigel caught the gnarled hand in both of his own. "You're not denying it?"

"No. It's the shock, that's all. First she comes back, and then this—Son." He wiped his eyes on his free sleeve.

"Then tell me all about it, please. How did a halfling become capable of siring a child, anyway? Magic?" Rigel released his father's hand.

"No, no. It happens. Our womenfolk never bear, but the males can be fathers, very rarely." Wasat smiled at last, shyly and uncertainly, exposing teeth worn down almost to the gums. "I've found two or three cases mentioned in the archives, but everyone 'knows' that halflings are mules, so most times the evidence is ignored. If a starborn has had more than one lover, she will twist the calendar to find a more credible explanation. If she hasn't, everyone else assumes she did, and she certainly doesn't argue. Miscegenation is always hushed up. Often the baby is disposed of—the guilt curse doesn't apply to killing halflings, you know. Electra refused to even consider that solution. When you made your presence known, you were a shock and a potential scandal. Your existence would have to be kept secret, but you had every right to live, she said, and she was delighted to discover that we were going to have a child." He looked up at his son with wonder. "How did you know?"

Rigel had been studying the old man's features, trying to find some trace of his own in them. The mouth, maybe. He turned to look at Izar, but the imp was happily whirling around the pond like an apprentice speedboat.

"Something the Pythia told me . . . But I suspected earlier. When I came here with Talitha, you already knew that I was going to be Izar's bodyguard. You showered the finest amulets in the royal collection on me and brushed off any talk of releases or warrants. You had all the authority you needed—a direct order from the queen! Mira had overheard the news about my appointment in the Gazebo, and when we arrived in Canopus she must have slipped away from . . . No?"

"No." Wasat showed his shy smile again. "She came to see me the previous night, through the Dziban root portal. 'I found him!' she said. 'He's here, in the Starlands! And he's a credit to you, old man, a great boy.'" He wiped his eyes again.

"Four!"

Praecipua came trotting across the sand. He scowled at the sight of Izar playing in the water and Rigel gabbing with Wasat. "Halfling, we must go."

"Later." Before the sphinx could argue, Rigel said, "This morning I heard Prince Vildiar telling Hadar to move the entire Family to somewhere called Zubenelgenubi. I assume it's in Phegda domain. Halfling Graffias must know more about it. Her Majesty would probably authorize a raid if you asked nicely."

"Zubenelgenubi? Why didn't you say so sooner? Get the amulets you need and leave!" Praecipua wheeled around and raced back toward the portal. He would be lucky to find as much as a stale crust at Zubenelgenubi, but at least it would keep him occupied.

"Three!"

"So, tell me the story, Dad. Where were you born?"

The old man smiled wistfully. "Somewhere in Eastern Europe. My mother was a beautiful dairymaid. Dairymaids were always the prettiest, because they caught cowpox, which gave them immunity to smallpox, so they escaped the scarring so many others had. My father was some unscrupulous, dissembling elf. He must have worn a charm amulet, because to the end of her days she was convinced he had been the local prince. When I was born, the priest ruled that I was the spawn of an incubus, and the bishop's court ordered me to be put to death. That was what happened in those days. Centuries later, my story helped persuade Electra to ban extroverting. I was lucky, though, because King Procyon had a squad of mages who watched the Pope's mailbag for such cases. They got to me in time, and introverted me and my mother. They found her a husband and lodged her in the slave barns, but she had a happier life there than she would have in the midst of all those human wars. Seven sons and six daughters!" He sighed, smiling at visions of the distant past.

"When was this?"

"I was born around 1520. I'm getting old for a halfling. When I grew up, I applied for status. That was the year Electra succeeded Procyon. Being a wild-stock cross, I was brighter than domestic halflings, so I had been given an education.

Electra sponsored me herself and found me a job in the palace records office."

Wasat paused to see how his son was taking his story. Encouraged by his smile, he continued. "She was lonely at the top, and I was a limber lad, and . . . You know it can happen. But with us it just went on happening, year after year, century after century. And I know that once we got together she never took any other men. Or elves. Not once! When she learned about you, she dragged me down to the Great Court one night and stood right on the Star to tell me so. Not once, she said. There could be no doubt that I was your father." He sniveled a little. "That was like her. Always kind. Apart from being a tweenling, I was old to sire a child."

Rigel chuckled. "Mom was not entirely honest with me. The way she told it, she was passed around like the baton in a relay race. I even wondered if Alfred could be my father."

"Alfred? *Alfred?*" Wasat cackled at the ludicrous notion. "He would have been a precocious ten or so, I'd think. No, Alfred's father was her secretary and his father before him, for eight or nine generations. When Electra returned yesterday, she just appointed the next in line. And I don't think any of those know-it-all confidential secretaries ever suspected what my duties were. Everyone thought the queen was an abstemious prude. Nobody ever noticed the office mouse who turned into a lion at sunset." He cackled again. "We would make love, sit up in bed drinking wine, reading poetry, debating history, and then make love again."

Rigel nodded. It was a bizarre image, but probably just the sort of private intimacy a royal personage might enjoy as a respite from the public scrutiny and endless ceremonies of her office.

An unnoticed tear ran down the archivist's cheek. "She was a lusty woman, your mother, but I could still satisfy her right up until . . ."

"Until I came along and spoiled everything?"

"Until I became an arthritic geriatric, older than half my archives." Wasat sighed, but that had not been what he'd meant. "Now she's gone. We had one of the longest love affairs in the history of the Starlands."

This ancient clerk was not quite the heroic, swashbuckling father Rigel had expected to find, but he clearly had love and loyalty and integrity in spades. *You will always be a servant by day and a lover slipping through the secret panel at night, but if you are big enough to accept that humble status and ignore the sneers, then your love can be very long term.* Electra had been thinking of her ever-faithful Wasat when she'd said that, wondering if Rigel was as good a man as his father was. Was he big enough? Did he have the strength of heart to serve his woman incognito for a lifetime, without public reward or recognition, as Wasat had served her?

"I'm not exactly a halfling, am I?" he said. "I'm a three-quarterling! I met the Pythia last night, and she warned me not to try to kill Vildiar when I got the chance. He claimed that his magic was stronger Saiph, but the Pythia told me to be merciful and I think she meant that I'm more elf than human. She was telling me that I'd be subject to the guilt curse if I killed a starborn. I would have died like my mother just did." *Minotaurs, sphinxes, halflings, but never full-blooded elves.*

Wasat shrank back in alarm. "That's quite possible! There have been cases of halflings succumbing to guilt. I wonder if any of them . . ." He turned to look at the enclosures where he kept the records.

"*Rigel!*" Izar was standing in shallow water with his hands on his minuscule hips. "Rigel! Come *on!*"

"The tyrant calls," Rigel said. "Time to go, Dad." They exchanged smiles. "I'd give you a loving hug, except I don't want Izar to know about you. He's a good imp, but it would slip out eventually."

"The hug can wait. Come back whenever you can get away, Son. I know I cannot hope for forgiveness for what happened in Winnipeg. The woman I had hired—"

"If there was anything to forgive, it is forgiven," Rigel said. He had been wrong in his initial reconstruction of the tragedy. The first-time father who had panicked and mislaid his baby had not been too young; he had been too old. "The main thing now is to cut Vildiar and his baboons down to size before they kill Talitha. And they'll want to get me too."

"Four!" The statue barely had the word out before Adhafera Sphinx's bellow rolled over the sand: "Halfling Rigel! You must come now!" He charged after it like a hungry lion.

Rigel jumped up. "The queen?"

Adhafera slid to a four-paw halt. "The queen is conferring with her senior officials. But Zozma wants you, urgently. Now! There is trouble."

Zozma could go chase his tail, as far as Rigel cared, but he didn't dare explain how much this meeting with Wasat mattered to him.

"I'll be there in just a minute." He waved for Izar to come join him. "Go and guard the door," he said to the sphinx.

"Just because you're the old queen's cub," Adhafera growled, and then stalked away muttering, tail thrashing.

Izar arrived, wet and angry. "You said—"

"Yes, I'm sorry. We have to go. Halfling, Izar Starling was robbed of all his amulets yesterday. What you may not have heard yet was that he inflicted the worst defeat on the Vildiar gang it has ever suffered. He killed three of them and wounded a fourth, using a Lesath called Turais."

"A dog. A HUGE dog," Izar explained, hands waving.

Rigel nodded solemnly. "Enormous. I mention this to show that the starling, despite his youth, is mature enough and responsible enough to be trusted with the strongest defense you can find for him." He might need it, and a new defender would be good for morale.

"Dog?" Wasat muttered, rising stiffly from the bench. "I don't have any serious dogs in stock at the moment, starling. How about a dragon?"

"Dragon?" Izar's eyes widened, and his ears twitched.

"A small dragon. About unicorn size, but able to blow fire a fair distance."

"That would do!" Izar looked ready to melt with joy.

"Then come with me, imp."

Rigel ran down to the pool for a quick dip. *Dragons?* Now he almost hoped that Hadar would take over the Izar file personally.

Chapter 40

M y dragon's name is Edasich," Izar announced. He was
riding on Kalb Sphinx's back, which on any other day
would be an epic honor, but it couldn't compare with owning
a dragon.

"Should you say that?" Rigel gasped. His four-footed escorts
were racing through the palace, and he was wearing himself
out trying to keep up. He had earned this punishment by lingering too long in Miaplacidus. "Won't that summon him?"

"Not him, her. She's a girl dragon, doesn't have a pizzle. But
saying her name won't bring her. I have to stamp my foot too.
This foot. That's her, there." His ears and fingers glittered
with amulets, but he was pointing to the pride of his collection, a slender jade anklet on his twiggy left leg. "She's a beautiful green color. I'll show you later."

He would certainly have to show someone, and Rigel had
brought that ordeal on himself. Then they turned a corner,
and he caught a whiff of something terrible.

The park was modest by palace standards, about half a hect-
are, and irregular in shape, with buildings on all sides, so it
was overlooked by many windows and rooftop terraces.

Among its lawns and flowers, fountains and trees of all shapes, a small crowd of gaping onlookers was being held back by more sphinxes, including the towering Zozma—sphinxes could not string yellow tape. Whatever they were guarding had the same foul stench as the dying Kornephoros.

When they reached the spectators, Rigel told Kalb and Algenubi to stay behind and look after Izar. They obeyed without so much as a miaow.

Praecipua opened a path for him through the crowd and led him around some shrubbery. The first corpse was a sphinx, whose neck and shoulders had already turned to black slime. The rear half of a red-feathered arrow lay beside it.

The female starborn was on her back. Most of her chest had rotted away, and her coppery hair had lost its former luster. The male beside her had lost his face and head, but his death throes had rucked up his cotton gown to expose his shins, which were covered in blue fuzz.

"The sphinx I do not know," Rigel said, fighting nausea. "The others were Starborn Cheleb and Halfling Graffias. You knew that, didn't you?"

"Doesn't hurt to have confirmation," Zozma rumbled. "This venom smells like whatever killed the regent. Do you suppose they used their own blood to poison their . . . What's wrong?"

A lot was wrong, terribly wrong. The Family had silenced the informer before he could incriminate Vildiar. They had struck down a mage of red rank, which must be a considerable feat. Had they known she was a member of the Red Justice coven, or had she just been unlucky enough to be guarding their chosen target? But Zozma was not referring to those troubles. He was asking why Tweenling Rigel looked like *that*, and Rigel looked like *that* because Saiph was throbbing violently.

"The killer's still around! Somewhere . . ."

Arrows? The sphinx had been shot from above. Rigel hastily scanned all the roofs and balconies all around the scene of the crime. "Izar! Get down! Kalb, cover him!"

The sphinx dropped and rolled, spilling the imp onto the ground and then pinning him with a paw when he shouted protests and tried to rise. Algenubi stepped over him as a living shield. The wiser spectators began bolting for the exits.

Satisfied that his charge was safe for the moment, Rigel resumed his survey of the windows and roofs. As he moved to peer around a palm tree, he was almost spun off his feet as Saiph struck aside an arrow that Rigel hadn't even seen. Before he recovered his balance, a violent crash against his head hurled him sprawling to the grass. A second arrow had ricocheted off his helmet.

The world was spinning . . . a silhouette on a high terrace . . . black against the blue summer sky . . . already nocking another arrow in his bow . . . Saiph was throbbing violently, useless because it could not strike against the enemy from this range.

Spectators were fleeing, screaming in terror.

Rigel scrambled to his knees, and, with a giddy lurch, forced himself upright. He hardly had to bother dodging and weaving to make himself a difficult target because he was staggering so much, but the arrows were probably cruise missiles, guided by magic, just like—

He hurled one of the knives Wasat had given him the previous night. Knowing that it couldn't possibly outrun an arrow, he ducked behind a palm tree and remembered to yell, *"Meissa!"* He was just in time, for the next arrow was already on its way. When it lost its target, it thudded into the tree instead of following him around the trunk and skewering him.

Feeling safe again, he peered up in time to see Hadar's bow shatter when the knife knicked the highly stressed wood. The giant staggered, but the blade itself did not seem to reach his person—magic against magic. Before Rigel could send a second missile, the halfling flipped him a finger in mocking salute: *Get you next time!* He turned and disappeared from view.

"Close off the treasury portal!" Zozma bellowed, but half his squad was already streaming away across the park. They would never catch Hadar. There would be no peace or safety in the Starlands until Vildiar was dead or crowned.

"Rigel!" Izar said, grabbing him with both arms. "Are you all right?"

"Yes, I'm fine," Rigel lied. "But now we need to go somewhere, don't we, Commander Zozma?"

~~~~~~~~~~~~~~~~~~~~~~~~

The safe house was named Nihal, and it was more calendar art—rambling fieldstone buildings with red tile roofs and walls draped in creepers nestled in among vines and fruit trees, both laden with fruit that had to be impossibly out of season. Everywhere, there were glimpses of distant hedges, trails, gates, livestock, and bonny hillsides, all of it much more skillfully rendered than Starborn Muphrid's crude efforts to depict scenery at Alrisha.

Nihal's managers, mudlings Marius and Olga, had produced a sumptuous spread in an enormous farmhouse kitchen. While Izar and his bodyguard gobbled everything within reach, Marius introduced them to eight or nine halfling imps—carefully explaining that Nihal doubled as an orphanage—and even more human children, who were the offspring of the human staff. Izar's eyes gleamed at the exciting prospect of bullying this new army into shape.

Nihal, Marius explained, also boasted hills, caves, creepy woods, hollow trees, a millpond with boats, a working smithy, a waterwheel, and two herds of unicorns—all stuff that would provide ample entertainment for an enterprising imp. To Izar, there was no time like the present. Indeed there was no time *but* the present.

Rigel groaned. "I need to digest."

The imp eyed him menacingly. "You said I could introduce you to Edasich!"

Rigel thought *Stars forbid!* and wondered how in the galaxy he could persuade his young ward that it was nap time. Izar was well rested, but Rigel felt like he hadn't slept in a year. Starborn Fomalhaut walked in, acknowledged the imp's and halfling's bows with a nod, and took a seat opposite them. He waved Olga away when she started to fuss over him.

"Turais . . ." Izar began.

"I heard he served you well, starling," the mage said and his golden eyes shone like twin summer suns.

The imp nodded vigorously. "I gotta . . . got another Lesath from an old halfling in the palace!"

"So I heard. I'd like to see that. Commander Zozma," Fomalhaut told Rigel, "has secured Nihal with two prides of sphinxes and a wing of griffins, and I have set the necessary occult bars on the portal. It should be quite safe for Izar Starling to do some exploring."

Izar actually remembered to look for Rigel's nod of approval before he launched himself out the door into an unsuspecting landscape. Bodyguard and mage were left alone, regarding each other in thoughtful silence over a table of dirty dishes, neither of them willing to try for first blood. The mage's eyes looked like chips of amber still cold from the Pleistocene.

Having the shorter life expectancy, Rigel spoke first. "You can see the future?"

The mage's smile would have frozen gasoline. "No. But I do get strong hunches. Yesterday morning something told me that the imp might find good use for a Lesath in the near future. I could be sent to the Dark Cells for giving him one."

"Legally so, but who would execute the warrant?"

Fomalhaut's second smile was more sincere. "Good question. But it is a good law. Today Hadar Halfling slew Cheleb Mage, our oldest and wisest mage. His father must have given him amulets far in excess of what the law allows."

He still had not introduced a topic for debate, but Rigel had a long list of questions waiting for him. Perhaps that was the agenda—it was payback time, be-nice-to-the-royal-half-breed time.

"My mother told me that you came to our rescue in the Walmart store because you were seancing Tarf. She also said that Tarf and co. had been seancing me from the Starlands for a while. I led them to her, and Tarf extroverted to deliver the Cujam." Electra had been talking obvious rubbish.

Fomalhaut pouted as if he had expected strawberry and tasted lemon. "Yes, your mother. A remarkable ruler, but nothing else in her reign will be remembered like that thunderbolt she dropped in the Great Court today. A royal halfling?" Fomalhaut sighed. "It is obscene! Earth decays and corrupts us also. But I grant you that you are a more tolerable depravity than Vildiar's litter, and a juvenile on the throne is less odious than that brainsick beanstalk would be, so you will have my assistance."

"I am honored and relieved, my lord. Just you or all of Red Justice?"

A long and deadly silence. "Red what?"

"My mother told me about Red Justice, starborn."

Fomalhaut nodded, thin-lipped. "She truly had diminished. That must have been just before Kornephoros died, so she may have been feeling the guilt curse even then.

"I cannot promise for the rest of our group. Some of them are so appalled by these events that they have faded. Whether they will ever return, I cannot say, and we are all sick at the thought of a publicly acknowledged royal halfling. But I will see what I can do to enlist their help as well."

"Thank you. In what ways?"

"To guard the queen and her son, our only other Naos. You will necessarily be involved. The scandal about you and Talitha is already spreading. Today Her Majesty's senior advisors repeatedly urged her to put you away as an abomination. She blistered their ears, and my vocabulary is not entirely metaphorical. She appointed you Marshal of Canopus, which gives you authority over the entire palace guard and stars know what else—you, a halfling fresh out of the wild! Four councilors faded at the thought."

"Will the collar match my eyes?"

The starborn flashed fury. "I do not recall; the office has been vacant for centuries."

"So my main job will be to assassinate Vildiar?"

"I did not say that!"

"Of course you didn't, but can Talitha ever be safe while he lives?"

Silence.

Rigel persisted. "Is there anyone else who can deal with him? And I do mean *kill* him."

Glaring, Fomalhaut shook his head. Evidently that was as far as he would go. But Rigel was officially a halfling, and Rigel had Saiph. After what had happened at Giauzar, it was doubtful that even Saiph could prevail against Naos Vildiar, but it was still the best chance anybody had. No one could force the prince into a Dark Cell. There was only one solution—and the guilt curse might kill a three-quarterling.

"You have not explained, my lord, how you turned up so opportunely to rescue Electra and myself when Tarf set the earthlings on us."

The mage clicked his shark teeth a few times. "We—Red Justice—knew that the Family was tracking several halflings. That is another illegality, as halflings are supposed to be rescued, not trolled as bait for a conscience-driven lost queen. When Tarf suddenly extroverted, I was able to follow."

"How? I mean how did you know? I understood that seancing was done in the Starlands to observe events on Earth. You are able to spy on people here with it?"

"No. That is not possible."

Rigel smiled triumphantly, just to annoy the old sourpuss. "So you were tipped off! You have penetrated the Family. Some member of Red Justice can dissemble as one of Vildiar's halflings?"

The mage flushed with anger at Rigel's line of questioning. "That might be possible transiently, but it would be insanely dangerous. If you need lessons in how magic works, halfling, I suggest you ask Starling Izar."

Rigel ignored the jab. "Then you have an agent in the Family? A servant? Or have you managed to turn one of Vildiar's own children?"

Fomalhaut showed his dagger teeth again, but not in a smile. "Domestic halflings are bad enough. I had forgotten how obnoxious they could be when reared in the wild. What Red Justice does is no business of yours, tweenling."

"With respect, my lord, it is very much my business." Rigel braced for trouble. "You moved the queen and me to Alrisha, and the next day somebody tried to murder us there. As Izar's bodyguard and Marshal of Canopus, I need to know whether you are a traitor, Starborn Fomalhaut!"

The mage drummed his fingers furiously on the table and drew a deep breath. His golden eyes burned. "In a thousand years, I have never apologized to a halfling or even dreamed of doing so. I apologize to you now, Marshal. Your inquiry is justifiable. Yes, we had an informer inside the Family. His name was Graffias. You were extremely fortunate to run into him and not one of his brethren when you raided Giauzar this morning. But then you went and enlisted his aid, and he was slain, ending his usefulness to us."

"No." Rigel thought back to the confrontations at Giauzar. "No, they had fingered him already. They knew. His father was anxious for him not to escape." Poor Graffias! "I suppose he tried to defect and asked for protection, but you and your mage buddies sent him back to be your spy?"

Angry silence. Fomalhaut was not going to admit to making a mistake.

Rigel said, "So Graffias reported that the Family was seancing me, and you started doing the same." How long had he been the box office hit of the Starlands? "Then Electra entered my life posing as Mira. Did you recognize the queen despite her dissembling, or did you just guess who she was?"

Glowering, the mage ground out the words. "We suspected. The next morning, when Tarf started the riot in that marketplace, the Cujam amulet did not affect her, so I knew that she was not human. I moved her to safety at Alrisha because it is a seedy, disreputable dive, not the sort of place anyone would look for her. I also knew that Talitha was visiting there incognito. Talitha had great trouble recovering from her enforced pairing to Vildiar, although she was being excessively stupid in hoping to find a reliable companion in a place like Alrisha. Electra would see through her dissembling, and if she needed help, I knew she would find it from Talitha. You, I did not care about."

"Understandably so," Rigel said, straight-faced. So Red Justice had also been watching over Talitha, the last surviving Naos? He wondered how much they had tried to guard the others who had died, but it would be unwise to ask. "And your story about the Moon Garden? All moonbeams?"

"Unfortunately it was," the mage admitted sourly. "It backfired. When Muphrid learned that your amulet was the ancestral Saiph, he knew exactly how to get back in Vildiar's good books. In truth he had never been out of them. He rushed over to Phegda with the news. Vildiar wasn't there, but Hadar's gang was, and they moved in to make sure that Saiph could never become a threat to them."

This sounded like the truth at last. Rigel nodded. "Thank you, my lord. Let us work together to remove, or at least confound, the Phegda evil."

The mage sneered. "Your good intentions vastly exceed your capacity. Now that I have admitted to possessing a modicum of prescience, will you not believe me when I tell you that only an early death awaits you here in the Starlands? I am certain of this."

A cold chill told Rigel that he believed this prophecy. "How long have I got?"

"Three months, maybe four."

"Remind me again when it gets down to a week, will you?"

Fomalhaut rose and stared down at Rigel with venomous dislike. "You are exhausted, tweenling. I will see that the imp is not molested, and perhaps put a few more safety catches on his Lesath. Go upstairs and sleep. You are in no fit state to perform your duties at present. Also, I have a repugnant hunch that you will need all your strength later this evening."

"Not if I am given any choice in the matter, my lord."

The mage snorted and strode away, but Rigel was serious. The dream was over. Talitha could not afford to jeopardize her throne with a major scandal right at the start of her reign. Maybe she could risk a half-breed lover in a century or two, but not now. She would have to enter a formal pairing with a true starborn, maybe Elgomaisa, or whatever his name was. Cue the violins—D minor, *doloroso*.

He took a tour of the building in the company of Olga and Sphinx Praecipua. He vetoed the sleeping quarters they had assigned, and chose others, where Talitha would have access to Izar, and any intruder would have to go past Rigel himself to get to either of them. His decisions were accepted without argument, a respect he found frightening. The last few days had changed him and he did not know this new, dangerous, involved person he had become. He had a cause to serve and that alone was unfamiliar. He had a duty that conflicted with his own impulses, which was even stranger.

He went outside for a hasty swim in the millpond and confirmed that Izar was in no trouble—he was just creating lots of it for other people.

Then he dragged himself up the narrow wooden stairs, flopped on top of his bed, and put what Izar would call his "self" into a bottomless sleep, devoid of dreams.

⸺⸺⸺⸺

He roused briefly when Izar slammed the door and stamped across the room toward the one that had been assigned to him. Talitha must have arrived, because nobody else would have managed to discipline the boy.

"Good night," Rigel murmured. Answered by another slam, he put himself back to sleep.

A dream came to him in darkness. He opened his eyes to see a woman leaning over him, a woman of unimaginable beauty clothed in a trillion stars, for her skin gleamed with them from the tips of her ears down to her hips. Her hair was a galaxy of multicolored flames.

Instantly awake, he barked, "No! Go away! You mustn't!"

"Mustn't?"

"Mustn't!" He clutched the sheet tight under his chin. "You are queen now. You cannot have a sordid love affair with a mongrel like me. You are too young to rule, but the starfolk will prefer you to Vildiar, for they all know of his crimes. Even so, they will surely turn against you if you flaunt a half-breed lover in their faces."

Mercifully she moved away. She sat on the edge of the bed and the eyes that stared back into his were deadly. "I am queen of the Starlands, and I will do anything I like with anyone I please."

Rigel moaned. "No! The diehards like Fomalhaut will not accept that. They won't." The mage had come close to telling him so.

Her starry aura burned redder, hotter. "You are telling me that one halfling lover is wrong but hundreds of mudlings would be all right? That's their choice."

"Vildiar does what he does for power. They all know that. You would be doing it for lust, or that's what they'll say, anyway." He was right, but oh, how it hurt!

"I need you," Talitha said. "I need you for Izar, because I know that Hadar will try to use him against me again. I need you to be here always, whenever I need you, to make me whole, to keep me sane, to tell me I am beautiful, to remind me yet again why life is worth fighting for."

"Then name Vildiar your heir and abdicate. You told me you didn't want to be queen."

She sighed. "Did I? But when Electra put the Light of Naos on me, I felt a bond sealed. I sensed the Starlands, in all their majesty. I was joined to them and all the starfolk . . . I can never abandon my people to Vildiar. He is a cancer, and he will bribe and conspire and traduce. Hadar will threaten and kidnap and slaughter. Without my rule, the realm will fall apart and fade into the void. But Rigel, Rigel, I need you!"

His self-control was snow in an oven. "I'm here," he said, "always. I'm yours, always. Whenever you want, and for as long as you want. But not this, please! If they suspect . . . I must be able to stand on the Star of Truth and say that I have never been your lover, that you let me kiss you only once—nothing more."

"I love you!"

Rigel groaned and tried to roll away. Invisible hands rolled him back.

He whimpered. "Please, please, Talitha, go away and stop torturing me."

She sighed again and stood up, her aura fading to dismal blues and purples. "You are right, of course, and I am being cruel. For now . . . But remember that I love you."

"And I love you," he whispered.

She faded into the darkness, leaving him in misery.

And now he had all the more reason to kill Vildiar.

End of Book One